The Keeper's Code

by

Barb DeLong

Keepers of Magic

Cover Art by *Lea Schizas*

The Wild Rose Press, Inc.
PO Box 708
Adams Basin, NY 14410-0708
Visit us at www.thewildrosepress.com

Publishing History
First Edition, 2025
Trade Paperback ISBN 978-1-5092-6106-2
Digital ISBN 978-1-5092-6107-9

Keepers of Magic
Published in the United States of America

Dedication

To all lovers of romance, herein lies the magic.

Acknowledgements

As book two, *The Keeper's Code* makes Keepers of Magic officially a series! Book one, the award-winning *The Witch Whisperer*, was released in 2023, and my acknowledgements inside that debut book revealed all the villages it took to create a final draft. Ditto for book two. Special thanks to my longtime critique friends Jann Audiss, Kathleen Harrington, Jaimee Friedl, Val Millette, Carol Persinger, JohnaMachek, and Ottilia Scherschel for your feedback and unending encouragement. Thanks to the O.C. Writers group and Lake Forest Roundtable Writers for the same, and DeAnna Cameron w/a D.D. Croix and DeAnna Drake for the beta read.

To my family—I so appreciate that you're as delighted as I am that I'm now a multi-published author!

To my awesome The Wild Rose Press editor Lea Schizas—thanks for believing in me and loving my stories full of magic and romance.

Chapter One

Skye Parker touched the pocket flap of the denim jacket where a new button camera recorded the street. "Can you hear me now? Vid on?" she whispered. "I'm at the corner of Central Park South and 6th. Traffic is heavy."

A bus roared by, followed by two yellow taxis running the light. Ten a.m. in a Manhattan rush hour that never ended and smelled like backward progress.

"Affirmative. Comin' in like a rocket blast. Don't turn so fast. You're making me dizzy. Over."

Jo's smoker-roughened voice in the earbuds seemed to come from the other side of the world instead of around the corner. A crowd waiting to cross had gathered at the light. Joggers wearing skin-thin pants and huge fitness gadgets, nannies, maybe actual mothers with strollers full of wriggling infants, all hell-bent on getting their Central Park fix in early on this coolish May morning. She should warn them about the park—not so much the danger, but the paranormal weirdness. Those eager, trusting faces. Best keep the Mage Believer's arcane stories to herself. For now.

She turned in a circle, pushing the glasses higher on her nose. People rushed by in both directions on the wide sidewalk. No tall guy, dark jeans, black hoodie jacket—the guy they'd had their eye on for weeks. The guy who'd walked right past her when she'd exited her building. "I may have lost him."

"You're gawking"—*static*—"much. Stick"—*static*—"mission. Over."

Skye smiled. "You're not at NASA anymore, White Fox." Jo took her techie job way too seriously, but that's what she loved about the senior hacker.

Skye turned back to the intersection. A line of delivery bikes with blinking rear lights, a million cars, and noxious buses passed by close enough to blow her ponytail back.

Boom. Black hoodie stepped beside her. He stood tall and straight at the curb. Her nerves caught a trip wire. Had he heard the conversation? She angled the button cam toward him.

"Holy shit." Jo's voice crackled in the earbuds. "Over."

Lucky for her Jo had wanted to test the new camera today. She'd be watching this live version of the man they'd seen only fuzzy images of from surveillance cameras at some reported paranormal events. *Yeah. This is the guy.*

His relaxed posture didn't fool her. He was focused, alert, oozing a dangerous competence. Leashed panther power. Under the black hood, the morning sun lit up a striking face of high cheekbones, straight nose, dark eyes. Very cool dude. Could that be rusty old stirrings of attraction in the girly parts? *Nah.*

Fizzle. Static. Hunnnnn.

She opened her eyes. When had she closed them? What—happened? Hoodie was gone. She whipped around. The wide sidewalk in either direction still bustled with pedestrians. Had her brain floated off somewhere? She touched her forehead. *Concentrate.*

"Jo, are you there?" *Nothing.* "Jo, did you see what happened?" The earbuds were deader than her expectations. She only hoped the camera was recording.

Something had happened. Something big. She scanned up the street where the last of the bikes wobbled precariously as the rider peddled too close to a slow-moving bus. Wait—the rear blinker light was out. No, smashed. There, in the road in front of her, sparkling red glass. Her breath escaped in a whoosh.

She rushed over to a jogger waiting at the light. "Hey, did you just see an accident?" The woman in tie-dye tights raised both penciled brows and took a step away. Okay, maybe dial back the frantic. "Sorry, I—I think there was an accident. Just now. With a bike." Skye pointed to the broken glass.

The light turned green. The jogger shook her head and took off, glancing over her shoulder. Probably making sure she wasn't being followed by a red-headed crazy.

Skye shouted to a man in a dark suit striding away toward the corner. "Mister, did you see an accident?" He gave no indication he'd heard her.

And what was she saying, anyway? That she'd missed some kind of bike accident in the blink of an eye? The same one that nobody else had seen? Or had it been more than a blink?

A sudden chill pimpled her skin. Was this déja vu all over again from when she was five? A feeling that something earth-shaking, something profound had taken place, yet having no memory of it?

Wait. There. Hoodie exited a building. "Jo. Jo, can you hear me?" Still nothing. She had to ask him what he saw. He would know—something. Skye power-walked, then broke into a jog along the sidewalk as she followed his long-legged stride. The small pack slapped against her back with each step. She dodged right, then left, as the grim-faced white collars came at her like an offensive line. Her cell phone vibrated in a pocket. It would be Jo. No time to answer.

He turned down the next street. She turned the corner soon after. The street ahead was empty. A side door to the next building was closing. Breathing hard, she rushed to catch it in case it needed a code or a key before bursting through to a small lobby with three elevators. One elevator door was closing. She ran and thrust her body through.

Hoodie stood by the panel, hand poised over the buttons. "Floor?"

What was with the searing gaze? Intimidation? Display of toxic masculinity? *Pfft.* "I'll ride with you. If I didn't know better, I'd think you were running away from me." She poked at her glasses and ignored the vibrating phone.

"I was running?" His voice, all smooth and sexy, slid over her like silky lingerie. A Jim Beam bourbon voice. A hint of woodsy cologne tested the air.

"Yeah. I just wanted to ask if you saw anything at the street corner just now. You were standing beside me."

"Like what?" He turned to the panel and punched button twenty-six.

The elevator shivered. The sensation of whooshing speed tickled her gut. He seemed much bigger, taller, here in the confines of the elevator.

"An accident. Maybe with a bicycle?"

"Why 'maybe'?" He swept the hood back. A

lightning bolt design was carved in his close-cropped, licorice-black hair just behind his right ear.

Interesting. Unexpected. "What's with the zigzag?" She pointed to his buzzed hair.

"The Flash. Big fan."

"Sure. That's it. Anyway, I saw some glass in the road."

His eyebrows rose. "I didn't see anything. Just traffic."

The elevator slid to a stop and the door opened. He nodded, exiting. She followed him down a wide, white-tiled hallway to a door marked "Ash Hunter, P.I." in gold lettering on the frosted glass panel. *He's a freakin' private detective.* "I'm not crazy. I know what I— sensed."

He slipped a key card out of a pocket, touched it to a panel, and pushed through. He turned. "Listen, I never saw a thing. Canvass the people at the corner."

She shouldered her way past into a foyer-turned-office area of a spacious, L-shaped apartment. In front of her, the glass-topped desk on thick, chrome legs looked straight out of *Architectural Digest*, as were the open shelves and abstract artwork on the wall behind it. To the right, in the long leg of the L, a rich, cow-brown leather sofa, easy chair, and coffee table seemed to float in mid-air on the polished marble floor.

Holy vertigo. Behind the sofa, floor-to-ceiling windows went wall to wall. The view was of the office building across the street, but still. How could a private investigator afford this kind of real estate? High-end clients?

"You're pushy, you know that?" he said. "You can close your mouth now."

"Occupational hazard," she said. "The pushy part."

He sat in one of those uber-expensive, ergo chairs she'd only dreamed of behind the desk containing one file folder, a laptop in a docking station, and a huge monitor. She slipped a business card from a silver tray into her pocket. Shelves of books shared space with a few potted plants. Decor items lined another wall. Laser printer. No file cabinets. What P.I. didn't have an overflowing desk, coffee cups, and at the very least, coffee rings on that pristine glass? Yeah, she'd watched too many of those old detective movies.

"Look," she said. "I'm really good at getting the information I want."

"I know you are, Nosy Parker."

"Huh. You know who I am."

"Pulitzer Prize-winning journalist. I realized it was you in the elevator."

"Nominated. I'll win with my next story."

He pressed the laptop's power button. "Can't help with that. If you'll excuse me, I'm really busy. Have a Zoom starting in a couple of minutes." A muscle twitched at his temple. He winced and touched his forehead.

"Is something wrong?" she asked.

"No. Please leave." He squeezed his eyes shut and whispered, "Too soon."

"What's too soon?"

A growly groan, like a grizzly in pain, issued through his clenched teeth. He stiffened in the chair and clutched the arms till his knuckles went white.

She shrugged out of the backpack and rushed around the desk. Was he having a seizure? *Crap.* "Hunter." She touched his shoulder. "Hunter, can you hear me? Do you have meds?" Should she call 9-1-1?

"N-no. Leave." Beads of sweat gathered on his forehead. "Just a—thunderclap."

Migraine on steroids.

A large, sleek cat, black as his hair, jumped onto the desk and yowled. Where the hell had it come from? Its glittering yellow eyes locked with hers for a moment. No hissing, no arched back with hackles raised. Maybe she wouldn't get ripped to shreds.

It walked its front legs up Hunter's left arm to paw his face. *Meow.*

"Soot," Hunter rasped. He released a hand and touched the animal. At least he had awareness somewhere in that sea of pain.

The phone vibrated again. She fished it out of her jeans. Jo's Wonder Woman avatar grinned. "Jo, I have a sitch." She glanced at Hunter's monitor. Elephants, zebra, and wildebeest migrated across the screen under the banner "Wild African Safaris."

"What happened to you? Audio vid went dark at ten thirty hours. I've been calling and calling."

Skye filled her in on the weird happening at the corner, that she was in Hoodie's office, where he was having a severe migraine attack. "His name's Ash Hunter. He's a private investigator." And apparently, he wanted a vaca in Africa.

"On it. White Fox out."

Skye pocketed the phone. The cat leaped into Hunter's lap. He loosened the death grip on the other chair arm, and the furrows disappeared from his forehead.

"Can I get you some water? A cold cloth?" She wasn't going to leave until she knew he was okay.

"The blind. Close the blind. There's a remote on the coffee table."

"Sure." She found the remote, pressing a button. A black shade descended from a pocket at the ceiling above the wall of windows, shutting out every bit of streaming light. They would have been in total darkness save for the soft, diffused glow from the hall through the frosted glass, and his monitor. A pride of lions now padded across the screen.

"Thanks." He stroked the cat's back. It arched up to meet his hand. He opened his eyes and focused on her. "Hey, I won't keel over dead. I'm fine. Really." Was that a tiny smile tilting the corner of his mouth? "You can leave now."

Every fused muscle in her body relaxed. "Going." She pulled one of her business cards out of the backpack and laid it on the desk. "Here. In case you remember anything odd from today, or any other time."

A single eyebrow lifted, framing his piercing gaze. "Not likely."

"You've been identified at the scene of a few reported paranormal events in this area. Again today."

"Well, I live here." He cocked his head. "Paranormal. Are you kidding?"

She flinched. *Skye Lie.* The childhood nickname taunted her. "Well-documented. You sure you're okay?"

"I'm good." He continued to pet the cat, the deep furrows between his brows registering pain.

She could hear the purr from where she stood by the door. "Um, your cat's name is Soot?"

"Yeah."

"Soot and Ash."

She let herself out, chuckling all the way along the hall to the elevators. Hard case Hunter had a cat, and a sense of humor that needed a magnifying glass to find, but it was there. Was he just an ordinary old P.I., or something more? She looked forward to finding out all about him. Jo was on the case.

****

When the office door closed behind Pushy Parker, Ash wanted to smash a fist through the glass-topped desk, but he needed both hands to hold his throbbing head. Why had the pain come so soon after the memory wipe? He should have had another half hour. Bad screw-ups today on too many levels to count.

"Stupid, stupid, stupid." Yet he'd had no choice. The child in the red snowsuit flashed across his mind. The sliding truck. The scream…

He shut his eyes on the images, but they weren't in front of him. They were seared on his brain and lodged in his soul.

Soot stretched out both front paws and passed his thoughts to Ash. *"You've done it now."*

He opened his eyes. "Yeah, Soot. I gotta call it in." Councilman Gray Hunter and the rest of the Bureau of Witchery would have what was left of his head when he did.

The cat jumped to the floor. Poof, he disappeared. "Don't be doing that," Ash said to empty air. His familiar must have made an ordinary entrance when the journalist was here, otherwise—well, he'd have to pluck that memory out of the Reg, too, and enjoy another thunderclap.

Sweat dampened his shirt. He took off the hoodie jacket, flexing tight shoulders, rolling his head from side to side. He grabbed the travel mug on the credenza, half full of tea he'd made from some mysterious herb that the Witch Whisperer prescribed for headaches. After downing the rest of the bitter brew, he began the light meditation exercise that the healer also recommended.

Ash went to his happy place—soft, white sand, warm waves lapping at bare feet, sea-salty breeze blowing through palm trees. A curvy, pony-tailed redhead in glasses, a denim jacket, and jeans strolled toward him. His pulse revved. Wait—was that Parker? Damn. She'd even intruded on the meditation.

The slam of a trip hammer became the soft thump of a mallet hitting his temples. Maybe he could function now. He'd call Myst. She was the optimist, talking him down off the ledge. Most of the time. He grabbed his cell from a pocket and punched in Myst's m-code number.

She answered on the second ring. "You're late."

"Yeah. I'm in my P.I. office. I'll be there in a minute. Can anybody hear you?"

"Not right now. I'm in the Sanctuary. I'm not going to like this, am I?"

He walked over to the kitchenette and took a bottle of water from the fridge. "I screwed up. I couldn't let the man die."

"What did you do, Ash?" She spat out each word.

"I saved a guy on a bike from the wheels of a bus."

"Tell me this happened on a deserted dirt road out in the country."

"Nope. Right outside. Central Park South. Ten-thirty."

The pause lasted a few beats too long. Would she

reach through the phone and slap him upside the head, or would she think up a way to help him out of this jam? He took a swig of water.

"Flippin' hell. You realize we Keepers cover up other witches' public displays of magic from the Regs, not cause them? There's more. Spill."

"I thought I recognized that Reg journalist we have on the watchlist, Skye Parker. She was standing at the curb. I got a closer look, and yeah, it was her." Yes, right down to the cute little scar on her nose that wrinkled when she squinted. A sexy librarian in those square-framed glasses.

"No shit?"

"Then these cyclists rode by. The last bike wobbled and fell against a bus."

"And being the noble savior you are, you worked your magic."

"Reflex, Myst. Reverence for life and all that."

"Bless the One Mother. Well, you are in deep caca. Wait till your father reads your report. You won't be able to dig yourself out of that overflowing latrine."

What happened to his opti-Myst? She wasn't about to get any sunnier. "There's more. The affected field was huge—Reg pedestrians, a few witches, traffic, surveillance cameras, cell phones. You know what it's like outside this building. I had to wipe the incident from everything and everyone. There's no way I can't report this." He left out the part where he failed to clean up the glass. His attention to detail went to hell standing beside the beautiful journalist. Stupid mistake.

"Crap. Your migraine—"

"Yep. Came like a bolt of lightning to the brain, and sooner than I expected. I rode it out in my office."

"You used a massive amount of energy. Are you okay now?"

"Yes, but I need to assign someone to keep close tabs on Parker."

"Why?"

"She followed me to my office. She's suspicious, and she witnessed my migraine."

"F—! Well, it was nice knowing you. I guess."

"Thanks." He powered off the laptop. "Coming down. Meet me in my Keeper office. And we'd better include Mort."

"Ash, you know I'll have your back. So will he. I'll grab a couple of shovels."

He clicked off the call and closed up. Once in the elevator, he held a finger on the first-floor button, which he'd intended to do until Nosy Parker barged through the closing door. He called on the magic, and a frisson of energy flowed through him.

Haven. Haven. Haven.

Mere seconds passed while his body seemed to drift off the floor, although he knew it didn't. *Ding.* The elevator door opened. He exited into the soft, ethereal glow of the Haven's wide, main corridor with its gleaming white marble tiles, a mystic realm somewhere yet nowhere "beneath" busy Manhattan streets. The walls looked solid enough but were merely suggestions. They shimmered with ever-changing scenic vistas. He paused when the scene of an orange grove appeared, and the rich scent of fruity blossoms filled the air. All traces of headache disappeared. Every molecule of the Haven owed its existence to the magic. Every mage who entered felt renewed.

Thank you, One Mother. If only she could shield

him from the wrath of Gray and ease the tension from his muscles.

The combined energies of passing mages, adults with children, some with their familiars draped around their necks or trotting alongside, buffeted him on the way to the Keeper wing. The scenic walls gave way to various offices and meeting rooms. The pulse and pull of the portal sites to the ancient homeland, Tae-wen, thrummed in the background.

Ash entered his glass-windowed office. He gave a nod to M&M, who sat in chairs in front of the desk. He went around to sit in his chair.

"So, Captain, what's the word? Myst said you're in a bind." Mort steepled his long, bony fingers.

Ash wanted to smile. All the darkly-clad Mortimer Payne needed was a pointy black hat and a straw-bundle broom. The six-foot-something gangly string bean with the lightning-struck dark hair was a cross between Ichabod Crane and Severus Snape.

Myst Avery was the exact opposite—short-cropped blond hair, one ear bristling with a half-dozen earrings, colorful clothes, sunny. Until you crossed her. A slender green snake was draped elegantly around her neck. Its forked tongue darted in and out, imbuing the air with its energy.

"Babysitting another familiar, I presume?" Ash asked.

She nodded. "Meet Beauregard. Belongs to a neighbor."

Ash massaged a temple. "Well, meet dead man walking."

She raised a brow. "You're sitting, so—and don't give up."

"Someone tell me what's going on," Mort said.

Ash filled him in on everything he'd told Myst, including the cat-and-mouse game with Parker. He had the feeling he was the mouse. "I just used up the last chance my dad gave me. He'll have my ass."

"That the Councilman will. I'm a pro at writing deviant reports. I'll help you." Mort stood and dragged his chair. "Shove over. Let's get started."

That's why Ash loved the guy. No nonsense. Let's get it done. "No one should be good at *Deviation Reports*, Mort. It means you screwed up."

"Bingo."

Myst stood. "I'll leave you guys to it. I'm no good with words." She threw an air punch, startling Beauregard from its stupor. "Now, if you need me to take on Councilman Gray Hunter, I'm your man."

"Stand down, Keeper." Ash rolled the chair sideways to make room for Mort in front of the computer. "Can't use you if they toss you through the portal. Go to Tech and dig deeper into Parker. I'm sure she's doing the same to me."

"Will do. And everything will be fine, Ash. Don't worry." Myst left and shut the door behind her.

"Love her positive attitude, but she better watch that temper," Mort said. "I've done a couple of reports for her."

"Yeah. Like me, she's walking a tightrope—do what you think is right, or rigidly adhere to the rules come portal hell or death."

"Dramatic, even for you. Number one rule: do not jeopardize the secrecy of our society. Period."

So much for the prime directive of reverence for life. Ash punched in the lengthy m-web instructions and brought up the Bureau of Witchery site. "Now you sound like Gray."

"And every other mage the world over trying to keep their magic on the down low from the Regs."

The Bureau's wallpaper took shape on the screen. The One Mother Tree spread her branches like a live oak, providing sheltering shade to a host of creatures. The image faded as various icons appeared. He clicked on the Keeper symbol, square with crossed spears, and then "Deviation Reporting." The report form was complex and intimidating. He pushed the keyboard closer to Mort. "Do your magic. Save my ass."

Mort took charge. "There's not a mage in the land, mortal or immortal, that has power enough."

Chapter Two

Skye checked her phone. The walk to her building from Hunter's had taken about twenty minutes. She entered around the back of the beige brick low-rise through a service entrance, went along the hall to a metal door and took the stairs to the basement level. No high-speed elevator. No skyscraper view. Not even a window. It was perfect.

At the door marked "Utilities Storage 5," she punched in the key code on the pad and pushed through the steel door to a long aisle of dusty metal shelving full of pieces of old piping, cables, and mysterious flotsam, all abandoned years ago. Trinket's sharp bark echoed off the block walls, sounding more like a dozen mini poodles than one teacup Yorkie.

The stale air wrapped around her like a shroud. At least the cigarette smell was gone. She flicked on the noisy ventilation fan to start some circulation and shrugged out of the backpack.

"Skye, you're not going to believe this." Jo's voice came from beyond the phalanx of shelving.

Her pulse kicked up. She rounded the end of the aisle and hurried across the cement floor to Jo's oversized desk, loaded down with monitors.

"What? Did you catch something on the cam? Was it the accident?" She dropped the pack and pulled the earbuds out. Trinket squirmed for attention on Jo's lap.

Skye kissed his tiny, furry face.

Jo's fingers flew over the keyboard. The streak in her fluffy white hair was purple today. "No. Something even more amazing." She zoomed in on an image on the screen.

She sat back, pulling Trinket closer as Skye leaned in and pushed the glasses higher on her nose. "What in hell…"

"I know, right? Does that jogger have a rolled-up sock stuck in his running shorts, or do you think it's the real thing?"

"Jeez, Jo." She unhooked the cam from the buttonhole.

Jo pointed to the screen. "And here, this gal in the tights. Look at the camel—"

"Argh. Not looking." But the images were seared on her retina. "So, you didn't record anything after Hunter stood beside me?"

"Negative. Audio and video went fuzzy."

The stab of disappointment sliced bone deep. She dumped the surveillance toys beside Jo's keyboard and went to the desk against the back wall. She slumped in the ancient office chair that squealed beneath her. "I know what I almost saw. And there was broken glass— hey, go back to the video. See if we got the street just beyond the curb before Hunter arrived. Shouldn't show any glass at that point."

"Monitor three," said Jo.

On a large screen mounted on the wall nearest Skye, a bumpy street scene played out from mid-chest perspective as she'd walked along the sidewalk, voice on audio saying, "Can you hear me now?" and Jo's reply. Then, the dizzying circle turn.

"Stop. Play that back in slow-mo."

Skye peered closely at the monitor. Pedestrians blocked the view of the roadway just beyond the curb where she'd seen the glass. "Damn. Keep going."

The video continued. There was no clear view of the road surface. And then Ash Hunter stood beside her.

"Stop." The strength of his presence, even from a computer screen, caused moth fidgets in the pit of her stomach.

Jo sighed, batting her eyelashes. "Even I recognize a hunky hunk when I see one."

"Yeah, well, he's got a lot going on, apparently." She fished his card out of a pocket. "A private detective with a multi-million-dollar office. Suffers from seizure-grade headaches. Has a black cat named Soot." She powered up the laptop docked into a PC port. "Now that we have his name, how much did you find out about him in like, five seconds?"

"Ash Hunter. No middle name. The only address for him is his office." Jo coughed and took a sip from a flask. "Thirty years old. Single. Comes from money. His old man, Gray, heads a brokerage firm on Wall Street. His mother runs the family charitable foundation. A married sister with kids in Seattle."

"That explains the fancy office with living space. There'd be a bedroom. I saw doors and a kitchenette."

"Ash studied criminal justice at NYU. No degree listed."

"How long has he been a private dick?" Skye searched online for *Ash Hunter, Private Investigator*.

"Dick." Jo giggled. "He got his license eight years ago. I haven't had time to get into his financials but looks like he successfully closed out a bunch of cases.

This list only IDs them by a number. No names or descriptions."

"Keep digging. I want to know if he's a paranormal or investigating paranormal events like we are. Even though I don't trust him, we might be able to use him."

Jo swiveled the chair. "You should have a 'trust no one' tattoo. But I know what you're really thinking."

"And what is that, oh wise one with more tattoos than a rock star?"

"Private dick. Your mom's alleged suicide."

Skye leaned back. Her mom's smiling face looked up at her from the walnut frame on the desk. Irish green eyes, long, red hair so like hers. Damned freckly face. Could it really be a year next Tuesday? Felt like yesterday. Like a lifetime ago. The pain hours fresh. "At the funeral, I made her a promise."

"Find out who killed her from all the possibles."

"I still think she was murdered to stop her from investigating the paranormal."

Jo gave her the side-eye. "I'm not ruling that out. I've seen some pretty wild stuff. Might have been smokin' a joint at the time, but…"

"Might?" Skye chuckled.

"As for hiring yet another P.I.?" said Jo. "I don't know. Up to you. Meantime, your Pulitzer awaits." She created air quotes. "'The Magic is Real, People,' by Skye Parker."

Skye harrumphed and clicked into her e-mails. *Damn.* One from her editor at the Gotham Gazette. *Parker, you're late again. Get me that article on crime in Central Park by Friday or we'll be forced to terminate your contract.*

"Shit. Shit, shit, shit."

"Hey, you can't be using my word, like, twenty times." Jo set Trinket down and used both hands to push up from the chair. She limped over. "I'm not one for soppy stuff, but…" She placed a hand on Skye's shoulder.

"Bob's going to fire me."

"Oh, shit."

"I've got three days to collate all that crime info you gave me, finish my own research, and write a brilliant article. He's too unreasonable. I need at least another month."

"I know somebody." Jo raised a fist and both brows. A long, gray t-shirt with the NASA logo stretched over her skinny chest, skimming the hips of a pair of psychedelic leggings. The bra was just for show.

"You know too many people. Well, thankfully this place is dirt cheap."

"The bitch bunker? If you need, Hetty and I have some savings—"

"No, thanks. I'm okay. I have enough." *Maybe.* "It's the humiliation, I guess."

Jo patted Skye's shoulder and returned to the chair. "You have nothing to feel ashamed of. Bob nominated you for a frickin' Pulitzer. He should be so lucky as to have you turn in assignments late."

Skye smiled. "Right. What have I got to show for that nomination? A rat bite scar on my nose and probably a termination." That prize had been her dream. Still was. She'd been so close. Even now, losing to that hack from the Milwaukee Post still had the power to set an ache in her chest. "Let's get down to business and investigate the frickin' hell out of all this paranormal crap."

"You'll be shoving your P-Prize right up—down Bobby-boy's throat." Jo's cell phone chimed. "It's Hetty." She held the phone to her ear. "Hey, sis. Yes, pick me up in half an hour. Lunch at Dooley's?" She paused. "My treat." She returned to the keyboard. "Hetty's seventy-eighth birthday. Oh, do you want to join us?"

"No, thanks. Tell her H.B." She and Mom had known the sisters for years. The pair, both spinsters, were in their seventies now. They looked like twins with their skinny frames and white hair. "Wow. Seventy-eight. Time has a funny way of passing, doesn't it?"

"Sure does. I'll keep on Hunter if you want to look up the latest Mage Believers posts. Read the one about the spilling wine that disappeared into thin air."

"And I'll see if anyone posted my incident this morning." Her stomach quivered. The earth had moved today, but she was the only one who'd felt it.

Trinket had curled up on the velvet pillow next to Jo's desk. His soft, fluttery snore and the clicking of fingers on keyboards were the only sounds. The bitch bunker was quiet, secure. The high ceiling with its exposed piping felt like one of those pricey lofts if it weren't for the lack of windows and pretty much every other amenity. Hey, it had a two-piece bathroom. Skye wouldn't lose the place, at least not anytime soon. They'd been there for six months. She'd just paid the building manager under the table for another six. They were good until at least the end of October.

Her cell chimed a text. Cindy again. She groaned. Her so-called friend had been trying to reconnect ever since Skye's fifteen minutes of fame when the Pulitzer finalists were announced. Skye had deleted every message. She wanted nothing to do with Cindy and her group of new moms, all mean girls from high school, so-called besties. The ones who'd called her Skye Lie after she'd confided her mystical experience in sincere wonder. Okay, so maybe a real magician was hard to believe, but Cindy had been like a sister. *Betray me once and you're dead to me. I don't do second chances.* Rough, but this mantra had helped her avoid a lot of disappointing "friends."

She tried to focus on the computer screen, anything *but* the scene in Hunter's office, his powerful presence even through the terrible pain he endured, the black cat—where had the damn thing come from? Was she really thinking about hiring him to investigate her mom's murder? She probably couldn't afford him even if she didn't lose her job. *Crap.*

Jo pulled herself up from the chair. She grabbed the Hurry Cane. "I'm off." Trinket awoke, stretched, and trotted over to the tote bag. "Hop in." He did, curling up in a little ball of fur.

Skye stood. "Need help with the stairs? You seem a bit stiff today."

"Nope. Been hauling this scrawny old ass up them for months. I now have a bionic hip, remember?" She bent and grabbed the handles of the tote. "See you in an hour."

Skye flicked Hunter's business card between her fingers. The card was simple—office address below his name in all caps, bold Arial font. A logo design of two spears that crossed at the center of a square sat in the upper left corner. *Does this mean something?* She'd do a search for symbols and see what came up. Sounded like more fun than killing herself on the crime article or looking for another job. She didn't have time for either.

Ash Hunter. Closed a bunch of cases. Must mean he's good at his job. Mom-with-the-perpetual-smile gazed up at her from the frame. Someone killed her. Someone connected to the paranormal or to the many conspiracy theories she'd believed in and loudly voiced wanted to silence her. No way would she ever have taken her life. And in that way. Depending on what else Jo dug up on Hunter, she just might empty her piggy bank to hire him. He'd investigate Mom's murder. She'd see what, if anything, he knew about all this paranormal activity in and near the park.

Were there people with magic or superheroes hiding in plain sight? Maybe they were behind some of the suspicious deaths as the Mage Believers claim. If so, her story, her *Pulitzer* story, would have the biggest impact on the world since that asteroid hit Yucatan.

****

Next morning, Ash sat in his Haven Keeper office scrolling through posts on the computer after searching the name *Skye Parker*. He'd already seen some of these posts. She was the real deal—a world-traveling, award-winning journalist, fierce and fearless and formidable. He'd love her life. Not the writing, but the adventuring. Walking through the stalls of a Bangkok market, riding a camel in Giza, snorkeling the Great Barrier Reef. He'd seldom left the state. *What I'd give…*

Not going to happen. He'd been stalling, anyway. He returned to double-checking the latest lengthy m-web login protocols that had been placed on the desk by tech. He got the series of alpha/numeric/symbolic codes correct by the third try. A chime sounded and the

Bureau of Witchery wallpaper appeared. The image of the One Mother Tree gave him no comfort this morning. Gray must have read the Deviation Report by now. He clicked on the icon and chose the DR. A counter showed that five Council members had read it but left no comments. Maybe the incident wouldn't be such a big deal. Soot thought otherwise. He'd refused to come with him today. Coward.

The door opened. Councilman Hunter and his powerful energy force stormed into the room. With a wave of a hand, he turned the windows opaque. He wore a fierce scowl that would stop a charging buffalo. Even the bushy white eyebrows glowered at Ash. Yeah, Soot was right. The DR was a *huge* deal.

Ash's jaw tightened as he set his back teeth. "Councilman." Years ago, Gray had asked him not to call him dad in the Haven, and Ash was only too willing to comply. He wore the formal uniform of the Council, including the damn bespoke One Mother vest, and a look that said *your ass is mine.*

Gray leaned forward and slapped both hands on the smooth, black surface of the desk. "How old are you?" Cold sarcasm dripped like melting icicles.

The lecture. He met Gray's furious eyes. "Thirty."

"You are not ten anymore."

Red snowsuit. Ash's gut twisted.

"You jeopardized all of us. Again." Gray straightened. "Thousands of us around the world. Think about that. You're a Keeper. One of the highest of the Elite mages. You didn't do your damn job. Keep our magic secret and safe."

"The cyclist would have died. The same with the woman six months ago. I wiped everything clean."

Almost.

"And that business last year with the Witch Whisperer? You were his warder. You were lax, if not negligent. Ravenwood breached a portal to Tae-wen under your watch. A bloody portal." Gray sat on the edge of a chair and ran a hand over his balding head. "You can't save everyone. Not with magic. Never."

"I can't turn my back. I'm not you."

"That was twenty years ago."

The memory was barbed wire in Ash's soul. "What happened to reverence for life above all? The One Mother oath."

"That was before we came through the portals from Tae-wen over three hundred years ago. Come on. Maintaining secrecy became oath number one damn quickly."

Ash couldn't reconcile the two tenets. Never had.

"You're a Keeper. This isn't just a job. With your unique talents, it's what you were born to. Being a Keeper is an obligation and a privilege."

A privilege? "So, cut to the chase. What's my punishment?"

"For one, I order you to watch the newest Armageddon video. It's been updated with all the latest nightmares our society would be subject to if the Regs find us out. Secondly, the Council has decided to temporarily suspend you. Those so-called vehicular murders you've been investigating—assigned elsewhere. You're off official Keeper duty and the Shadow Force for six months."

Ash held himself in tight check. Gray considered excess show of emotion a weakness unless it was his own anger. "The Council? You mean *you* decided. I *am* a Keeper. You said so yourself. Put me on the team investigating the increasing number of witches with problematic magic."

"I have another assignment for you. The reporter? Skye something? Keep close tabs on her."

"Already on it. I've assigned—"

"No, *you*. Get close to her. Romance her if you have to."

Ash stood so abruptly, his chair rolled backwards and slammed the wall. "You've got to be kidding. Romance her?"

"Whatever it takes. She's dangerous. She's one of those Mage Believers."

"Sounds like a Keeper assignment to me."

At the door, Gray turned to him. "You report back to me weekly. Daily if the situation warrants. Me only. Understand?"

Yeah, he understood. Gray wanted total control of his misfit son and the "situation." For now, Ash would comply. He'd have to start running in Parker's circles somehow. Mort followed the Mage Believers online to see postings that needed discrediting. He'd join the group, too, and see where that led him. Other than that, he had no idea.

As for romancing the gorgeous redheaded Reg?
Never.

And Never Ravenwood was who Ash had a date with—he checked the time—a half hour ago. His relief at being replaced as Nev's warder was short-lived. He'd soon regretted inviting the pain-in-the-ass Witch Whisperer to become an instructor last year in the magic arts, but with any luck, Nev would have been his usual impatient self and left. Ash had made last week's hologram training session seconds before that happened. He hurried to the Magic Arts wing.

He opened the door to the gym. Today the room was the size of half a dozen basketball courts, empty save for a fake forest of almost life-sized pine trees, boulders, and thick brush at one end. Too bad the trees weren't real. The place would smell green and woodsy instead of week-old gym socks.

Luck was a bitch. Nev, long hair a wild tangle below his shoulders, stood to one side of the door. The muscled size of the guy, clad in loose pants and a t-shirt, could be intimidating. Ash had never been impressed. Much. Hard to imagine this once-recluse with a wife and expecting a baby.

"Well, you decided to grace me with your presence. I was about to leave." Nev's gravelly voice echoed in the high-ceilinged gym. He strode to the middle of the room.

Ash followed. "Had a surprise visit from Councilman Hunter in my office."

Nev grimaced. "My favorite evil wizard of security. You aside, of course. What was he grilling you on now?"

"Oh, just another life saved. He said I should have let the S.O.B. die."

Nev's face softened. "Your job is like balancing on the razor-sharp edge of a sword."

Ash huffed. "Yeah. My Keeper job sucks sometimes, but he suspended me from official duty for six months, so there's that."

Nev whistled. "That's rough, I guess. I told you—walk away from all this."

"Wish it was that simple. But meantime, I still

gotta train."

"More than ever so you don't get rusty. Rustier."

"How's Willow? Still percolating your little demon?" Ash pushed up his shirt sleeves and flexed his fingers.

"*Baby's* due soon. Not soon enough for my sanity." He threw an anguished look skyward.

Ash laughed. "Sorry, dude. Let's get going. I have a special assignment I need to get to." No way was he going to tell Nev about Parker and the order to romance her. The W.W. would have a field day with that information.

"How are the headaches?"

"The usual ripper yesterday after wiping memories. High magic with sustained effort over several seconds."

Nev nodded. "Did you get one after last week's session when you created a half-assed hologram? That's high magic."

He'd felt a twinging ache. "No. I was fine."

"Right. Drink the lestrel tea afterward."

"Wait—lestrel. From Tae-wen?"

Nev paused and looked away. "Yes. I have a large supply of the herb. Years old but improves with age."

Ash didn't believe that for a second. If the W.W. had found a way to reopen the portal in Trowbridge House, he didn't want to know. The big guy wasn't his problem anymore. "Okay, Nev, how about you demonstrate your dazzling talent first?"

"I'll walk you through this duplication hologram. Remember last week. Take your time. Focus." Nev fixed his gaze on the faux forest and then closed his eyes. "Place the image in your mind. Every detail. Draw on your magic core. Concentrate." His nostrils flared. Jaw muscles twitched. He held out a hand, the muscles of his forearm bunching.

Across the room in front of the forest, an image of trees, bushes, and rocks wavered like a watery mirage in the desert. The image became fixed, and Ash couldn't tell the hologram from the real behind it. The orphaned Witch Whisperer didn't know if he was Elite, but the powers he demonstrated proved what he was.

Nev walked to the hologram and stepped through, rippling the image before it settled again. To Nev, he would have disappeared as surely as if he'd stepped through an opaque curtain. The hologram dissolved and he walked back to Ash.

"Now you try it. I'll keep quiet so you can concentrate."

Ash gritted his teeth, his feeble attempt last week foremost in his mind. He studied the pine trees, the low bushes, how the rocks lay among them, their distinctive shapes. He closed his eyes and stretched his arm out as Nev had done. He called on the magic, soul-deep magic. Warm tingles of energy traveled out from his core until his whole body radiated power. The forest in all its detail filled his mind, swamping his senses.

"Okay." Nev's voice was a jarring intrusion.

Ash opened his eyes. "Yes!" A rippling image of the forest played out across the room. It settled for a moment before the movement returned.

"Better than last week." Nev clapped him on the back. "We'll repeat this one next time. In a couple of weeks, we can try creating an original hologram."

Ash waved a hand, and the image disappeared. "I can see where a hologram would come in handy. I could create one to avoid anything lethal in dangerous situations."

"I've created them for all kinds of reasons. You want a sunny day outside the window when it's raining? Or vice versa."

The ache began in Ash's temples and quickly spread. Ash couldn't imagine conjuring holograms on a whim. Not when the consequences manifested in a thunderclap. He hurried away from the session, telling Nev he'd work on improving the skill, telling him to give his best to Willow. He needed to get to the upstairs office and make a cup of that tea.

Chapter Three

Skye hit the button for the twenty-sixth floor and experienced the same tummy tickle as last week when whooshing up in the elevator with Hunter. This time she had an appointment. The guy was an enigma. He had no personal Facebook page, only a sparse business page and profile on LinkedIn. No X or Instagram. No TikTok or Pinterest. What thirty-year-old business owner didn't have a ton of social media?

Jo had managed to hack into a lot of his more recent case files—Skye didn't want to know how—and determined that none were of a paranormal nature. That crossed spears logo on his business card? A protection symbol in many cultures, including the occult. Jo said not to read too much into it. Skye would proceed with an open mind.

When the elevator door slid open, she walked along the hall to his door. Her stomach still fluttered. She couldn't be nervous, not after ten years of interviewing the strange, the deranged, the dangerous. Until she and Jo could delve deeper into Hunter, she wouldn't know which one to label him, despite her first impression of him. Manila folder under an arm, she raised a hand to knock.

"Come in. It's open."

His smooth voice from beyond the frosted glass door sounded like warm brandy. She took a deep breath and entered the office. He sat at ease behind the desk, a stark contrast to the last time. He still managed to exude an aura of power, of *specialness* Mom called it. He was business casual today in a blue, long-sleeved collared shirt, making her ripped jeans and alien-from-Roswell sweatshirt seem juvenile. *I care why?* His dark eyes settled on her. *Hunky hunk. Yeah.* Her skin warmed. The damn moths still banged around in her stomach. She stomped them with her high tops.

"Have a seat, Parker." He swiveled his chair.

"Thanks. How are you?" She sat, placing the folder on her lap. Across the room, the cat lay curled up asleep on the sofa in a patch of morning sun. It opened one eye and flicked an ear.

"Fine. I have no new insights into whatever happened or didn't happen out on the street last week," he said.

"Yeah. Not here about that." *Right now.* "I want to hire you."

He raised his brows. "For?"

"I want you to find out who murdered my mother, Diana, and why."

He stilled the swiveling. "I'm sorry for your loss. Tell me about it."

She sat back in the padded armchair. A lump rose in her throat. She swallowed and lifted her chin. "A year ago this week, I found her in our home in Queens. It looked as though she'd hung herself. You know, scarf around the neck, overturned chair. Computer files full of so-called crazy theories." She could say the bare facts. The details would break her.

Hunter firmed his lips. "It must have been—still is—tough. What makes you think it was murder?"

"My mother was vital, fully into life and all its subtleties, all the gory, all the glory. She stuck her nose into every nook and cranny, saw the beauty in damn snail snot. Questioned everything. Took nothing at face value."

"The apple—"

"Right." She tossed the portfolio in front of him. "Take a look."

He opened the folder. She kept her eyes on his face as he sifted through the photographs. His only reaction was a slight tightening of his jaw. He stopped to read through the police report that included summations of the cause of death, and then closed the folder.

"They're saying she was likely mentally ill. Was she?"

"She was as sane as I am."

He nodded and smiled. "Do you believe in UFOs? I mean the kind from another planet?"

My shirt. Jeez. "No, not really. My mom did, though. I wrote an extensive piece on sightings for *Future Science Magazine*. I need to maintain credibility with the public, so watch what I put out there unless I have irrefutable evidence. I supported my mom, though."

"Besides your opinion of your mother's character, what else makes you think it was murder?"

"The scarf. If I didn't have any other reason, the scarf she used would be enough. I brought that scarf back from my visit to Beijing. She treasured it. She would never"—she swallowed the lump—"she wouldn't do that to me." *Dammit. No tears.* She adjusted her glasses.

"Sorry, Parker. Want to take a minute? Can I get

you some water?"

Boom. The cat jumped in her lap. She took in a sharp breath.

"Soot likes to comfort people in distress. Sorry if he startled you."

She stroked its back, black as a raven's feather. It arched up into her hand and meowed. "Thanks, Soot. Maybe I need to get a comfort kitty." She figured that's why Hunter kept the cat around. Soot turned in a circle and settled down, nose to tail.

"He likes you. He doesn't take to everyone."

"Animals gravitate to me. Must be my meek and mellow temperament."

His laugh softened the hard lines around his eyes and jaw. "They can see into our souls, deep beneath our chosen skins, so says my mother who has five cats."

"Yikes. All I need is another entity psychoanalyzing me." She wanted to shift in the chair, but that would disturb the cat.

Hunter sobered. "Before, when you talked about the scarf, you hinted at other reasons."

"Yes. She left no note. She'd certainly have something to say about her plans and why. There were a lot of her far-out theories to consider."

"Flying saucers? Little green men?"

"She had made a few enemies in industry and government, including the Department of Defense. She voiced her skepticism on everything from manmade climate change to JFK. Conspiracies were everywhere—cover-ups on the origin of Louisiana and Florida sinkholes, the secret contents of the chamber in Mount Rushmore. She believed in Bigfoot, the Lake Ontario monster. Called out government leaders she said were covering up either aliens among us or humans with extraordinary powers. Any one of them could have wanted her silenced."

"Extraordinary powers? Like what?"

She hadn't meant to talk about this right now. But the fact he'd homed in on this one topic out of all she'd mentioned, meant it struck a nerve with him. "She believed, and I do, too, that there are people who can manipulate their surroundings, move objects, maybe even control the weather and our minds."

"That sounds crazy."

"Maybe, but I experienced something amazing. When I was five, I fell off a steep bank into a river near our campsite. Next thing I know, I'm standing back up on the bank, dripping wet, and a guy, a hiker, is disappearing into the trees just as my mom comes running from camp. I remember nothing of actually hitting the water or how I got back up to the bank. I felt, well, disoriented like I felt last week after the incident in the street."

He frowned. "It's common to forget the details of a traumatic event, especially a kid, and fill in the gaps with fantasy."

"My mom saw it all. Years later she told me that the hiker stood on the bank while holding his hands out. I rose from below just like a magician's trick. He set me on my feet. When the guy heard my mom, he ran."

Hunter shook his head. "Like I said, that sounds crazy."

Skye Lie. Just like Cindy and her pals, ready to ridicule and deny. No one understood. That day on the high riverbank changed her life forever. The shared experience forged an even deeper connection with her mom than a familial one. She hadn't understood that until the day her mom told her what happened.

"You'd think after all this time, my memory would have blurred. The significance dulled. Instead, the event still fills me with wonder. After the river, our whole lives revolved around questioning what was real, what was not."

Soot stirred and stood. As he stretched, his nails dug into her thigh. "Easy, Soot, before you draw blood." She set him on the floor. "She was never quiet about her beliefs after that. A few years ago, she heard about the Mage Believers, an online group that shares stories of paranormal events, and we joined right away. Lately, some have posted suspicious deaths that may have paranormal connections."

He was silent. He was probably thinking he should run the other way, fast. The cat jumped onto his lap and rubbed against his chest.

"So, will you take the case?"

"Why me? You're the investigative journalist." He stroked the cat's back.

"I checked you out. You have a good closure record. I hit a dead end."

"I'm really busy, and expensive."

"Yeah, here's the thing. I can't pay you right now." *Or maybe never. No job. Damn Bob.*

"That's a problem."

"But you believe me? That my mother was murdered?"

He met her eyes for a long moment, as if assessing her words, what lay in her heart. She was determined not to look away first. Soot meowed, breaking the spell, or whatever the hell had been happening. He gathered the cat in his arms and cradled it like a baby.

"I believe you that she was murdered. The paranormal angle not so much. Is your mom's murder the big story you're writing for your next Pulitzer? You mentioned a story last week."

"Maybe I will. There are lots of stories out there. I'm glad you believe me. If you're taking the case, the first thing you should do is to interview the—"

"No. I need to go to the house."

"The house? It's been a year. There's nothing there. The photos—"

"I need to see it in person."

"Okay. I can make that happen. Send me your fee schedule. I'll find a way to make payments."

He nodded. "You still stay there sometimes, right? Do you want to be there when I go?"

"Of course. When?"

"I'll text you."

****

Back in the basement office, Skye poured a cup of dark roast, took a sip, and made a face.

"Hey," Jo said. "That's good stuff. Sure to curl your short ones, if you have any." She chuckled.

"Not going there. So, Hunter is taking the case." She sat at her computer and logged into the Mage Believers Facebook page. Still no chatter about the bike incident from last week. "He wants to see the house. Maybe he has a sixth sense about crime scenes, or he's some kind of sensitive."

He said he didn't believe her story about the mysterious man in the woods who had saved her with magic when she was five. She'd have to work on convincing him somehow. Or maybe he wanted her to think he didn't believe.

"Feel any woo-woo vibes from him this morning?"

"I felt—something. He's very introspective. Quiet."

"Calculating?"

"Maybe."

"Sexy in a dark, mysterious way?"

Skye smiled. The long length of him, lounging in his chair, stroking the cat. Panther power. Dark eyes assessing, heating her skin. "Very."

Chapter Four

Ash shut down the computer just as the phone pinged. Old Sam, his trusted mage Uber driver, was downstairs to take him to Skye's place in Queens. He was to meet her there. He couldn't imagine how she'd felt finding her mother's body, and the fact that she'd taken her own life. He agreed that the circumstances were suspicious. What did he hope to find at the house after a year? More like what he might sense.

And then there was her own incredible encounter years ago with a witch who'd saved her from drowning. He'd always known there were more mages like him who couldn't turn their backs on human suffering regardless of the risk to their society.

Was that paranormal encounter the Pulitzer story she was writing, or her mom's murder? She said she needed to maintain credibility with the public. Regs would never believe the witch story, whereas a murder cover-up could make great journalism. Ash grabbed Parker's folder.

Soot jumped off the sofa. *"Come with."*

"No, you can't come. Stay here and behave."

Yowl.

"You think being a cat sucks? You're a witch's familiar. You don't know how good you have it. Be thankful you're bonded to me and not Myst. Her cat shares her with dozens of other witch's familiars."

Soot lifted his nose in the air. *"Lucien is a wuss. A dark, fluffy mush ball."*

"That looks like he would kill you if you messed with Myst. You're jealous because Lucien is a giant Maine coon and you're just a domestic shorthair."

"I'm no common domestic. He can't even transport."

Ash shook his head. Damn cat. Always in his face, offering opinions. Soot liked Skye, though, despite some doubts the familiar voiced about her motivations. Ash locked up and rode down in the elevator.

Taking Parker's case would keep her close, just like Councilman Hunter wanted. It couldn't be a better setup, even though his initial focus was supposed to be on her interest in paranormal activities and the Mage Believers. The Bureau of Witchery would explode if her next story exposed their society, even if the vast majority of the world's Regs didn't believe her. He only hoped he wouldn't have to use magic in front of her like last week. The fallout had been huge. The tech team was still running interference with social media postings. Parker probably suspected that he was hiding something about the incident.

He'd filled Mort and Myst in on his Keeper suspension and new assignment to keep tabs on Parker. Myst had detected breaches in his P.I. business files. His personal profiles had been probed. But no matter how good Parker's tech team was, they'd never be able to access the m-web. Only a mage could do that.

He shoved open the door to the street. Warm air and the smell of exhaust fumes smacked him in the face. He got in the back seat of the small Toyota.

Sam turned, "Morning. So, Queens today. I have

the address in my GPS." Sam gave him his signature round-faced smile full of mustache and mischief.

Sam didn't need GPS. A map of the whole New York City area was imprinted on his brain. Sam tore away from the curb into traffic, weaving and dodging and considering traffic lights to be merely suggestions. Parker said it would take almost an hour to get to her place. With Sam at the wheel, Ash shaved fifteen minutes off that estimate if they survived the trip.

They soon pulled up in front of a typical older Queens house, red brick, two stories with a third dormer on top. The houses crowded one another on the street, and like the others, Parker's place had the usual closed-in front porch.

"Wait for me, Sam. I won't be long." He grabbed the folder.

Ash walked up the few cement steps to knock on the porch door. Parker opened the door, thin-lipped and hollow-eyed. No glasses. She probably hadn't slept. Her hair hung in messy copper waves around her face. Reliving this tragedy was hard on her.

"You okay?" he asked, walking past her through another door to a sparsely furnished living room. A large, glass-topped coffee table fronted an overstuffed gray sofa and easy chair. A bed pillow lay on one arm of the sofa.

She followed close behind. "I'm fine. Yeah, I know. I look like hell." She tried to tuck a slab of hair behind an ear but failed.

He smiled and handed over the folder. Their fingers touched as she met his eyes. He pushed a mild mesmer onto her frazzled nerves.

Her face relaxed before she looked away.

41

"Welcome to my home. I actually live here. Sometimes."

He nodded. "Looks comfortable." Her face was more charming than classically beautiful. A hundred freckles had come out from hiding since she wore no makeup. No rip in the jeans today, but his blood heated, anyway.

Romance her. His dad's words. If only she were a witch.

"Um, I'm glad you texted me so quickly after our meeting yesterday," she said. "I wondered if the story of my life-saving magician would give you second thoughts."

Yeah, the story had shaken him on a lot of levels. "No. An opening came up today. I had time."

"So, you have a bunch of clients you're working with right now?"

He smiled. "You know I don't."

She raised a brow. "Caught me. I won't apologize. I've got to know who I'm dealing with."

"Understood. No apologies from me, either. I spent hours last night going over your background and the information in your mom's case file. I have a talented computer geek who helps me with my investigations."

She smiled. "Me, too. Maybe my geek can meet your geek. Compare hacks."

He'd like to see where she worked, who she worked with. "Might not be a bad idea."

She nodded, and the smile disappeared. "Jo downloaded the last three years of files from my mom's computer. Too many conspiracies, but some worth big money. I've only read through a fraction of it. Jo included the password so you could open it." She handed him a thumb drive that he slipped into a pocket. "I always say follow the money. But don't overlook the less obvious. There are some suspicious deaths that she's listed under 'Mage Believers'."

She walked ahead of him into a hall. A door led to a home office crammed with bookshelves, file cabinets, and a heavy wooden desk loaded down with stacks of paperwork. "Here is where my mom worked on all those conspiracy theories. Some of them had actual merit."

Above the desk, a glittery sign read "Magic is real!" A pulse ticked in his jaw. Skye believed those words. Ash fingered the thumb drive in his pocket. "I'm glad she documented a lot on her computer. I'd hate to wade through all this."

"Yeah. Jo and I have spent countless hours lost in all these files, hard copies and electronic." Skye turned for the door. "Let's go upstairs."

He followed her up the staircase, scuffed from many years of many feet. "The floors look like original hardwood."

"They are, from the twenties."

Family photos lined the wall. He had the urge to straighten the crooked ones. Some of them were Parker at different ages. None of her with a guy that looked boyfriend-y. Her dad passed just after she was born, apparently, drawing mother and daughter into a tight bond. There was one of her in a campground. She looked around five. He stopped.

"Is this the camping trip where you thought you had that experience?" he asked. Parker at five was an adorable little girl, tomboyish, dirty faced. Her long red hair was a tangled mess.

"Yes. My life *was* saved, Hunter. By magic." She marched up the rest of the steps.

The witch slipped up by not erasing the mom's memory. He didn't take the time. So many fumbles by witches, him included. How long would their society remain a secret? Now he was sounding like his dad.

They stood on the landing. He detected the faint energy signature of mages who must have been in the home, but who and when? "You don't have to go any farther. Just point to the room."

"No, I'm fine." She led him to a room on the left.

She let him precede her through the door into a large bedroom with a vaulted, beamed ceiling. Bare floors. Queen-sized bed with a coral bedspread, a small nightstand on either side. A pretty room, wallpapered in pale peach flowers. Neat. Clean. Not a place for violent death.

A place where the energy fields were much stronger. Someone had used magic.

Parker sat grim-faced on a small vanity stool and opened the folder. Why did she torture herself? He looked up to a beam that met the wall. *The* beam. "Where's the chair she used?"

"Correction—the chair someone put in place. I threw it away."

Yeah, he would, too. He turned his back and closed his eyes, fully opening his senses to the rarest of rare Elite talent. The different energies separated, three of them. He grabbed the unique signature left by each mage, a kind of sharp note of which no two were alike. If he met them on the street, he could identify them. But there was one, a fourth—a fuzzy-edged, blurred signature, like a badly smudged chalk drawing. Was it being deliberately masked? What mage had that kind of power? Why would they use it? A frisson of alarm jangled his nerves. He'd come across this type of unidentifiable signature a couple of times and not in good circumstances.

"How many people have been in this room?"

"You mean since that day?"

"Okay, let's start there."

"Cops, EMTs. I called 9-1-1, and somehow—somehow, I got her down. Two cops showed up first. Then paramedics, but…" Parker took a shuddering breath, face pink as tears welled. "I screamed and screamed at them that she wouldn't do this. I lost it."

He laid a hand on her shoulder. He didn't need to be one of the empaths to feel the strength of grief. When her body shook, he urged her up and folded his arms around her. She hesitated a second before wrapping shaky arms around his waist and leaning her head on his shoulder. He pushed another gentle mesmer onto her senses. There'd be no Deviation Reports on these breaches of the code. If any Reg needed a bit of magic right now, it was Parker.

She trembled. "It was a year ago today. My mom was all I had. She was my world."

Tears soaked into his shirt. He breathed in the flowery scent of her hair. The warm body pressed against his stirred more than just blood. She was not skin and bones like his ex, Amanda. Parker had luscious curves…

What a jerk I am getting turned on while she…

Parker squeezed him before leaning away. "Sorry." *Snuffle.* "Look what I did to your t-shirt."

He could only look into her eyes, red-rimmed and

sparking green glittery bits. Her face had blotched, melting several freckles into one, yet she was still beautiful. Her full lips parted. When she lifted her head, he lowered his mouth to within a fraction of hers. Their breaths mingled before he eased back. He wanted more. "I'm sorry. I—I don't—"

She tilted her head with a trace of a smile. "Don't be sorry." She pulled away and picked up the folder.

He could still feel the warm imprint of her body. He hoped the physical signs of his desire weren't showing.

"I wanted you to kiss me," she said.

"But you were—are—vulnerable. I took advantage."

"Really? I'm no shrinking violet. Okay, that moment, talking about what happened, got to me. But no one, no man, takes advantage of me."

"Got it, Parker."

She tapped him on the arm with the folder. "Don't look so serious. It's all good."

Yeah, it was good. She'd wanted his kiss. "Uh, back to the case, I need to know everyone who's been in this room."

"I'll e-mail you the list. A few are named in the reports. A couple of others I only know by occupation."

"That's fine. We can get those."

She led the way out of the bedroom and down the stairs, pausing at the porch door. "Why do you need to know all these people?"

"Because sometimes a killer hides in plain sight. He or she comes back to the scene of the crime to check if they did a good enough cover-up. I can bounce the list off what we find on the thumb drive."

Her brows furrowed. "A long shot, and a lot of people to investigate."

"That's okay. I have a really good—"

"Geek. Yeah, I know."

The death-defying ride back to his office tried hard to distract Ash from arousing thoughts of their almost kiss, how she felt in his arms. How he'd never let that happen again, even if she still wanted to. And then there was the disturbing discovery that someone had used magic in that room. Someone had blurred their energy signature. Maybe it was the same mage he'd encountered before. But why? Was there a connection? He hoped the answers lay in Diana's files.

****

Ash sat in the Keeper's office petting a needy Soot while he surfed the m-web. The cat had appeared as soon as he'd settled in the chair and punctuated heavy purring with annoying teasing.

"Listen, quit nagging. I just left Parker three hours ago. I don't know when I'm going to see her again." But he wanted it to be soon. Her body pressed close, her scent…

Soot rubbed a cheek against his arm. *"Hmm. Loving the pheromones."*

"Pheromones? I don't have pheromones." He didn't want to see Parker again. Nope. Not if Soot was picking up sexy chem vibes. And for other reasons. Number one? She was a Reg. Number two? He was still smarting over Amanda dumping him for the final time.

Huh. Smarting. Not lovesick, not even hurting. More like humiliated? Whatever. Dating was too complicated. Too demanding. Too…

He checked the computer clock. Where was Mort?

It had been a couple of hours since he'd copied the thumb drive to his computer and given it to him. Ash was anxious to figure out who might have gone after Diana. Someone had used magic in her house. *Please, don't let them be one and the same.* His phone pinged. Mort wanted him to come to tech right away.

He set Soot on the floor. "Stay here or go back to my office upstairs."

"You're not my boss."

"I *am* the boss of you, dammit."

Ash strode along the wide, main corridor of the Keeper wing, skirting the edge of the Magic Arts. He'd missed a hologram training session there yesterday and was avoiding a pissed-off Never Ravenwood. He passed the Sanctuary sector with its private meditation spaces. Everyone he met on the way nodded and smiled those soft-eyed, aw-isn't-that-cute smiles at him. Why? When he got to tech, he found out. Soot scampered into the huge computer room ahead of him. The damn cat had followed him, probably playing the part of some adorable comfort animal. Soot could have just winked out and appeared in here. No, Soot had to embarrass him by trailing behind him, probably strutting that high-tailed tip-toe thing all the damn way.

"This isn't 'embarrass your witch' day," he whispered. "Watch it, or I'll trade you for a mouse." The Witch Whisperer's wife, the healer Willow, had a mouse familiar. On second thought, that mouse had attitude, too.

The fake-windowed room currently held around twenty simple white desks arranged in two neat rows containing at least two monitors each. Only a couple were occupied. In an hour, the room would expand to forty desks full of disproving hackers all clicking away. Protecting the secret. All rooms in the Haven and the Haven itself, expanded and contracted as needed.

Mort raised a beckoning hand from the far desk. Poof, Soot disappeared. The cat didn't like Mort. Why? The guy was a softy at heart.

Myst, a bright canary in an eye-burning yellow t-shirt, perched beside Mort, who wore his usual bat black. Their combined Elite energies washed over Ash when he reached their side.

She summoned a chair from the next desk. "Sit. We're just getting into Diana's files. What a nutcase." She winced. "Um, bless the dearly departed."

"I can tell you're no empath," Ash said, sitting. He crowded her to get a look at the screen while tucking his legs under the chair. Lucien lounged his huge fluffy body on the floor under the desk. "Before we start on Diana's files, Parker told me an incredible story this morning. I'm glad you're sitting down." He told them about Parker's brush with magic when she was five. She truly believed that someone with superpowers saved her life and wiped her memory but didn't wipe Diana's. That's why they'd had gotten involved with the Mage Believers.

"Holy shit," said Mort. "Do you think the savior was a Keeper?"

Myst's eyes were wide. "Probably. That mind-blowing experience changed her life."

"Yeah. Just another example of how hard it is to keep who we are a secret. It's like someone blasts a dyke with a scatter shot every day. Not enough fingers to plug all the holes."

There was silence for a moment, then, "What's that

on your shirt?" Myst poked Ash in the chest.

Damn. Forgot about the stain. "Parker got emotional in her mom's bedroom."

"So that's, like, tears and snot?"

"Yes. Yes, it is." Ash waved a hand, and the stain vanished.

"Be careful. The London Bureau nulled the magic of a friend of mine before she could marry a Reg." Myst fiddled with one of six earrings. "Rules."

"How did we go from snot to marriage?" *Romance her.*

"Focus people." Mort adjusted the twin monitors. "Back to Diana. You look at the other monitor." He scooted his chair farther away and clicked furiously on the keyboard. "Okay, it wasn't hard to find people and businesses she royally pissed off, even the government. She was a big-time tin foil hat. But this one, Cleaver Chemical, stood out."

A blog post written by Diana appeared on the screen nearest Ash. It was dated a few months before her death. He scanned through it. She had savaged Cleaver Chem for more than just its alleged dumping practices.

Myst leaned toward the screen. "Am I reading this right? She said Edward Cleaver is a closet member of the furries?"

Mort guffawed. "I'd kill someone to keep that a secret."

Myst jabbed him in the shoulder. "I can picture you dressed as a mighty raven, or um, maybe a bat. But kill? You wouldn't hurt a flea on a tick, Mortimer."

Mort lifted his chin. "Reverence for life—the One Mother code. And, smarty, a bird is not furry."

"Okay, what are furries?" Ash asked. *Do I really want to know?*

"It's a subculture thing. Dressing up as the creature of your choice, like a bear or a lion. Could even be a lizard, smarty Mort. They have conferences, events, etc. Some town councilman resigned a few years ago after he was publicly outed."

"You know too much." Ash pulled his chair closer to the screen to see a small photo. "Cleaver likes monkeys, I guess. Can you look him up in the database, Mort? See if he's a witch?"

"Already did. He's not. Why?"

Ash looked around. The nearest occupied desk was out of earshot, but he lowered his voice anyway. "Because I detected energies from four mages in the bedroom where Diana supposedly took her life. Three of them were unique and distinct. I'd be able to recognize the mage. The fourth was muzzy. I think someone deliberately masked his or her energy signature."

"What? Why would they do that?" Myst asked.

Mort sat back. "To cover up that they were there, I assume?"

"And here's the most interesting part. Magic had been performed in the room."

"Wowzer. Way to use your superpower." Myst tapped her fingers on the desk. "But think for a sec. Sounds like some of the cops or paramedics, or whoever came to the house, were mage. One of them wanted to hurry up so did a hocus pocus to make their job easier."

"That makes sense," said Mort. "Sounds more logical than what I think you're implying."

"That a witch killed Diana? Smashed our code?" Ash realized the absurdity of the words as he said them. "The One Mother code is inviolate." But now, according to his dad, reverence for life now took second place to keeping their society a secret.

The worm in his gut twisted.

"Right. So, maybe since a killer witch is off the table, we concentrate on this Cleaver guy to start with," Myst said. "He's rich, could have hired someone to off her. Another Reg."

"One more thing. Somewhere in Diana's Mage Believer's file are references to suspicious deaths."

"I'll check out that file and sift through Cleaver's online dirty laundry. Every move he made prior to the murder." Mort's fingers flew over the keys while Myst powered up her tablet.

M&M weren't on his team that were investigating two other suspicious vehicular deaths. *Huh. I'm not now, either*. Should he tell them that he'd detected magic and fuzzy energy signatures at the scenes of those suspected murders? He'd dismissed those details as coincidental, the result of cross-contamination from maybe a Keeper using magic to wipe some unrelated record in the vicinity. But why would the Keeper mask his or her signature?

"Listen," Ash said. "I—"

"Hold on, I've been waiting for a text," Mort said. He grabbed his vibrating phone from the desk and checked the message. He looked up, his face creased with concern. "Frick, life is cruel. I'm needed at my Brooklyn clinic. No one else can handle this."

"What happened?" Myst and Ash asked in unison.

"A woman in my grief counseling group, a Reg.

Her husband just died. She lost a son only a month ago." He stood and pocketed the phone. "She's spiraling."

"Go. Myst can take over."

Mort raised an eyebrow. "You sure? Your keystrokes—"

"Really?" Myst moved over into Mort's chair and flexed her fingers. "You are a pain, Payne. Go."

He nodded and hurried across the room.

She scooted the chair closer to the desk. Lucien protested when her feet invaded his space. "I don't know how Mort can live there and absorb all that despair every day. He's one hundred percent empath. It would help him if he had the mesmer like you do."

"He's a trained clinician. If he'd stayed another semester at NYU, we'd be calling him doctor."

"Pfft. And wouldn't that be fun? He's already full of himself." Her fingers punched the keys.

Ash decided he'd wait to bring M&M in on his half-baked theory that was more like raw cookie dough. Maybe the deaths were as advertised—two accidental car crashes and one suicide. Councilman Hunter had taken him off the vehicular cases, but he still had access to the investigation. He needed to cross-reference the names of everyone who had been in the bedroom after Diana's alleged suicide with the mage database.

"I'm going back to my Keeper office. Let's get together at nine tomorrow. Hopefully, Mort can join us."

Myst nodded. "And then you can tell us more about how her bodily fluids ended up on your shirt."

He gave her the finger.

When he entered his office, Soot greeted him with

a yowl. "No, Soot, that wasn't funny. I didn't appreciate you dogging me all the way to tech."

Snarl.

"Yeah, I said 'dogging.' You missed your friend Lucien. He was there with Myst."

Ash logged into the case files for the two car crashes. He'd do another deep dive into both witches who lost their lives and the circumstances of the accidents. What had he missed?

Chapter Five

Skye exited her office building into the gloom of a cloudy, misty morning. When had this started? Earlier at the Queens' train station, she'd wished for sunglasses. She hurried along the sidewalk to the Bean Scene Cafe, a chill chasing up bare arms and the smell of pavement petrichor pinching her nose. It was only a block. How wet could she get?

When she left the coffee shop fifteen minutes later, a hot latte-no-foam in each hand, the mist had turned to a light drizzle. With head down she charged up the street, no free hand to wipe the foggy glasses.

She could almost hear her traitorous hair slurping up the moisture and curling into long, tight ringlets like one of those large, super-mop dogs. Soon, the white blouse clung as watery rivulets trickled between her breasts. She thanked the sweet universe for the good bra today because it was now visible in all its pastel pink lace glory.

She turned the corner and gave a quick glance in each direction before stepping off the curb into the street. Only a smidge of coffee had bubbled up through the hole in the lids in the rush back to the office. *I'll take this one small victory.*

Something loomed in her periphery. She turned. Like a slow-motion train wreck, a silver car bore down, silent except for the tires shushing on wet pavement.

The wipers swiped back and forth, back and forth. The driver was shaking his head, eyes wide, mouth working like a landed fish. He yanked on a steering wheel that didn't budge. The car surged ahead, straight for her.

She leaped. One cup lid flew off, then the other. Rain pelted her face. The opposite gutter reached out with a bone-jarring promise. *This is going to be painful.*

Oomph! Her right shoulder landed first, then her whole side. She lay there while brain fuzz cleared. Her heart walloped her chest. *I'm alive.*

"Skye." Someone knelt and touched her shoulder. "Are you okay? I've called 9-1-1." The familiar voice, urgent, and smooth as liquid honey, somehow relaxed her. *Hunter.*

"I think so. I wasn't hit." She rose on one elbow. By some miracle, the glasses hadn't joined the lattes. The pavement scraped across an arm. She felt no real pain anywhere at the moment. Shaking like a wet dog, she scootched over onto her butt and sat up.

Hunter pushed the sodden hood back. "I saw you fly in the air. Maybe you should—"

"No, I'm fine. Just rattled."

A tall, thin man rushed over, his sneakered feet splashing through shallow potholes. Water dripped off his long, pointed nose. He gestured wildly. "Oh my God, I'm so sorry. The brakes. The wheel…"

The car, one of those electric models, sat at the curb in front of the next building.

"I walked into the street. It's not your fault. You didn't hit me." She held up an arm. Hunter grabbed it and hauled her up. For a moment she had the insane thought of nestling into his warm arms like yesterday. *Jeez, I must have hit my head.*

A siren sounded in the distance. Hunter turned to the man. "You got the car stopped."

"I can't explain it. Suddenly the brakes worked."

Hunter sprinted up the street. The man shrugged and followed him. Hunter opened the car door and sat inside. No way she'd be left out of this investigation. She gave herself a quick inspection for damage. Tear in the blouse, jeans dripping cruddy water into her loafers—what one might expect from playing dodgeball with a car. The body aches would come shortly. She walked toward the car on shaky legs while finger-wiping the glasses. She smudged them worse than before. The rain had slowed to misty dampness.

Oh, the lattes. Both cups had been flattened beneath the tires of the runaway car. A siren screamed around the corner ahead of a white police car with blue NYPD lettering. It stopped beside her, and a cop leaned out the window. "Someone call 9-1-1?"

"It was for me. I'm okay. Fine. I walked out in front of that car. Didn't hit me, though. Wasn't paying attention."

"You don't want us to call a bus?"

"No. God, no. I'm fine." She rolled her shoulders. "Just wet." *And mad about the lattes.*

The cop nodded to his partner behind the wheel. The car rolled up the street to stop behind the electric car. She couldn't summon the energy to walk any faster and met Hunter on his way back just when a bone-deep chill set her teeth chattering.

She rubbed her arms. "Hey, you look like you could stomp kittens." Besides the angry slash to his mouth, the eyebrows had a puzzled tilt to them.

"You look like a drowned—I won't say it. Let's

get you inside."

Rat. He was going to say rat. Once through the glass door, she squeezed out sopping hair and wove it into a single braid. "I wish you'd have stayed there. I wanted to hear what the cops said."

"They're calling for a tow truck." He removed the dripping jacket and held it away from his body. "They won't let him get behind the wheel until the car gets checked out."

"That's good. Maybe some intermittent electrical problem." The damp t-shirt clung to his muscular pecs in a swoony way.

"You sure you're okay?" He reached out, hesitated, then dropped his hand. His mouth tilted in a side smile.

Hmmm. That smile. "I'm not gonna lie. I'll be sore tomorrow." *Bra.* She crossed her arms. "What are you doing here?"

"Decided to grab that list of names in person. Check out your office."

"Oh, yeah? Without an appointment? I'm really busy."

"And wet. We're both really wet."

"Jeez. Come on. Hope you have something for me." *Not your fee schedule.* What she didn't have for him was any money. She led the way along the hall and down the stairs, ruined leather loafers squelching. She keyed the pad outside the door and opened it wide. She expected to hear Trinket's bark, then remembered he was at the groomer.

"Welcome to my bunker. Not exactly a stunning office with an awe-inspiring view, but we like it." He walked past her into the aisle of metal shelving.

"Love it so far," he said.

"Who the hell is that?" shouted Jo. "I'm a conceal carry."

"Stand down. Hunter is with me." She edged by him, grabbing his jacket. He arched a brow. "Don't mind Jo. She's old, ex-military, and we've never had visitors." She hung the jacket on a hook at the end of the aisle.

Skye walked across the room to Jo's desk, Hunter following close behind.

Jo was half out of her chair. "What the hell happened to you?"

"Oh, I dodged a speeding car and landed in the gutter."

"She's lucky to be alive." He extended a hand to Jo. "Ash Hunter. You're the 'talented geek?'"

"Geek, eh? White Fox, aka Jo Wilson." And under her breath, "Not *ex*-mil, but don't tell her." Jo shook his hand and sat down with a grunt. She tucked a pink-streaked strand of hair, behind an ear. "So, no lattes?"

Skye exchanged amused glances with Hunter. "Sorry. They were collateral."

"Nice bra, by the way." Jo winked at her.

Crap. "Hunter, have a seat." She avoided his gaze and waved in the vicinity of a pair of plastic-padded kitchen chairs lined up in front of the desk.

She hurried behind a tall bookshelf at the back that served as a room divider. She hadn't made up the bedding on the cot for days. Well, he wouldn't be seeing the makeshift bedroom anyway. She threw on jeans from the clothes rack and a bra from the suitcase. Pain radiated from a shoulder when she raised both arms to maneuver into the sweatshirt. *So, it starts.* She cleaned the glasses with a tissue and grabbed a towel on the way out.

Jo gave a nod. "Hunter is impressed with our setup here. He was filling me in on your dance with death."

"I'm already starting to feel the pain."

"See how you are tomorrow and the next day. Don't hesitate to go to urgent care." He sat on the chair, long legs stretched out, managing to look as relaxed as a sloth, which irked her for some reason. Her nerves still quivered.

She handed him a towel. "Sorry. We don't keep men's clothing here." *Gah.*

He smiled and took the towel, running it over his short-cropped hair with its zigzag cutout, down bare arms, biceps flexing. He lay the towel across his knees.

Stop staring. I'm out of control. She'd been standing there drooling like some sex-starved nitwit. She got her libido under control and sat in the chair beside him.

Jo grinned. "That was fun."

Skye shot her a killing glance. "Hunter would like that list of names we've been compiling."

"Coming up." Jo's fingers worked the keyboard.

Skye shifted the chair at an angle with Hunter's. "Any viable leads so far in my mom's files?"

He straightened, waking up the sloth creature. "Yeah. One guy stood out. Edward Cleaver."

The name made her skin cockroach crawl. "Cleaver Chemical. Jo and I helped Mom investigate them."

"Seems like he has motive. Follow the money, right? If the company's illegal dumping practices were ever proven, they'd lose a ton of money, probably go out of business."

"And don't forget ol' Eddie's monkeying around," said Jo. "That furry reveal made it personal."

"My tech is delving into him and the company. Maybe he hired a hitman."

Skye tapped fingers on the desk. "I've been over that ground, but maybe you'll find something new. Plus, there are so many others she's pissed off. Are you looking into the suspicious deaths in her M.B. file?"

Hunter nodded. "On it."

The only sound for a couple of moments was Jo's keystrokes. Hunter seemed lost in thought, his eyes narrowed, and brows furrowed. She'd love to have one of those superpowers right now and read his mind.

"Done," said Jo. "Want me to e-mail the list to you or save it to a thumb drive?"

"E-mail." His phone buzzed. He stood and removed the phone from a back pocket. "It's after nine. I'm late for a meeting with my team." He handed her the damp towel. "Thanks for inviting me in."

She stood, holding his gaze for a couple of beats. The deep-thinking lines across his forehead melted away. He gave her that side smile, half knowing, half innocent. All sexy. "We're not fancy here, but we get the job done."

"I can see that." He turned to Jo. "Nice to meet the super tech behind the scenes."

"Let's just call me what I am. A hacker. And a damn good one." She beamed. "Great to meet you, Hunter. Oh, love your hair, by the way."

He laughed. "I love yours. Pink looks good on you."

She had to break up this damn love fest. "We all have work to do, Hunter."

He nodded. "We'll talk tomorrow. Be careful out there, both of you." He grabbed his jacket and let himself out.

Skye flopped on the chair. "Be careful? Why did that sound like more than looking both ways before we cross the street?" Even though she hadn't given a statement to the cops, she'd call the police station tomorrow and follow up on that car. Just in case.

****

On the elevator to the Haven, Ash called on the magic to dry his clothes and shoes. In an instant, his comfort level rose to acceptable, at least physical comfort. Inside, his gut churned. Someone, a witch, had tampered with the car that almost hit Parker. But there was more.

He hurried to his office where man-in-black Mort and multi-colored Myst were standing, waiting. The Keeper teams really should have a dress code, especially since Myst wore a chameleon familiar on her shoulder. He wondered if the mottled creature was having an existential crisis trying to pick what color on her shirt to turn. "Sorry I'm late."

"Nine-thirty." said Myst. "You're never late."

Mort shrugged his thin shoulders. "What she said."

"Let's meet somewhere else. Myst, leave now, take the route by the cafeteria, and go to the Sanctuary, Pod Number Seven. Go inside."

"What?"

"Go. Wait for us there."

She gave him a puzzled frown, nodded, and left the room.

"Something bad happen?" asked Mort.

"Yeah. We need total privacy to talk." Ash

couldn't be sure of his own office. "Okay, go along the west corridor and join her. I'll be there in a couple of minutes."

Mort hurried out the door. Ash waited a beat before he left. He strolled by the cafeteria that wafted bacon and maple syrup and freshly baked bread smells. He'd been hungry earlier, but his appetite got crushed beneath the wheels of a car.

The double door entry into the Sanctuary wing stood wide open like the welcoming arms of the One Mother. He stepped over the threshold, triggering the walls of the corridor to fill with images from places he longed to visit, but never would—striding African beasts, like giraffes, elephants, and zebras; waves lapping the shore of a white sand beach. Soft music, some classical violin composition, played on the air. His taut muscles and clenched jaw relaxed, gut settled. He decided he didn't come here often enough.

He passed no one in the corridor but heard voices behind the doors to the main meeting hall. He turned a corner that led to rows of private pod doors. One could use the pods to meditate or meet a mentor or counselor in complete confidence. Anxiety was high, not only in this Haven, but in others around the world. It was becoming more and more difficult to maintain the secrecy of their vast mage society. The pods were soundproof, perfect for what he had to discuss.

At number seven, he knocked twice, paused, then gave one rap. The door opened and he stepped inside the room. Mort set a protection spell on the door. This pod was maybe fifteen by twenty, with a large, fake opaque window on one wall that could be made to show daylight or darkness. False sunlight shone through the gauzy curtains. The walls were a pleasant pale blue, the upholstered easy chairs plump and comfortable.

"Let's sit." Ash indicated the chairs. "Thanks for turning off the sensory walls in here."

"Had to. My Taichi images fought with Mort's crochet patterns." Myst mimed working needles through yarn. The chameleon's bulging eyes swiveled in opposite directions.

"Freaks me out that they can pluck something from our brains and throw it up on the walls." Mort shuddered.

Myst shook her head. "Mort, you of all people need some calm and tranquility." She turned to Ash. "But I guess we won't be getting much of that right now."

"No. A car almost hit Parker this morning. That's why I was late."

"Is she okay?" Myst asked.

"She's fine. Maybe banged up. She dove out of the way."

"That's scary," Mort said. "Does she need to talk to someone? I can—"

"Thanks. Don't think so. But it was deliberate. The car went straight for her. The driver had no control. When I sat in the driver's seat, I sensed magic."

Myst let out a breath. "Was the driver a witch?"

"No. And what struck like those proverbial ton of? Whoever had performed magic on the car, fuzzed their energy signature."

Myst's eyes widened. "No way. So, a witch may have offed the mom and now wants the daughter?"

"Cleaver, maybe?" Mort leaned bony elbows on his knees. "He's as rank as his sewage. We said he could have inadvertently hired a mage hitman, or maybe it's someone else in Diana's exposé file." He huffed. "Diana—impressive and yet so loony."

Ash shook his head. "Remember I told you about those two car accidents I was investigating? Now we have four incidents where magic was performed, and someone fuzzed their energy."

Myst stood and paced in a circle. "We need to find a connection."

"I think I found one, but I want you guys to talk me out of it," said Ash. "It comes back to the Mage Believers."

Mort stiffened. "Really? I've been through those suspicious deaths Diana listed in her Mage Believers file. "Suspicious" is a stretch for all of them. I'm pretty sure they can be discounted."

"Well, I had to do a deep dive into the backgrounds of the man and woman, both witches, who were killed in separate car crashes a while ago. Both had issues with their magic in some way that had manifested in public and reported on the Believers' website. Both were quickly discredited by our tech."

"Did they ever seek a magic healer? Maybe that Witch Whisperer is behind this." Mort leaned back in the chair, stretching his Ichabod legs out in front of him.

"Never Ravenwood remains incarcerated at Immortal Trowbridge's estate, except when he's here teaching holograms. He's still healing broken magic with his online clinic. His focus right now is on his wife Willow. They have a baby on the way."

"Ash is right. I saw Nev and Willow at her sister's wedding last year, and they were both totally into each other. He's not right for this. Especially with the baby."

"This might sound as crazy as some of Diana's way-out conspiracy theories, but maybe a witch is going around eliminating threats to our society. Targeting Regs and witch alike."

"Hmmm. Another stretch. Wouldn't that endanger our secrecy even more?" asked Myst. "Aside from freaking breaking the One Mother oath, as well as human decency."

"Yes, it would." Mort steepled his long fingers. "I'll keep looking into Cleaver and my next in line from Diana's files, Everett Winsdale. According to her, New York's esteemed mayor reeks of corruption."

"I don't know. You haven't convinced me that my theory is whack. This needs to be kept among the three of us. If I'm right, the killer could be here in the Haven." Ash stood. "We'll divide and conquer. Myst, I'll send you the list of names of everyone who's been in Diana's room since the murder. Cross-reference it to the common witch database. I'm looking for four names."

"Got it," she said.

"Mort, poke around more into Cleaver and do a dive into the mayor. Let's see if there's anything concrete there or rule them out once and for all." Ash placed a hand on Mort's shoulder. "This next is a big ask. You can say a hell no."

"Anything," said Mort. "I only need about four hours a day next week at my clinic unless a disaster happens. Always a possibility."

"That's fine. On the Bureau of Witchery's m-web is an encrypted database containing the name of every witch and whether they are a Quaint, a Special, or an Elite." He paused, waiting for Mort to freak out. He didn't. "That classified database also lists what special magic they possess. As a Shadow Force leader, I don't even have clearance to access it."

Mort nodded. "I get it. You want me to hack into the database and see who has some kind of power that could mask their energy signature. I've never heard of that power myself."

Myst shook her head.

"Me neither," said Ash. "You know the penalty for breaching a secure protocol?"

"I'm guessing a one-way ticket through the portal to Tae-wen."

Myst flopped on the chair. "Our ancient homeland. Mort, you wouldn't last a day in that place. No coffee maker, no microwave, not to mention most of the Malgren race still hating on magic."

"That's why I asked Mort, Myst. He has the skills. You'd shrivel up and die without your tablet and your animals."

"Hey, I'm okay if he sacrifices himself for the greater good," said Myst. "What are you going to do, Ash?"

"Kick back and get drunk while you guys do all the work."

"That I'd love to see." Mort stood. "You need a break, too. Seriously. Take the rest of the day off."

Ash laughed. "Right. I'm going to dig into the Mage Believers and keep a close watch on Parker just in case that attempt on her life wasn't a one-off." His phone buzzed a text tone. He groaned. "Councilman Hunter. He wants to see me in his office." He pocketed the phone. "He needs a report. I need to decide how much to tell him."

Myst punched his arm. "You got this."

The chameleon had turned bright red. Ash wondered if his own dread showed so plainly. He forced a smile. "Not worried. Just getting all this sorted out so he'll understand." He went to the door. "You two leave a minute apart. Send me what you have as soon as you can."

Ash walked back along the Sanctuary corridor that featured a band of wild horses galloping on the walls to a lively country-western tune. This would be as close to his dream of a dude ranch getaway as he'd get. He waved a hand. The walls settled to quiet undulations of blue.

The Bureau of Witchery council rooms were located far to the back of the Haven, back being a relative term for walls that could move with a touch of special magic. It took him a ten-minute brisk walk before he reached the hallowed Witchery halls. He gained access by pressing a finger on a touch pad and pushing the magic. It took him a moment to subdue the vibrational waves from the various Elite Council members that sizzled along his nerves.

He took a deep breath at Councilman Hunter's office, knocked, and let himself in. Standing in front of Gray's massive oak desk was Employment and Disputes Council member Jada Gladstone. Jefrem, her preening, pretentious, insufferable son, stood beside her. Yeah, he didn't like the SOB.

"Jada," Ash said, coming beside her. "Nice to see you." He gave a nod to Jefrem, who wore business casual like a tux and that slicked-back hairstyle Ash hated. Jada always looked like she floated on air, thin as a strand of hair in black and white. "How's Willow?

Nev?"

"My daughter is fabulous now, no thanks to you."

He wanted to smile. She was so damned forthright. As the exiled Witch Whisperer Nev's warder, Ash had faced a considerable challenge. Nev and Willow's stubborn spirit had bested him. Few let him forget that fact.

Gray cleared his throat. "People, let's get on with it. Jefrem Gladstone, here are your papers. Welcome to the Council. You'll work directly under Cecil Camford." Gray handed over a document pouch.

Ash stiffened. *The Housing Council?* They were responsible for adjusting the Haven's size, for providing and maintaining accommodations for everyone who wanted to live here. A huge job for a second in command. Jef was not up to the task. Jada had pull, as Ash well knew.

"Thank you. I'm looking forward to jumping in." Jefrem turned up his snooty nose. "I already have plans to improve the deplorable Keeper offices."

Ash smiled. "Not necessary. I—"

Gray held up a hand. "Hunter, you're late with a report."

Jada arched a brow. "Not surprising. Thank you, Gray. We'll talk later." She directed Jefrem to precede her out of the room.

Gray's enormous desk was meant to impress, but instead, it made his dad seem smaller by comparison. He wore that damn vest over a pristine white shirt.

He looked up from his papers. "Well? Why are you late?"

"Wanted to double-check some information."

"Sit. Tell me."

Ash remained standing. "I'm in with Parker. She hired me to investigate the death of her mother."

Gray glanced up from his papers. "Great. Stick close. I want to know the minute she talks about writing anything to do with those Mage Believers. She must be stopped."

"Yeah, someone did try to stop her. Permanently."

Gray raised an eyebrow. How was that his only reaction?

"She was almost hit by a car this morning. She dodged out of the way."

"I don't understand."

"The car had been tampered with. I checked it myself."

"What—"

Ash held up a hand. "There's more. Someone had used magic to freeze the controls and aim the car straight for Parker. I wouldn't be able to identify the witch because he or she obscured their energy signature."

Gray was silent for a moment, his face expressionless. "I've never heard of that kind of magic, obscuring your signature."

"Neither have I. I think the same witch has killed others. The two witches who died in traffic accidents, Parker's mother—all involved magic and a witch who fuzzed out his or her unique aura. All had something to do with the Mage Believers."

"So, what are you saying?" His dad rose from the chair.

"A witch is murdering whoever is jeopardizing our secrecy."

Gray turned toward the opaque window behind his

desk as if viewing some kind of vista. "Who else knows of this?"

"Just M&M. They're helping me figure out who it might be."

Gray faced him again. Deep lines creased his forehead. "I know we don't see things the same way, Ash, but this was bound to happen. Someone may be zealous about keeping us secret from the Regs, especially now when there are increasing magical malfunctions. We can't let the Regs know of our powers."

"Zealous? Murder is just someone being zealous?"

"Maybe that's the end of it. Those, how many? Three? Besides, you might be mistaken about a cover-up. String Parker along about her mother or find a scapegoat and stand down on any further investigation of some rogue witch. I'll keep an eye on that situation myself. Focus on preventing Parker from revealing us."

"You can't be serious." Ash had heard enough. He held up a hand and ignored Gray's shouts as he strode through the door. He would continue the investigation. He would find out who the killer was despite the Councilman's objections.

Why tell him to stand down? The impossible answer clawed its way up his spine. His dad just didn't care.

Chapter Six

Skye's spidey sense sent creepy crawlies skittering across her skin. Someone was following her. From a bistro chair in the Bean Scene, she sipped a latte and sniffed the fresh-baked cinnamon rolls.

"Are you watching your six? Over." Jo's rough voice sounded in her earbuds.

Jo had suited her up with a different button cam before she left the office. Skye agreed this would be standard practice for the foreseeable future.

"Can you see the room? I'm against the wall," Skye whispered. She poked at her glasses. "The stalker."

"Affirmative. Navy rain jacket with the hood over his head."

Yeah. She'd been keeping an eye on the guy seated near the door with his back to her. There was something about him—his stiffness? Alert posture? He wasn't enjoying what should be a lazy Sunday morning.

The large coffee house was bustling despite the threatening rain. Most would be heading into Central Park across the street. No suits today, just jogging leos and backpack babies. Some spring tourists, mainly seniors. A few customers sat in other chairs with their backs to her. The guy in the navy all-weather jacket seemed out of place. Or she was just paranoid?

She rolled the aching shoulder beneath the

raincoat. Yesterday's dive into the curb saved her life, but she paid the price in pain today. The office cot she'd slept on last night hadn't helped. She'd been lucky that car hadn't hit her. Hunter's arrival had somehow settled her nerves.

What the hell's wrong with me? She didn't need a man to pick her up from the ground and kiss her boo-boos. Make everything all better. She could handle herself very well, thank you.

She checked the phone. Hunter was going to call sometime today. Hopefully, he was onto something. That's the only thing she needed him for—to find out who killed her mom. Why was she targeted? She still had an unsettled feeling, like something was off about him. Too bad because Hunter was kind of easy on the eyes. Tough on the willpower.

Wait. Had navy guy turned to look at her? *Jeez.* She'd just looked away for a second. "Jo, I'm on the move."

"Affirmative."

Skye grabbed both lattes and meandered across the floor, weaving among the tables, eyes fixed on the back of navy guy's hood. When she came beside him, he shifted away. She pretended to trip, launching both lattes in his direction. The lids popped off. Liquid splashed on his shoulder and down the jacket sleeve.

"Oh, my God," she said. "Sorry, mister. Let me—"

He got to his feet and turned. *Hunter.* Her breath hitched. Coffee dripped off his fingers to the floor.

His nostrils flared, lips forming a thin line. "Parker."

Jo's shrill laughter pierced her ear.

Blood rushed to Skye's face. "What are you doing

here? Are you"—she lowered her voice—"spying on me?"

He glanced around the room, but most of the patrons ignored them, except for a barista headed their way armed with paper towels. "Let's go outside." He started for the door.

"But I—I…" Skye shrugged. "Jo, on the move." She hurried after him.

"Affirmative, klutz." *Chuckle*.

Skye found him seated at one of the outdoor tables underneath an overhang. She plunked her butt into the chair. "You were following me."

"I was." He gave her that charming half-smile. She wasn't falling for it. "Guess I'm no good at undercover protection," he said.

"Protection?" Her voice rose on the last syllable. "I can take care of myself." When he raised both eyebrows, she added, "Yesterday was an accident."

"It was deliberate."

"What aren't you telling me?"

He sat back in the chair and studied her. Was he reading her mind? Looking into her soul? Into his? Those eyes…

"My team and I are still investigating."

"The cops didn't find anything wrong with the car. I called them this morning."

She let him take her hand. Well, it was like her hand had a mind of its own. His was warm, smooth, held hers in a light, gentle grip. The tight muscles relaxed into puddles.

"Parker, do you trust me?" The eyes, soft brown…

That word "trust," loaded with lies and betrayal. "I don't trust anyone." A rude squawking sounded in her ear. "Oh, except Jo. At this point."

He nodded. "I don't blame you. You don't know me. But trust your gut. Your life is in danger."

"You think it's Cleaver, don't you?"

A pulse beat at his temple. "Could be. We're looking into him and a couple of others that Diana more than pissed off."

There. Right there is why she could not trust him. His eyes had lost focus, shoulders had tightened. The "could be." She pulled her hand away. Time to follow the "no second chances" rule.

"Well, look," she said, standing. "This has been peachy. I gotta go back inside and get Jo her latte or she'll kill me. I'm afraid of her."

"Yes!" Jo cackled.

Skye waved a finger. "Do not try following me again. I can spot a tail." She moved to walk past him.

His goofy grin got her back up. Skye gave him the finger and headed toward the shop door.

"Charming dude," said Jo.

"Do you want that latte or not?"

"You're a hard case, Parker." Jo coughed. "No foam."

A few minutes later, Skye exited the shop with a latte in each hand. Hunter was nowhere to be seen. "I guess I told him."

"He's really into you, you know," said Jo. "He cares."

Jeez. "Sorry, you're breaking up. Phtt. Breaking—"

"Get back here with my latte. Alive. White Fox out."

Rain threatened, but Skye took her time. No

rushing headlong into the street like yesterday. She crossed with her head on a swivel, made it downstairs and through the bunker door in one piece, heart thumping. Trinket greeted her with a sharp bark from Jo's lap.

She handed a latte to Jo and set her own on the desk.

"Dying for this," said Jo. "Oops. You almost did, so thanks."

It wasn't lost on Skye that her red hat had kept the pink streak in her hair today when she usually changed it up day to day. Jo had fallen for Hunter's charm. She removed the button cam from the jacket. Trinket wriggled his butt and whimpered.

"Okay, fur face." Skye grabbed the drink, gathered the dog up in one arm, and carried the little bundle to her desk.

"Don't forget dinner tonight at my place. Bring the wine," Jo said. "Hetty is making her famous lasagna. She just texted me."

"Hey, I won't forget, not for her lasagna." Trinket settled on her lap after turning around a half dozen times. She'd only taken a couple of sips of the latte when snorty snores fluttered from Trinket's lips. If only she could sleep that deeply, or at all.

"Can't wait to share this," said Jo. "Don't get up. I uploaded some vid snippets I compiled to our shared drive."

Skye logged into the drive and clicked on the video. The first one, dated last year, showed their mysterious figure, aka Ash Hunter, in a gray hoodie jacket walking away from the camera. It was captioned, "Levitating Credit Card—Anecdotal." She'd seen that one before. And the next one, and the next one. She hit pause.

"Seen these. That's how I identified Hunter."

"Look at the last one. I grabbed it from Mage Believers just now."

The last video captioned "WTH?" was a long shot looking across a busy street to people on the sidewalk. She zoomed in. "That's me. And Hunter is walking up beside me." Her pulse kicked up. "Ten days ago, Central Park." Traffic whizzed by in the video, creating a stop-action effect on those being filmed. The tie-dye leotard jogger she'd questioned stood at the corner.

"Wait for it…" said Jo.

Bicyclists rolled past. A bus obscured the view of her and Hunter. The screen went whiteout for a few seconds, turning to heavy flurries. Skye squinted at the screen. "I can almost—is that Hunter lowering his arm?" The screen turned white again. When the scene cleared, Hunter was gone. She stood there, frozen in place, feeling that disorienting vertigo. Vehicles continued to rush past between the videographer and her. But there in the street, the early morning light glinted off red glass. The video ended.

Skye let out a breath. "The glass. Yes!" She pumped a fist in the air. Trinket stirred. She looked over at Jo. "For once, I don't like what I'm thinking." She replayed the last few seconds. A "n-o-o-o" echoed in her head and in her heart. "He *is* some kind of paranormal."

"Take a breath, sister. Consider this rationally." Jo always supported, but always encouraged another perspective.

"Rationally? Something happened to put that

broken glass in the street where it wasn't before."

"No evidence of what really happened. You are an investigative reporter. You follow the evidence. Hard evidence." Jo tucked her pink swath behind an ear.

"What do you bet that very soon the video will be challenged and disproved? There will be a post that the image was altered or manipulated." Skye played with Trinket's top knot.

"If—when that happens, I'll see if I can trace who posted the fake news item. I'm working on who posted this video, too."

Skye nodded. Her immediate need was to confront Hunter. Like now. She grabbed the phone and texted him.

Not five seconds later, a loud rapping sounded on the bunker door. Trinket stirred and yapped.

"Who's that?" Jo asked, pulling out the drawer that held her Sig.

Skye hated the sharp jab of fear. She picked up Trinket and stood. "Don't shoot yet. Let's see."

She deposited the dog on Jo's lap and walked to the door, body gone shivery cold. Loud rapping sounded again, making her jump. Trinket set off on a round of staccato barks. Damn that Hunter for striking fear into her already paranoid self.

****

Ash pocketed the phone and stood waiting outside Parker's office door, clad in the damp, stained jacket.

"Who is it?" Her muffled voice made it through the heavy fire door.

"Hunter. You texted me."

"Wait, what?"

The door opened with a jerk. A dog's shrill bark

echoed off the walls. A red stain traveled up Parker's neck, and nostrils flared. She poked at the glasses. "What the hell, Hunter. You followed me from the shop?"

"I did. White Fox's latte was in jeopardy."

"Jeez. Get in here."

She held the door wide, and he stepped through. She wore a green "Oregon—Bigfoot Country" t-shirt. The image of Bigfoot was a damn good likeness to the real thing, a Tae-wen kasnatch. He walked ahead along the aisle of shelving and to Jo's desk, aware of Parker's steam behind him.

"Hey, Hunter, thanks for keeping an eye on my latte," Jo said, brushing the pink hair with her fingers. The dog on her lap had stopped barking, and now wiggled and whined. "This is Trinket."

He scratched the dog behind a fluffy ear. Trinket's eyes closed. "Love your bow." A tiny blue bow held a tuft of fur into a peak on the top of its head.

"I didn't call you here to love up the dog." Parker stood beside him with arms crossed, green eyes narrowed. "You've been lying to me, probably about everything."

Groan. "What's this about?"

Parker turned to Jo. "Throw that video up on the big wall monitor."

A hard knot formed in the pit of his stomach. What the hell had she found?

The video started with a tilted camera shot across busy traffic from one side of a street to the other. *Damn. Central Park South. That day.* "What am I looking at?"

Parker huffed. "I know you know."

He shook his head. And then there he was, standing beside Parker. The stomach knot twisted as a bus started to pass the wobbly bike rider. The video went snowy for a few long seconds. The instant after he'd set the bike back on its wheels, he'd thrown a pinpoint eraser to all electronic and human memories, both of which would go fuzzy. The video paused at a frame that showed red glass shards sparkling on the asphalt. The damn glass from the bike's broken blinker light. He blamed the beautiful woman he'd stood beside for his own memory blip.

Parker walked to the wall monitor and pointed. "There. The glass. At the start of the video, no glass."

"We had this discussion days ago. I have no idea. I saw nothing." Lying was coming all too easy. It was just another one of the things he hated about the job. But this constant fibbing to Parker had his soul cringing and wishing he was on that African safari. "Maybe the glass was already loose. Maybe it just fell out right when he passed us."

"Yeah. That's it. Why didn't I think of that, Jo?"

"Hey, sounds good to me," she said.

Parker thinned her lips. "So, all at once our cam quit working, the camera used in this video whited out, as well as one of the building's security cams, and my memory. You, apparently, weren't affected at all. Get creative, Hunter."

He didn't need the ability to read Reg energy signatures, if they had any, to know she was beyond agitated and frustrated. "I don't know. Power surge? Solar flare?"

Jo snorted.

Skye locked eyes with him. He got her silent go-to-hell message. "Ash Hunter, are you a paranormal with special powers?"

"What? Me? I wish." He attempted a disarming smile while acid flooded his stomach. "I'm just a regular person struggling through this crazy world just like you, trying to find lost keys, losing track of a cell phone, dropping pizza on the floor. All that happened last night."

Her shoulders sagged. The fight left her eyes. "Well, thanks for not laughing in my face."

"I would never do that. I know you believe in magic, Parker." He wanted to touch her in the worst way and smooth out the furrowed brows.

"Well, now that I'm here"—he turned to Jo—"that file of names you sent me, the ones who'd been in Diana's room, all checked out as non-suspects. *Except for the one who blurred their energy signature.* "From Diana's personal file, that Cleaver dude I mentioned before. He's prime. My tech is still concentrating on him. He has a couple of strong arms that do his dirty work."

"Give me their names. A few months ago, I did background checks on some of his employees," Jo said. "I'll share what I have."

"Hell-o." Parker waved a hand. "Still pissed you were following me."

Ash put on a sunny face, aware he was sending them on wild goose chases. "Sorry, I'm all out of suggestions for—whatever." He pointed at the screen. "If that's all, I'll get back to my office and dig in." He turned to go.

"Hunter. Don't shadow me. Don't lurk outside my door, or even this building."

"Yes, ma'am."

"I'll fire your ass. Probably don't need you at all."

"Harsh," said Jo. She hugged Trinket close.

Parker didn't need him. She was dead wrong.

****

Soot appeared on Ash's lap as soon as he sat at the desk in his twenty-sixth-floor apartment. "Yeah, I'm feeling rejected. Almost got fired. Deserve it."

Soot circled his lap and curled up. *"Tell her what you are. Problemo solved."*

"She already suspects I'm mage. I hope I've convinced her I'm not. She's a Reg. She can't know about us."

He shot Mort a text to send Jo the names of Cleaver's heavies for her to compare notes and help on the deep dive. After powering up the computer, he went through the login protocols for the Bureau of Witchery site on the m-web twice before he got them right. He clicked on Diana's database that he'd copied from the thumb drive and logged in her password *TrustNoOneDP5*. Mort had gone through a lot of Diana's blogs contained in many folders labeled by issue. *Polluters. Political Corruption. Climate Crisis. Sinkholes. Mt. Rushmore.*

Mage Believers. "Let's see what Diana has in here."

Soot yawned and unfurled, claws flexing way too near his crotch. Ash shifted in the chair. With a sardonic side-eye, the cat jumped onto the desk and stretched out on the cool glass beside the computer.

"Sorry I'm boring you, my dark demon." Ash clicked on the M.B. folder. Mort said he'd already been through it, but Ash was curious.

Lots of sub-folders with sub-folders containing many files. He clicked on "Paranormals by Kind." More folders. And then one titled "Murder Files."

"Murder Files. Cute." He opened the first document out of six. "Adam Williams, thirty. Official cause of death undetermined. Date: August 3, 2018." He scanned the blog Diana had written, the newspaper write-up that listed the death as a heart attack, and the Mage Believer's posting of the story. Their version, anyway. Body, still warm, found in his ground-floor apartment. No evidence of foul play. "A witness swore they saw someone run past in front of a window. Garden showed no footprints. Williams was a member of the Believers."

Soot opened one eye.

"Yeah, I agree. Not enough there." He scanned through the next few files. Two car accidents due to some fault with the vehicle, yet no fault was found. Just like Parker's near miss. "Victims were Believers." The accident stories were all too familiar. Nerves tripped. He had the urge to run back to Skye's office and plant himself there, no matter what she said.

One bathtub drowning of a Mage Believer. Suspicious, but not definitive. Another "phantom person" sighting on the scene but no physical evidence of a presence. A drug overdose of a supposed non-user. Not a member of Mage Believers that Diana could find, but the group posted the story on their site for some reason.

"Diana did one hell of a detailed research job on all this, Soot. Police records, coroners' reports."

The last file was the death of a woman who'd mixed up her prescription drugs. "Wait. The date on this file is the day before Diana's murder." The file was incomplete. "She'd been researching this one."

He clicked into a subfolder called "Notes and Map." The street map of New York City and environs was marked with colored dots at the location of each death. The dots were identified with the victim's initials, the date of death, and were color-coded by cause of death. Six dots. The hairs on the back of his neck stood on end. Central Park lay almost dead center on the map. What else hovered there below Reg consciousness? The Haven.

His stomach soured. Mort hadn't put much stock in these events once he got his claws into the corruption files, but Ash did. He hated to put any more on Mort's plate by sending him back into the Murder Files to do a deeper dive. If Ash could visit a couple of the scenes on some pretext, he could see if any of them still resonated with aura.

And Councilman Hunter? Ash would keep Diana's findings on the down low from Gray for now considering he didn't want Ash investigating any of this.

Diana's copious notes, in a daily journal style, followed the map. She summed up the murders with a statement that was just formulating in his own mind. He read, "Any one of these deaths taken on its own elicits a 'that's interesting.' Taken together, they cause awe, shock, and outright fear. Who will be next?"

Diana and the Mage Believers were convinced someone with paranormal powers was committing murder. He had to agree. The final note dated the morning of her death read "Update Skye tomorrow with latest files and notes for her Project Pulitzer."

He stroked the sleeping cat's sleek fur. "Sorry, Parker. I'm going to have to shut you down." Project Pulitzer would never see print. Was that what the killer was trying to do?

Chapter Seven

Skye knocked on the door of apartment number 420 precisely at six, a bottle of cab clutched in one hand and a gift bag in the other. Trinket began his shrill yapping.

The door opened and Jo held out a hand. "Cover charge to Club Wilson is a bottle of booze." She'd changed into a jazzy mid-calf dress, all zigzag black stripes, cinched with a thin leather belt. Trinket wriggled his way between her legs, whining for attention.

Skye handed her the bottle and rattled the gift bag. "I also come bearing gifts." She crouched to kiss Trink on the nose before walking past Jo into the roomy apartment, the luscious aroma of tomato sauce undercut with baking bread filling her nose. "Why are you dressed up? And where's your cane?"

"Hate that damn thing. Makes me look old. Besides, my hip is almost healed."

Her hair was done up all pretty, too. Pink streak intact. *Hmmm.*

Hetty hailed her from the kitchen, open to the living area. "Skye, I need a taste tester."

Ha! Hetty wore the badly stained bib apron from the restaurant where she'd retired as head chef. Skye set the bag on the counter. "Before I do, open this."

"You brought me a gift? You didn't have to do

that."

"Oh, I think it's time, and I missed your birthday."

Jo joined them at the island. Hetty tossed the tissue aside. She pulled out a pure white bib apron adorned with a name and logo. She held it up. "The Ebony Truffle." Her pale blue eyes teared. "I love it. Where did you find this? The restaurant has been closed for years."

"I kind of pirated the design from their old files and had the apron printed. I was going to wait till Christmas, but I can see my timing is just right." The truffle image replacing the letter "o" of Ebony always looked like a fossilized dinosaur turd, but she wasn't about to change the iconic design.

Skye helped Hetty off with the soiled apron. She tied the new one on over a soft pink silky blouse and long skirt. "You know, guys, I really feel underdressed in this sweatshirt."

"We love Bigfoot," said Hetty. "Here, taste this. I used it in the lasagna." She dipped a ladle into a pot of red sauce, then held it out.

Skye sipped. Tomato, oregano, garlic. The flavors swirled on her tongue and made every taste bud dance. "Delicious. Let me know if I can help."

A knock on the door set Trinket yapping again. The clutch of fear that grabbed her by the throat annoyed the heck out of her. The dog scrabbled across the hardwood floor. "Are you expecting anyone? Check the peephole, Jo." She thrust the cane into Jo's reluctant hand and hustled to keep up with her.

Jo opened the door wide without checking. "Shut up, dog. Come on in. So glad you could make it."

Hunter. Skye groaned. Why the hell had they

invited him, and why did he have to look so amazing? She pushed her glasses higher. He wore a pale blue denim long-sleeved shirt, rolled at the cuff, and dark jeans. He'd had a trim before he came, the thin lightning bolt etched in sharp detail. *The Flash. Right.*

After a scratch behind the dog's ears, he straightened and locked eyes with her. He smiled in what he probably thought was a disarming way, crooked with a slight head tilt.

Heat rose up her neck. "You are like the proverbial thorn in my ass."

"Hi to you, too," he said, venturing into the room. "My contribution." He handed a bottle of wine to Jo, who tried to hide the cane behind the folds of her dress.

Skye's fingers curled. "Didn't I make myself clear like, five minutes ago?"

"Five hours. And I came because Jo so graciously invited me."

"I figured that out. You should have said no."

"Ahem. Corners, people." Jo thumped the cane and handed her the bottle. "Welcome to our home, Ash Hunter. The young lady over there in the kitchen is my sister, Hetty." She laid a hand on his arm and ushered him to the large sectional.

Skye shook her head. *Be civil. For now.* At least he had the decency to bring a very nice Pinot. She set it on the counter.

Hetty waved a large bread knife. "Nice to meet you."

"Are you twins?" Hunter sat and placed an arm along the sofa back.

Jo giggled and sat beside him.

Did she actually giggle? Sheesh.

"No. We're a couple of years apart. I'm the younger one."

Hetty huffed.

"We've lived together ever since our parents died and Hetty got divorced. What is it now, Hetty?"

"Fifty-odd years. Too many," said Hetty.

Skye sat at the far end of the sectional, away from Hunter. Might as well contribute to the small talk. Jo would get an earful after Hunter left. "Jo retired from NASA. Tell him about your different jobs there."

Jo lifted Trinket up on her lap. "In the early '70s, I started out with their IBMs. Moved on to programming. Couldn't resist the challenge of those I's and O's.' Did some tech work for a hush-hush Government ops team through the '80s, '90s. Can't provide specifics or I'd have to kill you." She laughed along with Ash. "I've worked special assignments, one-offs, until I semi-retired a few years ago."

Jeez. It took several years of knowing Jo before she'd learned all of this, and Hunter got the inside scoop after one day.

"Love all the artwork—close-ups of planets." He pointed to a huge art piece hanging on the opposite wall. "Saturn."

"Yes. And over there's my pride and joy." She pointed to another large picture.

"That iconic photo of a moon footprint?"

"Personally signed by Neil Armstrong himself."

Skye watched while Hunter and Jo talked. Hetty interjected a comment or two into the conversation from the kitchen. It was as if he'd known them for years. He sat with so much ease, something she'd noted about him. But unsettling undercurrents ran beneath his composure. She was good at reading people from years of experience. So was Jo. Somehow, Hunter had managed to charm the caution right out of her hacker.

"Dinner is ready," said Hetty.

Skye transported a basket of warm rolls to the long dining table set for four before helping Hetty carry the plates of lasagna. Hunter escorted Jo and sat her where she indicated. He chose the chair beside her.

"Shall I pour the wine?" he asked, picking up Skye's bottle of cabernet.

"All around," said Jo as Hetty took off the fungal apron and sat.

"Fill mine to the top." Skye picked up the wine glass and tilted it his way.

He arched a brow. "I knew there was a reason I liked you."

"Only one?" Her face heated again, probably melting every freckle into one congealed mass. What was wrong with her?

"Definitely not." He topped off the glass.

"I see what you mean, Jo," Hetty said. The grin stretched across a face so smooth and wrinkle-free, Skye suspected a recent Botox injection.

The delicious meal continued with little chit-chat but for Hunter declaring Hetty's lasagna the best he'd tasted. Skye agreed. When dessert time came, she followed Hetty into the kitchen.

"Has Jo been talking about me and Hunter?" she whispered.

Hetty took the lid off a strawberry cheesecake and precision cut generous slices. "She may have mentioned that you two look so cute together. And you do."

"Jeez. No, we don't. Not cute at all."

Hetty touched her arm. "You may not see it now, my dear, but be open to the possibility. It's early times yet. Trust your heart."

Trust. Yeah, she had a hard time with trust. Especially where Hunter was concerned. She carried a cheesecake plate to Jo and stacked up dirty dishes.

Hunter joined her in the kitchen and placed a plate in the sink. He leaned in. "Are we an item?"

"You, too?"

His dark eyes held a gleam. She thrust a slice of cheesecake at him.

"Thanks. Talk later?"

"Sure."

The cheesecake was devoured around talk of Hetty's time at the Ebony Truffle, the excitement over the Michelin star while she was head chef, the momentous visit from POTUS and FLOTUS in 1985. She donned the apron again to show Hunter.

By eight all was put away and cleaned up. Skye was ready to go. She'd ordered a ride on the app. *Why doesn't Hunter leave?* He was talking to Jo in front of the footprint picture. She didn't want to walk out with him like they were a couple or something.

"Thanks for dinner, Hetty, Jo," she said, heading for the door. "See you tomorrow, Jo."

"Oh, hey, let me walk you out. Thank you, ladies, for the wonderful evening."

Argh.

"What are your plans for tomorrow," he asked, as the elevator glided to the first floor, and they exited into the lobby.

"We're going to dig into who posted that bike incident video on Mage Believers, see what pops up on the site to refute it, trace that post." She judged his expression.

He nodded, not a flicker of reaction as they walked to the door. He held it open for her. "Are you going home from here?"

"Yes. I need a good night's sleep for once." That cot in the office with the too-thin mattress had her waking up grumpy and muzzy-headed. And the house was close by.

She stepped out into damp darkness, streetlights haloed by mist. A dark blue car sat idling at the curb. "Well, my ride is here. Keep in touch."

He opened the car door, and she slid in. He crowded in right beside her.

"What?" She moved over, annoyed at the intrusion while her body parts, damn them, responded to his nearness. "We're ride-sharing?"

"Sam, meet Skye Parker. Sam's my Uber guy."

He knows the driver? The man twisted around, a grin spreading across his face, crinkling his eyes. The dark curving full mustache and the beard shot with gray reminded her of an aging elf.

"Nice to meet you, Ms. Parker."

"Same."

Hunter gave Sam the address and they sped away from the curb. Hunter's thigh lay along hers. She could have moved over but didn't. *Why am I so weak?*

"What did you do with my Uber?"

"Sam persuaded him to pursue other rides."

"Uh-huh. So, we're back to shadowing me."

"For the time being."

She let out a huff. "You are so stubborn."

"So are you."

She chuckled. "Yes, I am. Tenacious, motivated. Got me where I am today."

"And where is that exactly?"

"Hmm. Loaded question with too many answers."

"I'll be specific. Tell me about the Pulitzer you missed out on, and what your next project is to ensure a victory?"

"You mean you didn't read my exposé of the rat-infested New York City underground? A classic. Got me on the short list."

"Missed it, sorry."

"I started investigating the rats when Mom and I discovered nests of them under the house. Moved on to horror stories from the subway system, the sewers, the Hudson River. I crawled into places even you wouldn't go."

He laughed. "For sure."

"Early on, I came whiskers to nose with a rat the size of Trinket. The thing bit me." She poked her glasses with a finger and pointed to small scar on the side of her nose.

"Shit. And still, you didn't give up."

"Like I said, tenacious, motivated. Maybe reckless. I wanted that damn Pulitzer."

The car came to a stop. Timely because she was sure he was going to remind her of the second part to his question.

"I'll walk you to the door," he said, getting out.

She slid out. "It's just right there."

He walked ahead of her up the three steps and waited under the porch light. *Yeah, stubborn.*

She thanked Sam and followed, fishing the key from a pocket. She turned it in the lock. "Good night.

Like I said, keep in touch."

"I'll see you inside."

He held her gaze, dark eyes searching. She had to smile. He was so serious. She stepped into the dimly lit, closed-in porch, Hunter right behind. He glanced around, probably looking for a deranged murderer lounging on the wicker rocker.

"Safe and sound," she said. The pale light shadowed the angles of his face, making his dark eyes even darker, his appeal laser bright.

"I hope so." He stepped closer, keeping his voice just above a whisper that brushed her cheek. "Can I send Sam to pick you up in the morning?"

"Hunter, really?"

"Really. You can't take the subway. Too dangerous even if there wasn't a possible threat."

She held his gaze. The danger? His nearness. The threat? That she'd weaken and fall for him. But her hands strayed up to his broad shoulders anyway. His warmth seeped into them. He placed a light kiss on her lips, a sweet cheesecake-y wine kiss. Her arms wound around his neck, pulling him in, deepening the kiss, dislodging the glasses. His tongue played with hers. A thrill, sharp and needy, shot through every girly part. His body pressed closer, arms went around her. *Was that his heartbeat or mine?*

What am I doing? She groaned and pulled back from the kiss. His breathing was rough, like hers. She unwound from his neck. He took her chin in a hand, adjusted the glasses, then placed a soft kiss on the scar.

"You should go now." Her voice was raspy.

"I know."

"I don't even like you."

He smiled. "I know."

"I don't trust you."

He nodded. "Wish we could work on that."

He wishes? Before she could ask what he meant, he turned for the door. "Sam will be here at 6:30 a.m."

She locked the outer door and went through to the house. She recognized his very real worry about her safety so would let Sam drive her. But Hunter himself was the real threat. To her heart.

Chapter Eight

Ash turned away from the computer screen that compounded the headache thrashing his brain and stroked Soot. The cat lay across his lap like a limp dish rag. An hour ago, an unthinking witch had used magic to stop his child's ice cream cone from falling on the ground. Ash had to run into Central Park to wipe the memories and electronics of a large crowd.

"Thanks, you jerk."

Soot tensed.

"Didn't mean you, Soot."

This particular pain was endurable, not like the thunderclap migraine last time after the bike incident with Parker. He hadn't felt the need to close the blackout drapes in the living room yet.

A jolt struck his temple. Maybe the whole shitty mess of murders, cover-ups, and lies was getting to him. The lies to one special redhead bothered him the most. She'd outright asked him if he was a paranormal. He groaned. Gray said the Keeper job was an obligation, a privilege. He was trapped in that burden of birth. He'd give anything to step away.

Soot stirred. *"Find your stupid happy place. I vote for Tahiti. Or, deal."*

"You're pushy even for a familiar. All right. I'll meditate."

He closed his eyes. Delicious lasagna dinner at Jo

and Hetty's. Was that three days ago? The even more delicious kiss at Parker's. She'd said she didn't like him. Now there was a lie. Could you like someone and not trust them at the same time? More than like?

Soot intruded. *"Sure."*

"Stop reading my thoughts. But you're right, Soot."

His attraction sent him careening down a dangerous path. He'd have to end any involvement with Parker eventually or risk having his magic taken away. How did a mage live without their power? It was one thing to want civilian life, quite another to carve out your soul. He stroked Soot's silky fur. The cat melted on his lap.

"Don't worry. I'm watching over her while keeping my distance. At least she has the common sense to allow Sam to drive her everywhere."

He opened his eyes and logged back into the computer. The danger wouldn't be over until they found out, then neutralized the mystery witch who was fuzzing out his or her aura. Mort had come up empty for all the risk of hacking into the classified database of what powers each witch had. It had taken him three full days to go through thousands of names in New York City and environs. Not one listing had hinted at the ability to mask their aura. Either the ability was so rare, or the mage lived far outside the area.

There was still Cleaver to consider, at least. He could have hired a witch without knowing it to get rid of Diana and Parker. That mage didn't want to be identified. Both Mort and Jo had named two strong arms as possible suspects, but neither were witches. Jo didn't know that, of course. She'd put forward the possibility of opportunity on both counts.

But what about the rest of the murders and the ones in Diana's files, if they were murders? He hadn't yet been able to get out to any scenes of the crime to check auras, but he was sure a witch was out there eliminating threats to their secrecy. Parker would be right on top of the hit list. His stomach hollowed out.

"Sorry, gotta go." Soot disappeared before he could scoop the cat off his lap.

He hustled down in the elevator. Out on the busy street, the noon sun beat down on an unseasonably warm May day. Pedestrians heading to Central Park crowded the intersection, while the usual Manhattan traffic flowed past. He ignored the pinpricks of dread along his spine, resisting the urge to break into a headlong run. *Keep calm and focus.*

He sensed some who passed were mage, nodding to those he recognized, including Sam who sat in his car outside Parker's building. Ash kept his eyes sharp when crossing the street and entered the building. He sensed no auras, fuzzy or otherwise except his own, descending the stairs.

He texted Parker—*I'm outside the office*—then knocked.

A minute passed. Was she going to see him or what? He let out a breath when the door opened. "Hi. Just checking in."

Under an open jacket, she wore a long "shit happens" t-shirt and leggings, and a frown.

Shit.

"I'm kind of busy, Hunter." She nudged her glasses.

"I'm here to talk to Jo." He wasn't. Her red hair

hung loose in spectacular waves. His mind galloped off somewhere, leaving his body to overreact, catch fire, and melt.

"She caught an Uber for home a half hour ago. Hetty called. Trinket's sick and is at the vet."

A few working brain cells kicked in. *Trinket. The dog.* "Oh, poor Trinket. Hope it's not serious. I'll talk to *you*, then."

She blew out a breath. "Listen—"

"I know what you're going to say. Can we talk inside?"

She hesitated a few beats, then opened the door wider. "Just for a minute. I'm busy."

"So you said." He followed her along the aisle of shelving and into the room. He sat in Jo's chair and swiveled.

She stood, arms crossed, looking like a fiercely beautiful warrior. "Okay. Shoot."

"First, why the hostility?"

"I…" She lowered her arms and went to her desk. "Sorry. I'm not being fair. I was deep into something here." She glanced at the computer screen.

The Pulitzer story? He stopped swiveling. "And that other thing? The elephant in the room, namely me?"

She smiled. "Picturing you as an elephant."

"Not unflattering."

"I've been avoiding you," she said, standing. She clearly didn't know what to do with herself. "We can't have a repeat of Sunday night."

"So, I'm irresistible, is that what you're saying?"

A flush rose up her neck. "In a maddening way, yes."

He wanted to go to her, taste her lips one more time, or one last time. Instead, he said, "As much as it pains me to agree, I do. We need to keep our relationship strictly business." For many more reasons than she could ever know.

She nodded, her uncertain gaze holding his for so long he wanted to say eff this and take her in his arms.

Her cell rang. "It's Jo." She clicked into the call. "How's Trinket?" A pause. "Jo, what's wrong? Are you okay? Jo?" She turned to him, face crumpling. "I couldn't understand what she was saying, and then she hung up."

Ash stood. "Could they have lost the dog?"

Parker grabbed the backpack. "Sounded worse. Is Sam outside?"

"Yes. Let's go."

He led the way up the stairs and out to the car. He got in beside her.

Sam raced through the streets. Parker was so busy on the phone trying to reach Jo that she made no comment, or maybe never noticed that the green lights along the way were unusually long and the reds short. Not his doing. Sam's. An ambulance sat out front of the apartment building.

"Oh my God." Parker clutched his hand as Sam parked behind the vehicle. "Something's happened to Hetty or Jo."

"We don't know that yet." Uncertainty raked his nerves.

They rushed to the lobby and into the elevator. A couple of neighbors had gathered outside the open door. They parted for Parker as she ran along the hall and entered the apartment, calling for Jo. Ash shut the door on the gawkers.

He followed Parker through the empty living room to a very purple, lacy bedroom. She rushed over to Jo, who sat on the edge of the bed. Two of three EMTs knelt on the carpeted floor beside a prone Hetty. Ash was no doctor, but by the deathly stillness and grayish tone of her skin, he could tell she had passed. He sent up a silent prayer to the One Mother.

"I'm so sorry," Parker said, her arm around Jo.

Ash looked away as the two close friends cried. A lump the size of Manhattan lodged in his throat. At least one of the EMTs was a witch—a Special, judging by the energy signature. The mage gave Ash a nod. There was another tickle on his senses he couldn't identify, but magic had been performed here very recently.

"Any idea the cause of death?" Ash asked him. Both ladies looked up.

"My guess is heart attack. We called for her doctor. He'll be here shortly."

Jo shut her eyes a moment, releasing more tears. "She had a bad ticker. But took all her meds religiously."

A female EMT walked toward them to talk to Jo. Parker patted Jo on the shoulder and stood. "Hang in there, my friend. I want to speak to Hunter for a sec."

Parker approached him. Her eye makeup had smeared and run down her face. He handed her a tissue from the nightstand. She sniffled into it. "The living room," she whispered.

He followed her out of the bedroom. "What's up?"

She took a deep breath and blew it out. "Someone killed Hetty."

"What? She was old, with a bad heart."

"Convenient. She looks like Jo. They thought she was Jo."

"You're not serious?" He had to admit, when she'd failed to reach Jo again, he'd thought for a moment that her hacker had been a target.

"Deadly serious. Think about it. How hard is it to bring on a heart attack? Or to poison someone? I'm telling Jo to insist on an autopsy."

"You're right. Too much similarity to one of the deaths in your mom's files."

"So, do you believe us that someone with certain powers is killing people?

Crap. "No, I won't go so far as to say that."

While Parker was talking about an autopsy, Ash called on his senses to identify the other aura in the room. A witch had been in the apartment earlier this morning. The energy signature remained amorphous, without edges, without heft. His chest grew tight.

That same mage, the one who fuzzes his aura, had murdered Hetty.

****

Ash stayed with Jo and Parker throughout the day. He texted Sam the sad news. Sam would wait with the car as long as needed. Hetty's doctor had come and gone, agreeing with the EMT that the cause of death was a heart attack. He said there was no basis for an autopsy. Ash knew an autopsy would be a waste of time because the witch was skilled at covering his tracks, judging by Diana's murder files.

He texted M&M to keep on those files. Find him *someone*. A funeral home gathered up the body with a sensitivity that brought fresh tears to the ladies and did nothing to lessen the balloon in his throat.

After lunch, several of Jo's relatives arrived. Ash took Parker out onto the roomy balcony lined with pots of blooming flowers and climbing tomato plants. Sam's car sat at the curb four floors below. Parker leaned her elbows on the railing, face turned to the sun. He stood beside her and let her have a moment. Soon enough he'd add to her tragically altered world.

She sniffled and blew into a tissue. "This is all my fault. Because of me—"

"It's not your fault. Some crazy is out there for what reason we don't really know."

"I can't believe Hetty was murdered," she whispered, glancing through the closed slider.

He wished it could be otherwise, to take that guilt off her shoulders, but she needed to be afraid, needed to be terrified she might be next. "They probably thought she was Jo. An autopsy would be useless." He took her shoulders in both hands. "Listen, you and Jo are in real danger. The guy, and I'm leaning toward a man, will soon find out he killed the wrong sister and will try again for you both." He was tempted to push a mesmer onto her frazzled nerves, but she needed to be hyper-alert.

"We'll hunker down in the bitch bunker for a while. I'll hire real security." Her smile was forced.

"Not good enough." He removed his hands from her shoulders and paced.

"What could be more secure than a basement fortress with a coded entry, steel door, no windows, and an armed ex-military, trigger-happy old broad with a killer dog?"

"He could take out any guards, just wait you out."

Of course, the witch could just draw on some basic magic. Bypass codes and locks.

Her brows drew together. "Wow. Just—wow. There's more to this than you're telling me."

"You and Jo can come to my place." His mind churned with the possibility. The logistics. The risks. Could he handle such an arrangement?

"What? Your steel tower?"

"I have a killer cat."

The slider opened. Jo's cousin stuck out her head. "We're gathering up some of Jo's things and taking her with us to Springfield for a few days."

"Okay, Cynthia. I'll be right in." She turned to Ash. "Massachusetts. What do you think?"

Diana's map showed only suspicious murders locally. He hoped the guy didn't travel beyond the subway. "Might be good. How about you go with them?"

She scoffed. "For how long? A couple of days? Weeks? Not happening, Hunter."

"Steel tower, then." He didn't want her out of his sight, anyway. She held his gaze for a moment but thankfully didn't argue. "We'll go to your office so you can get a change of clothes. Leave your laptop there. One more thing, ditch your cell phone. We'll get burners."

****

What he hadn't figured on was Trinket. The vet had texted Jo just before they all left the apartment that the dog was ready for pickup. Trinket just had a tummy upset. He recommended a different dog food. Parker told Jo not to worry. She'd get the dog after a stop at her house and look after him.

So now he rode up on the elevator to his place loaded with Parker's stuff, the dog's stuff, and a worried Parker. Soot would be another problem altogether.

The cat proved his point as soon as they'd shouldered their way through the door. Hackles raised, he stood on tip toe beside the desk. Trinket tugged hard on the leash to get as far away as possible from the angry beast. Parker picked up the little dog, coo-cooing baby talk. The cat hissed.

"Knock it off, Soot." Ash wheeled the small roller bag past Soot and gave the cat a nudge with his foot as he passed. *We'll talk later. This is only temporary.*

Soot pushed his thoughts onto Ash's mind. *"Like an hour temporary? With that suitcase? What's with the blue bow?"*

Ash ignored him and continued to the bedroom, Parker following behind. He stashed the bag inside the walk-in closet and shoved a bunch of shirts over to make room on a rod for anything she'd like to hang up.

"I can't stay in your room," she said, turning in a circle. "But wow, it's gorgeous, in a modern-masculine-minimalist kind of way."

"You have a writer's way of putting things. I get it. I like white. Sleek. Clean."

"And no clutter." She set Trinket down and unclipped the leash. He ran around sniffing the oatmeal-colored carpeting. "Your cat won't attack Trinket, will he?"

"Trinket won't throw up on my floor, will he?" Ash stood in the closet doorway. Parker was staring at his king size bed. *Is she thinking of the two of us together, naked, tangling up the sheets while we have hot—*

"Yeah, he might." She scooped him up again. "Anyway, I can't sleep in here. I'll take the couch."

Not going to happen.

"Hey, while we're in here, I want to show you the other exit from the apartment. A secret exit. You know, just in case. Never had to use it yet."

"Whoa. You had me at secret."

He went deeper into the closet, parting shirts way at the back, and slid out a low shoe shelf.

"Funny. I thought your closet would be full of hoodie jackets."

"I can be fashionable when I want to be."

"Uh-huh."

"Look." He showed her how to press a certain molding strip on the wall. A half door near the floor silently swung open.

"Holy crap. Nice."

"You have to go on hands and knees. When you close the door after you, it automatically slides the shoe rack back against the wall. It's a tight squeeze along a narrow corridor. At the end is another half door to a utility closet for the office cleaners. The closet is near the back stairs. No one ever uses the stairs. At any floor, you can cut in and take one of the elevators."

"How did this place end up with a secret exit?"

"The original owner of this place added it when the building was under construction."

"Lucky you."

He followed her out of the closet. Trinket wriggled, so she let him down. Ash touched her arm. Her wide, green eyes, clouded with concern, held his. "Listen, this guy, this killer, is brutal and persistent, whatever his motives. He is too good at making murder look like it's not and covering his tracks. Take no chances."

She nodded and left the room. With a final glance at the bed, Ash followed.

She hovered by the desk. "I'm lost without my laptop. Can I use your PC?"

Nope. "I have a laptop you can use." He pulled a case from a shelf and set it on the desk. Nothing on this one to incriminate him. "Can I take your jacket?"

"No, thanks. It's cool in here."

Trinket had his nose to the floor and began a nasal assault on every inch of the space. No Soot. Wherever he was, the fur ball knew better than to wink out of sight in front of a Reg.

"I guess you don't have another one of those fancy office chairs." She dragged the padded armchair closer and sat.

It was too low to type comfortably. He could conjure one in seconds, but instead offered her an overstuffed pillow from the couch. "You could have mine, but you won't take it."

"You're right," she said, placing the pillow on the chair. She sat and removed the computer from its case. "Perfect." She gathered her hair back into a low ponytail, securing it with a scrunchie.

He sat in his "fancy" chair and powered up the PC. A migration of African beasts tramped across the screen. "What are we working on?" He could only see the top of her bent head as she tapped away.

"Well, if I had an actual job—oh, by the way, the paper fired me, so you are pro bono right now. I'm in the cloud delving deeper into my mom's database. I'd love to make something of those Murder Files involving Mage Believer victims, but I can't quite get there. Neither could Jo or any of those other useless P.I.s. Only six or seven questionables over how many years?"

"At least six years." *Damn. I've gotta check those scenes for magic.* But now, he couldn't.

"I'm trying to find what angle a killer would have in these cases, if there's only one killer." She tapped away on the keyboard.

"You're stuck on the paranormal. You know how *that* sounds. But the usual course is to follow the money or the power concentrating on whoever she pissed off in business or government. Our killer is in there somewhere."

She drew her brows together. He hadn't convinced her.

Rowl. Hiss.

Trinket came tearing around the corner from the living room and leaped into Parker's lap. Soot pranced into the office area after him, tail high.

Ash tried to ignore the messages flung at him but failed.

"This is why I hate dogs. They snot up the place, contaminating my markings."

"Sorry, Parker." Ash stood and glared at Soot. "Bad cat."

He pushed his thoughts to Soot. *Listen, you're being an asshole. Knock it off or I'll send you to the Haven office.*

"Bad cat? Asshole? I've been called worse."

Parker cuddled Trinket. "Maybe this is a bad idea. I can go to a hotel."

Yeah, a really bad idea, but somehow, they had to

make it work. He picked up a stiff-bodied Soot and brought him over to Trinket, who quivered in Parker's arms. "Soot, make nice."

"Make nice? Are you kidding me?"

Ash gave the cat a squeeze. "You like Parker. Parker likes the dog."

Parker smiled. "I love your reasoning, Hunter." She stroked Trinket's back.

"Yeah, Parker is okay."

A rumbly purr vibrated along Ash's arms. Soot went slack, leaning a nose toward Trinket. After a few seconds, the dog inched closer until they touched noses. Trinket stopped trembling and began sniffing.

Soot tensed again. *"Make it stop. Please, make it stop."*

"Okay, that's enough for now." Ash put Soot down. The cat sauntered out to the living room.

Parker got back to work. Tap, tap. The dog jumped down and tiptoed away.

Ash would wait till he was in the Haven office for the Bureau's m-web. He logged into the Mage Believer's social media page. There were several new posts since the last time he'd looked—a flock of "possessed" birds flying as one and creating an intricate spiral up into the sky. Not magic. Just starlings doing what starlings do. A fountain with reversing water. Debunked. By Mort?

Parker let out a huge sigh and sat back. "I can't stop thinking about Jo. Hetty was more than just a sister to her. She was a best friend. At some point, I'll have to tell her we think Hetty was murdered."

"When the time is right."

"When will that be? How long will I be here,

Hunter?" Her voice registered both impatience and frustration. "I can't just stay here forever while we flail around looking for some phantom murderer."

"You've only been here less than an hour."

She blew a raspberry and went back to the laptop.

What were his options? Soon he'd be out of any. He needed to consult with someone fast. Not M&M. He needed them to focus on the investigation. Certainly not Councilman Hunter.

Immortal Elizabeth Trowbridge.

No. He couldn't. Could he? He'd been in her presence quite a few times, spoken to her maybe a half dozen. Last time was after the Witch Whisperer fiasco last year. Trowbridge was ethereal yet powerful. Gentle yet fierce. Always fair. Still beautiful at nearly four hundred years old. She was a native-born Tae-wenian and a distant relative. He could trust her, unlike Gray.

A quiver of anticipation, maybe apprehension, triggered his nerves. He powered off the computer. "Listen, I have an appointment."

Her brows drew together. "You just remembered now?"

"I'll only be gone an hour." *I hope.* "Stay inside. Keep the door locked. Text me the second anyone comes to the door. I'll bring back food. What do you like?" *Don't say Thai.*

"Thai. Anything Thai."

Groan. "Okay. I'll be back as quick as I can."

He glanced up and down the hall, calling on his powerful magic to set a protection spell on the door, impenetrable except by the highest powers.

Only a privileged few had E.T.'s cell number. He wasn't one of them. To sneak in to see Elizabeth

Trowbridge without the proper protocols and permission was punishable by a stay in the security cells, or worse. He could be stripped of all rank.

Hey, not a bad idea, then.

Would she be available? Would she accept him without raising alarm? They were blood after all. He said a prayer to the One Mother. She'd better be listening.

Chapter Nine

Skye cradled the burner phone between cheek and shoulder while clicking through more of her mom's files on the laptop, looking for anything she might have missed.

On the fourth ring, Jo picked up. "Hello? Who's this?"

"It's me. Ash just left. I'm on a burner."

"An abundance of caution. I like it." Jo coughed.

Skye hoped she wasn't smoking again. "How you doing, girlfriend?"

A sigh. "Fine. We just got here an hour ago. Already all these mushy aunts and cousins are smothering me. And, God, there's a baby here. A goddamn two-year-old. He ran off with my cane."

"Ha! That'll keep you young. Listen, Trinket's fine. We've got him on new kibble the vet recommended."

"Thanks for looking after the little lint ball."

"Hetty's service?" A heaviness settled in her chest. They hadn't had any time to mourn together.

"She's being cremated. We're planning a memorial for one day next month."

"I'm so sorry. I loved Hetty."

"I know. We all did."

"Well, I'm at Hunter's place. He insisted."

A bark of laughter. "Right. I was going to ask

where Ash left from. You want to be there, or you wouldn't have gone."

"Only because I'm nosy. Do you know he called me Nosy Parker?"

"Not original, but accurate. Occupational hazard." Keyboard clicks sounded in the background. "I retreated to a bedroom. I'm on my laptop. Checking out some of the mayor's shady dealings lately. After that, I'll look again at the Murder Files because I know you want your mom's killer to be in there."

Too soon to tell her she's sure Hetty was murdered by the same guy. "Good. You're keeping busy. Listen, I'm wearing the button cam that matches a different jacket. I've placed it lower down. Hunter hasn't noticed. Hopefully, it's recording. We'll check it when we get together. Gotta go. I have some snooping— investigating to do. Take care, Jo. Love ya."

Skye scraped the chair back from the desk and stood. Hunter had been gone ten minutes. It was probably safe to have a look around, check out the artwork, the small kitchen, his room.

Yeah. Snoop.

She considered she still had her investigative reporter hat on, the slouchy, soft felt fedora one, and the belted trench coat with the oversized magnifying glass in a pocket. She wanted to figure Hunter out. If not a paranormal, just who was he? Oh, she really wanted to trust him cause he was hot, but couldn't quite get there. Maybe there were clues in this sterile office residence. Maybe she'd learn his secrets.

She scooped up Trinket in one arm and perused the few shelves in the desk area. Trays kept the usual office supplies in some kind of order. The dozen or so books looked like a curated collection of law school tomes probably from his college studies, criminal investigation manuals, a couple of mystery novels. There were no file cabinets to rifle through. So disappointing. He must keep everything electronically.

She moved on to the bedroom. Moody art prints of New York skylines hung above the upholstered headboard. Dare she look in the night table drawers? Would there be a weapon?

Oh, just a peek. She slid one open. A tissue packet. *Trojans. Nice. Trust Hunter to be prepared.* She slid the drawer shut. The bathroom held a bit of color, with teal tiles in the huge shower and matching towels. A long, dark walnut vanity held two gleaming sinks and chrome faucets. She slid open a drawer while holding Trinket tight. No snotty nose splotches allowed on the sparkle.

Holy pharmaceutical. Every extra-strength OTC drug for migraines filled the space. Even a couple of prescriptions. How often did he have those headaches, and why? The one he had when she first met him was a doozy. Maybe Hunter was just a regular guy like he said, one with a health issue.

A low rumble sounded from Trinket's throat. He squirmed in her arm as she closed the drawer. *Omigod. Hunter already?* Tip-toeing to the bedroom door, she listened. Someone was trying the front door. She held Trinket's mouth closed to muffle any barks. She scooched along the living room wall and peeked around the corner to the desk area. A dark form moved out in the hall beyond the opaque glass. The doorknob jiggled.

She jerked back. *The killer?* Her heart slammed so hard against her ribs it might have broken one. Trinket struggled, but she couldn't let him down or loosen his muzzle. No way would she let anything happen to Jo and Hetty's precious pet. Crap, the burner phone was in her bag beside the desk.

Her ears started buzzing like a swarm of murder hornets in the brain, followed by a pulse of air or energy against her body, or something that didn't disturb even a hair on her head. *What the hell was that?* She didn't wait to find out. She hurried back into the bedroom and closed the door, then to the walk-in closet, closing that door behind her. Soft lighting came on. Deep in the closet was the shoe shelf. She slid it out from the wall.

"Trinket, shhh. No barking," she whispered. The dog quivered like her favorite vibrator and issued tiny whimpers before she put him down. He stuck by her side.

She crouched under a rod of shirts. *Shit, where is the spot?* Someplace on the molding. She adjusted her glasses and ran shaky hands along a trim strip. Her breath came in shallow pants like the dog's. She pressed every couple of inches. Nothing. Better lighting would help.

A sound. She stilled. The bedroom door opening? Her stomach liquified. *Shit, shit. Where—?*

Then the secret half door opened soundlessly. She pushed Trinket ahead and crawled through. She shoved the door closed, plunging the narrow, low corridor into the darkness of a tomb.

She sat, gulping in stale, fetid air. Her nose pinched against a foul odor. She knew that smell. *Rats.* The shiver traveled along her spine and shafted soul deep. New York skyscraper rats, even on the twenty-sixth floor. *Yep.*

Click, click. *Please let that sound be dog's nails on the tile floor.* She had no idea how long the corridor was. Never had time to look before closing the half door. Hopefully the shoe shelf closed too, like he'd told her. Hunter never said anything about the lack of lighting or the length of the corridor. Was he still in that just-remembered meeting, or would he walk in on the intruder?

Her heart rattled her chest, breaths coming in doggy pants. *Keep moving.* On all fours, she felt along the gritty floor, blinking in hopes of capturing some tiny sliver of light from somewhere. Trinket's nails clicked ahead of her. One knee pressed down on something sharp. *Ouch. Mother clucker!* She scrabbled faster, sweeping at the floor ahead of her.

Fur brushed her hand. The image of a rat, all sharp claws and dripping fangs, spasmed her lungs and sent her head up to bang on the low ceiling. She bumped into the furry body. A whimper. *Just Trinket.* Her breath whooshed. He was as blind as she was.

She stilled again, listening. Errant sounds from other units came through the walls just inches from her—bangs, muffled music, loud voices somewhere. There was no telling now if anyone had come through that secret door after her.

How much farther? She continued into the endless darkness. *I can do this. I can do this.* Hell, she'd endured worse. That New York sewer, dark and dank and dangerous. Full of her subject rodents and rotting garbage. She hadn't gotten the stink off for days.

The liquid in her stomach turned to acid. Sweat beaded her upper lip. The light jacket felt like a down parka. Was the camera still working? Did it record the intruder? *Please, please let it be recording.*

Her knee burned. That sharp thing had put a hole in her leggings. *Wait.* A pinprick of light appeared ahead. She quickened her scrabbling pace. Yes, the end of the corridor lay just ahead, and the light became the outline of a panel much smaller than the half door she'd come through from Hunter's closet. A decent-sized man would have difficulty squeezing through it. Trinket was waiting for her. She placed a hand on the surface.

Bang. Clank.

She jerked back her hand. Someone was in the utility closet. *The killer?* Fear had a stranglehold on her throat.

Shit. He's waiting for me.

No. That didn't make sense. Unless he knew about the secret door. But Hunter said no one knew about it. Rationalizing did nothing to stop the shaking. She sat and gathered Trinket in her arms, nuzzling in his fur. He relaxed against her. Soon her runaway breathing slowed, tense muscles eased.

More banging and shuffling from beyond the panel. Then humming in a high, yet masculine tone. She strained to hear. That tune—she knew it. What was it? "Born This Way."

She sagged, smiling into Trinket's neck. She pictured a cleaning person with earbuds, twerking in the utility closet, a mop for a partner. He needed to leave so she could escape this place, and whoever had broken into Hunter's apartment.

How *had* the intruder gotten in? That pulse against her body—some kind of a new chemical explosive device that issues an energy blast but no sound? Maybe a Cleaver chemical?

The humming stopped and the thin slivers of light went out, plunging them into total darkness again. A door closed. She set Trinket down as her heart rate revved. She'd have to wriggle on her stomach to get through the opening. She lay flat and pushed on the panel. It gave an inch. She shoved harder, straining, digging toes into the floor. Something was against the panel on the other side. Could be anything—shelves, boxes, cabinets. It was obvious no one had used this escape route for a long, long time, if ever.

The noises through the walls from other units seemed to surround her. Or were the noises coming from within the tunnel? *Shit!* Sounded like it. Would thick, hairy hands grab her feet and drag her back? Circle her throat, choking her while her eyeballs bulged? She shook her head. Damn that overactive imagination. *Thanks, Mom.*

She rolled onto a hip and slammed a shoulder against the panel. The panel slid another inch. *Slam. Slam. Slam.* Pain radiated down her arm. *Slam.* The panel slid a few more inches. She rolled onto her belly again and shoved with both hands. Trinket rushed past her through the small opening. She followed at a wriggle into more darkness and the sting of cleaning solvents, forcing the panel open with her body. A heavy carton of some sort had been against the panel. Trinket's nails clicked on the floor.

She straightened vertebra by vertebra, waving her hands above her head in case a shelf lay above the opening. She blinked several times. Light seeped through the edges of a door at one end of the utility closet. Her poor sight sought it out and drank in the meager glow. Ghostly floor-to-ceiling shelving with dark square shapes lined the walls of this maybe twenty-foot by eight-foot room. She shoved the panel closed and moved the heavy carton back against it before shuffling toward the door. She wiped gritty, sweaty hands on her clothes.

"Okay, Trinket," she whispered, feeling for him, and picking up the bundle of fur. "Let's blow this joint." The dog lathered her face with a sloppy tongue. "I know, lovie."

She opened the door a crack. The blast of light blinded her, causing her to tear up. Silence on the landing. She stepped through the door. To the left, the closed double doors to the office corridor. She imagined Hunter even now fighting off the intruder way down the hall. To the right, the stairs, and escape. She hurried to the stairs, tempted to race down them, but took her time. It wouldn't do if she broke a leg.

Trinket wriggled, but she held him tight. He'd lost his cute bow. "No playing on stairs this time, little one."

They continued down, down. At the seventeenth-floor landing, she cracked open the door to the hall. No one in sight. She hurried to the nearby elevator. The main elevators to the lobby were at the other end of the building. Hopefully this one was by the rear service exit. Minutes seemed to crawl by like a cat at nap time, but it was only seconds by the time the doors slid open. The oversized, padded elevator swiftly descended to the first floor.

On the way down, she'd decided to go directly to her basement office and lock herself in, try to reach Hunter before calling the police. The cops weren't an option yet. She had no way of knowing if the apartment had been broken into, really. She thought she heard noises—felt something weird. Had she? Or was that her creative mind again?

Throwing open the back door to early evening dusk, she gulped in kind-of-fresh, familiar New York air and hurried along the deserted sidewalk, hugging Trinket close as vehicles whisked past. The streetlights were on, hardly needed yet as the lights from a thousand windows in the tall buildings all around lit up the area like daytime. She'd take this route rather than duck over to the pedestrian-heavy main street. She didn't know who this faceless murderer was, so the crowds there would freak her out. Any one of them could pull a shiv, slide it between her ribs, and move on.

She kept vigilant, skin pebbling more from nerves than cool air. She saw her reflection in a parked car window. Hair half loose from its ponytail, dark streaks across her face. Filthy clothes. Oh, yeah, ripped tights. A little blood. Who would lend a phone to someone who looked like they'd just gotten up from the gutter?

Slap, slap, slap.

She glanced behind. A jogger in a blue tracksuit advanced on her.

Or is he a jogger? Her heart leapfrogged into her throat. She moved on splintered legs to a nearby door, readying her mind and muscles for a fight.

****

Ash hurried through the Haven's west corridor to avoid the busy cafeteria and tech areas where he might run into Mort and Myst. He didn't have time to explain about Parker stashed upstairs, never mind the plan to talk to Elizabeth Trowbridge. Truth was, he didn't want to hear their arguments against. They'd call him an idiot. Which he was.

Slow down. Relax. His gut churned sour butter.

Using the code with a push of magic, he opened the side door to the Bureau of Witchery's council rooms. This narrow corridor was empty except for the rush of powerful mage energy that buffeted him like skyscraper wind tunnels. He focused on identifying E.T.'s unique signature. She was not anywhere nearby.

To the right at the far end were the Council offices, including Gray's. To the left through two other entrances was the housing wing lobby. He turned left. The final entry led him to the vast, pillared room that always reminded him of the marble lobby of an expensive hotel with its soaring, coffered ceiling. The place bustled with adults and children with their familiars of all kinds—a dog, a few cats, a pot-bellied pig, a crow, an owl.

The impossibly green lawn stretched away from the huge sliding doors to his right. A faux dusk was falling. Lights flickered on outside, the scene so real, it would fool the first-time visitor into thinking they were witnessing a real sundown.

The check-in desk stretched the length of another wall with people on phones or computers. How many gatekeepers would he need to go through before gaining access to E.T.? He relaxed tight shoulders as he approached the desk with a carefree air.

A young woman with glasses and long, blond hair looked up from the computer. A chunky green iguana the size of a decent meatloaf lounged on her shoulder, its tail wrapped around to tuck over her ear. It blinked lazily, then stuck out a fat tongue. The name tag on her navy vest read *Lorraine.*

"Can I help you?" She looked up and pushed the tortoiseshells higher on a sharp nose.

An endearing Parker quirk. She waited for him upstairs. He had to hurry.

"Yes, Lorraine. Hal Simpson. I'm here to see Elizabeth Trowbridge." He displayed his biggest smile. Charm he had in spades.

Her well-manicured eyebrows rose as she tap-tapped at the keyboard. "You're not on the list. She doesn't receive casual visitors." The shrug and head tilt meant "sorry, you schmuck."

"Can you at least tell me if she's home?" Big smile again. She wasn't in the Council wing, and he didn't have time to search the rest of the Haven for her.

Lorraine heaved a long-suffering sigh. "She is at home."

There was no sense in asking for directions to her apartment. Besides, the coded doors to the residences could only be opened by specific mages. Again, he wasn't one of them. He thanked Lorraine and strolled away as if, yeah, he'd only wanted to share a nice cup of tea with the oldest immortal in the Haven, no problems. No rush. No killer.

His jaw tightened. There might be another way. He followed a couple out the glass doors to the flagstone patio, their two cockatoo familiars fluttering between them. Walkways fanned out throughout the park from this central point. More lamps on tall stands winked on. On the far horizon, past lawns, fountains, and flower gardens, a curving high hedge gave the impression the whole place was walled off from the rest of the world.

Beyond the hedge lay only the imagination of the mage.

The dozens of condos with their white fencing enclosing private patios stretched out to his left. He'd have to walk past them all, open his senses to the energy signals of each occupant, many of them immortals. He knew E.T.'s well.

Wait. There, about thirty condos away. A tall hedge jutted out beyond the other patios and appeared to wrap around the corner. Not a white fence, but a live green one. He took off in that direction and controlled his pace, as if out for an early evening stroll, as if he belonged. A bunch of kids kicked a soccer ball around on the grass, their youthful energy signatures on the low spectrum till they would come into their magic. He wanted to join them in the worst way.

He approached the gate set in a tall hedge. The air throbbed with a strong protection spell that encapsulated the property. The view through the filigreed ironwork revealed lush garden plots of roses and other blooms, flowering bushes, giant pots overflowing with greenery. The combined heady fragrances, a portal vibe, and E.T.'s intense aura flooded his senses. Animal statuary of all kinds competed with fountains large and small. Water tumbled down through a jumble of rocks into a small pond. Thousands of tiny lights winked on throughout the garden. This place screamed Elizabeth Trowbridge. The immortal mage had always been fair, listened to all sides of a story. He took a chance she wouldn't immediately call for security.

Clearance as a Keeper allowed him to breach many protection spells, but this one was especially powerful, like the one he'd set on the office door. He called on his magic core and focused. Power surged along nerves, heating his blood. Fingers tingled for long seconds.

Nothing. The gate remained locked.

"What the hell, Hunter?" a voice barked.

He turned. *Shit. Jefrem Gladstone, newly minted housing director.*

Jef tapped him on the shoulder with a long, rolled-up scroll of papers. Probably the blueprints for hell. Ash balled a hand into a fist.

"Why are you sneaking around the Trowbridge gate?" Jef asked.

"You're questioning a Keeper?"

"Of course. I have a right as a Councilman."

Jeez. Didn't take long for the position to go to his swelled head.

"You are not my boss." Ash leaned in close to his face. "Get lost."

Jef sputtered and stepped back. "We'll see what *your* boss, Gray, has to say about this." He turned and hurried along the walkway toward the lobby doors.

Shit and shit. Ash closed his eyes. He summoned the magic, fixed it laser-sharp toward Jef's retreating head. Like a gifted neurosurgeon with a scalpel, he excised the memory of their meeting clean out of Jef's mind, then refocused on the gate. With energy juiced, he powered the magic, setting his intention. Within seconds, the latch clicked. He stepped through the gate onto a glittering stone path. He replaced the protection spell with his own.

Squawk. "Halt, intruder."

Ash stopped. *What—?*

A raven the size of a hawk hopped into view on a branch just above his head. Was it in molt or just old?

Feathers stuck out at odd angles and bare patches revealed pimpled skin like a plucked chicken. It looked down on him with a head tilt. "Intruder-r-r-r," it screeched.

Ash covered his ears, a slight headache beginning to pulse in his temple from the effort of magical surgery. The scruffy thing was better than an alarm system.

"Strike, knock it off." A figure approached from the corner of the building.

Elizabeth Trowbridge strolled toward him with a welcoming smile, removing a gardening glove and tucking it into an apron pocket. Tall, erect with a full head of long, white hair gathered at her nape, she was almost 400 years old but could pass for seventy-five. Last time he'd seen her she was in ceremonial robes. Today, purple leggings and flowered tunic. She turned down the intensity of her energy signature, which reminded him why he was there. He'd been star-struck at the sight of her. The blue eyes, so direct.

"He's not on the list," said Strike. Hunter recognized a bit of E.T. in the bird's voice.

She extended a hand. "Welcome, Ash Hunter."

He shook her hand, firm and warm. "Sorry for the intrusion." He glanced at the bird.

"Last time I saw you, you were before me in Council."

"Because of you, I got to keep my job. Thanks. Can we talk in private, Ms. Trowbridge? I need your advice."

"Of course. Call me Elizabeth. Let's go to the patio." She walked back the way she'd come, removing the apron. Ash followed, senses picking up the intense vibe of a nearby portal entry. Even closed, the portal gave off detectable signals. The bird sputtered and fluttered ahead, one wing bent so badly Ash expected it to crash land.

They went around the corner of the building onto a tiled patio surrounded by flower beds, small trees, and another fountain featuring a One Mother statue. More stone animal statues sat among the bushes or peeked out from the flowers. White lights twinkled throughout. *A freaking fairy garden.*

Ash sat on a padded chair across a low table from Elizabeth. Two cocktail glasses with ice floating in a dark liquid appeared in front of them.

"Jack on the rocks," said the raven. "She knows." The bird only had one eye. The other was an empty, crusted socket.

Elizabeth held up her glass. "It is. And I didn't properly introduce my outspoken familiar, Strike. He's as old as I am but hasn't held up nearly as well as me." Strike squawked, and she laughed, the lines around her eyes deepening. Her incredible life story was etched in the lines on her face. All that she was, all that she'd endured, all that she'd suffered—the joys, the sorrows, the triumphs—all there for anyone to interpret.

Ash took a sip, the liquid smooth and fiery as it slipped down his throat. "Thanks for this. Drink up. You're going to need it."

"Indeed, if you felt you had to sneak in here to see me." She took a swallow. "You impressed me at Council with your impassioned plea for the Witch Whisperer and yourself. Let's hear it then."

"Yes, this better be good because I'm missing my supper." Strike hopped to the back of her chair and angled the good eye toward him.

"What I'm going to tell you must be held in strict confidence." Ash raised a brow and glared at Strike.

"Hey, I won't say anything. My lips are sealed." Then the bird cackled. "Lips."

"Strike, I'll send you inside. Go ahead, Ash."

"A witch is murdering both mage and Reg in order to keep our society a secret."

Elizabeth stiffened. "Murder? Who is this witch?"

"I don't know. I've detected the same fuzzed-out energy signal at several so-called accident scenes where magic had been performed, even a murder that was made to look like suicide."

"I know of your gift for recognizing energies. I've not heard of any mages who can alter their energy. There must be some other explanation. Reverence for life."

"My team and I have been looking at every piece of evidence. A couple of weeks ago, Councilman Gray assigned me to keep tabs on an investigative journalist, Skye Parker, a Reg. Last year, her mother was murdered, staged as a suicide. Last week there was an attempt on Parker's life. This morning, her tech assistant's sister was murdered. Fuzzed auras at all three. I brought Parker to my place."

Strike hopped from one leg to the other on the back of the chair. "Get the mage. Bless the One Mother."

"Yes. He must be stopped." Elizabeth tapped the table with long fingers. "This journalist, Skye Parker, why is she targeted?"

Ash sat back. "She and her mother, Diana, had spent years investigating paranormal activity. Diana was compiling a list containing many suspicious deaths, all in the Manhattan and surrounding area. The last entry was dated the day before her death. Parker's working on a story, an exposé, about people with magical powers. Gray wants me to make sure she doesn't." He told her Parker's story of being saved from drowning by a "superhero" when she was five.

Strike ruffled his motley feathers. "You like Parker. A lot."

Ash groaned. Could the damn familiar read his pheromones, too?

"Ignore him, Ash. He fancies himself a matchmaker. So, Skye Parker is at your place." She stood, paced to the edge of the patio and back. "Is she alone right now?"

"Yes." A flicker of apprehension zapped his nerves. "I put the strongest protection spell on the door. I've only been gone twenty minutes."

"If you don't know what magic the witch is capable of, your spell might not be enough. You passed through my gate. He's proven he can make himself virtually invisible to us."

Fear was now a jab to the gut. He fished out the new phone and called Parker's burner. It rang several times, then went to voicemail. "No answer."

Elizabeth put a hand on his arm. "I'm sure she's fine, but you'd best make sure. Between the two of us, we'll have to come up with a way to truly protect her till we catch this witch. One option is a last resort."

Strike squawked. "Bless the One Mother."

"You might have to bring her here to me." She touched Ash's arm. "Let's share phone numbers. Keep me updated."

They did, and he ran along the garden path. He

wondered how his legs still moved when his brain had seized. *Bring her to the Haven? No way that could ever happen.*

Strike flapped awkwardly ahead of him. The bird landed on the gate. "Forget what she said."

"Damn right." Ash hurried through the gate, slowing his pace on the pathway and through the housing lobby so he wouldn't attract attention.

He called Myst's m-number while walking the west corridor. "Where are you?"

"In your office with Soot, waiting for Mort."

Soot probably left his apartment to get away from the smelly dog. "Tell Soot to pop up to my place immediately. Text Mort. Meet me at my elevator. Hurry." He clicked off but kept his head down to the screen to avoid eye contact with the foot traffic. A meeting had just let out and people streamed past.

Myst waited for him at the end by the elevators when he entered the corridor. The orange grove video on the walls and his favorite scent of orange blossoms did not soothe this time. He willed them away. He came beside her and punched the button.

She raised both eyebrows. "What's up? I texted Mort. He's in Tech but is coming as soon as he finishes a large download."

"I just came from E.T.'s place. Fill you in later. It's Parker. She's upstairs at my place. Or was. She's not answering her phone."

"Really, Ash. E.T.? I'm sure Parker's all right. I'll send another text to Mort."

The moment they stepped into the elevator, Soot appeared at Ash's feet.

"She's not up there. No one is. Not even that sucky

dog."

"Shit." He tried her phone again. It went to voicemail. *Where the hell is she?*

Chapter Ten

Spiky energy waves hit Ash as soon as he stepped off the elevator into the hall with Myst. "Somebody's used magic after I left." He hoped to hell Parker had gone through the secret door.

He started to bolt, but Myst grabbed his arm. "Wait. They might still be there."

"Soot says no." Where was the damn cat? He'd winked out somewhere on the ride up.

"Better safe than…" Myst whispered.

His muscles bunched. Everything told him to race to the door except better judgment. He heightened his senses and crept along the hall through an invisible miasma of energy thick as a peat bog.

They both flattened their bodies against the wall when they reached the apartment. Light shone from inside through the opaque glass. The doorknob and code panel looked normal. Nothing fried. He touched the panel with the access card. Click. He touched the knob under the opaque square of the window. Electricity crackled through his fingertips, sizzling along nerves like the zap from a light socket.

Myst touched his arm, hand-signed that she would enter first, for him to hang back a sec. He shook his head, turned the knob, and plunged through the open door.

Soot sat on the desk. *"Nice entrance. Told you no*

one was here."

Myst crowded in behind him. "Holy dog meat. You could have come out in the hall, fleabag."

"All her stuff is still here." Ash rummaged in a tote and brought out the burner phone that showed several missed calls and texts. "She left in a hurry. Let's check the closet." *Please be in the closet or through the hidden door.*

"I still can't believe you have a secret exit from this place." Myst followed him as he strode through into the bedroom and walk-in closet.

At the back of the closet, he crouched down, pulled out the shoe shelf, and then touched a spot on the molding. The half door swung open. "Parker, you in there?" Nothing.

He summoned a streak of light that barreled down the tunnel. The grit on the floor had been disturbed the whole way. "She went through." But a witch had not. Relief loosened every tight muscle. Someone called from the other room.

"It's Mort." Myst stood and laid a hand on his shoulder. "It's okay, Ash. Parker's resourceful."

She left him sitting on his butt. He closed his eyes to concentrate on the auras, the mage signatures in the closet. Myst's was a distinct mark, all hard edges, solid red. The other one, the billowy gray smoke—the killer's stamp made of invisible ink. He let it drift around in his mind, separate into tendrils like long, amorphous fingers, stroking, seeking. The killer witch had been in here but hadn't followed her through the door.

Parker had probably grabbed Trinket, then escaped before the intruder saw where she went. Ash cleared his head and stood. He met Mort and Myst in the living room.

"I filled him in on the awesome secret door," said Myst.

"Mort, someone got in here, past my security, past my protection spell, someone powerful."

"First, I'm sure she's fine." Mort squeezed his shoulder. "She's tough. Have you read some of the stuff she's been through for her stories?"

"Thanks, my personal empath. But she hasn't come up against a witch. She can't defend against magic." Ash's phone dinged. "It's a text from Parker." He took a huge breath in and let it leak out. He held the phone so M&M could see the message.

Parker: —*You ok, Hunter? I'm fine, safe. Have Trinket. Someone broke in. Didn't see who. Went through the hidden door. In my office using Jo's PC to msg you. Police?*—

Ash typed: —*No. No cops. I'm good. Be right there.*—

The cops were all they needed. "She thinks she's safe and secure in her basement office." He texted Sam to pull up outside. "I'm heading over there."

"We're going with you," said Mort.

"No. You stay here and watch the place. Hop on my computer and keep digging for the identity of this witch. We need to stop him. Elizabeth Trowbridge's orders."

Mort nodded, a grim set to his mouth. "I haven't had a chance to tell you. I've been working all day, hacking into street cameras, at least, the ones that still had old footage. That same witch—I swear it is—is on camera in the vicinity of some of those deaths in

Diana's murder files. I'll check all the cameras in this area. I told you to install surveillance cameras in here."

"Didn't want everything I do captured on film." *Hell no.* "Myst, come with me. Soot, stay here."

Myst grabbed Parker's tote bag and backpack from beside the chair. "It's, uh, eight o'clock. What's the plan? Do we stay in her bunker overnight? All three of us?"

Ash tugged open the door. "Right now, I have no idea."

Myst grinned. "I love this plan."

Sam pulled up in front of Parker's building in less than five minutes. It saved them a fifteen-minute run down the street for a couple of long blocks.

"Sam, can you wait here till I text you?"

"Sure thing." Sam put the car in park and turned off the engine. "As long as you need."

Myst had the building's outer door open, and they both descended the stairs.

"No fuzzy energy signal in here. She wasn't followed." Ash never wanted to go through the same panic he'd felt moments ago when he'd stepped off the elevator on his floor.

He banged on the steel door. "Parker, it's me and Myst." The dog yap-yapped. The door opened, and Trinket jumped up against his leg.

Parker's glittering green eyes were huge. "You didn't tell me the damn tunnel would be black as a vampire's coffin. And where's my damn Thai takeout?"

Dirt streaked her cheeks, clothes, the "shit happens" t-shirt. Her hair—he groaned and crushed her to him. "I'm so sorry," he said into her mass of tangles. "I should never have left you."

"Mfffldsuffmffld." After a moment, she pushed against him and made a space. "Suffocating. Whew." She sent him a crooked smile. "I'm a mess. Look worse than I feel. I only had time to wash my hands."

"You look…" Words choked the back of his throat. He slid a hand to the back of her head and leaned in for a kiss. Soft, willing lips met his as arms wound around his neck, setting his senses, blood, and every other part of his body on fire.

"Ahem. 'Scuse me, lovebirds. I'll just…"

Ash felt Myst's hand on his back, giving a gentle shove to move him into the aisle of shelves while she scooted past them. The door slammed shut.

He pulled away with a groan. "When I couldn't reach you, I nearly went crazy."

She tugged him by his shirt along the aisle of shelving to the open office area. "The damn burner was in my bag right by the damn desk. I was in your bathroom when I heard someone."

"You're limping."

She let the shirt go and leaned over to pluck the legging away from a bloody hole at the knee. "No biggie. Just a scrape."

He let out a breath. *No biggie.* She'd just scrambled on hands and knees over filthy crap, blind in the darkness, to escape a killer. Myst was sitting on a plastic chair in front of Jo's desk, clicking away on her cell. Parker's bags sat beside her. "This is Myst, by the way. She's my right hand. One of my tech wizards."

Myst looked up from her phone. "You're right. He'd be a whimpering mass of masculine helplessness if it wasn't for me, Parker."

He smiled. "Truth. Anyway, tell me what

happened."

Parker sat across from Myst in Jo's chair. Trinket leaped onto her lap. Ash pulled a stool close beside Parker. He didn't want her too far away. He ruffled the dog's fur. The little bow was gone.

"After I heard the noise, I peeked around the corner of the living room. Through the opaque glass in the door, I saw a shape, a man I think, trying the knob."

"How tall?" asked Myst.

"Maybe six foot but he might have been leaning over. I couldn't tell." She took a breath. "But here's the wacky part. A wave of some kind of energy, or something, swept over me and my ears buzzed."

Ash shot a glance to Myst. *Magic blast.* Would he need to relieve Parker of that snippet of memory?

"Must have been some kind of chemical or other silent explosive. I didn't wait to find out."

He'd hold off on a memory wipe. "I've heard of devices like that."

Myst stood and paced. "Very cutting-edge stuff."

"That effing tunnel was—"

"'Black as a vampire's coffin.'" He wanted her in his arms again, to smooth out the deep frown lines, to somehow make up for what he put her through.

"And rat shit. Rat shit, Ash." Her body shuddered. She hugged Trinket close.

"Oh yeah," Myst said, "You wrote that great story on the sewer rats."

"And look what it got me?" She pointed to the scar on her cute nose.

Her Pulitzer nomination. He had to make sure that a magic reveal wouldn't be her next one. "The tunnel spit you out in the utility closet?"

"Had to wait till the janitor finished his playlist, but yes. Then I booked it here. Oh, out on the street—a guy was jogging behind me. I was ready to take him out. Lucky for him I didn't overreact."

"She has a brown belt in Krav Maga," Ash said.

Myst wandered over to a bank of shelves loaded with tech equipment. "Badass. Hey, I love your digs. Hacker basement. Very retro."

"I'm glad to have this place." She handed Ash the dog, stood, grabbing the purse and bag. "Pardon me while I clean up. Need a change. This t-shirt proved way too prophetic." She limped to the room divider and disappeared behind it.

"I'll bandage that knee," he called after her.

"Pathetic." Myst tsked. She returned to sit in the chair. "Check your sleeve."

"What?" Ash brushed at both long sleeves of his shirt. "Dog hair?"

She leaned over the desk and whispered, "Your heart."

"Ha. Very funny." He stood, setting Trinket on the floor. The dog ran behind the divider. "Wipe that smirk off your face."

But yeah, he did care for Parker, more than he should. Councilman Hunter's command to get close to her might backfire on both him and his dad. He couldn't allow himself to fall in love, not with a Reg. Especially not one that didn't trust him. If he'd had nothing to offer his ex, Amanda, he was in negative territory with Parker. And there was that magic null rule to consider if a mage wanted a long-term relationship with a Reg, which Myst pointed out in a warning text to him after he'd visited Parker's house.

A moot point, because very soon he might have to reveal his true self, and that of his whole secret society to protect her. Then he'd have to learn to trust *her* in a very big way while she'd turn further away. Could he somehow avoid a big reveal by taking her somewhere while E.T. and M&M find the killer? That might take too long to never. Elizabeth suggested the Haven. *No way.*

Parker came out from behind the divider in a pair of loose-fitting jeans and an oversized denim shirt, her flaming hair in a high ponytail. "I feel as good as I'm going to get until I can have a shower." She put on the librarian glasses.

"So, what's the plan?" she asked.

"Oh, we have no idea." Myst looked up from the phone. "Or do we, boss?"

"Parker, you can't stay here. Grab whatever you need for overnight."

"Where are we going?"

"I'll figure that out once we're out of here. Myst, you don't need to, uh, pet sit tonight?"

She pulled on the neckline of her loose top. "Have with. No worries."

He didn't ask what creature clung or coiled or curled up under that shirt. "Right. You stay here with Trinket. Hop on Jo's computer and work with Mort if you want. Or just chill with the dog."

"Huh. Like I can chill." She came around the desk and sat in the office chair. "I just need the password."

"Jo changes it daily, but this is the last one I know." Parker rattled off an alpha-numeric code with a few symbols thrown in. She slipped the burner phone in a back pocket, then grabbed a large tote bag and backpack. "I guess my roller bag is still at your place."

"Sorry. Never thought about it. I can have Mort grab it." Ash took the tote from her.

"Okay. But I'm not sure I want to be out there at all, in the open. Here seems so…"

"Out there where no one can trace us is better than in here. You don't have a secret back door, do you?"

She smiled. "No. Now I wish I had."

"The killer knows this place. He'll be back."

"Can we call this guy something else? Every time you say 'killer,' I get the chills. How about perp?"

How about murdering witch? "Perp. Okay, let's go." He'd promised to keep E.T. updated. He'd do that when he knew more. The last thing he wanted was for her to demand that Parker take refuge in the Haven.

****

"How's the pad thai?" Ash tasted a generous forkful of the spicy stir-fried noodles. An explosion of flavors burst on his tongue. Not bad.

"Mmm. The best." Parker paused chopsticks halfway to her mouth. "I've never been to Manhattan's Chinatown. On my radar now. It's so close to the office."

They sat by the window inside the tiny, smoky restaurant, the only patrons left at eleven. He smiled. "That subway. Always an adventure."

"I know, right? Love the subway. The people watching. That tingle of anticipation, the apprehension. You can travel the same subway every day and soak in a new experience." She continued talking about the subway rats, human and animal. How you could never fully trust either one.

He loved watching her talk. The face animated,

eyes alive with excitement. She was full of passion, curiosity, and yeah, mistrust.

His burner on the table pinged the text tone. *Mort.* Mort had put a face to the dark-clad figure on the surveillance videos. He was searching databases for a name. A photo appeared. Ash didn't recognize the guy. Sharp nose, chin dimple. Streak of white in muddy brown hair.

He texted Mort: *—Find out all you can on this guy and whereabouts. Keep me updated. Call Myst. —*

He hoped this was the kill—perp. For the first time in days, he felt they were getting somewhere.

"What's the sigh for? Good news?" Parker put the chopsticks crosswise on the empty plate.

Tell another lie or the truth? "Maybe. Mort, my other tech guru, is looking into the identity of a guy seen on surveillance a couple of times." He showed her the photo.

"I don't know him. Hard to tell if he's the one who broke into your office."

"He's been seen in the vicinity of some questionable deaths."

She straightened. "Hetty's? My mom? Anyone in the Murder Files?"

He paused, uncertain of what to reveal. He needed to steer her away from the paranormal aspect of the Murder Files. "Hetty's. Not your mom's. No cameras in that area. But there was another death he's looking into."

"I knew you were hiding something. You know a lot more than you're letting on." She tossed the napkin on the table and stood. "I'm going back to my office."

"Wait. You can't." He signaled for the check. "If

you come with me, I promise to tell you everything I know so far."

"Blackmail." She narrowed her eyes. "So where are you taking me?"

The server brought the check, and Ash handed him several twenties. "Keep the change." He grabbed Parker's bag and headed for the door.

She followed. "So, where to, oh cryptic one?"

"Across the street. The Mayfield."

"Hotel?" She stopped mid-way out the door. A restaurant worker encouraged her the rest of the way so he could lock up.

"I made a reservation in the car on the way here."

Her nostrils flared and lips firmed. "You know, I should just walk away right now. No, run."

"But you won't. You're too curious. Maybe scared."

She shook her head and stomped ahead of him to the crosswalk.

A headache began behind his eyes, and he hadn't even wiped a memory. Now he had only minutes to figure out how much to tell her. Both their lives might very well change in the coming hours and not in a good way.

Chapter Eleven

It didn't matter to Skye that the sixth-floor room had two queen beds. She didn't plan on sleeping a wink even though she'd had little sleep last night. Meantime, a hot shower beckoned like a spa day at the Bamford.

Hunter prowled the large suite with its comfy loveseat, serviceable desk area, checked the mini-fridge in the kitchenette, and stuck his head in the bathroom. Soft rain pattered against the window. He drew the drapes closed against the damp darkness.

"Is everything secure, captain?" she asked. His head shot up. *Was it something I said?*

"Just wanted to make sure the place was up to our high standards, milady. It's not fancy, but it's clean."

"Better than a lot of places I've stayed in around the world. I'm going to take a shower. I'll let you know if there's hot water." She grinned, trying to draw him out of the funk he seemed to be in.

"Don't use it all. I'm next." His mouth tilted in a sexy smile.

His dark eyes held hers, the message clear. He'd love to join her in the shower, get all soapy and hot, and…

Or maybe not. She had a wild imagination.

"I'm going to…" She broke eye contact, grabbed the bag, and hurried into the bathroom.

She'd thought about taking the phone in, sending

Jo a quick text, tell her about the death-defying escape from a killer, but Jo didn't need more stuff to worry about.

Twenty minutes later she emerged, body cleansed from rat residue, feeling like a new person. She rubbed the ends of her hair with a hand towel to stop the drips. It would soon start curling like a bitch. With her glasses on, everything came into focus. Hunter held up a long-sleeved, navy-blue t-shirt. A pair of jeans and—were those boxers?—lay folded on the bed.

"Where did those come from? You had nothing."

He looked over at her and stopped, eyes widening. She was fully dressed, right? Same oversized denim shirt, but instead of the jeans, she'd put on comfy lounge pants, a last-minute addition to the bag. In the bathroom, she'd threaded another fully charged camera through a different buttonhole. The twinge of guilt she swallowed tasted like bitter gourd. But he was hiding something, a lot of somethings. She had a nose for that sort of thing, and he'd promised to talk. She wanted it on the record.

"Uh, yeah. Sam brought me a change while you were in the shower."

"All I can say is, I need a Sam." She tossed her stuff on the other bed. "I sure wish I had my laptop. I have research to do and need to work on my story."

"Which one?"

Should she tell him? Why not? Time for them to come clean. Ha. Showers. Clean. Maybe she should try to sleep. He promised to spill. So would she. "I'm writing about my experience when I was five and some of the Mage Believers' posts we've investigated out of the hundreds of incidents they've documented."

"Those posts have been discredited for one reason or another."

"Yeah, about that. Mom was convinced there was—is a group or government entity that systematically refutes all these claims for reasons of, oh, I don't know, national security, privacy, secrecy. I want—need—to write this story, to validate my mom's life's work, and mine. To validate what happened to me. She was murdered to keep her quiet. *They*, whoever they are, don't want to be outed. They'll kill to prevent that from happening."

Hunter fussed with the sleeve of his shirt. "So, you don't think it was some corporate bigwig trying to hide his furry fetish? Your story will try to convince the world that these paranormal events are real? You're in serious danger no matter what."

"Apparently. I talked to Jo before that perp sent me through the tunnel of terror. She said she's fine, by the way, and anxious to keep busy. She's never laughed at my beliefs in the paranormal, so she's going back into all the investigations we did of the deaths. She's looking at the money/power angle, too."

"I'm glad Jo's ok. Losing a loved one is rough." He gathered the clothes in his arms. "If you write that story, you'd be opening yourself up to national, maybe world-wide ridicule."

"Not if my proof is irrefutable."

"Irrefutable. Hmm. I'm going for my shower."

"I recommend the hotel toiletries. The lavender body wash and matching shampoo, heavenly."

He was not amused. His frown was back along with deeply troubled eyes. She knew what she'd be in for once the story broke. But first, she needed the positive evidence. "Hey, I have questions for *you* when you're done."

He nodded and walked into the bathroom, shutting the door. She went through the backpack, extracted a notepad and pen, then sat at the desk. She'd go old school. Sometimes a blank sheet of lined paper released some spark of creativity that an electronic screen didn't. Before long, she'd filled three pages with notes.

She looked up from the notebook when Hunter emerged from the bathroom in a wash of fragrance. Barefoot, he wore the change of clothes Sam brought him. The t-shirt molded to his chest. Tall and lean, his whip-cord strength flirted with every one of her girly parts. The melting hot kiss at the bunker door awhile ago set more than her lips on fire.

She sniffed the air. "Didn't I tell you? The hotel stuff is amazing."

He smiled. "Regular spa quality."

He strode to the kitchenette where an ice bucket and—*wait*—a bottle of whiskey sat on the counter.

"Did Sam also bring the Jack Daniels?"

"Yep. I take it on the rocks. You?"

"Definitely." She swiveled in the chair. "You *will* share Sam, right?"

He laughed. "I've known Sam for years. He can anticipate my needs. I needed this." He swallowed half the glass and poured a generous amount of the amber liquid in another tumbler of ice before topping off his own. He handed it to her.

"A toast is in order," she said, lifting the glass.

"What the hell for?"

"I lived."

His face sobered. "You did." He clinked his glass

to hers.

She sipped the drink. The fiery liquid burned its way down to her stomach. She moved to the loveseat and patted the spot beside her. "Now, get comfortable, Hunter. I have questions."

He placed his phone on the coffee table before sitting touch-ably close. Putting an arm along the back of the sofa, he stretched out long legs and cradled the drink in the other hand. Hunter appeared to be the picture of casual nonchalance until you studied the set of his jaw, the tic at his temple.

"Shoot," he said.

"This may take a while. So many questions. Some will be personal." She took another fortifying drink of Jack. "Let's start with just who the hell are you? Where were you born and all that?"

"You already know a lot about me. But, okay. Born right here in the Big Apple. Dad runs roughshod over a brokerage firm. Mom is busier than all of us with charitable events and running a household with my dad in it. An older sister in Seattle is married with children. I'm thirty. Went to NYU. Played a little b-ball. Not married. No children that I know of."

"Do you have a girlfriend?"

His jaw relaxed as a smile formed. "No. I had a serious relationship for a couple of years. We broke up last year."

"Sorry. Is your heart broken?"

"Maybe. Or maybe just my ego. How about you? Boyfriends?"

"Hey, this is about you."

"Just this one."

She poked the glasses higher. "I've had a few.

146

None stuck. I was always so busy traveling, writing."
And weren't they all just a little bit boring?

"Ever think about marriage? A family?"

"Hell, yes. Everybody else's."

He laughed. *I love when he laughs.* Delicious tingles invaded her stomach. Or maybe it was the alcohol. "Truthfully, I can see a husband and maybe a kid in my future. But, enough about me. You work full-time as a private detective. Can't live the way you do on that. Daddy's money? Trust fund?"

"I love my P.I. job, and I make good money. But when I run short, I tap into my trust fund."

"Cool. You have two tech people, hackers, who help you. Myst and—Mort was it?"

"I call them M&M."

"Cute. What *exactly* have they found out about the, um, perp who killed my mom, Hetty, and tried to kill me—twice?"

He took a deep breath, then let it out slowly. He swirled the melting ice cubes in the glass. "I need another drink." He stood and took her empty glass, too.

"Bet I can drink you under the table. I've won that Nepalese shot challenge that Marion in Raiders won."

"Ha. I bet you did." He refilled both their drinks, then returned to the loveseat.

She took the glass and sipped. The fire had turned to warm embers slipping down her throat.

"Parker, you continue to amaze me."

"Aw, thanks. My question. Waiting."

"I've told you all we know. We don't have his name yet or if he was hired by Cleaver or any of your mom's other so-called enemies or acted alone. That other death is from the Murder Files. M&M are on it.

Like most importantly, where is this guy right now?"

Thunder rattled the windows. Skye set the drink on the coffee table and rubbed the goosebumps from her arms. She wasn't cold. Afraid? Maybe. "Why aren't we bringing the police in on this?"

"And tell them what? There's no evidence that someone killed your mom, or Hetty, or tried to run you down, or even broke into my apartment."

"Right." Tweaked nerves sent shivery fingers trailing along her spine.

He downed the rest of the drink and put the glass next to hers. Gone was the I'm-too-easy-for-my-clothes guy. He turned in his seat, thigh brushing hers, and took her warm hand. "I won't let anything happen to you."

She searched his eyes, earnest creases across his brow, the serious set of the mouth. "*We* won't. Together."

The mouth twitched. "I forgot you could probably have me on the floor in one move."

She'd like to have him on the floor. His thumb rubbed the top of her hand in a soothing—strike that—arousing way. Scattered sparks flared through body parts. "I have another question. What do you want out of your life? What's your dream? Be honest."

"Hmm. My dream. I'd like to travel the world. Go on an African safari and walk among the elephants. Swim with turtles in some tropical place. Chase cows on a galloping horse at a dude ranch in Montana."

His face lit up as he spoke. The smile, tentative at first, turned into a grin. Yeah, he was being honest. She'd seen his screensaver.

"Why don't you? You can afford it. Go do all those things."

He blew out a puff of air. "Duty. Work ethic, I guess." He played with her fingers.

"You're your own boss. Take time off. Where have you gone?"

"L.A., other places in the U.S., London a couple of times. As a kid, went with family to a cabin in Colorado to play in the snow."

"That's it. You need to play. You're way too serious, dude." She squeezed his hand. "After this is all over, I'll take you to Luna Park on Coney Island. Rollercoasters, junk food. So much fun you'll puke."

He laughed. "I'll take you up on that."

"See, even thinking about it made you happy."

"When you're not driving me crazy, you make me happy." He tugged her close. "And other things."

Her tummy did a crazy swoop. "Like what things?"

"Too many questions." He cupped her chin and placed a soft kiss on her lips. The glasses fogged.

She ran her tongue along the seam of his lips. When they parted, she slipped in, played with his tongue. He moaned low, and she came undone. She didn't want soft or slow or indecisive. She tossed her glasses, pushed him down on the sofa, his long, hard body beneath hers. His arms wrapped around, pulling her closer. The kiss deepened, chin stubble chafing in a delicious friction. Warm hands under her shirt, setting her skin on fire. No bra. Ripples of need coursed through her, chasing doubt and common sense out the door, down the street to the subway.

He pulled back. "Mmm. You taste so good. Like whiskey."

"So do you. Smell good too. We both smell like lavender and liquor." She chuckled, running her hands under his shirt, over hard abs, up to pecs, heavy breathing a match to his, too.

He sucked in a breath. "Should we be doing this?"

"Oh, yes." She leaned back, undid her denim shirt, and let it drift to the floor. No recording *this* scene.

Hands splayed up from her stomach to cup her breasts, nipples hardening. He took one in his mouth. Her moan this time. She reached for the button of his jeans.

The phone rang. Skye jerked her hand away from his pants. Hunter swore. The ringing continued. "You going to get that or…?"

He stretched out an arm and snagged the phone. "I *do* have to get this. Sorry. God, I'm sorry." He clicked into the call. "Hi. Hang on."

Skye rolled off him and moved his legs so she could sit to put on the shirt. She didn't trust her legs. He walked into the bathroom, shutting the door.

Well, holy ding dang. Almost coitus interruptus. Whoever that was—M or M?— their timing sucked, but could have been worse. Her overheated body tingled. She groaned. It had been so long since she'd been this close to having sex. Maybe they could still salvage the evening and finish in bed what they'd started.

Pasting an ear to the bathroom door would be wrong, but the idea tempted her. Her hair hung in a tangle of ringlets. She managed to make it to the tote bag on the bed and rummaged around for the brush. Hunter opened the bathroom door as she gathered her hair back and up into a ponytail.

"So, what was—" She stopped. The hooded eyes, the scowl drawing his brows together and mouth into a tight line—not good news.

"Later." He crossed to the other bed, sitting with his back to her, stiff, unyielding, and tossed the phone onto the nightstand.

"Hey, don't dismiss me like that." *Not after what we just shared.*

His voice softened. "Sorry. I need to think. Go to bed. Get some sleep."

"Does this have to do with me? The stalker-at-large? I'm really good at processing. I can help."

"We'll talk in the morning. After coffee, or something stronger." He stretched out on the bed, eyes closed, body language closed.

The letdown, the rebuff was both physical and mental. Her body sagged onto the bed. She was just beginning to place a modicum of trust in him, but he was making it very difficult. The night would be a long one. In the morning, she *would* get answers.

****

Skye awoke to the smell of fresh coffee. Someone moved around in her bedroom. A shot of adrenaline stiffened her muscles. She opened her eyes. *Not my room.* That someone was Hunter. She relaxed and sat up against the padded headboard, wondering how the heck she'd managed to fall asleep at all. The clock on the nightstand read six. Pale light leaked around the edges of the drapes.

"Morning." She shoved a blanket away. Hunter must have laid the cover over her sometime in the night. He'd lost that haunted look from last night but was still guarded and stiff-shouldered.

He poured two cups of coffee and brought her one. "Morning. Did you sleep well?" His smile was

151

tentative, just a tug at the corners as if he couldn't quite bring himself anywhere close to joy.

"Want the truth? It would have been a whole lot better if you'd have joined me." She tried coquettish eyes over the rim of the cup.

He raised a brow. "Neither of us would have gotten *any* sleep."

"I know, right?" She took a sip of the steaming coffee. "Wowza. As Jo would say, this stuff would curl your short ones."

He chuckled. "I like Jo. A lot."

He sobered and took his coffee to the loveseat, the site of last evening's almost love fest. Or whatever. She tested her legs. Steady as a rock. *Wish my heart was the same.* In that la-la-land between sleep and awake she'd dreamed of him, of them, him handing her a rose, proposing on a sunny beach. Just like the TV show. She wasn't that far gone, was she? No. She liked him. A lot. Wanted his body. That was all. •

Time to get serious. "You have something to tell me. Let me go to the bathroom, brush my teeth." *The camera.* She had to change into the shirt and check the camera. What he had to say might be important to save.

He nodded, his thoughts a mile away or a thousand. She couldn't tell.

She emerged from the bathroom after putting on the shirt and jeans, re-taming the feral hair. The button cam indicated that it was recording. With a fresh cup of coffee, she sat beside his rigid body, sipped, and waited. Looked like he was being careful not to touch her with any body parts.

He cleared his throat. "I've been trying to think of an easy way to tell you."

"Tell me what."

"There is no easy way." He let a deep breath seep out through pursed lips. "That experience you had as a kid. The mysterious stranger who seemed to have saved you from the river."

A bumble of butterflies knocked around in her stomach. She set the cup on the table.

He glanced at the ceiling then at her. "He was mage."

"Mage? He saved me with some superpower?"

"With magic. He was a witch."

The butterflies threatened to fly up and tear out of her throat. She placed a hand on her stomach, mind careening. How did he know this? She closed her eyes and got the rapid breathing under control. "I was right. I *am* right, dammit." *A witch, though?* She stood, paced, then stopped in front of him, remembering the camera. "You've been lying to me all along. Just who *are* you?"

"Someone who's trying to keep you alive. This killer is a witch, too."

A chill spread through her bones and, weak-kneed, she sank onto the sofa. "Are *you* a witch, a mage?" She searched his dark eyes, knowing the truth before he said the words. Knowing whatever feelings she had for him were dying word by word. Knowing he'd just kicked trust in already-broken teeth.

"Yes, I am. That guy in the photo, the suspect, has special powers, and he's using them to kill people who jeopardize our secret."

One simple *yes* had the power to upend her world. "That's why he killed my mom. He wants to silence me, too."

"He's obsessed with keeping the secret. You and

others were too close to the truth."

"And why does this truth sound so much bigger than the killer's identity or just three random witches in the world?"

"Because there are more than three witches. Many, many more. A whole society."

Her lungs squeezed, voice a croak. "How many?"

"Thousands."

She closed her eyes. *Thousands*. Not just as few people with paranormal powers like she and her mom had thought. The implications were mind-boggling. Were some others she knew really witches? Could this be real? She and her mom read, researched, and documented hundreds of events over many years, same as the Mage Believers. Isn't this why she was writing her story? The story that would shift the world on its axis? The questions tumbled around in her brain like tennis balls in a dryer.

Magic is real.

"If there are so many, how have you remained a secret?"

"Obviously, it's been difficult to hide what we are from the Regs—people with no magic like you. It's worse in this electronic age, with the Mage Believers, other fringe groups, cameras everywhere. Look, the story of my society, its governance and faith, is a long, complex one. I'm overwhelming you right now." He stood. "Let's take a break."

"So, that lightning pattern in your hair—not a superhero mark?"

"No."

"The crossed spears logo on your business card and website really is some kind of protection symbol."

"It's complicated. Both the hair and the logo let other witches know I'm one of them."

"I was right about you from the start. Talked myself out of it as I got to know you." He'd lied to her. The coffee churned and burned in her stomach. Her wrecked heart dropped in with a splash.

He stood. "You can't write your story."

The story. Her thoughts traveled along myriad pathways leading to one stunning question. How would the world react, all the Regs like her, to the spectacular news that thousands of genuine witches lived among them, and that magic was real? She'd been programming herself for this day since she was five years old but hadn't really thought the whole staggering prospect through beyond that magnificent Pulitzer and validation on several levels.

Was his revelation on tape the irrefutable proof she needed? Not quite.

He approached carrying a plate and mug and set them on the table. "Buttered toast, fresh coffee. Killer in the wind. Worlds colliding. But one must eat."

"I never heard room service."

"No room service." He flicked a wrist. A white napkin appeared out of thin air and drifted down to her lap.

"Oh, your clothes last night. The whiskey—not Sam."

"No."

Her mouth flapped open. No words came out. Thinking about magic on an intellectual level was one thing. To witness it was something extra-terrestrial. Had she gotten his magic on camera? "Is this food, like, real?"

"It's delicious. Trust me."

Looked real. Smelled real. But trust him? Nope. "I'm sure it is, but I don't think my stomach could handle it right now." She leaned into the sofa and closed her eyes. "I need time to think." Time to rein in the galloping thoughts, get some control back. Time to put on the investigative journalist fedora and ferret out the facts. The whole damn 5Ws1H of Journalism 101. She wanted her computer in the worst way. And Jo. She'd call her as soon as possible. How much to tell her? Damned if she knew. But all this was being taped.

Magic is real. Take that, Cindy, and the mean girls.

His burner pinged an incoming text tone. "It's Mort." He texted while pacing the floor.

"No secrets from now on, Hunter. What's he saying?"

He glanced over, face impassive. "The suspect has a name—Thomas Blakely. Apparently, he's been vocal in our support group meetings about threats to our secrecy. We know he's been spotted near the scene of at least three suspected murders and attempted murders."

"Shit. Do we know where he is now?"

Hunter shook his head. "Myst says Shadow Force is combing the areas Blakely frequents. He lives in Brooklyn and works at a bar in Queens."

"Okay. You lost me at Shadow Force."

His mouth tightened. "The Force is a team of Elite witches that neutralize threats to our society, and other…"

"Define neutralize."

"Non-violent means of eliminating the threat." He paused, as if thinking about how much more to tell her.

"Don't you hold back on me now. You've lied enough."

He gave a curt nod and relaxed his shoulders as if surrendering to the inevitable. "Our ancient belief, our prime doctrine, is reverence for life, with equal importance given to the sanctity of secrecy. The killer, he's only focused on the latter."

Hard, metallic puzzle pieces settled into place in her brain. Gears shifted, levers clanked. Time clicked backwards. "I was right again. You did something with a bicycle out on the street the day we met. And then, somehow, you—goddammit, Hunter. You blipped it from my memory." She stood, pressure building behind her sternum.

"I was wondering how long it would take you to get there." He rested a hip against the counter, as nonchalant as you please now, and sipped the frickin' coffee.

Heat raced to every freckle. She rushed him and got in his face. "Sneaking into someone's mind is inherently immoral, and snatching a memory is nothing short of vile."

His nostrils flared. "And yet, necessary."

"What else did you excise from my memory banks? Wait, the guy that saved me from the river. I had the same weird, disoriented feeling as I did on the street with you. He wiped my memory. Holy shit." She hugged herself despite the heat and took in deep breaths.

He put the mug down and touched her sleeve. "You're hyperventilating. Breathe slowly. Very few have the power to erase memories, but there's a cost to the mage."

"What cost?"

"Some get headaches. Debilitating, depending on the scope of the wipe. You witnessed one of the worst when we met."

"What did you do in the street with the bicyclist?"

"He connected with a bus and was toppling over. He would have gone under the wheels. I stopped that from happening but then had to wipe the memory of anyone there who might have seen it. My magic also focuses on masking or removing the event from any surveillance in the area, like cameras, cell phones. I don't know where or specifically what is being affected. My magic does it all and doesn't tell me."

She wandered to a desk chair and sat, steadying the quiver in overstrung nerves. She'd given him so many chances to come clean. He'd lied to her face like a professional con man. But how *could* he tell her, really?

His phone rang. He fished it out of a pocket and answered, dark, unreadable eyes on her. "Yes, Elizabeth, we're still here. She knows. Mort just updated me. He has identified a Thomas Blakely as a major suspect." He straightened, shaking his head. "Are you sure? Myst mobilized Shadow Force to locate him. It's only a matter of time." He listened for a moment while a tic pulsed in his jaw. "I understand. Right away." He clicked off.

"Who is Elizabeth?" *Another secret witch no doubt.*

"Hang on. I need to text M&M." His fingers tapped out messages. He pocketed the phone on his way to her. He crouched and pried a hand from her sleeve. "All this has been a lot for you right now." He gripped her hand and rubbed the back.

"Don't you *dare* wipe my memory."

He gave her a crooked smile. "Never again. I promise. But we need to leave here. I'm taking you somewhere safe until they catch this guy. You'll meet the amazing Elizabeth Trowbridge and learn the rest of our story. She knows some of yours."

His earnest, handsome face, all hard angles, hooded eyes, convinced her that he sincerely had her welfare at heart. That, and the fact he'd shared with her the biggest secret in the entire universe. She smoothed a hand down the shirt, wishing with all her heart that Jo was at the receiving end of the recordings. She would know what to do, could counsel her. Skye had to call her.

Her life was no longer her own. It was like she'd been set adrift on an alien planet with zero gravity.

Mom, I wish you were still with me. We were so right, and I need you now.

Chapter Twelve

Ash kept watch for anyone suspicious on the busy, early Friday morning rush of Chinatown streets while Parker got in the back seat of Sam's car. He stowed the bag and backpack in the trunk and slipped in beside her. The car held the light, sweet-spicy fragrance of Sam's pipe tobacco.

Sam turned. "To the office, then?" He directed a kindly smile at Parker.

"The office? Which office?" Parker sat rigid and red-faced on the far side of the seat.

"Mine. Take it slow, Sam, not your usual Le Mans speed."

Sam nodded, edging the car into the stream of vehicles. Ash had sent his trusted friend and driver a short "she knows" text when he'd asked Sam for a pickup.

He wanted to take her hand, maybe push a gentle mesmer onto frazzled nerves, but she sat as far away as she could without falling out the door. He'd resisted a mesmer back in the room. At the time, he'd needed her to understand the full implications of this monumental revelation.

"I'm taking you to a special place, an amazing place, a safe place."

"Your office? With Soot? Hardly safe."

"I have another office at the same location."

"Jeez, Hunter. Anyway, I need my laptop."

"We have lots of computers you can use."

She shook her head and closed her eyes, mouth a tight line. Parker was the type of person who did not give up control easily. She took the burner from a pocket and began typing.

"Are you texting? Who?"

Her eyes glittered. "None of your business."

"You can't tell anyone any of this."

"I know. I'm just asking Jo how she's doing. Tell her I'm safe."

"Tell her I won't let anything happen to you."

She shot him an *are-you-kidding* glance. Parker had to keep everything she'd heard, will hear and see a secret. Like, for the rest of her life. And what about the big story she was writing? He'd let E.T. impress on her the absolute necessity for complete secrecy.

He was very afraid of the unknowns, like the whereabouts of the killer, his dad's complacency about the deaths, what the Council might ask him to do. He'd always had a problem with the contradictory nature of the Keeper's code. Secrecy and sanctity of life sometimes clashed in life-altering ways.

The car pulled up in front of the building. Parker's hands-off posture threw up an invisible, prickly shield. She insisted on carrying her own stuff. M&M stood inside the side door when they entered.

Parker's mouth turned down. "Myst, where's Trinket?"

"Don't worry. Your adorable dog is in Ash's Keeper office."

"Skye Parker, this is Mort Payne," Ash said.

Mort stuck out his hand, smile more a grimace.

He'd texted Ash his extreme dislike of the whole idea of revealing who they were to a Reg and appalled at the very thought of bringing one into the Haven. He wore the same black pants and long-sleeved shirt he had on yesterday. The poor guy had been working all night.

Parker hesitated, then finally offered a hand. "I guess you are all—you know—witches." The final word a whisper.

Myst had changed at some point into a blue swirly tunic and leggings. "Yep, we are. You'll get used to the idea."

Ash didn't think so, at least not for a long while. Thinking that magic was real like that sign had said, and then witnessing it, were as far apart as believing in UFO's and actually seeing one. "Let's get down there. There's no precedence for sneaking a Reg into the Haven, but I'll tell you about the flimsy plan in the elevator."

Ash held the door open as they entered the elevator. Mort pressed and held the first-floor button. Parker tensed, eyes huge.

"Parker, when the door opens, I want you in between Myst and I. Mort, stay close behind. With the combined energies of three mages, no one will detect that you're a Reg."

"What? What does that even mean?"

"I'm sorry. There's so much you don't know. But until we can get you to Elizabeth Trowbridge, please just act normal, like nothing you see is surprising."

"I hope you're not the fainting type," said Mort, displaying an almost genuine smile this time.

Parker pulled back her shoulders and lifted her chin. Good. She was getting over the shock. When the sensation of movement ended, Ash pressed the *door closed* button. "This place is called the Haven. Right now, it's as big as a town. We've just come through a portal. Stick very close to us. We'll head along the west corridor to the housing wing."

"A portal. In an elevator." Parker snorted. "Just like that alien movie MIB."

"Hey, yes." Myst gave her a playful punch on the arm.

The door slid open. The three shuffled out into the main hall ahead of Mort. Watery blue undulations wavered along the walls while soft music played on the air. Was Parker feeling the calm? He didn't think so. Her head was on a swivel.

He whispered in her ear. "Relax. You're going to meet an extraordinary woman."

They walked along the hall, passing the occasional witch they knew with a nod or a quick hello. The west corridor was least traveled, and they arrived at the Bureau of Witchery's side doors in just a few minutes. He kept his energy signature on max to overpower Parker's energy void. They continued through to the left to the massive housing lobby, almost empty compared to the last time he was there. This time he wouldn't need to sneak through the gardens to E.T.'s place.

"Keep calm. Don't talk. Pretend you belong here," he said as they approached the same blonde desk clerk with the iguana scarf. To her credit, Parker kept her face a mask except for the twitch by an eye.

He smiled at the clerk. Maybe she wouldn't recognize him. "Lorraine, we're here to see Elizabeth Trowbridge. She's expecting us."

Lorraine looked up from the computer screen and pushed at her glasses. "Name." The lizard's thick tongue lashed in and out. He was being assessed.

"Ash Hunter."

She squinted at him. "Wasn't your name Al or Hal?"

Argh. "We're late already. Look up Ash Hunter. Please." Another smile.

She heaved a sigh and consulted the screen. "Yes, you're on the list." Tap, tap, tap. "Wait by the door over there. I've summoned Blunt."

He had no idea what a Blunt was. E.T.'s assistant? Butler? He ushered the three across the lobby to a far door, then turned to M&M. "Mort, when someone shows up to escort us, go to tech. Keep trying to locate our perp. Myst, my office. You can hop on my computer and keep the dog company."

Mort smirked at her. "Doggie-do-do duty."

She made a face at him.

Parker's face had darkened to brick red. "May I speak now?" she said through tight lips. "No one can hear unless you all have Superman hearing."

Ash smiled and shook his head.

"If somebody doesn't tell me right now where in hell we are, I'll go full-on Krav Maga." She jabbed Ash with an elbow.

"Not where. More what." Ash glanced around the cavernous space. "Look, this—"

The door opened a crack. A bald guy with a terry headband and scraggly mustache poked his head out in a wash of intense energy. "Blunt. Come with me." His voice was deep like the bark of a mastiff, eyes milky white. The man was blind.

Mort cradled Parker's hand in his. "I know this is input overload for you, but trust Ash. He's the best. And, E.T. is like the Goddess herself to us." He turned to Ash. "I'll run to tech now. Last thing we need is Blakely inside the Haven with his unique powers. Good luck."

Myst nodded. "He's right. Don't worry about little Trinket. Soot, Lucien, and I will keep him good company."

M&M left, their good-natured banter loud as they crossed the lobby. He wished he was going with them. Wished that he wasn't in the Haven with an illegal Reg. Wished he didn't feel that rush of longing whenever he remembered the feel of her lush body covering his. Wished she would feel the same about him. Never gonna happen now and shouldn't.

****

The bald guy, Blunt, held the door open. Hunter's gentle hand touched the small of her back as Blunt ushered them into a long, wide hallway lined with many numbered doors. They followed his tall form, clad in a white t-shirt that stretched across massive muscles, long legs in loose-fitting workout pants. He was blind, judging by the pale eyes, but you'd never know it from the confident stride.

Skye's heart rate had long ago spiked at heart attack, then leveled off a notch below full-on panic mixed with trembling excitement. This was how humans felt when they'd been abducted by aliens and taken aboard their spaceship. Could she be dreaming? This wasn't a nightmare. Some things were too amusing, like that lizard lady. What was with the weasel poking out of someone's jacket? And the giant

Blunt himself with a workout headband.

She'd glimpsed a vast lawn, maybe gardens through glass doors on the far side of the lobby. She prayed all this was taping but couldn't wait to document everything as soon as she could in the notebook, or if she was lucky, a computer, then relay the info to Jo. She glanced at Hunter's resolute face. Regardless, she'd remember everything, provided he didn't prune her hippocampus.

Blunt entered a code at the end of the hallway and showed them through a heavily carved wooden door into a roomy foyer whose arched ceilings soared thirty feet. A heady floral scent filled the space.

He took Skye's bags from her after a brief tug. "Wait here," Blunt boomed.

The home of a witch. Skye was vaguely disappointed. So ordinary. Like a well-to-do grandma's place. A vase of pretty, multi-colored flowers sat on a doily on a round, walnut table in the middle of the space. Built-in walnut cabinets lined the roomy foyer walls. They were stuffed with knick-knacks. She poked at the glasses and peered through the glass doors. Most were animal figurines from around the world crowding other souvenirs, like miniature Dutch wooden shoes, a set of nesting dolls, a tiny metal Eiffel Tower. Hundreds of chotskies.

She straightened. Yes, ordinary. What had she expected? A creepy, dark dungeon full of bats, and a black cauldron boiling with green slime?

Kind of. But still, ordinary, or not, her body quivered with the strangeness, the immensity of this reality.

"I don't know how this is even possible." What had

Hunter said? They'd come through a portal. "Is this under the streets of Manhattan?"

He smiled. "If that makes it easier."

"Hello. Welcome to my home."

A stately woman with silver-streaked hair approached them wearing a thigh-length t-shirt over leggings, followed closely by the giant. "Pardon my clothes. Blunt and I have been doing our daily yoga routine. Ash I know." She stuck her hand out. "You are the famous Skye Parker. I'm Elizabeth Trowbridge."

Skye shook hands. "No. Yes. I mean, I'm Skye, but hardly famous. Nice to meet you, Ms. Trowbridge."

"Oh, call me Elizabeth." She could be in her eighties, and her broad smile crinkled the corners of pale blue eyes. She was lovely and elegant even in workout clothes. "Come on back to the patio. I have some refreshing iced tea waiting."

No whisky straight? She could use a stiff drink or three. It was noon somewhere.

Blunt went ahead through a great room dominated by a floor-to-ceiling fireplace with an oversized mantel crowded with more curios. Somehow a wall of windows in front of him slid back when he waved a hand.

Magic again right before her eyes. Her knees knocked together. *Get a grip, Parker.*

"Oh, I'm sorry, this helpful gentleman is Blunt." Elizabeth touched his beefy arm. "What he cannot see he more than makes up for in intuition and tenacity. I could not run my household without him."

Blunt nodded his head. "Truth. The scones are ready for the oven."

Scones. Her stomach gurgled. Maybe they had

magic jam.

While Blunt headed for the kitchen, Elizabeth led them out to a flagstone patio lush with greenery and dotted with bubbling fountains. They sat around an iron bistro table. A slight breeze ruffled the leaves, stirring the rich, sweet scent of many roses. A stone statue of a dragon with dragonfly-shaped wings sat on a pedestal surrounded by yellow marigolds. The fairy statues, fountains and flowers reminded Skye of an enchanted fairy tale. Maybe she was Alice and she'd tumbled down a rabbit hole.

Hunter looked up into the fruit trees. "Where's Strike?"

Elizabeth poured tea from a frosted pitcher into three tall glasses. "He's sulking in the ficus over there. I told him to wait until I give the signal to join us."

A loud caw-cackle came from the tree. Skye couldn't see a thing. "Strike is a bird?"

"A raven with a smart mouth." With a smile, she handed Skye a tall glass. "He's my familiar."

"Familiar? Like a witch's familiar?"

"Same as Soot," said Hunter, watching her closely. "And the other animals you saw when we walked through the halls."

He was probably wondering if she was about to freak out. She was but got her breathing under control and put on her sleuth fedora again.

Be calm. Be focused. Be strategic.

Elizabeth sobered. "I can understand how disorienting and unreal all this may seem to you. I want you to feel free to ask me any questions you want. But first, I need you to promise me something."

"I know what you'll ask."

"Yes. You cannot give away our secret. Cannot speak about it, write about it, or in any way divulge that witches and magic are real, that this place, the Haven, exists."

The squirmy, uncomfortable feeling she'd get as a kid whenever she tried fooling her mother had her stomach in knots. "My mother and I have researched paranormal phenomena since I was a child. Did Hunter tell you what happened to me?"

Elizabeth nodded.

"I've been steeped in the arcane my whole life. We already have hundreds of files, posted many stories, talked to many people." She pushed at her glasses. "I'm an investigative journalist. How can I make that promise? Doesn't the world have a right to know?"

Elizabeth opened her mouth to speak but Blunt came through to the patio carrying a tray of delicious smells and set it on the table.

"Fresh-baked blueberry scones, a variety of preserves and freshly whipped cream," he said, his baritone lending a musical quality to the dessert menu. He wore an extra-large lacy bib apron dusted with flour. A raucous cackling came from the ficus.

Elizabeth handed out small plates and napkins. "Thank you, Blunt. This looks delightful. Take the rest of the day off and visit your friend Crystal, why don't you?"

A pink stain crept up Blunt's neck. He nodded, turned, and left. Elizabeth clapped once. "You may join, Strike."

A huge black bird flap-flapped from the tree, careening sideways and losing feathery bits along the way. It made an awkward landing on the back of

Elizabeth's bistro chair and cast one beady eye on the dessert tray, the other crusted socket empty. "I don't really need all the fresh this and fresh that, but no worries. I'll choke it down."

"Did—did the bird really talk?" Skye placed a hand firmly on a knee to stop the leg bounce.

Elizabeth laughed. "Ravens can be taught to talk, whether mage or not. But being mage, Strike has a mind of his own and vocalizes his thoughts whether we want to hear them or not." She offered the bird a piece of scone with a spot of raspberry jam. The sweet disappeared in the thick, slightly curved beak.

"Soot, being a cat, can't talk," said Hunter. "He pushes his thoughts onto my mind, and I speak or push mine onto his. Not all familiars communicate with their witches in that way."

Skye shook her head. So many questions. Where to start? Ravens that talk like humans, telepathic cats, and a portal to some weird trippy place were just at base camp, Mount Everest. The rest of the mountain loomed.

"Okay. I promise not to tell anyone about any of this." *Until I see the video, the irrefutable proof.* There was no doubt a story like this would catapult her onto the world stage. Validate everything she was.

Elizabeth and Hunter pinned her with their eyes and the bird with his good one, no doubt looking for insincerity. She was very good at feigning credibility. Didn't they know to trust no one?

Elizabeth broke off a piece of biscuit, added a dab of jam and whipped cream. "Ask whatever questions you'd like."

"Where, or what, is this place you call the Haven?"

"From the beginning, it became obvious that our

society could not function as we once did. We created small sanctuaries we could retreat to when threatened, or for spiritual refreshment and schooling for our children, to assess those who break our rules. Other purposes."

"Created—like with magic? Accessed through some kind of portal?" She glanced around. So, all this wasn't real, even the sky, the clouds.

"Yes. High magic." She took a bite of biscuit.

"Your beginning—how far back? And what do you mean you couldn't function as you once did?"

Hunter looked up from his plate at Elizabeth, a speck of jam on a lower lip. Even now, how could she long to lick off the jam? He'd be wondering how much to reveal to a Reg, a journalist at that.

Strike ruffled his motley feathers. "Careful, E. This one is not trustworthy."

"Our beginnings." She sighed. "Many thousands of years ago in a distant land we were called Majiste, witches. The Goddess, the One Mother, gave us magic, with the promise to revere all life, renounce violence. Over there among the roses is a statue of the One Mother. There are others scattered throughout the garden."

"I've never heard of the Majiste. Where is this distant land?"

"It's called Tae-wen. You won't find it on any of your maps."

"What map will I find it on?"

"Might as well tell her. She's a ferret," said Hunter.

Elizabeth sat back against the chair. "Tae-wen is our ancient world. We visited Otherworld, this earthly plane, many times over millennia, so we were familiar with it. We came to your world en masse over three hundred years ago when a brutal race threatened to wipe out all mage, and then began attacking us. Due to our nature, we couldn't fight back with the ruthlessness required."

Strike screeched. "Now you've done it."

Skye stiffened. Every nerve prepared for a freakout. "You're from another planet? You are all,"— she swallowed hard—"extra-terrestrials?"

Chapter Thirteen

"Extra-terrestrials?" Elizabeth laughed. "No, although I'm told they call me E.T. for short. Tae-wen is more like another dimension of Earth, wouldn't you say, Ash?"

Hunter nodded, regarding Skye intently. "And as real as our world. Tae-wen is peopled by different races, some similar creatures, some different. Many of the people speak English."

Elizabeth continued, "Those on Tae-wen who know about mage portals call this Earth *Otherworld.* They speculate that Otherworld was borne as a child from Tae-wen, thus the similarities in some cultures and language. It seems the two worlds have bled into each other since time began."

Another dimension of Earth. Never mind Mount Everest. The simple fact that magic was real skimmed the surface of a bottomless ocean, and Skye felt like she was drowning. A strong pulse beat in her neck. Did she really want to know more? Could she handle the truth?

Hell, yes.

"How are there many thousands of you, like Hunter says?"

"There were not this many when we came through portals from the Majiste land of Lumeria. We have multiplied across the world since the 1690s. At first, we settled in mainly Caucasian countries so we could blend in with existing populations."

"Wow. Tough time in history for witches, or those who were thought to be. A lot of countries persecuted witches, hunted them, burned them. There are witch hunts even today, although there are some—would they be Regs?—who call themselves witches. They're open about it, sometimes form covens and follow Wiccan rituals."

"You're right. They are Regs, not mage like us."

"But tell me, how is this world any better than the place you left?"

"We wondered the same thing. Still do. But there was no going home, even though we held out hope through the ages. We hid our magic because the people of this world would not accept us, as you stated. We formed the global Bureau of Witchery. Local Councils govern us, maintain our secrecy, and ensure our magic didn't interfere with Reg life unless absolutely necessary."

Hunter shifted. "I'm what's called a Keeper. A Keeper of magic. Same as Mort and Myst. Because I have some unique talents, I'm suited to the job of ensuring any public displays of magic are dealt with."

Yeah, like the bike incident. "I can't imagine how you've remained secret this long. Your powers—can everyone wipe memories like you, Hunter?"

"No. We have magical spectrums. Quaints have lower powers, like kinetic abilities. Specials have higher powers and can transform one object into another, among other things. Elites have the greatest powers and can create something from nothing, manipulate the elements to a greater degree than the Specials. A few are empaths like Mort, who counsel and calm. Fewer still have the rare ability to heal, wipe memories, recognize each witch's energy signature."

Strike rocked back and forth behind Elizabeth's shoulder. "Tell her about the cost. Magic comes with a cost, don't you know."

"I thought you didn't want her knowing everything, bird." Hunter popped a final morsel of scone into his mouth.

"That giant Disney cruise ship has sailed." Strike bobbed his head.

"I know about Hunter's headaches, migraines." Skye wiped the condensation from the glass and sipped the tea.

Elizabeth nodded. "Most experience fatigue, some have stomach upsets, even shortness of breath, and other side effects."

Hunter's burner phone chimed. He stood and pulled it from a pocket. "It's Myst." He answered the call. "What's up?" He walked out of earshot.

Skye needed to write all this down until she could check the video. Every detail that had been disclosed only led to more questions. So many questions. Like, why weren't they all wallowing in riches? What other powers did these people have? Could they read minds? If they could, she'd probably have been locked up somewhere already.

Maybe they had no intention of letting her go. Maybe Hunter had brought her here to be "assessed" and then locked away.

The bird shuffled its feet along the back of Elizabeth's chair and tilted its good eye toward Skye. "You look about to go crack-up. What are you thinking?"

"Me?" *Is this a test? Can the damn bird read minds?* "I wondered if I was brought here to be locked away."

Elizabeth looked up from brushing crumbs off her shirt. The oh-my-God expression seemed genuine. "Absolutely not. We're trying to keep you safe. We must catch this witch because every life he takes in the name of keeping our society a secret is a blasphemy against the One Mother, against humanity. Every death could have the opposite consequence of revealing us to the world."

Skye watched Hunter across the patio on the phone, his back rigid, handsome face scowling. She wanted to believe the woman, but from day one, Hunter had fed her a web of lies with such cool mastery she'd almost fallen for every one of them. And almost fallen for him.

Okay, she had fallen. For like five seconds.

Squawk. "You're in love with him. Your face—an open romance novel. Same as his."

"You are so wrong." And how crazy was it that she was arguing with a raggedy raven?

Elizabeth booped the bird on the beak. "Stop that." She stretched a hand across the table to her. "Don't mind him. He fancies himself a cupid. Too many Hallmark movies."

Hunter strode over, pocketing the phone. "You okay, Parker? You're pale."

"Well, let's see. I learned that a bunch of my neighbors, maybe some close friends and colleagues, are witches with who-knows-what powers, and some deranged witch wants me dead. I'm in a place somewhere between sleep and awake, a veritable

176

Neverland. I don't—"

"We get the picture. I'm sorry you had to learn about us this way."

"I'll bet."

Hunter squatted beside the chair and took her hand. She wanted to pull back, but he began a soothing massage with a thumb across her knuckles. He owed her way more than a lousy massage. *Hmm, not so lousy.* He was good. Very good. In fact, she bet her pale-face-with-freckles look had turned pink from the sudden warmth, maybe even melted a couple of those angel kisses.

"Myst told me they closed in on the, uh, perp, but he slipped away. He's still in the wind somewhere in the city. They'll get him."

Strike stretched out a tattered wing. "You could use Super Strike out there on aerial patrol." He took off and hovered a few feet above Elizabeth, listing to the left, then the right.

Elizabeth smiled. "No, I need you here on *my* patrol." She stood, scraping back the chair. The bird swung higher and soared off. "Skye, I have a couple of guest rooms. You both should stay here where you're safe."

Sounded like an order. Skye wanted to object, but somehow, she couldn't summon the emotional energy. All this talk of magic and portal worlds had drained her. Hunter, crouching so close with his masculine scent, earnest dark eyes, soothing fingers, had the effect of a comfy, weighted blanket on a cold and dangerous night. Or like she'd just popped a Valium.

"Thank you, Elizabeth. I could use a lie down right now. Didn't sleep well last night for some reason." She made a face at Hunter, who let go of her hand and stood. If she got some alone time, she could jot notes, document all this craziness. Including the fact that, while she'd been making eyes at Hunter, the table had been cleared of dishes without anyone leaving the patio. Caught on tape? She hoped so, although the amount of video she had already would be more than enough.

Magic is real.

Holy shit. I'm swimming in a deep, deep ocean for sure. The Mariana Trench.

Elizabeth showed them through the apartment and down a hallway to the bedrooms. Skye's room, painted a soft green, was spacious. Her bags sat on a king size four-poster. Beside a desk on one wall, a sliding door led onto a private patio. Another open door led to a spa-like bathroom with a claw-foot tub.

"This is perfect."

Skye moved through the room, examining the framed photo artwork hung on the walls. She'd visited every one of the places in the pictures. It was as if…

She turned to Elizabeth and waved at the walls. "Is this just a coincidence?"

Elizabeth smiled and tilted her head. "No, my dear. I've read your articles and essays, and about your many adventures. I created this room while we enjoyed our iced tea and biscuits."

This silver-haired octogenarian, a witch, created this room while I sipped tea. Wonder and awe filled the hollow space carved out by betrayal. Yet, uncertainty jangled her nerves. How long would she be in the Haven? She'd only thrown in the tote enough for one night away. Maybe they had a mall down here.

"I'll leave you to get settled. Please, make yourself

at home. Have a rest. I'll collect you at lunch." Elizabeth turned and softly closed the door behind her.

A door in another wall opened and Hunter stuck his head through. "We have adjoining rooms." He glanced around and chuckled. "Love how she curated your room. Here, I have a surprise for you." He came through the door holding a wriggling Trinket.

"Trinket!" She gathered the little dog in her arms. He licked and wriggled and whined. She smiled. "Thank you. I needed him."

"I know. And whether I needed my pain-in-the-rear or not, I got Soot."

The black cat tiptoed into the room, tail high, nose in the air.

"Soot says 'nice digs.'"

The fact that she took the feline comment in stride meant that a freak out was not imminent. She set the squirmy dog down. He raced to Soot, licking the cat's face and dancing around him.

"Soot, watch the language," said Hunter.

Her laugh turned into a yawn. "I hope we're only here for the day. I didn't bring a change."

"I'm hoping so, too. Go lie down. Soot, let's go."

And poof, the cat disappeared mid-jump on the way to the easy chair. Skye blinked several times. No cat. *Holy shit.*

"Oh, forgot to mention that he can transport at will."

"You mean, disappear and reappear somewhere else?"

"Yes. But he knows never to transport in front of Regs. Since you know about us, and you're here..."

A tight, prickly ball of panic formed in her gut, but

immediately dissolved into a puddle of what-the-hell. After he left, she turned off the button cam, sank onto the bed and stretched out with the dog. She'd never sleep again, but maybe she could try to rest. Her life had been turned upside down and inside out by a sexy guy in a hoodie, a freaking Keeper of magic, someone she had no future with nor could trust.

In Sam's car she'd texted Jo. Just a quick "I'm safe" like she'd told Hunter. But she'd left her with the exploding head emoji. Jo replied with a series of question marks. Skye had typed "later." She needed her friend and partner in crime in the worst way. First, rest the brain, then somehow find the words to bring Jo in on this wild adventure.

She hugged Trinket tight, then kissed his furry head. This secret witch society was built on so much trust. If not, it would fall apart. She suppressed the pinch of guilt that nipped at her conscience like a feral fox. Maybe they would never let her leave the Haven. Maybe trust was a two-way superhighway.

Rest brain. She closed her eyes, focusing on even breathing in and out.

Magic is real. This was truly a case of "be careful what you wish for."

****

Ash shut the door between their bedrooms and went in search of E.T. He wasn't the least bit sorry he'd pushed a mesmer on Parker. She may have braved a riot in the Philippines and a rampaging hippo on the Mara in Africa, not to mention a nose-gnawing rat in a New York sewer, but she was not prepared to learn the existence of an alternate Earth. He didn't want her to have a coronary in her sleep.

He found Elizabeth sitting behind an ornately carved antique desk in her office. A museum's worth of artifacts and ornaments that she'd gathered throughout her eons in this world sat on shelves throughout the room. The power of her magic had infused them and the very walls with a vibrational energy. He adjusted his sensitivity.

"This reminds me of Trowbridge House in Connecticut."

She looked up and smiled wistfully. "It does. I miss that old barge. Never and Willow Ravenwood are taking good care of the place and all my collectibles."

"More like the knick-knacks are taking care of them."

"Yes, they will do that. Our magic is truly wonderful, isn't it?"

He might disagree sometimes. A lot of times. "Parker's resting. When she wakes up, she'll be full of more questions. How much are we prepared to tell her?"

"We'll answer her questions. She doesn't know enough *what* to ask. But she's astute. It's a wonder she didn't realize you were mesmering her."

"She'd deck me if she knew. It's bad enough she knows I erased a fragment of memory from the bicycle accident."

"Sit. We need to talk." Her phone chimed. "It's Councilman Hunter. He wants to see us. I can decline."

The esteemed Immortal Elizabeth Trowbridge answered to no one. She could tell Gray to take a hike. "No. Let's go. See what's up." His dad. Never good. How did Gray know he was with E.T.?

"He said he'd meet us in the inner boardroom."

"Alone?"

She frowned. "Likely not." She grabbed a notebook and pen.

Shit. "I'll tell Strike and Soot to keep watch over Parker. If Soot senses anything out of the ordinary, he'll pop into the meeting."

After giving the familiars their instructions, he caught up with E.T. at the entrance to the Bureau's offices. They walked in silence to the boardroom while his stomach threw acid on the four scones he'd wolfed down. Elizabeth went ahead into the room.

The grim-faced Councilman, dressed in his usual vest and white shirt, sat at the head of a long conference table, attention on a laptop open in front of him. He was alone except for the waves of dark energy surrounding him. Ash dulled his own power receptors. Three powerful Elites in one room was like a surround sound stereo on full blast.

Ash exchanged glances with E.T. as she sat to Gray's right. He took a seat beside her. Her mouth twitched. She should be at the head of the table. Always had. But today, Gray wanted to exert his power and she was going to let him. For now. The Councilman looked up and gave a nod to each of them before returning to the screen. The least he could have done was stand when Elizabeth entered. Show some respect for the ancient immortal. Ash glared at the bent head.

A door on the far wall opened and Jada Gladstone walked in, awash in high energy and self-importance. If the morality monitor was here, it meant a serious breach of the rules of conduct had occurred. Ash stood briefly, then sat, forcing tight shoulder muscles to relax.

They know about Parker.

Gray pushed the laptop aside. "Whatever is discussed here must not leave this room without my approval, understood?"

Ash gave a curt nod. E.T. and Jada murmured assent.

"Ash, you should be in a holding cell right now awaiting Council trial."

"For which offense? Been a few."

Gray's face mottled red. "Let's start with revealing our existence to a Reg, and then bringing her here to the Haven."

"How did you know?"

Jada leaned forward and looked down her sharp nose at him. "Surveillance video. I recognized Skye Parker, an investigative reporter no less."

Gray swung the laptop around. He hit a key. A video feed in the Haven corridor showed Ash, Parker, and M&M exiting the elevator. The next one was from somewhere in the residence lobby. Ash and Parker were disappearing through a doorway with Blunt.

E.T.'s face morphed into a mask of suppressed fury. "Who authorized surveillance in the Haven and how long has it been in place?" Her voice was quiet and controlled, like the eye of a hurricane.

"Some of the cameras have been up for at least three months. Jada and I conferred and felt it was best for security as well as monitoring compliance to rules. There have been increasing reports of a breakdown of magical powers that requires our attention, too."

Jada shifted in the chair, lips pinched. "We've needed surveillance for a long time. It's standard practice everywhere in the world."

"The cameras will be taken down immediately. I

forbid electronic spying on each other in this place, this sanctuary," Elizabeth said with force.

Gray closed the laptop lid. "Fine, fine. We'll consider it. But now we have an unidentified rogue witch on the loose somewhere in New York. If he ever comes to the Haven—"

"We'll deal with that if it happens." E.T. stood. "Are we done, then?"

"No. *Hell* no. The reason we're here is because a Reg, a damn reporter, knows about us and was sneaked into the Haven."

Elizabeth sent an *I tried* look to Ash and sat in the chair. "I told Ash to bring her to me for protection, which meant revealing to her what she already suspected."

Ash leaned in. "Parker's life was in imminent danger. That killer was closing in."

Gray let out an exasperated breath. "Ash, you were supposed to report regularly to me. I'm head of security. I needed to be in the loop. Why the hell wasn't I?"

Because you would rather see her die. Too harsh? "I couldn't waste time arguing with you."

Jada rapped the table. "What's to be done with her now is my domain."

"What do you mean 'done with her'? I'm seeing to her. Only me."

Gray held up a hand. "Hold on. Ash, when I told you to romance her, I didn't mean fall for her. You have, haven't you?"

Gray's question floored him. He looked at E.T. with her eyes gone soft, and Jada with brows winging up into her hairline.

"You have," said Jada, as if he'd been kicking dogs.

"Doesn't matter how I feel. I've shattered what little trust Parker had in me. There's nothing there."

"That's good, because she's the biggest direct threat to our secrecy that we've encountered." Jada set her shoulders back. "We have two solutions. One, Ash will erase her memory of this place and magic as far back as possible. With your talent, only *you* can do this massive wipe without us bringing in another from L.A. Discredit all her claims of our existence. Ridicule—"

"No!" Ash jumped to his feet. "Never going to happen."

Elizabeth laid fingers on his arm. "Easy, Ash." She handed him the notebook with a pointed look.

The mesmer began as a warm tingling on his nerves. He jerked his arm away and sent her a warning look.

Jada continued. "Two, send her to Tae-wen."

His gut clenched. "Have you all gone crazy? Who are you? Dad? Elizabeth?"

He'd heard enough. He shoved in the chair with a thought and strode from the room, Gray calling after him. He willed the door to slam shut behind him.

He hurried along the hall lined with Council offices and through two coded doors to the housing wing, his mind chaotic. Had E.T. lured him into bringing Parker here so they could lock her up, erase her memory? He didn't want to accept that idea. No, E.T. wouldn't be a party to either of Jada's so-called solutions. Would she? And what was up with this notebook? He glanced inside. A scribble of words—a chant—and directions.

Thank you, E.T. He tore out the page and pocketed

it.

As soon as he entered the housing lobby, Myst rushed to his side. "I was about to text you. The guy we've been trying to follow? He's here. We're sure of it." She thrust a tablet in front of him. "I just learned about the surveillance cameras from a guy in tech."

A video of a guy wearing a dark jacket and backpack exited an elevator in another part of the Haven. Looked like a white streak in his hair. He walked away from the camera.

"Damn. A surveillance camera. Hate to say that Councilman Hunter may have been right to install them. Looks like the guy is deliberately keeping his head down and avoiding eye contact with anyone."

"See the lean to his left shoulder?" Myst asked.

"Yeah. It's him." A pulse pounded in his temple. He handed her the tablet. "Get Mort and Shadow Force. Grab this guy. *Now*. I'll make sure Parker is safe."

Myst nodded and turned toward the lobby door. A trio of Gray's smartly uniformed Haven security guards, all beefed up and earnest as hell, stood in the hall beyond the glass doors. A fourth joined them.

"Stall them. They want Parker."

"What? Why—"

"I'll tell you later. Show them the video. Tell them this killer needs to be found. Sound an alarm or something."

She headed for the men, while he headed for the outdoors and the gardens. No Blunt or E.T. to let him in through the coded doors. He kept his stride just short of a dead run along the stone walkway.

He glanced in all directions when he reached E's gate. The last thing he needed was that weasel Jefrem

Gladstone to catch him again. He removed the pulsing protection spell and dashed through the gate. He took a few precious moments to place a more powerful spell behind him.

Something dive-bombed him from a nearby tree, sharp claws raking the top of his head. Luckily his hair was too short to grasp.

"Shit, Strike. It's me." Ash raced along the path with the bird flapping beside him.

"Sorry, Keeper. Instinct."

Ash appreciated the familiar's vigilance. He had the urge to shout for Parker. Was she even awake? Strike landed on the back of a patio chair.

Soot appeared outside the patio's sliding doors. *"What's up?"*

Ash pushed his thoughts. *Security is coming to get Parker.*

The cat disappeared. When Ash opened the bedroom door, Soot was pawing Parker awake. Ash rushed to her bedside and tossed the notebook. "Parker, get up. Quick. We have to leave."

She sat up, rubbing her eyes. "Leave?" She shoved a hand through thick, red curls. "How long have I been asleep?"

He rushed the magic, but managed to produce a long tunic, rough-spun pants, and short boots. "Get up. Hurry. Security is on its way."

Soot kept shooting Ash questions and comments, all of which Ash ignored. Trinket jumped down from the bed where he'd been curled in a tight ball. Parker stood on wobbly legs. Ash reached out a steadying hand. Maybe the mesmer had been too strong.

"Security? What's happened?" She put on her

glasses.

"You know how you said to trust no one? You were right. That killer, the Council, and I thought maybe even Trowbridge herself—they want you 'dealt with.'"

"Doesn't sound good."

"The killer is in the Haven somewhere. E.T. came through. She's on our side. My dad, who is Chief Security Officer for the Haven, is definitely not."

"Your dad is Chief of Security? I thought he headed a brokerage firm."

He focused on the clothes for Parker. "He does, part-time."

"He's your dad. Why isn't he helping you?"

"Long story. Not enough time."

A tunic and pants appeared on her body, short boots on her feet. The clothes she'd had on lay in a heap on the floor. He called the magic for himself— long shirt and rough pants, boots.

Parker's eyes widened as she looked down. "What the hell, Hunter. Why am I in this getup? And you?" She pulled on the tunic to straighten it. The pants were an inch too short. "At least you left me with my bra and panties underneath."

He groaned. He wished he could spend the whole morning contemplating Parker in her underwear, or out of it. He hated performing clothing magic "Follow me. Soot, stay here with Trinket. That's an order."

"Where are we going?" She went to grab her bags and phone.

"Leave them. You won't need anything." A lie, but he could take care of whatever came up. "We're going somewhere safe." *Relatively.*

He hurried out into the living room with Parker following close behind. He didn't really need the directions to the portal site that E.T. had written on the note. The pulse of the site grew stronger as he approached the door set deep in a back hallway. He thrust her through the door into a large storage room painted stark white and lined with shelves along three walls. Cases of bottled water, backpacks, Tae-wen clothing—all manner of provisions filled the shelves.

"A storeroom? We're hiding here? No windows. I'd be right at home if I had my damn computer."

"We're not staying in this room. Can't take any electronics. Here is where you're at least going to have to trust *me*." He grabbed two knitted caps from pegs on the wall. He put one on and pulled it down over his ears. He handed the other one to Parker.

"Hunter, where are we going?" Her eyes were bright with anticipation, but her lips firmed. She stood rigid, legs planted.

"Put on the cap and pull it down over your ears."

Ash pulled the scrap of paper from a pocket and began the ritual to call forth the portal. There were many portals in the Haven. Even one in the Keeper wing, which he'd prefer to use. But they had to use this one, had to go now. A swirling eddy of rainbow colors and flashes of light took shape against the blank wall.

She touched a hand to her chest. "Hunter?" She pulled on the cap and tugged, adjusting the glasses. A mass of red curls stuck out like one of those wig hats.

"We're going to Tae-wen." The irony wasn't lost on him. Wasn't this just what Gray and Jada wanted?

She gasped. "Through that? What happened to an elevator portal?"

The eddy had become a thrashing vortex of light ten feet high, its pull as strong as a rainbow-colored black hole.

"No, it's not. I've been through these a few times, just not this one. Funny sensation, but nothing to fear. We'll end up in a cave." He held out his hand. "I won't let anything happen to you."

"When are we coming back?"

"Honestly, I don't know."

She placed her trembling hand in his. "Hey, I'm so not going to pay you."

"It's time."

The portal tugged on his body, thrashing the headache that throbbed like a bastard. He pulled her beside him, and together they stepped into the maelstrom.

Chapter Fourteen

Skye's body tingled like she'd touched a low-voltage outlet. Colored lights flashed behind closed eyelids. A rush of blood pulsed through her heart, coursing through veins; cells separating, floating, combining. A slow-motion tumble like that free fall skydive last year tickled her stomach.

"Oomph." She landed hard on her butt, and her eyes popped open. The vortex churned beside her, throwing off its rainbow colors to be swallowed by the dark rock walls of a cave. Daylight bent around the corner of a tunnel, and along with a slight breeze, reached them in what appeared to be a dead-end anteroom.

"Are you okay?" The smooth voice beside her. *Hunter*.

"Yes, I think so."

He gently supported her elbow and helped her stand. She brushed at the tunic, then checked the woolen cap. "I didn't even lose the hat. Or my glasses." *But damn, no hidden camera*. What she wouldn't give to have video proof of this alternate world. And she'd never gotten to talk to Jo.

"You don't actually roll around in the portal." His teeth flashed white in a smile. "I don't think. As many times as I've been through this past year, I can't tell."

He turned to the vortex and mumbled some

gibberish words. The swirling conical rainbow grew smaller and smaller, then disappeared.

Her stomach quivered. *Holy shit. I'm in some other dimension.* Solid rock walls and hard-packed earthen floor held a damp, dirt smell, and something funky.

Not a dream.

"Wait." She pointed to the back wall where a huge pile of sticks, dead foliage, and tufts of fur were made up in what looked like a nest. "This cave is some creature's home. A bear?" She stiffened, eyes focused on the exit.

"No bears in Tae-wen. That I know of, anyway." Hunter groaned. "I think that nest belongs to a kasnatch. Bigfoot."

"Bigfoot. You're kidding me."

"They're a mage creature and more afraid of us than we are of them."

"Mage—meaning they have magic powers?"

"They can make themselves invisible. That's how they snuck into our world through active portals in our early portal history. Maybe they still do, and that's why one has never been caught in either place." Hunter turned in a circle and whispered close to her ear, "Could be one beside you right now."

Skye's heart banged against her ribs. When he grinned, she punched his arm. "Let's get out of here. This place gives me the creeps."

"Okay. We're in Faenstar and we'll head for the Faen town of Moonstone, about two miles from here."

"Faen?"

"They're an elven-type race who look like us except for dual-pointed ears. That's why we're wearing caps over our ears. If we come across any Malgren, we can hope to pass as the neutral Faen. Malgren can null magic. They'll hunt us if they think we're witches."

"Holy…" She swallowed. "But there aren't any of you here anymore, right?"

"Very few. Might be some that were banished for serious crimes, maybe a Shadow Force member or two on special assignment. Malgren are always on the lookout."

"What do Malgren look like?"

"Us, except for bumps on their foreheads. Some are sympathetic to mage, others aren't. We're going to keep hidden, anyway. Stay in the trees and avoid a chance meeting. Probably not going to come across my Malgren buddy Gryph. He now uses another portal to report to us."

"Okay." So many questions. No notebook. Great memory, though, unless Hunter decided to wipe it clean. But he promised never to do that again. *Trust— gah.*

"Hang back a sec while I check outside." He disappeared around the corner.

She clasped her hands together to stop them from shaking. Why the overstrung nerves? She'd been through a world of dangerous adventures. Just not *this* world. One with Bigfoots—Feet. The unknown walloped her in the gut.

He soon returned. "Let's go. Keep close."

She followed him out of the cave mouth just large enough that they didn't need to stoop. She blinked in the bright light. Was that the same sun as back home? They stood in a rocky clearing surrounded by dense bushes and a mix of broad-leafed trees and thick-needled pine. At first glance, this place could be anywhere in any American woods.

The pine-scented air smelled heavenly. All the tight muscles began to relax with the familiar as she followed behind along a narrow trail hemmed in by thick underbrush. Heavy tree branches arched overhead with maple leaf shaped leaves as big as an elephant's footprint. One tree sprouted huge, waxy flowers like magnolia blossoms that reached toward the filtering sun.

Hunter stopped, and she plowed into him. "Oh, sorry," she whispered.

"Watch out along here." He unhooked his pant leg from a thorny bush. "This is part of the Sudden Woods. Full of thorns and the odd hell creeper."

"What the—hell?" Her muscles corkscrewed. "Full disclosure, Hunter."

He reached for her hand, but she pulled it away. "No more hand-holding. Give it to me straight."

A frown pulled his brows together. "A hell creeper is a carnivorous flower kind of like that one in the movie."

"Little Shop of Horrors?" Her throat constricted.

"It's about the size of a cow and sends out vines when it feels vibrations in the ground. The vines wrap around legs or bodies, squeezing and dragging the victim to the flower's mouth. A giant-sized Venus fly trap."

She swallowed. "Not a good way to die."

"So, keep moving. Fast. And watch where you're going." He turned and continued along the rocky path.

She scooted beside him on the widening path, wishing not for the first time that she could fly. No feet on the ground meant no vibrations. But, hey, she had a witch with her. No worries, right?

No worries except the one that surrounded her like a death shroud. "Hey, I need to know. You said they want me dealt with. How were they going to 'deal' with me? Give it to me straight."

He shot her a quick glance. "Wipe your memories, banish you to Tae-wen, or maybe both."

Her heart stuttered. "And here we are. Goddammit, Hunter." She stopped and grabbed his arm.

He turned to her, tight lines around his mouth softening. "You're here only until they catch the killer and put him away. I won't let them keep you here or erase even one memory. Never."

She searched his eyes as her own grew moist. In them she read sincerity, confidence, and a spark of—what? Longing? His gaze strayed to her mouth. He leaned in.

Rustle. Crash.

Hunter jerked back, shoving her into a crouch beside him. She caught a flash of something on two legs. Something huge, brown, and furry. It leapt across the trail in front of them and—poof—disappeared. Except for the smell. The same fetid odor as the cave. Her breaths became shallow, heart pounding in her ears.

Hunter lifted her chin. "Kasnatch. So rude." He smiled and planted a kiss on her lips.

Before she could respond, he was helping her up. "We better get moving. Something startled him. Or her."

The trail narrowed, forcing her to walk behind him. The rock soon gave way to a rutted, meandering path littered with leaves, pine needles, and crisscrossed with roots. *Good ones?* At least the roots didn't move. She focused on the ground, keeping her arms tucked close to avoid the wicked thorns. Birds trilled overhead, but she didn't dare look for them. They crossed an intersecting trail.

Hunter stopped again, putting a hand behind him. He pulled at a tiny scrap of fabric caught on a bush. "Someone was here," he whispered. "And not long ago. Must've come from that other trail."

He pointed to the ground. Some of the roots were scuffed bare and the leaves flattened. "More than one. They're up ahead somewhere. Don't know friend or foe."

Adrenaline still rushed her veins from the Bigfoot encounter, shivering her stomach. "What'll we do?"

"Keep moving, but quieter and slower."

She followed him for long minutes, treading lightly. She listened so hard for voices or twigs snapping or any unnatural sounds she thought her teeth would break. The trail widened. The dense, thorny bushes gave way to less lethal, scraggly underbrush, some with clusters of small berries and tiny white flowers. Many of the trees looked like live oak with their heavy branches growing at odd angles and reaching for the ground.

Voices sounded ahead around a bend. Hunter stopped. So did her heart. She couldn't make out what was said, only that they were male. Hunter gestured they go to the right through a gap in the bushes. He pushed her ahead of him. She picked her way over the woodsy litter, trying to avoid snapping a twig, his gentle hand at her back.

The voices receded, and then silence again except for the weird call of some bird. Or was it a bird? She hugged her body. The underbrush became denser, the trees closer together.

He tugged on her tunic. "Crouch between these bushes. Keep quiet. I'm going to check the trail."

She nodded and found a spot to hide free of thorns. A small, winged beetle on a leaf studied her with several eyes on the ends of two long feelers. A many-forked tail waved wildly in the air. She pulled back a safe distance. This world, as much as she'd seen of it, was strange and familiar all at once.

Something bumped her foot. She shifted position. A bright green vine as big around as a wrist and covered in oozing red boils snaked around her right shin above the boot top. *Hell creeper!* A scream climbed up her throat.

Keep quiet. Hunter, where are you?

She sat on her butt, grasped the tough vine with both hands and tugged. Fingers slid in the pus. Her stomach roiled. She'd need an ax. The creeper wound higher. *Jeez, knee now.* Another, thinner vine snuck out, seeking the other leg. She pounded on it, kicking it away. *Shit, more coming.*

She got to her feet, kicking and stomping at the dozen fingers. *Too much noise. Too much vibration.* But what else could she do? Adrenaline spiked her nerves.

"Hunter," she called, keeping her voice low. What was worse, Malgren or hell creeper? "Hunter." Louder.

A violent tug on the right leg threw her backward. Her glasses flew off somewhere. Pressure like a tourniquet would soon cut off blood flow. The vine pulled. Her body scooted along the ground. She dug in her heels, grasping a slender sapling with one hand.

Okay, time to shout like a girl.

"Hunter! Hell creeper!"

She pummeled the vine with one fist as she shouted for him again. Blood-red pus flew. When a finger-thin vine captured a wrist, she had to let go of the tree. "Get. Off. Me."

She bit into the vine. Bitter liquid flooded her mouth. The trailer let go. She dry retched. Her body slid along the forest floor, still held captive by a leg and a wrist. Where was this goddam mother flower?

There, through a gap in the bushes, one gargantuan, angry looking—cabbage—about ten feet away. Dozens of creepers, slender and stout and seeking, waved in the air. Some snaked along the ground like blind boa constrictors.

Shit, shit, shit.

She flailed with a free arm. Punched. Yanked. Still, she was drawn forward into the open. The green folds of the cabbage, big as an SUV, unfurled. From a gaping maw, a sinuous, malevolent tongue like the arm of an octopus, sought a cheek. And licked. Rotting flesh halitosis slammed her senses, pinched nostrils closed. She held her breath, punching the tip of the dripping tongue in rapid jabs.

Closer, inch by inch.

She panted, heart bursting. Punch. Punch. She dug in again with one heel. She could no longer feel below the gripping creeper that encircled the other leg. Pokes at her back. She twisted. The ground around her writhed.

She closed her eyes. She'd never screamed in her life but let loose. "Hunter!"

The stink enveloped her like a thick fog. Creepers

choked off voice. Her air.

I don't want to die. God, not this way. Never got to write my story...

Chapter Fifteen

Ash followed the pair of Malgren men for a time, keeping silent and to the dense brush. Dressed in spiked leather vests, they were armed with bows and arrows, probably poison-tipped, and sheathed knives at the hip. Not the friendly-to-mage type. Dark Raiders. They talked about the everyday, one with buzzed hair about annoying children, the other wearing a leather-like, metal-studded tunic, about what's for supper. And they took their damn time along the trail, always choosing the one that led to Moonstone. He needed to get back to Parker. Pick another route to Flip House. Thankfully, the throbbing in his head had become a dull ache.

A far-off shout.

Shit. Parker.

Ash didn't wait for the Malgren's reaction. He bolted out of the brush and back down the trail. More Dark Raiders? The creeper? He ran. Minutes passed. Had he come this far? Pounding of feet chased after him with shouts of "Faen, Faen, hold on." A blood-curdling scream came from just ahead and to the side of the trail. He dove into the brush.

Scarlet creeper vines like the oversized capillaries of a giant beast crisscrossed the ground. *No!* "Parker!"

A push of magic sent a searing jolt of power to shred a path. Bloody pus flew. He broke into a clearing. Parker, body encircled by choking vines, struggled weakly in front of the gaping mouth. He rushed to her.

"I got you, Parker." He blasted the thick vine encircling her waist, legs, and arms, then pulled her limp body to the edge of the brush. Her face was a sickly yellow, lips tinted blue. The monstrous flower's yawning, noxious mouth flapped. It sent out more tendrils. Loathe to kill the thing, half beast, half plant, he kept up a barrage of energy blasts that repelled the snaking vines.

He patted her cheeks, then rubbed both arms. "Parker, can you hear me? Skye."

Shouts sounded behind him. The two Malgren burst through the brush and stopped. Their faces registered shock as vines wound around their ankles. They grabbed knives and hacked away as more advanced on them. Creepers yanked them off their feet.

He was about to give Parker mouth-to-mouth when she gasped. Her eyes opened, and she flailed her arms. Her voice was a raspy cry.

"It's okay, Skye. I've got you." He gathered her up and stood. She wound her arms around his neck, eyes wide.

The more the men shouted and stabbed at the vines, the more entangled they became as if the flower were angry at losing a tasty Parker morsel and doubled down on the pair.

"Help us, Faen." The voices had become hoarse with pleading.

Ash would have to use magic. He couldn't let the pair die when he had the power to save them. He held no illusion that they'd be grateful a witch saved their lives.

Forgive me, One Mother.

He directed a laser blast deep into the gaping mouth. The thing exploded. Red pus, pieces of vine and cabbage-y bits rained down. With Parker held firmly in his arms, he stumbled through the brush.

Where the bushes were too thick, he used a push of magic to part them, then closed the foliage behind. He did his best to erase signs of their passage and mask their noise. Before long, Parker squirmed. He slowed.

"Put me down. I'm okay." Her voice was whisper-hoarse.

He studied her eyes. The pupils were normal, breathing less labored. He stopped and set her on her feet, holding steady to one arm until blood flowed back to the legs. "You have bruising already." He touched the bright red bands that encircled her arms. "These will be purple soon." If she were mage, a unicorn could heal the damage. But she wasn't a witch, and unicorns were elusive as wishes come true.

"I'm sorry I took you through the portal. If I—"

"If you hadn't, I might be sitting home wondering where a good portion of my life's memories went."

He grimaced. And, they might have sent her right where *he'd* brought her. Right where he risked her life. "At least you're alive. Meantime, Parker, I'm not letting you out of my sight."

She gave him a crooked smile. "I liked before, when you called me Skye."

"I did?" he said, keeping his voice low.

She nodded.

He unwound, softened. "Call me Ash, then."

"Okay." A hand went to her face. "Wait. Where are my glasses?"

"Shit. I thought there was something different

about you, rotting sludge aside."

She groaned. "I lost them when that thing threw me to the ground."

"How blind are you without them?"

"Well, you look unnaturally handsome right now."

"Funny. I can try making you a new pair." It would take strong magic, and the promise of another headache.

"Wow. Yeah, how hard could that be, right?"

Ash held out a hand, closed his eyes, and focused on an image of wire-rimmed glasses like the kind Eldrin sometimes wore when he thought no one was looking. He called on the energy, the power, the magic. Warmth spread outward from his core, down arms to fingers that tingled with voltage. *Shapes. Wire. Glass. A zing of current. A swirl of color.*

In a few short moments, he felt a weight on his hand. Skye gasped. He opened his eyes. A pair of wire-framed glasses sat in his palm.

"Oh my god, you did it." She took them and wiggled the arms over her ears. "The prescription is not quite right, Doctor, but they'll do for now."

"You look like a librarian. A sexy librarian." Through the glass, her oversized green eyes sparkled.

She smiled. "And you are back to your homely old self. With fuzzy edges." She wiped slimy pus from her tunic and pants. "Is there a stream nearby? This stink is making me sick."

He waved a hand toward her body, then over his, with a brush of magic. "There. Clean enough for now. Let's get moving. I can hear them searching for us. Keep as quiet as possible."

He directed them down a rough animal trail that led

in the opposite direction to Moonstone. Maybe the men would give up since the Faen town seemed to be their original destination.

He went slowly at first to give her legs time to recover. They were still being followed judging by the faint noises back through the trees. A witch in Tae-wen was a rarity, Never Ravenwood's visits to collect herbs aside. The Malgren wouldn't give up easily on him and Parker—Skye—even though a mage was a tough adversary.

They broke through the thick woods onto a deserted dirt road rutted with wagon tracks, Abbott's Trail, if he remembered a map he'd once seen of Faenstar.

"Which way?" Skye adjusted the tangled mop of hair under the knit cap. The welts on her wrists and arms had turned crimson.

He was responsible for the suffering as if he'd used brute force himself. "To the right and miles past that curve in the road is the start of Moonstone and the property of a Malgren-hating Faen named Quinn. I wanted to sit tight at Flip House in Moonstone without the Malgren knowing we were there. I don't want those men we met to chase us into town. Risk innocent Faen lives." He turned to the left. "Maybe two miles down this way is the abandoned land of Lumeria, the forbidden land. I've never set foot there."

"This way, then." She turned left and marched up the side of the road toward Lumeria.

He smiled. This lady was game and gutsy. "Let's cross to the other side. I'll erase our tracks."

He jumped into one rut then another. She followed, stepping where he stepped. After they crossed, he erased their prints with a push of magic. Keeping silent and an eye on the road, they continued through the sparse woods for a couple of miles, stopping to rest and take a drink from a stream.

Skye sat on a log and rolled up a pant leg. Burgundy welts crisscrossed her calf. "Doesn't look as bad as I thought."

"Does it hurt?" He spoke low as if his voice could add to her pain.

"Only when I touch the bruises."

"Wish I had the healing. Or a unicorn." He rubbed a temple, wishing he could heal himself.

She laughed. "Now I know I'm adjusting to this whole witch magic and other realm shit when your words just washed over me."

"Welcome to my world."

A low rumbling vibrated the ground.

"Get down." He crouched to peer through the brush.

A wagon led by a team of chestnut horses lumbered by on the road. The driver was Faen. In the back, the Malgren men sat on crates, arrows nocked in bows. They'd likely realized that the mage and the woman weren't headed to Moonstone, so they hitched a ride in the opposite direction. How did they hope to overpower a mage? Just engaging would reap rewards with their leader. The ancient feud lasted to this day, and they knew they would never be killed by a witch. Reverence for life above all. *Bless the One Mother.*

Ash didn't want a confrontation.

"Stop the wagon," one shouted.

When the wagon rolled to a stop, the two men jumped down.

Ash put a finger to his lips and signaled Skye to move back through the sparse trees. The cover was lousy here. *Okay, Nev, let's see if I've mastered your hologram lessons. If I have any magic energy left.*

He studied the trees, shrubs, and landscape, setting the image firmly in his mind. Hands out, eyes closed, he called on the deep magic. A tingle of warm energy spread outward from his chest, powering the magic along arms, hands, and fingers. When a floating sensation began, he opened his eyes. The hologram, a perfect replica of the landscape, stretched before him. He couldn't see Skye through the image. He walked through it. Now the Malgren wouldn't see him, either.

When he caught up to Skye, he turned around. The men were heading back to the wagon. They called out to the driver to take them to Glendon, a town in the Malgren land miles in the opposite direction to Moonstone.

"What did you do? They can see us."

"No. I created a hologram of the area. You can't see through holograms from the other side."

"Holograms? Jeez."

Her mind was on overload. "I just learned how to make them. It was a gamble."

"Really? A magical gamble." She hugged herself.

He unwound an arm and held her hand. "Are you okay? Your eyes are huge."

"Hey, sure. Just keep the surprises coming." She pulled free. "Which way now?"

He pointed to the left. "Let's get into better cover. They could keep searching for us until we get to the Lumeria border." Even if they didn't follow, he wanted to continue. He was curious about the ancient homeland.

"What happens at the border?"

"They won't enter the land. The Malgren consider Lumeria cursed." Maybe it was.

He led her further into the woods. The path became smoother. "The border is less than a mile. Can you walk faster?"

She nodded.

"Let me know if you're hurting. Follow me."

He picked up the pace along another trail. Skye kept up, but he bet she was in pain. He knew the instant they passed onto Lumeria land. Some trees had lost their leaves. Others looked dusted with white powder. He stopped. The bushes were spindly ghosts, the weeds and grasses a sickly yellow.

"What happened here?" Skye's breathing wasn't even labored. She came beside him and gazed around.

"We've crossed into Lumeria. Majiste land." He removed the knitted cap and shoved it in the belt.

"Where your ancestors came from."

He nodded. "No real cover from here to the city. But then, no one to see us, anyway."

"City?"

"Elysium. Capital city. Once home to thousands."

"Why are you forbidden to come here?"

"You'll see soon enough." The penalty for entering their ancient land could be as severe as nullification of powers. Councilman Hunter wouldn't go easy on him if he found out. *Just one more offense to add to the list.*

****

Skye ignored the throbbing ribcage and the shudder of pain through bruised muscles with each step. She kept close to Ash as dusk fell over the valley consisting of wide fields of what looked like corn. The silver stalks reached toward the sky on either side of them, concealing their passage from, well, no one, apparently. The husks hugging tufted, well-formed ears were also silvery, like the color had been leached from them. She rubbed a soft and supple leaf between her fingers. It sprung back when she let go.

"Suspended animation," said Ash.

"For three hundred years?"

"And counting."

A light breeze ruffled her clothes, setting off goosebumps along bare arms. There was only the scent of dirt on the air, not the green of growing things. "It's getting kinda dark under the stalks" She didn't know why the whisper.

He stopped and turned. "Hold on. I'll get us some light. The sun will be setting soon."

He closed his eyes and held out a palm. She studied his face, the long lashes, well-shaped nose, strong chin. He was lean and whip-cord strong. A pulse beat in his temple. He was drawing on his powers. She bit her lip. *A magic man.* Her pulse quickened.

A ball of light appeared above his palm as he opened his eyes. No, a flame that spun, danced, and grew, but threw off no heat.

"Holy shit. Okay. Okay. I can handle this." She kept her breathing even. How would she ever make anyone believe all—this. She couldn't wait to try, and she had to, right?

He pushed a hand up and forward, sending the flaming orb a few feet ahead of them where it whirled in the air like a mad dervish. Her eyes had twin spots, so she looked away.

"You couldn't conjure up a lantern?"

"Easier for me to manipulate a natural element like fire than create a piece of equipment. Your glasses and that hologram weren't a slam dunk, you know."

"None of this seems 'natural.'"

His smile was crooked. "You'll get used to it. Let's go." He started off, the ball of flame keeping its distance.

Soon they left the cornfield and climbed a steep embankment to a wide, hard-surface road that led the way into the setting sun far in the distance. Her breath caught. That golden orb, a giant replica of the one Ash commanded, was sinking behind turreted buildings casting them in shadows. She imagined grand castles with towers and ramparts in the dark outlines. The stuff of fairy tales.

"Elysium," she whispered.

"Bless the One Mother." Ash's wide, moist eyes, the slack jaw, reflected both awe and reverence.

An upwelling rush of emotions swept through her. She hadn't stopped to think how being here in this sacred land, seeing the ancient city for the first time, would affect Ash. She took his hand and squeezed. He cupped her cheek. His gaze was like a kiss, until he leaned down and placed his lips on hers for real. A gentle pressure, then firmer. *This is what magic tastes like.* Her glasses fogged.

He drew his lips away and wrapped strong arms around her, lay his chin on top of her capped head. She read a wealth of meaning in his sigh—longing, regret, worry—while she relaxed into his warmth.

He stiffened. "Holy shit, to use your words."

She pulled away. "What?"

He nodded toward the cornfield below them. Even in the waning light, she could make out their path, a narrow trail of green, through the vast, colorless cropland.

"Holy…"

"This is why we're not to come here."

"You somehow awaken the sleepers."

"If Lumeria is roused, the Malgren would know that mages are back. We don't want them overrunning our land."

"Can you use your powers to put the field back to sleep?"

"Only immortals can order the long sleep, but eventually, sleep will return when I leave. I don't know how long it takes."

"Uh, back up. Immortals?"

He winced. "I thought Elizabeth told you."

"Huh. So much you're keeping from me."

"Only because to reveal everything all at once would overwhelm you."

"Bullshit. Overwhelm me? I'm no delicate, freaking orchid blossom. I'd like to deck you right now." Her hands curled into fists.

His lip twitched. "I can see that. Go ahead if it makes you feel any better." He stuck out his chin.

"Jeez. Let's get to the city. This isn't the yellow brick road, but I see Oz." She grabbed his hand and tugged. "There better be some kind of food you can awaken there. I'm starving."

He smiled, his white teeth gleaming in the light from the floating flame. She held his hand, warm and strong, as they strode in silence along the middle of the road that was about four lanes wide, the flame guiding them. Fields on either side gave way to some kind of buildings or farmhouses hulking in the darkness to the right and left. Maybe the Elysium burbs. Side roads intersected and disappeared into the gloom.

The taller structures of the city loomed ever closer. Now, towering white cypress-type trees, slender and stately, lined the road like formal sentries at attention honoring their passage.

"Looks almost like winter, with a dusting of snow. All the foliage is white or silver. Kind of sad."

"It is, but they'd better stay that way. I'm far enough away that I shouldn't affect them."

"You, Ash Hunter, are one major witch dude."

"Huh. Wish I was more."

"Doesn't everybody? We do the best with what we have." She wriggled tired toes in the short boots that were a half size too big. "From what I've been told, you're classified as an Elite, right?"

"Yes."

"And Elizabeth Trowbridge?"

He hesitated. She hated when he did that. "She's one of the immortals with the highest of Elite powers. They are rare."

"Immortal. Define."

"Long-lived. Immortals can and will die eventually. Unless disease or injuries take them, they can live hundreds of years. They age normally after birth, but then stop aging after around eighty. Immortals can beget immortals along with normally aging children. The older immortals find permanent homes in the Havens around the world because there's a danger they'll be noticed."

"Crackers. When was Elizabeth born?"

"1665 I think."

Skye's brain seized. She was excellent at processing unusual stimuli and freaky input, but all this, a sleeping land in another dimension, voracious man-eating plants, magic, and immortals had her stupefied.

"Are you okay?" Ash jiggled her hand in his. "See? I've said too much."

She pulled her hand away and adjusted the glasses. "No. No, I'm fine. Like I said, no damn violet. Don't hold back information. I know you are."

He frowned and looked away from her, up at the multi-storied stone buildings they were now passing. Was he wondering if he could trust her? He couldn't and shouldn't.

"As Strike said, that mighty cruise ship has sailed." He stopped at an intersection that was probably a bustling business center hundreds of years ago. "You think I'm holding back. You can read minds now?"

"I know a ton about your society, even if you don't tell me another thing. I'm certainly a threat. That won't change once the wacko killer is caught."

"So, you'll write your story?" The flaming light on his face created a shapeshifting, sinister phantom.

He wouldn't hurt her no matter what she said. "Oh, I can write the story, but I'll need irrefutable proof that magic is real, or I can't publish it." The video, untouched, unaltered. That was her proof.

His rigid shoulders relaxed. "Then I have nothing to worry about."

"Right." She felt like a reluctant betrayer, all itchy and guilt-twinged. Because she knew all hell would break loose when the witch society was exposed to the world. She had to come to terms with the ultimate consequences.

"We'll head left here. It's not far to Elizabeth's old place." He waved two fingers at the old-fashioned lanterns on tall posts that lined both sides of the street. They flickered to life, whatever was inside them flaring brightly. He closed a hand with a snap and the flaming ball disappeared.

She walked beside him. "How do the lanterns light after all this time?"

"Keen oil. A naturally occurring super fuel that's pulled from the sand on the other side of the Beset Mountains. A teaspoon can light and heat a house for a week."

"Too bad we don't have such a thing." *Omigod. What if...*

"I heard your little gasp. It can't be transported through the portal. People have tried."

"Well, luckily it can't. Otherwise, magic be damned, this one commodity would be exploited to hell and gone."

"You see our dilemma. We must keep our magic a secret. The portals would come out next, then Tae-wen and all it holds."

Well, hell's bells. The world had the right to know. Or was she just thinking about herself, her fame and fortune as the revealer of a hidden society? She shivered in the light breeze. In the next instant, a soft knitted cloak settled across her shoulders. Ash stopped and tugged on the lapels, drawing her in front of him. He fastened the button at her throat.

She placed two hands on his chest, gazing up into his dark eyes. His heart beat strong and steady. He shifted his focus to her lips. She wet them with her tongue.

He groaned. "Full disclosure. I'm seriously turned on right now."

"I like when you're open and honest." She wound her arms around his neck and pulled his head down.

He parted her lips with his tongue, setting off a serious heat. The cloak was now too warm. Her stomach growled. They laughed and broke apart.

"We better keep moving." He bussed her nose and started off, extinguishing the streetlights behind them.

The stone buildings grew taller. Some had elaborately carved wooden doors and etched frescoes of people and animals above arched porticos. The turreted building she'd seen from outside the city was up ahead on the right. It was set way back from the street. *A damn castle*. A dry fountain nearly the size of the Pulitzer Fountain in Central Park sat in the middle of a lawn of pale gray grass and garden plots of sleeping foliage. A wide, stone tree-lined walkway led to broad steps and enormous double doors. Skye imagined the park-like grounds would have been spectacular back in the day.

Ash turned up the walk. "E.T.'s place."

"Place? More like a palace." The multi-storied home had rows of arched windows on the first floor and tall, peaked turrets at either end. "Did E.T. rule Lumeria?"

"As Aris, she was one of six immortal leaders. They scattered to different locations around Otherworld when they went through the portals." Ash opened one of the doors and ushered her inside. "Immortals can telepath with each other. The six set up the Havens and coordinated the new rules and guidelines for our world."

Telepathy. Why didn't that surprise her? The total darkness unnerved her for a second until wall sconces and a giant iron chandelier hanging high above illuminated the space. *Keen again? Probably.* Their steps on the terrazzo-like tile floor echoed in the grand foyer. Twin staircases curved up to a second floor. The walls of the foyer and the next rooms they entered were lined with built-in glass cabinets filled with knick-knacks or artifacts of some kind. She passed open double doors to what might have been a ballroom. Framed artwork—landscapes and portraits—hung on the walls.

"Elizabeth was, still is, an avid collector of crazy stuff. Anything that strikes her fancy."

"I can see that." She wanted to stop and examine some of them, but Ash forged on until they came to a kitchen twice the size of the bitch bunker.

Rows of pale green cupboards and overflowing open shelving hung above long counters. Two hulking iron wood-fed stoves side by side dominated one wall, patinaed copper pots and pans hung in hooks overhead.

"Sit. You must be exhausted." Ash opened a pantry door and disappeared inside.

Skye sat on a high-backed chair at a long wooden table scarred and stained. She expected the whole place to be coated in dust, cobwebs, or whatever creatures in this land would make cobwebs in an abandoned house. The table, counters, floor—everything was as if the cleaning crew had just left. She removed her glasses, new glasses fashioned with magic, and polished the spotted lenses with the edge of the cloak.

Ash reappeared carrying a couple of covered

dishes.

"Found bread and butter." He placed the smaller crock in front of her along with a broad-bladed knife.

She paused over the lid, then grasped the glass knob and lifted. A milky glob sat in the dish. "I don't think so."

"Wait. I'm doing the bread." He had both hands on a piece of linen covering the larger dish. In less than a minute, he removed the cloth to reveal a sliced loaf of crusty bread.

"Did you—"

"I awakened it. Takes less of my energy to manipulate real things than create from nothing, like I did the toast and coffee at the hotel. Hand me the butter."

She scooted the crock across the table. He placed the dish in both hands for a moment. The glob turned pale yellow within moments.

"You try it first," she said.

"Don't mind if I do."

Two small plates appeared on the table. He buttered a slice and took a bite.

His face screwed up. He coughed and sputtered, then swallowed hard. *Cripes. He poisoned himself.* She started to rise. He took another bite and grinned.

"You faker." She slumped in the chair. "I once thought you had no sense of humor. Guess I was wrong." Two tumblers of clear liquid appeared on the table. "Fresh water, I hope?"

"I hope so, too." He took a sip. Then another. "Ah. Drink up. We haven't had any hydration."

She sniffed at a piece of bread, and then nibbled around the crust before taking a small bite. "Okay. This

is pretty good. Yeasty and fresh like it was just baked."
She finished the slice dry, butter holding no appeal. She
ate another while he puttered around the kitchen.

He found a stoppered canvas-looking flask, filled it
with water, and tucked it under his belt. "If you've had
enough, we should keep moving."

"We're going to make our way to Moonstone?"

"Yes, but I need to check on something first. The
map I saw showed the library in a separate building
with the sacred garden in back."

"We're visiting a library and garden?"

"Briefly. I don't want to wake up the whole place."

She'd love to see everything in this castle as it once
was. Housekeepers scurrying around dusting, sweeping
the grand halls. The bustling kitchen staff preparing a
feast for special guests gathered in the ballroom. Or did
they use magic for everyday, mundane tasks? Who
were those guests? What sort of formal duds did they
wear? The name Majiste conjured all sorts of images of
sumptuous robes, lacey veils, and priceless jewels. She
rubbed the rough-spun cloth of the Faen tunic. Tae-wen
comprised races of people on some sort of hierarchy.
Couldn't get away from gaping class disparity even in
an alternate world.

She followed him through a back door off a
butler's pantry and onto a stone walkway. The lanterns
on lampposts lighted as they walked and winked out
after they'd passed. *Ash magic.* The pillared and domed
library building shared the sleeping castle grounds.
They entered a work room of sorts by a side door. Wall
sconces lit one by one around the room. Here at least,
the smell of paper, aging wood—that old library scent
she loved—delighted her nose.

"No locks on any doors?" she asked. Shelving loaded with books lined the walls. A large table in the middle of the room held stacks of shabby books in need of repair.

"No need. Everyone had magic, and a strong moral code."

"Right."

They continued into the main library with two walls of enormous, arched windows that in daytime would fill the space with glorious light. Large sconces between each window flamed to life. Dozens of rows of shelves to the right met the main hallway.

She walked over to a shelf. What kinds of books did the Majiste read and write? "Hey, there's a lot of empty space on some of these shelves."

"We don't have time to stop and read. Elizabeth—Aris—took as many as she could with her to our world when she fled Lumeria with the Majiste."

"Crazy. Where are the books now, in the Haven?"

"Most are at Trowbridge House in Connecticut, her old home before she moved to the Haven."

They reached the far side, and he held another door open for her. She looked back at the stacks before he extinguished the lights. How arrogant she'd been, thinking she had the world all figured out. She felt like she'd entered the "Upside Down" where soul-shattering surprises lurked around every bend. She could hardly wait.

Chapter Sixteen

Ash followed Skye through the library door onto the wide stone steps leading to the garden, lighting all the lanterns on posts throughout the grounds with a thought. Skye pulled the cloak tighter on the chill breeze.

There it was, the One Mother tree, in the middle of the grounds. He stilled, opening his senses to its energy. Yes, a faint vibration shivered along his nerves. The sacred tree only snoozed.

Skye took a few steps down and turned. "Why did you come here? Look at this place. It's sad."

The once-lush garden looked as if someone had poured bleach over it.

"I wanted—needed—to do this for Elizabeth."

And me.

"Okay, but I hope she wasn't playing you."

"She's not. I trust her." But for a moment back in the meeting, he hadn't.

He followed Skye along the pathway that wove among the plantings. Some flowers looked as if they'd withered and died. Some, like the roses, could be perfect blossoms in full bloom except for their sickly gray color. He returned his focus to the tree. It dominated the garden, its huge heart-shaped leaves creating a canopy that would shade a large crowd in the hot sun.

He picked up his pace on the path. "Can't stay long here. I've already affected the plants." He'd noticed his powers, his vibrations, seemed enhanced since he'd entered Lumeria lands, like someone was slowly turning up the amperage.

"Crap. You have. Look at those roses. They're turning pink." She wandered over to a large bush with giant blossoms. "Can you wake this up? I want to see what these flowers look like."

"Romy blossoms. They look dead, not asleep. Might be too far gone." He approached the tree. "I need a minute. Find a place to sit."

She nodded and found a huge, flat rock by the garden wall to park.

Ash flexed his fingers and took a deep breath, letting it out slowly before placing both palms on the rough bark. He closed his eyes. The tree's low energy bee-buzzed along nerves, grew stronger, sizzled through the bloodstream. Images dissolved one upon the other in his brain like a mystic slide show. Gray in his vest, mom in ritual robes, Soot asleep in his lap, then Skye in his arms. Anger, peace, happiness, love chased each other through the images.

Red snowsuit. Despair.

He wanted desperately to open his eyes, to take his hands from the tree. Make the image of the child in the street disappear.

"Keeper Hunter. I am the One Mother."

Holy—is this happening, or just my imagination?

"I'm glad you sought me out."

"I—I didn't believe I could."

"I know. You are full of doubts. The last to speak with me here was Aris. She was like you. Honorable,

brave, powerful, and yet uncertain, not trusting herself or her future."

"Elizabeth had a lot to fear back then, and now in Otherworld. My job, Keeper of magic, is difficult. I'm not sure I…" He should shut up.

"I feel your soul-deep pain. Trust yourself, Keeper. Trust that you will seek the right path for YOU. Trust your heart."

One Mother was all-knowing. She knew about the child in the snowsuit, his gut-wrenching battle between insuring their secrecy and reverence for life, his rift with Gray-don't-call-me-dad. His desire to quit the Keeper life.

"Trusting myself is as hard as trusting others." Maybe harder.

"And yet here you are with a companion who jeopardizes her life, yours, and our entire society. That is trust both ways on a high level."

"I'm hopeful."

"You are hopeful because this companion has a piece of your heart, and you have hers."

He couldn't tell her it was likely just a physical attraction. What else could it be? "I just need to keep her safe. Too many enemies."

"I understand more than you know. Safe travels."

His body warmed. Tension drained from taut muscles. The headache drifted away. He recognized a mesmer and didn't fight the serenity that swept away uncertainty and hurt like a breeze clears away the smog.

Within moments, the tug of powerful energy diminished. He removed his hands from the fissured bark, took in a deep breath and let it out. His heart returned to a normal rhythm from its staccato beat. He appreciated Skye's silence, letting him have recovery time from this experience of which she had no idea the profundity, the karate kick to his psyche. He opened his eyes, blinked to adjust to the lantern light. The leafy canopy was greening.

He turned and ran gritty hands down his shirt.

She still sat, bouncing a leg, and nudging her glasses higher. "So, Hunter. I'm going to pretend that talking to trees that apparently answer is a common witch thing, but what are you torn about?"

"Was I talking out loud?"

"Yep."

He walked over to her. She let the boot on the end of the bouncing leg fall to the ground and leaned over to massage a stockinged foot.

He crouched and took her foot in his hands. "Let me."

"Jeez. Really? This foot?"

She smiled, then her eyes closed for a moment. "Ah. Heaven. Did you know that a great foot massage is as satisfying as an orgasm?"

"It is?" He kneaded the arch with both thumbs. "Feel free to let go."

She moaned low in her throat. Skye in ecstasy fired his imagination and his blood.

"Wait." She shifted. "The rock. It's moving."

He dropped her foot and stood. She jumped up. The rock quivered and slid a couple of inches.

"What's happening?"

He moved her back. The rock slid a few more inches. The air shivered with a buzzing sound that grew louder. A small, green lizard-like creature crawled out of the opening and onto the rock, flexing long, phosphorescent wings. Two sharp horns curved up from the top of its head and one from its nose. Many more of the creatures poked spiked noses out of the crevice.

"Is that a dragonfly or a reptile?" Skye's eyes widened. "Wait. I saw a statue in Elizabeth's garden."

"Dragonite. Shit. E.T. will kick my dead body." Words took shape in his mind. The scaly creature, body the color and texture of asparagus tips, was trying to communicate. "Shh. I need to focus on what it's saying." He crouched beside the rock inches from the dragon-like head and blood-red eyes.

"...must be mage. I'm Tarig, leader of my kind."

"Ash Hunter, mage Keeper. Sorry I awakened you."

"I will not be put in the long sleep again." The dragonite snorted a puff of sooty smoke.

Ash coughed. "I couldn't even if I wanted to." Oh, yeah. He wanted to. "I'm not an immortal."

Skye crouched close to him. "What's it saying?" She held out a palm.

"Be careful. They can spit fire."

"Cool." Her hand was steady, face full of wonder like a kid watching a magician pull a rabbit out of a hat.

"Who is this? Not mage or Faen. Not Malgren."

"Right. Skye Parker. She's a friend."

Tarig climbed onto her palm on four sturdy legs and seemed to assess her with his fierce glare. *"You are very brave."*

Ash told her Tarig's thought message.

"I am. There's not much that can scare me, except maybe a hell creeper."

"You are wise, too."

Ash stayed silent. It wouldn't do to give her a

swelled head.

"Tell her, Ash Hunter. A female always needs praise and encouragement."

Right. "You're wise," Tarig says. He left out the creature's misogynistic viewpoint.

"Thank you, Tarig." Skye stood, lifting the dragonite with her. "You're heavy. Can you really fly?"

Tarig fluttered his wings and buzzed into the air, hovering a foot from her face like a squat, ugly Tinkerbell.

She laughed. "I guess you can."

"They are mage creatures. I think there's a bit of magic involved," said Ash.

"Fairy dust, maybe?" Her open-mouthed smile showed pure delight.

Tarig flitted among the dormant plants, then returned to sit on the rock, his wings hanging low. *"My garden. What happened?"*

"Elizabeth—Aris—put the garden, the whole of Lumeria, into dormancy. I've stirred a few things awake temporarily in my passing," said Ash.

"I'll have to move my swarm out of this land. We need to feed."

Ash groaned. "Be careful. Malgren still hunt mage."

More dragonites filed out of the crevice and took off, filling the air with a raucous buzzing. Tarig called for the rest. Ash moved Skye back under the One Mother tree as hundreds streamed out from under the rock.

Skye covered her ears while a grin split her face. Wind from thousands of wings ruffled her hair. "I can't believe I'm seeing this," she shouted.

"Neither can I. How am I going to tell Elizabeth that I woke up her pet, and put the entire species in danger?"

The swarm blotted out the stars as they moved up and out of the garden, the drone gradually fading as they flew out of sight.

"Let's get out of here. It must be midnight." He extinguished the garden lanterns.

"Where to?" She slipped on the boot and followed him out a side gate onto a stone walk.

"We passed an inn. We can stay the night there." He lit the streetlamps as they passed in front of the library and E.T.'s place. The cool night air brushed his skin, bringing the faintest odor of stone and earth, not flowers, not late-night cooking odors, not smoke from a chimney. The dead smell of a graveyard.

The small inn sat in the middle of a city block, a row of businesses they'd walked past earlier. The sign hanging over the sidewalk read "The Cozy."

"I hope so," Skye said. "I'm ready for some comfort."

He ushered her through the door and lit the keen lamps lining the walls of a small, neat lobby. He half expected that a clerk would appear at the desk if he rang the bell. All the rooms were on the second floor.

"I'd prefer street level," he said. "Easier escape."

"Escape from what?" She smiled in the dim light. "Maybe there's a secret door. I'm an expert at those."

He grunted and took the lead up the stairs. The first room they passed was a bathroom of sorts. Ash lit the wall lamps, and with a push of magic, added water to a washing basin.

"I'll come back to this," Skye said, after sticking

her head into the small room.

Ash tried a few doors until he found a double. He lit the wall sconces and table lamps. The plaster walls were painted white except for one wall that was papered in a dusty rose floral. An area rug, worn but clean, covered the wide plank floor.

Skye sat on the edge of the bed nearest the window and stroked the damask bedspread. "Amazing. No dirt, no dust. It's as if the housekeeper just left. I mean, it's no Mayfield, but it'll do." She removed the cap and gathered her mess of red hair back into a ponytail. She somehow managed to secure the tail with a twist.

"Sorry, there's no en suite. I guess we share that bathroom down the hall with the ghosts."

"I'll be back in a sec."

Skye left, and Ash walked to the window, parting the heavy white drapes to peer at the street below. Empty, dark, the way he liked it. He returned to the bed nearest the door and kicked off his boots, removed the flask from the belt. He focused a hit of magic on the Faen clothing. The loose shirt became a belted tunic of heavy, gray cotton. He changed the rough-spun pants into the same soft fabric. He could wear these to bed and during the day tomorrow. He wiggled his toes. What was it about fresh socks that trumped every other change of clothing for comfort? Not quite orgasmic, but they'd do until the real thing. The best he could hope for right now would be one of those foot massages.

Skye needed pjs. He amped his magic core. Lacy lingerie? Yeah, tempting, but no. He used some extra bedding stored on a shelf to create warm flannel in a fun print and folded them neatly on her bed.

She came through the door carrying the shawl and

a towel. "The privy was barely adequate," she said in an English accent. "But the soaps—wait—you changed clothes."

"Literally."

"You look like a kung-fu master."

He laughed and pointed to her bed three feet away.

She hurried over and lifted the long-sleeved top. "Pajamas. Pink llama pajamas." She rubbed them on her cheek. "Omigod. And socks. Thank you."

The smile lit up her face and his insides.

"Turn around. I gotta get out of these funky rags."

He did, making a show of turning back the covers on his bed and punching the down pillow while listening to the rustle of clothes, imagining a naked Skye.

"Okay. How do I look?"

He turned. She stood, eyes wide and arms outstretched. Her breasts strained the buttons. The bottoms puddled at her ankles.

"I'm a lousy tailor."

"You are, but I love them." She hugged herself. "So snuggly."

He wanted to find out in the worst way. Instead, he said goodnight and lay on his back on the bed, pulled a thin sheet over his body, closed his eyes.

Her bed creaked. She sighed. Rustling of covers. Another sigh. He lowered the lights with a push of magic. Had it really been only twenty-four hours since they'd last spent the night together in the Chinatown hotel, when she'd found out that everything he'd been telling her since they met was a lie. She still didn't know the whole story.

****

Something weighed him down. Something warm. Soot? He opened his eyes straight into a pair of sleepy green ones. He was on his side. The weight was Skye's arm around his waist. Daylight leaked through the curtains.

"Hmm. You're certainly better to wake up with than the cat. You smell better, too."

"Well, thank you. You set a low bar."

He traced a finger down her nose. "Your freckles sprouted."

"The sun hates me."

"Why…"

"Am I here? In your bed? You were dreaming and thrashing."

"I was?"

"And talking. Something about a snowsuit."

Well, shit.

She rubbed his shoulder. "Tell me about it. I'm a great listener. Lousy as a life coach though."

He rolled onto his back. She scooted closer, running her hands under his top and over his chest, tugging on chest hair.

"Hmm. Just continue what you're doing. Won't relax me, but I like it."

She circled a nail tip around a nipple, making his body tighten. "Have you ever talked to anybody about it? The dream, or nightmare?"

"A nightmare that's real. No one except my don't-call-me-dad, Gray. Wasn't so much a conversation as a confrontation."

Her arousing hand stilled. "How so?"

Don't tell her. She'd condemn Gray, maybe his whole society. Hadn't he done the same? "We had a difference of opinion, putting it mildly."

"Over?"

Her hand on his cheek, the gentle touch, released something inside him. The words hurled out like they'd sat for years fermenting in his gut. "I was ten, walking with my dad one January day. Icy 86th Street. Busy rush hour. A little kid in a red snowsuit—he might have been three…" His chest squeezed, driving the barbed wire deeper. "A taxi was sliding in slow motion. Sliding. I tugged on my dad's coat. Use magic. Use magic." The seconds had stretched out in his mind since that day, each one sharp and painful and cruel.

"You didn't have your powers yet."

"No. He could have saved that boy with his magic." His throat constricted. "He said there were too many witnesses. No Keeper nearby to wipe memories."

"This is where reverence for life challenges the secrecy of your society." She said it without outrage, without rebuke.

He nodded. "My dad and I—always knocking heads. He said we can't interfere in Reg lives by using our magic in public, even if a life is at stake."

"Tough one. You probably saved that bicyclist's life when I first met you." She removed her other hand from under his shirt.

"I've been blessed—or cursed—with special powers."

"Like wiping memories and electronics. Perfect for a Keeper." She traced a finger along the *Z* shaved in his hair. "I have the feeling you interfere a lot when a life is at stake."

He turned on his side and cupped her face. "I do, as you can see. I leave a lot out of the reports I file."

She smiled. "I sense you'd rather not be a Keeper at all. You want to be free of all this and go run with the animals in Africa."

Would that be following his heart, as the One Mother said? Ditch the role he'd been born to play and become just another mage in a Reg world? "You're a keen observer, Parker. Perfect for an investigative journalist." He gave her a quick kiss. "Enough talk for now." His soul wouldn't stand much more, anyway. "We need to get going to Moonstone."

She swung her legs over the side of the bed and groaned. "I hurt in places I didn't know I had."

"A hell creeper will do that to you." He wanted to pull her back and kiss away the pain. The idea was both exciting and dangerous. They had no future together. Especially since his future probably involved an austere cell in the Haven.

Chapter Seventeen

Skye felt like a new person in fresh pants and a long shirt in the Faen fashion, courtesy of Ash magic. He was getting better at tailoring. The pants didn't drag like the pjs. She adjusted the wire frame of the glasses and followed him out onto the empty street in front of the inn, a vaguely unsatisfied feeling tugging at her insides. It was either the last piece of bread she'd choked down hours ago, or the lack of follow-through in bed. *Hmm. Definitely the latter.*

She ached for him after hearing his life-defining story of the child his dad wouldn't save. And here she'd been saved by someone who didn't hesitate to drag her up from the river with magic. Her life-defining moment.

He pointed down the street. "We'll head out this way. If I remember the map, this road eventually leads to a rough track through some fields to the Lumeria border that's closest to Moonstone."

The early morning sun warmed her skin as they walked side-by-side past storefronts. A barbershop, sweet shop, apothecary. She lagged a few steps, peering through the windows. A bookstore. Okay. She'd duck in here for one sec if the door wasn't locked. Just a quick peek.

The door opened easily. No locks because, you know, magic. The low sun found its way inside, partially lighting the small room. The smell of books, old wooden shelves, and plank flooring brought back the libraries of her youth. Low beamed ceiling, plump, comfortable chairs invited patrons to curl up a while and read. She selected a leather-bound book with weird symbols on the cover—runes of some sort.

The door opened, and Ash stepped in. "Hey, don't disappear like that."

"I was only going to stick my head in, but books." She held up the one she'd picked.

"Hey, I'd love to sit and read with you, but we have to keep moving."

Out the window, a tall figure hurried by on the sidewalk. "Ash, duck," she whispered. She crouched and pulled him down, cold pricks of fear chilling like an ice bath.

"Who?"

"He was so quick. I think maybe a Malgren."

"Here? In Elysium?" He cursed. "Stay put. Do not move."

The last time he'd told her that and disappeared, she'd almost been eaten by an ugly cabbage head. A shudder rattled her teeth.

A couple of minutes felt like an hour. She forced her legs to unfold and scooted along a wall to the multi-paned window. She looked down the street and saw nothing, heard nothing.

A gritty hand covered her mouth. A large body pressed against her back. Her stomach fell. Pulse spiked. Something sharp poked her spine. A knife?

A guttural voice near an ear whispered, "Keep still, mage. I could gut you before you use your power."

Malgren. With foul breath like liver gone rancid.

He thinks I'm a witch. Wish I was. He knew she wasn't Faen. The ear-hiding cap was still in her belt.

"We move outside." He shoved her to the door.

Her legs shook but they got her to the sidewalk. He stood behind her and removed his hand from her mouth. Ash and a Malgren wearing leather came out a door further along the street. The Malgren smiled at Ash. then clapped him on the shoulder. *What?*

The knife quickly moved to her throat. Fingers brushed her nape. "Mage, Gryph Kazlo, don't move."

Both men started.

"Let her go!" Ash held out both hands.

The Malgren named Gryph reached for a knife in a sheath. "Bings, don't—"

"Stop, you filthy betrayer. I'll null her magic or slit her throat. I'll let her go when I knows you not be followin' me."

Gryph kept his hand on the hilt. "Don't be doing anything stupid, Bings. You'll call down the mighty wrath of the Majiste."

Bings. It would be cute if she didn't feel the pinprick of a blade against her jugular.

Bings spat. "The Majiste? Extinct as the dragonite."

"I am Majiste," said Ash, his face a dark scowl. She felt the tension in his muscles from twenty feet away. "And this woman can turn you to powder with a thought."

"You both are Otherworld scum." He pressed cold fingers into the back of her neck and pinched the flesh. "I have nulled her magic. In seconds she will be drained."

"No! Not my magic. You've ended me." She

slumped. The knife left her neck. In one swift move, she grabbed the arm with the weapon, twisting and laying a hip into the man's midsection. He flipped up and over her back. *Thud*. His body slammed into the ground, head hitting the stone walk with a crack. Her glasses went flying. Every welt from the creeper burned. Ribs screamed.

Skye wrenched the long, curved knife from the Malgren's grip as his eyes blinked, then closed. She sucked in a breath, then another, lungs spasming.

Ash took the knife. "Relax. You didn't kill him."

"Wanted to. You better tie him or whatever."

"Already did. Bonds of magic." He set the glasses on her nose. "This is my friend Gryph. He's with a Malgren group of mage sympathizers called the Defenders, and an important member of my Shadow Force."

The large Malgren approached and held out a hand. "Ash called your ass bad, but he did not say you could take down an ox with your bare hands."

"Ass bad? Oh, you mean badass." She smiled. The small lumps across Gryph's forehead gave him an alien-race-from-outer-space look. One bump had been sliced off. Handsome dude, though. She shook his hand. "Nobody puts Baby in a corner."

Ash and Gryph gave each other a blank stare. She shook her head. "Classic movie of all time. Phtt. Never mind."

Bings groaned and opened his eyes. She hadn't really seen him while he held her. Half on his side, he struggled to release hands tied with invisible bonds behind his back. His forehead sprouts were different sizes, but it was the crooked honker of a nose that dominated the pocked face. A spot of blood above his right temple soaked into wild, stringy hair. Ugly as Gryph was hunky.

Gryph hauled him to his feet. "Don't try anything. I can bring you back to the Defenders' Tribunal breathin' or not."

"I thought the Malgren never entered Lumeria," Skye said.

"They don't. Just this dolt and myself. He parted ways with his lugs at the border. They would not cross. His gang of Dark Raiders stormed my town and stole weapons."

"You said you have a horse stashed somewhere?" Ash pulled on his cap, so she did, too, after a struggle with the ponytail.

"Patch is back this way along with Bings' bruiser." Gryph shoved the beefy Bings ahead of him. "Just outside of town there be a shortcut to the border. Follow me."

Skye walked beside Ash trying to ignore the awakened pain in her side. "I noticed that horses here are like horses back home."

"Almost exactly. Maybe here they tend to have longer manes and tails if they aren't trimmed." He leaned close and whispered in her ear. "Are you okay?"

"A little shaken. But damn, I'm sorry he took away my magic."

He smiled. "No, he didn't." His fingers touched hers.

Warm sparks tingled along her arm and traveled to her heart.

Really? Warm sparks? Yeah.

The commercial buildings gave way to quaint

houses set back from the street. The stone walkway led to a hard-packed earthen road. Gryph led them behind one of the cottages.

The familiar, pungent odor of horse twitched her nose, and was welcomed. A last, something that smelled. A beefy chestnut and a pretty pinto stood with heads hanging, probably wondering what happened to the grass. Normally they'd be munching away. As everywhere else she'd seen in Lumeria, the grass, the trees, bushes, gardens—all were varying shades of white and gray, not unlike New York City.

"Can you ride?" asked Ash.

"Sure can. Spent a summer on a Montana ranch. Rode with real cowboys every day."

"For a story?"

"Yep."

She rode behind Ash on Bings' chunky chestnut while Gryph rode his pinto named Patch, for one eye ringed in black. Their long manes and tails were lush. Both tails reached the ground. Bings was forced to march ahead of them, still with hands tied behind his back. He kept up a steady stream of invectives until Ash told him he'd turn his pecker into an earthworm.

The saddle was some kind of roomy version of the standard Western kind, so she was able to snuggle up close and wrap her arms around him. His warm, solid body somehow soothed her aches, calmed jangled nerves after Bings' sudden attack. She smiled. Yeah, she was one badass.

Ash turned his head. "Listen," he whispered. "I told Gryph I'm going to wipe Bings' memory of Lumeria as soon as we cross the border into Faenstar. We made up a story. You and I are Faen. Keep quiet.

Go along with it. No one can know we've been here."

"Got it." Would her memories be next? He'd told her he would never take a scalpel to her hippocampus. Could Elizabeth? Maybe they'd be forced to by the damn council of whatever. She pulled her cap down low.

It wasn't long before they reached the border. It was like someone had thrown up an invisible fence. The Lumeria side was bleached white, the other, Faenstar, was verdant green, and smelled like the forests of home. They rode until Lumeria was out of sight. Ash pulled the chestnut beside the pinto, nodding to Gryph. Bings belched and grumbled as he stumble-walked ahead of them. Ash's hard muscles tensed under her hands. He must be focusing on the memory wipe. His breathing changed from slow and deep to rapid and shallow.

Bings went silent, staggered, then got his feet under him. He shook his head. Ash let out a deep breath and put a hand to his temple. He'd be in for a whopping headache.

Before long, they reached Abbott's Trail. She startled when three riders, Malgren, burst from the trees. Bings cowered on his knees. The leather-clad Malgren were all smiles, whooped and hollered, so her nerves settled quickly.

One of the men with a bow and quiver full of arrows on his back rode up next to Gryph as they eyed her and Ash. "The rest of Bings' scabby crew are on their way to Lyall Hill with Sid and the others. I knew you'd get this dake whelp."

"Got him afore he reached Lumeria." Gryph jerked a thumb in Bings' direction. "He's had quite a knock on the noggin. He's crazier than he ever was."

Bings mumbled that he couldn't remember a thing.

All eyes turned to her and Ash.

"Who might these be on Bings' horse?" asked another man astride a fancy gray.

"I'm Ash. This be Skye. Faen from down Hollyrose."

"Long way from home."

"Got lost in the Sudden Woods."

"I gave them Bings' brawny horse. I'm going to see them to Moonstone. Take this swine. He won't mind walkin'."

The men laughed. One used his horse to nudge Bings upright. They headed in one direction while Gryph lead them in another along Abbott's Trail.

Ash half turned to her. "You all right to move faster?"

"Sure."

"Let me know if you're uncomfortable."

She squeezed a smile out of him. "I will."

He nudged the horse into a slow canter along the hard packed earthen road beside Gryph's Patch. The big chestnut loped in an easy, rocking horse gait, shifting her body in a sensuous rhythm with Ash's.

Okay, I'm uncomfortable. In a delicious, naughty way.

They ate up the miles this way, no one speaking. They slowed to a walk when Abbott's Trail ended at another, wider road. They turned right.

"This be Twilda Road. Remember when you were here last time, Ash? We pass by Quinn's place."

"Quinn? The guy who hates the Malgren?" Skye cast a concerned glance at Gryph.

Gryph smiled. "Oh, I run with witches, so he just tolerates me."

"As we all do," said Ash, rubbing the back of his neck. He took a swig of water from the flask and handed it back to her.

"What Quinn does not know is, I have mage in my blood." Gryph lifted his head. "Ancestors past. How did you describe it, Ash?"

"Romeo and Juliet. Forbidden love. Shakespearean tragedy."

"There's a story right there," Skye said. She drank and handed the flask back to Ash.

"Don't even think about it, Nosy Parker. She's a writer, Gryph. Parker's Big Adventure will never see print, right?"

She gave him a squeeze while her mind was filled with images of amazing book covers, exciting scenes, passionate love, heartbreaking tragedy, and a Pulitzer.

"I should not have told you, then. You must not tell anyone I have mage blood." Gryph pinned her with his eyes. "My life depends on secrecy."

She nodded. The combined secrets among them would fill a football stadium.

Gryph pointed to a field where some kind of leafy green vegetable grew in neat rows. "On the left we come up on Quinn's land. The house is set back there among the trees."

A few hundred yards away, a round wooden building with a bunch of attached domed structures, additions maybe, sprung out of the ground like a plague of giant warts. She would have loved to see the place up close. A rickety fence—no, racks of some sort—partially encircled the homestead. The racks held hundreds of small lumps.

She squinted. "What are hanging on those racks?"

"You don't want to know, missy," said Gryph, kicking his horse into a canter.

Ash whispered. "What Malgren hate, but you love. Rats."

Omigod. The story just keeps getting better and better.

Chapter Eighteen

More yurt-style homes appeared as they approached the outskirts of Moonstone. "Why are all the buildings round?" asked Skye.

"The Faen favor the circular shape," said Gryph. "Part of their faith that a circle holds power and life everlasting."

"We can go straight through the village? We don't have to sneak in to"—Ash groaned low in his throat—"Flip House?"

Skye ran gentle fingers along his ribcage. He must be in so much pain from the memory wipe.

"The only Malgren in Moonstone right now be my Defenders but keep your caps and your story tight 'til we see what guests are at Eldrin's inn."

"That Malgren pair we met with yesterday knew I was mage. They headed for Glendon. Hope they didn't double-back."

"Ah, Glendon," said Gryph. "Stronghold of the Dark Raiders. They were goin' there to report you."

Well-balanced cairns of round, smooth boulders ten feet high sat one on each side of the road where the town began. Horses nickered from a stable and their own mounts answered. A hand-painted sign on the barn announced "Moonstone Rentals. Deals by the Month."

The wide road became cobblestoned and the clop, clop of the horses' hooves rang out. The town was quaint as any Hobbit hamlet. The round wooden and stone structures—shops and homes—reminded her of a fairytale village in a story her mom would read to her. A woman in a high-waisted dress and apron waved to them as she swept the area in front of a shop called Mapin's Bakery. Skye made out dual-pointed ears peeking through gray hair pulled back in a loose bun. Somehow, she thought the Faen would be wee folk, but not so. The sweet, rich aroma of baking cinnamon bread wafted on the light breeze. Her mouth watered.

They wound through the town, Gryph calling out greetings to the Faen out and about. A buckboard wagon pulled by a team of black horses trundled by them. A man drove and the woman beside him held a small child on her lap. All wore similar clothing to her own.

A couple of men lounged on chairs outside of The Lazy Dake Pub and Rooms. Tinkly music played through the open doors.

"I could use a beer," she whispered in Ash's ear.

"Me too. And drugs."

"Migraine? You don't have any meds."

"I'll live. What's really bothering me, and in a good way, are your hands on my body."

She laughed. "Yeah, you'll live."

A huge two-story, rounded dome structure loomed ahead. Clinging to one side was a partially constructed addition. A skeleton of curved beams and ribbed roof rose from a foundation of round stones that looked like they'd been in a fire.

They pulled the horses up to a hitching rail in front. The horses immediately dipped their mouths into a trough of water, drawing deeply. A large sign over the double doors declared this to be Flip House, "Best Inn in the Land!" Five gold stars underlined the words. Gold stars must be the universal symbol of greatness. Yes, this place was no Hobbit house.

Ash dismounted and helped her down. She slowly slid the length of his lean, hard body, and although his eyes held hints of pain, they sparked with heat.

"Ready?" Gryph tied both horses to the rail and pulled a canvas sack from the saddle.

Skye reluctantly moved out of Ash's arms. "You've been here before, right, Ash?" Skye tugged on her tunic, straightened the cap over hair gone wild.

"A few times. The Flips know me. Know I'm a witch. They can be trusted."

Gryph held open one of the doors. She followed Ash into a huge, wood-beamed great hall with a high curved ceiling. A staircase led to an upper floor that ran in a half circle above her behind an intricately carved railing. Thickly upholstered chairs sat in front of a massive stone fireplace that dominated one curved wall. A friendly flame sparked and spit. Traces of piney smoke, cedar, and baking bread smelled like comfort and welcome.

They walked to a high wooden counter with a bell across the room from the fireplace. Through an open door, a man the size of a mountain strode toward them. An untamed mane of dark hair tumbled past burly shoulders. His long, thick beard shot with gray would make a great nest for a couple of sparrows.

"Travelers. By the spirits." His voice boomed and echoed in the room. His arms opened wide as he hurried around the desk to engulf Ash, then Gryph in a back-thumping man hug. "You be back once again.

Can't get enough of my hospitality, eh?" He stood away from the men and eyed Skye. "Ah, a sweet lass. Who this be?"

Ash took her hand. "This is—"

She gave Ash a side-eye, pulled her hand free and stuck it out. "I'm Skye Parker. Nice to meet you." Her hand was swallowed in his large, rough one.

"Skye. A name from the Gods. I'm Eldrin Flip. This be my—er—me and my wife Freya's inn."

Did eyes twinkle? His brilliant blue eyes held a dancing light, and a knowing smile teased his lips. He'd sized up her uncertain relationship with Ash at a glance.

Gryph leaned in close to Eldrin's ear. "Where can we speak in private?"

"Through here, my friends." He led them through another door into a large storeroom with shelving piled high with flour sacks, crates, and various containers. The smell of hoppy ale lay heavy on the air, with undertones of garlic, onion, spices.

This room had right-angled walls. Muted light filtered through a small window with opaque glass. Tall barrels with some kind of symbols burned into the lids lined one side. Eldrin led them to a barrel that held a small keg with a tap.

"Afore you tell me what 'tis I should not be hearin', let's imbibe." He took four glasses down from a shelf.

Gryph clapped his hands. "Now you be talking."

"I could use a drink." Skye glanced at Ash, who winked at her. *Hmm.* She'd prepare for a gut burn.

Eldrin handed each of them a glass full to the brim with an amber liquid. Skye sniffed. Her eyes watered.

Eldrin held a glass high. "To my friends, old and

new. Maybeshteekemalva, maybeshteekusita."

"May you find peace, may you not puke." Gryph tossed the drink down. "Gah!"

Skye laughed. "That isn't what it means, right?"

Ash shrugged, tossing his back, too. He grimaced, then burped. "That should kill my headache. What are you waiting for, Parker, winner of the Nepalese challenge?"

"Watch this." She put the glass to her lips, tilted it, letting the fiery liquid slide down her throat. *The burn of a thousand suns.* No way would she let them see her discomfort. Maybe the brew would kill her aches and pains, too, or make her forget them.

"Impressive, lass," said Eldrin. "Now, my friends, I am half ready to listen."

Ash held his glass out for more. Eldrin obliged. "We need a favor, El, the biggest. It may put you at risk, so, say no way in hell, and we'll find another way."

"I be always in peril. 'Tis the times."

"Skye is not mage. She's a Reg from Otherworld, and in danger."

Eldrin's bushy eyebrows rose. "A Reg you say. First I have ever seen in person. The first in Tae-wen, I'd wager."

All eyes were on her. She swallowed, aware that her overheated face was probably blotchy from the drink.

Ash explained why they were in Tae-wen and had come to Flip House. "I'm thinking Skye and I pretend we are Faen, guests staying here at the inn. I'm hoping this might be only for a day or two."

Skye wanted to ask how he figured that timeframe,

but she'd talk to him later.

Eldrin nodded. "We have Sandie guests. Although they be not enemies of mage, best keep those funny ears of yours covered, mind. I shall let Freya know to make up three of our finest rooms."

"Gryph is leaving tonight to wait by his portal for word from the Haven. We only need one room. For me and Skye. I need—want—her to stay close."

Ash held her gaze for a fraction before lowering it. She was up for another night with Ash, as unwise as that was on a lot of levels. They had unfinished business.

"'Tis done."

That twinkle was back in the Faen's eyes, putting ideas in Skye's head of a suitable backstory for her and Ash. Oh, she'd have fun with this.

"Come meet Freya, Miss Skye. She'll have my arse if she finds us in here swilling. I want you to meet my babe, all of four months old now, and with a cry to bleed your ears."

They filed out of the storage room into the great hall to be greeted by a tall, striking woman with pale hair intricately braided and pulled into a long side tail, leaving one dual-pointed ear exposed. The back of a pink, fuzzy baby head poked out from the top of a lumpy cloth pouch strapped to her chest. Skye wanted to feel the fuzz in the worst way.

Freya gave Eldrin a stern look and spoke low. "You be filling our guests with your lusty brew, husband?"

"Ah, but see our guests, Freya? Ash has returned with the hero Gryph and has brought a lass. Skye be her name."

Freya's scowl morphed into a huge grin. "Welcome back, my friends. I'd hug you all, but it might wake Alain. I've just got him asleep." She took Skye's hand. "Aren't you a colorful one, and a beauty. I've not seen such red hair."

'Don't mind her now, Miss Skye. She speaks first."

Freya let go of her hand. "I'll leave the intrigue and nonsense to you men. You need rooms, eh? How long will you be staying?"

"Only one for a couple of days. For now." Skye glanced at Ash, who gave her a crooked smile. "And when you have time, you have to show me how to braid my hair like yours."

"I surely will." She turned to Eldrin. "Fetch the keys and show them upstairs to the end room. The Sandies are top of the stairs. I'll put Alain down for his afternoon."

Freya was a woman after her own heart. Proud, take charge, forthright, all the while with a newborn strapped on. Skye was looking forward to her stay here at Flip House, and learning all she could about this land, its people. She only hoped the stay was temporary.

****

The lowering sun filtered through the gauzy curtains in their room. When the dinner bell rang out, Skye's stomach growled. Freya had brought them clothing and toiletries after Eldrin had shown them to their quaint, curved-wall room with the log cabin-y feel. She'd told Freya that she was a Reg from Otherworld. The Faen had marveled at the thought of having a Reg guest. Skye wanted her to stay and talk, but Freya had dinner to prepare. There were other guests at the inn

247

besides them. Who were they? *What* were they?

Both she and Ash had taken turns in the privy room bath. Afterward, Ash threw on one of the shirts, then went in search of Eldrin.

Skye spent more time with her hair than she had in months. A braid here, a twist there. Nothing like Freya's artistic do, but better than she expected. She tamed the fuzzy tendrils that framed her face with some kind of paste or pomade she found on the dresser. She was careful that her ears were covered, feeling lucky for the first time that she had a Wookie's worth of thick hair. She decided to leave the glasses behind and hoped she wouldn't break her neck going down the stairs.

She pulled up on the revealing bodice of the long dress a size too small, trying to hide a creeper bruise. The girls strained the pretty blue fabric. *Yeah, boob-i-lishus*. She had a lot more meat on her bones than the slender Freya. Most of her life had been a battle between keeping healthy and fit and a love of double-double cheeseburgers. The ankle-length, high-waisted dress pulled in with a tie in the front. Simple, feminine, and so unlike her.

The tinkly bell rang again. She slid into a pair of oversized cream slippers, drew in a hyperventilating breath, and opened the door. Downstairs, she found the dining room through double doors that opened off the great hall. Eldrin's boom dominated among the many voices. She paused in the doorway, the aroma of roasted beast and exotic spices set off the stomach gurgles. Ash, Eldrin, and Gryph were just sitting down at the long, wooden table that could easily seat twelve or more. It was laden with brimming bowls, platters, and goblets.

Across the table sat two figures, mature yet youth-sized, swathed in beige fabric from head to toe. The clothing was similar to the thawbs worn by the Bedouins she'd traveled with in Morocco. She squinted. Only their deep-olive-skinned, unisex faces were visible, fine-featured with chiseled cheekbones and piercing green eyes. Gorgeous people. They chattered away in high, lyrical voices. Were these the Sandies? Was she really about to break bread, or whatever, with these disparate races from another dimension?

Freya motioned for her to come sit, and then all went silent as six pairs of eyes watched her walk rubber-kneed to the table. Ash stood, his hand on the back of an empty chair. His gaze traveled her body, a light stain creeping up his neck. She raised her eyebrows. He snapped out of whatever reverie he was in and pulled the chair out. She sat. His fingers lingered on a shoulder for a fraction before he dropped into the chair.

"Welcome, friends," Eldrin said. "Introduce yourselves as the repast is passed." He laughed and grabbed a bowl of white fluffy stuff. *Mashed potatoes?* "You all know me, Eldrin Flip, the humble helpmate to goddess of this establishment, Freya." He handed his wife the bowl and picked up another.

"Pfft. Humble?" She scooped a dollop of the stuff onto her plate. "He has introduced *me* correctly."

Everyone chuckled. It was Skye's turn with the bowl. She cleared her throat. "I'm Skye and this be my husband, Ash. We're newlyweds from Hollyrose traveling about on our honeymoon."

Ash coughed. His knee bumped hers.

"I could tell," said one of the Sandies, the woman,

judging by the soft tone. "We, too, are bound. I'm Tara. This is Scud, my shanta. Husband, as you say."

Scud pushed back the wrap covering his head, revealing closely shorn black hair not unlike Ash's, rounded ears like hers. "We are taking our celebration travel. Tara needed to see trees. I deny her nothing."

"Trees? You don't have them—" Another kick under the table. Skye looked at Ash's frowning face. A bowl full of green and white striped asparagus-looking stalks passed into her hands.

"You have not heard of us? Sand people— Sandies—from the desert region of Whittensand. Beyond the Beset Mountains."

Jeez. I'm Faen. I should know this.

Ash put a hand on Skye's, his smile annoyingly indulgent. "My dear wife does not think straight. I fault Eldrin's hell fire drink."

"I thought as much," said Freya. "Eldrin, do not befuddle our guests with your swill."

"Love will befuddle even the brightest brain." Tara's sweet, lilting voice turned the words lyrical. She took Scud's hand and held it to her cheek. They looked deeply into each other's amazing green eyes.

They needed to get a room. Skye needed to know how to find love as big as the Beset Mountains. While the others at the table talked about Eldrin's homemade booze and passed dish after dish, Skye leaned toward Tara, saying in a low voice, "What's the secret to a love like yours?"

Tara laid down her fork and drew pencil-thin brows together. "I believe it is allowing your suhm— your soul, your spirit—to accept the other completely." Even her sigh was a song. "To trust with a faith beyond the Gods."

Skye started as if she'd been poked. *Trust. I may never love.*

"You will get there." The Sandie smiled. "I can see it."

Later, after the meal was done, Freya excused herself to feed the baby. Alain's cries carried all the way from wherever their private rooms were located. A young Faen server named Min began clearing away the dishes, so Skye got up to help. The Sandies had left, probably up to their room. Skye chuckled to herself as she gathered dirty plates, glancing at Gryph and Ash deep in quiet conversation, something about a Malgren force of Dark Raiders on the move.

Eldrin pushed back from the table and stood. "Miss Skye, guests don't need to work for a meal."

"I need something to do while I wait for Freya. I'm hoping she brings out the baby."

"Knock on our door. 'Tis under the stairs. She will be glad of your company." He turned to the men. "Shall we return outdoors to the new wall studs 'afore it gets dark? I need your wisdom."

Ash came beside her, a teasing smile on his lips. He whispered, "Newlyweds? Honeymoon? I hope you packed some sexy lingerie." He winked, then followed Gryph and Eldrin out the door.

Jeez. Her fun little lie might come back to bite her. If she was lucky.

Min took the plates from her hands and urged her to go seek out Freya. She found the door and tapped with a knuckle. In a few moments, the door opened. Freya had the baby swaddled in her arms.

She smiled. "Skye, come in. I'm so anxious to talk

with you."

"I hope I'm not disturbing you."

"No, no. Not at all. Alain drained me quickly, as he does, and now wants to sleep. So like a man with a full belly."

Skye laughed as she stepped through the doorway into a large sitting room stuffed with comfy chairs. A rustic stone fireplace, where a low fire crackled, dominated the space. Dark, rough-hewn beams spanned the high ceiling.

"I didn't get a chance to see Alain. May I hold him?"

"Surely. Mind, he's a lump and may mark you with drool, or other fluids." She handed the baby to Skye, then sat in one of the chairs. "Come sit. Would you like a cup of whister? Like a tea."

"No, thanks. I drank too much at dinner, which was delicious, by the way. I don't know what I ate, but I cleaned my plate."

Freya looked pleased, a smile playing about her mouth. "I didn't have a moment to tell you at dinner that I love your hair. You hid your ears well and did a fine job of the braiding. Truly beautiful."

"Thanks. I tried. I don't normally fuss with my hair like that." Skye picked a chair close to Freya in case she had to toss Alain to her in a hurry. "First baby I've held in—honestly, can't remember." She had no mothering instincts but was curious to see what a baby Faen looked like. She pulled back the cloth wrapping. Large eyes opened, warm brown like his mother's, mouth puckered in a bow, blowing bubbles. The sweet face, and oh, the tiny ears with twin buds on each that would blossom into points one day.

Her heart filled while a funny ache lodged beneath her breastbone. She was like the Grinch with the kick-started soul. And then, he smiled.

"If you could see your face, Skye. You like him."

"He's precious." Skye's throat felt tight. *Crap, I'm not about to cry, am I?*

Alain flailed a fist in the air, kicking with his legs. He wore a long, pastel green nightshirt and booties.

"Did you make these?" Skye caught a foot in the air.

"Yes. Knitted them years ago for another wee one lost. I despaired we'd never have two little feet to wear them, but the Gods took pity on an aging Faen." She smiled and whispered, "Ha. We know the Gods had little to do with it."

"I don't know. This little boy looks extra special."

"What are your plans, eh? Ash being mage and you Reg?"

"Phew. Damned if I know. We're attracted to each other. Physically." Freya said what she pleased, so Skye would do the same. "But I can't trust him. I just can't."

"What has he done?"

"It's all this secrecy sh—stuff. Their society must remain a secret from the rest of the world. The Regs. He's had to lie to me so many times. He still is, and he's keeping a lot from me."

"He's protecting you. Eldrin told me there someone in Otherworld wants to kill you."

"There's that. Ash doesn't trust me, either, and shouldn't."

"Why?"

Alain's eyes were fluttering closed. Skye tried folding the cover over him like it had been but ended up handing the whole messy bundle back into Freya's arms.

"I'm an investigative journalist. I write about topics the world has an interest in, has a right to know. A secret witch society? I am—was—am writing a story about magic in the world, people who have paranormal powers."

Freya gasped. "Would your story not destroy their lives? Perhaps this world, too? Ash and others have said as much." She gathered Alain up and stood. "Follow me while I put him abed. You have more to tell me."

Skye followed her through a doorway, then down a hall, turning in at a cozy nursery room. The rough plastered walls were painted a soft green. Skye kept her voice low. "I'm looking at all the different possible outcomes." One being the journalistic recognition she deserved. She told Freya about the encounter with a witch who saved her life when she was five, ever influencing the trajectory of her life and her mom's, their years of investigating funny business that ran through business, finance, the government, some magical, some pure Reg shenanigans, all leading to her becoming a journalist. Somehow, all that put her life in danger.

"In any case, I would need some kind of irrefutable proof of magic before I could write the story of the witches in my world." And the proof hopefully resided on her computer back home.

Freya, a frown knitting her brows together, led her back out to the sitting room where she lit more lamps with a flaming taper. The sun had set. "In all of this, there is Ash to consider." She settled into the chair. "I heard what Tara said to you about trust and love. I would say the same. I see how Ash looks at you. You are special to him."

"We only met a little over two weeks ago. He's new to me, as is his world of witches. Worlds. I'm—overwhelmed."

She nodded. "And yet you are drawn to him, as Ash is to you. We have known him for a short time, too, perhaps a year. He is honorable, steadfast in his convictions, brave, yet conflicted, as you are."

"I know. We're practically twins." The child in the snowsuit left a splinter in his soul. Skye sighed. "Well, here's hoping I live long enough to make many more bad decisions."

A knock sounded on the door. "It's me, Ash."

"He comes to check on your safety." Freya went to the door. "Come in, sit."

Ash took a step inside as Skye stood. "Thanks, but I think I'll turn in." He shot a glance past Freya to Skye and smiled. "Gryph just left for his portal. We've had a busy day."

"So I heard. And by the scent of spirits, you've been into more of Eldrin's fiery brew."

"Oh no, I couldn't handle another finger of that rot gut. We had civilized ale."

"Civilized? All right, then. Off you go."

Skye laid a hand on Freya's arm. "Thanks for the talk. Alain is precious. I loved holding him."

Freya beamed like any proud mother. "I wish you many of your own. And, Miss Skye, I know you will make the right decisions."

Skye nodded, then followed Ash out the door, up the stairs. She was thirty-two and had no so-called biological clock ticking in her girly parts. But something had shifted when she held Freya's baby, like when Hetty and Jo first showed her a tiny bundle of fur that grew into the adorable Trinket. The irresistible appeal of puppies and babies. The similarities were uncanny.

"Did you?" Ash opened the door to their room. The keen oil lamps were lit, casting a soft glow over the room.

She stepped inside, and he followed. "Did I what?"

"You didn't hear a word I said. You're deep in thought." He pulled off the knit cap and tossed it on the dressing table.

"Sorry. Mind's blown. Not convinced I'm not dreaming or delirious."

"Does this feel like a dream?" Ash took her in his arms, pulling her in close. "Or this?"

His kiss was gentle, lips hinting at hops, causing a tug of desire low in her belly. He drew back and smiled that crooked smile. The one that spoke to her *jeez, he's cute* side.

"Uh, still dreaming," she managed through a tight throat, and leaned in for more.

This time, the kiss was firmer, more insistent. Might have involved tongue. He wound a hand in her hair, tugging her closer. For one second, she thought of the intricate braids, all the taming and fussing and—oh, his body. Warm. Hard.

Then she was lifting his shirt, and he was pushing the dress from one shoulder, raining kisses on the bareness, one tender kiss on the purple-y bruise. Did she say *raining*? Yes, she did. Her hands slid up his taut belly to his chest, where lean muscle quivered under her fingers. The raining continued across the top of one breast. A slight tug on the bodice and the breast was free. His lips found the tip, then his tongue. There was moaning and whimpering. Pathetic surrendering noises. All hers.

He lifted his head, fingers still playing in her hair, causing delicious tingles to travel up and down her spine. "Should we be doing this?"

"Hell, no."

"Should I stop?"

"Hell, no." She pulled the shirt over his head and ran her hands up to his pecs, the chest hair crisp and arousing.

He undid the tie under her breasts, pulled the dress from the other shoulder, letting it fall to puddle on the floor. "Did I tell you how incredible you looked tonight?"

She shook her head, aware of the granny panties and sloppy slippers and a patchwork of welts. *How incredible is that?*

But she *felt* incredible. Tingly, quiver-y. Hot. Liquid.

He moved them a few steps to the edge of the bed, and she fell back, taking him with her. The weight of him, the lean, hard length of him, pressed her down until he propped up on one elbow to gaze into her eyes. She'd called his eyes unfathomable, but the message now was damn clear. He wanted her.

Yeah. Her whole body wanted him, too. Her magic man. Her amazing witch. Her naked mage. Where had his clothes gone?

He placed gentle kisses on the purpling bruises on a shoulder, working his way down, taking his time, setting her on fire. Before long, the want turned to need.

The slow and gentle just wasn't cutting it. He got the message. Maybe it was her moans. Or her insistent hands.

And then she was lost in the movement, the delicious friction, the sweet words in her ear.

How was this not a dream?

Chapter Nineteen

Ash woke with the tattered remnants of the nightmare fading into mist. Early dawn leaked through the curtains. Skye lay curled beside him, asleep, naked, and warm, hair a messy tangle of fiery redness. His body responded. He wrapped an arm around her. Last night he'd kissed every single bruise and welt on the curvy body, maybe a few hundred freckles. The desire to repeat kicked in like a sugar addiction.

Had it only been a couple of days since he'd revealed who—what—he was? Seemed like weeks ago. She'd accepted everything that had happened to her, everything she'd learned, with a wide-eyed wonder, with bravery, and a fierce spirit. He hoped she wasn't storing all the data away for the great exposé, the one that would change the world forever. It killed him that he wasn't sure.

Her eyes opened, and she smiled, leaning in for a kiss. "Morning, magic man."

And he was lost in a mad jumble of emotions. *Crap*. He recognized this feeling—the helpless ache, the longing so strong, it swamped the senses, swamped reason. He wanted her, not just now, but forever.

I'm in love. But he couldn't be. *The consequences…*

The only consequence would be his own heartache. He needed to step on the brakes, walk back the desire.

She tilted her head. "You tensed up like a cat spotting a bird. Regretting last night?"

Say yes, or you're an idiot. "Never."

"Never? Wow. I like." Frown lines appeared between her brows. "You realize we didn't use protection, unless you used, you know, magic."

Shit. He sat up and leaned on the headboard. "Sorry. Farthest thing from my mind at that moment. I acted like some kind of randy teenager."

She scooted next to him, dragging the sheet up to her waist. He tried to ignore her beautiful breasts just to prove he wasn't a sex-starved teen.

He took her hand and played with her fingers. A heaviness settled in his chest. "Odds are I didn't get you pregnant, right?"

"Right. Not my time."

"But if you are—"

A knock sounded at the door. Muffled words. "'Tis Gryph. News."

Ash scrambled up, along with Skye. "Just a sec."

He threw on a loose shirt over pants, tugged the cap over his ears, then pulled on boots. He checked that Skye was dressed before stepping into the hall. "Gryph, glad you're back in one piece. Let's go to the storeroom." He kept his voice low.

Gryph nodded and led the way down the stairs. In the storeroom, the scent of spilled liquor and ale lay heavy on the air. Eldrin's fault.

Ash willed the keen oil lamps to flame in the weak dawn light. "What did you learn?"

The door opened. "'Tis just me, Eldrin." The Faen walked in with Freya following close behind, the baby strapped to her chest facing in. "And Freya, as you can see."

"I was up with Alain," she said, shifting the load and sitting in a flour-dusted chair. "No use in you telling your tale twice." She waved a hand in front of her face. "Whew, El. 'Tis a brew house in here. You'll swagger the babe."

"Perhaps you should leave, then, lovie." He motioned with his hand.

She sent him that universal eff off expression. He'd seen that same look on Skye's face more than once.

Gryph cleared his throat. "I have news. Risked my life if anyone is interested."

The door opened and Skye walked in. She'd drawn the mess of flaming hair back to cover her ears and into a low tail. She pushed at the wire glasses. Ash's temperature rose knowing that hidden beneath the baggy Faen tunic and pants was a gorgeous body he'd spent hours ravishing. Loving.

"Is there anyone else?" asked Gryph. "The Sandies, maybe? Any beggar from the street?"

Ash dragged his attention away from Skye. "Go ahead."

"They caught the killer in the Haven. Sunshine— er, Myst—herself came through the portal to tell me. 'Twas all I could do to dissuade her from comin' here with me. She gave me the blather you must say to open that portal." He handed Ash a folded piece of paper. He shoved it in a pocket.

"They caught Thomas Blakely?" asked Skye.

"Yes, that's the name. They have him in a Haven lockup."

Ash opened his mouth, but Skye got there first. "Did he confess?"

"No. Denies all. Never heard of this one or that one."

Everyone started talking, giving opinions on guilt, innocence, and justice. Ash held up a hand. "Wait." They all quieted. "I'll return to the Haven. Alone."

"No way. I'm coming with you." Skye lifted her chin.

"Too risky. What if Blakely isn't the one? I need to question the guy myself."

"It's risky for you, too. You might be thrown in a cell right next to him."

"That's another reason to go alone. I know the Haven. I can avoid getting caught."

Again, with the talking, some agreeing with him, some not.

Gryph leaned in, his faint mage energy a tingle on Ash's senses. "I'll take you to the portal site. After dark be best. Myst said she will stay close by on her side. Await your return."

Skye was busy talking to Freya and Eldrin, cooing over a fussy baby. Ash whispered to Gryph, "Your portal will drop me deep within the Keeper wing. Much less risky than the cave's portal to E.T.'s, or others in the Haven. I'll go right after breakfast. Tell me how to get there. I need you here to watch over Skye."

"Pity the bugger crosses her path," Gryph scoffed. "But I'll draw you a map and stay."

Freya stood. "Are we done? What's decided? Breakfast needs making. Min may already be in the kitchen."

Ash faced Skye. "I'm leaving after I eat. Gryph will stay here with you."

Freya nodded, shooed Eldrin and Gryph from the

room, then closed the door behind her.

Skye stayed rooted to the spot. Her neck turned blotchy. "You can't leave me here. Shit shows happen when you leave me. Jeez, I sound pathetic right now. I'll follow you."

"Gryph is staying with you."

She got up in his face. "As my jailor or my babysitter?"

"Backup to your badass."

"Flattery will get you—"

He cut her off with a kiss. She pushed at his chest even as she deepened the kiss, parting her lips to allow his tongue inside. Then her arms circled his neck and her body molded to his. Heartache be damned.

She moaned low in her throat and said through mashed lips, "I want you to shtay."

He pulled his lips from hers despite the need roaring through him. "I've got to hear Blakely's story, and fast before they move him. I'll be back as soon as I can."

She removed her arms and stepped away. "I don't like this half-assed plan. Wait. It's not even *one* buttock."

"Funny. Don't worry. I'm good at improvising."

She nodded, that busy brain probably working double-time. She'd better not do something stupid, like try to follow him. A bell sounded and, like Pavlov's dog, his stomach growled.

He dropped a quick kiss onto pouty lips. "Time to feed the beast." He steered her toward the door. He hoped Gryph and the Flips remembered to keep their mouths shut about the Witch Whisperer disaster last year. Skye didn't need to know anything about that particular shit show.

****

Ash had made sure Skye was surrounded by friends when he turned Gryph's flashy pinto, Patch, along Twilda Road. One last glance back showed her being led inside the inn by a smiling Freya and yacking away. She'd be safe with Gryph and the fierce fighter Eldrin. *Huh. She's a warrior herself.*

It was at least two hours by horseback to the Keeper portal, toward the Beset Mountains. Quicker with this swift horse, and safer than trying to get to the cave portal leading to Elizabeth's storage room. He touched his heels to the animal's flank, and it broke into an easy canter. He tugged the cap on tight to hide the ears from any Malgren passing by on their way to the town. Flip House was the last building in Moonstone, and soon he was past Eldrin's fields, with woods to the left and other Faen farmland to the right. He kept a lookout for the wide trail called Dead Man's that met the road to the left. He didn't want to know where the route got its name.

The early morning sky threatened rain with more heavy storm clouds spreading out over the foothills where he was heading. The wind picked up, stirring the scent of forest and field crops, bringing a hint of moisture. Just when fat raindrops started to fall, he came across the trail and turned Patch. He could shelter from the worst by staying under the trees to one side.

The deluge started within minutes. Not even overhanging limbs protected him. Soon, chilled water dripped from nose and chin. His hands were slick on the reins. Head down, Patch slogged on as the hard-packed trail, ever ascending, turned to mud, then a trickling stream. So much for making good time.

Lightning flashed across the sky, and thunder followed by a second, sending reverberations through his body. The horse didn't flinch. This was the mount Gryph likely rode into more than one fight. Ash gave the animal a pat on the neck while he concentrated on stopping his teeth from chattering.

The terrain changed from heavy, leafy trees on either side to pine interspersed by brush and rock. The sheer drop-off Gryph had told him about appeared to his left. A misstep here could plunge him and Patch over the side and into a deep, rocky canyon. Maybe that's where Dead Man's got its name.

He looked to the right for a heart-shaped boulder the size of a large whiskey barrel, or as Gryph put it, somebody's bare arse sticking up in the air. This was no New York City with an exact address on a certain street.

Thunder rumbled. The steady downpour changed to drizzle as he spotted the rock. He turned Patch into the trees and found a faint kuda trail. To be sure he was on the right track, he fished Gryph's soggy map from a pocket. The guy couldn't draw worth a damn. Nothing was to scale, but Ash was fairly certain he was heading in the right direction. *Look for the fallen tree caught in the fork of another. Check. The giant boulder with one sheer side. Check. Carcass of a dead hell creeper in a rocky clearing.* He smelled the stench long before he saw it. *Check and check.*

Patch picked his way along the narrow, rock-strewn trail. The faint current of electricity from the portal site buzzed his senses. He was close. Gryph said to look for a massive boulder that had split in two somewhere beyond where the trail intersects with another.

Voices and footsteps. *My luck. Malgren again.* So much for this being the safer route.

The cross trail was just ahead. He pulled on the reins and directed Patch into the trees. The cover wasn't ideal, but if the men weren't paying attention, and the horse kept quiet…

The voices stopped. A roll of thunder rumbled in the distance. The storm had passed, but trees dripped water down his neck. He shivered and waited. A twig snapped behind him.

"You, on the horse."

Ash twisted around. Two Malgren men, one as big as an ox and sporting the usual forehead lumps and bumps, stood among the trees behind him, arrows nocked in bows. They weren't the pair he'd saved from the hell creeper. They wore a lot of wet leather, tooled with markings of the Dark Raiders. *Shit. Might need some help here, One Mother.* He directed Patch to face them.

"Not Malgren, Dilly," said the biggest one in a low, guttural voice. His dark mop of salt and pepper hair matched a full beard, all dripping. "Why do you travel this trail, Faen?

"I'm lost. I be looking for Moonstone."

The clean-shaven one giggled and shifted from one foot to the other. "You be lost, that's sure." His hands shook, making the bow quaver. Ash amped up energy in case he'd need instant magic.

"Wrong way. Go back the way you came." With a nod of the head, the big hairy one indicated the trail Ash had been traveling.

"Thank you. I be on my way." He signaled Patch to back up, away from the pair.

"Wait. I wasn't done. Leave the horse."

No way in hell.

"'Tis a fine horse," said Dilly, all smiles. He lowered the bow.

"Ain't for you, Dil. I be the one with the bunions."

Ash resisted a snort. "This horse belongs to another. I can't give him up."

"Ha! You stole the beast." Dilly shifted feet like an antsy five-year-old. "You took 'im."

"I borrowed it on a promise to return. I keep my promises."

The hairy one drew the bowstring taut. "Get down offa it. Now."

Ash held both hands out. "Let's talk." He took a breath, focusing on the high magic. Warm, sizzling power welled up from his chest and traveled down his arms to his hands. *Focus. Focus.*

The ground shivered right up through the horse. Patch stirred. Both men looked to the ground. Another shake, and the trees quivered, sending a shower of water on their heads. Their eyes went wide.

"Sig, what that *be*?" Dilly's voice rose an octave on the last word. He hopped from one foot to the other.

Ash pretended fear. "Quaking earth. The curse." He pulled sharply on Patch's reins, causing the animal to throw its head up and dance, adding to the chaos.

"Curse?" Sig set his feet apart as the shaking began again with a long, low rumble like thunder. The trees swayed, leaves and needles rained down.

Dilly's face paled. "Our fault, Sig. We looked upon Lumeria."

"Shut up. Don't speak of it."

A bit of luck had come his way at last. Ash didn't have to make up a curse. He ignored the ache building behind his temple and focused. The ground shook violently, almost knocking the men off their feet. Boulders lifted and slammed down. The heaving earth was too much for the steady Patch. The horse reared. Ash held on. Dilly took off screaming into the woods with Sig racing after him, bunions the last thing on his mind.

Sounds of the pair crashing through the brush receded. Ash settled the earth and the horse. He'd need to hurry in case the two returned looking for him. He urged Patch along the trail past the intersection. He piled on the power, clearing rock and fallen brush from the trail to make the going easier.

The portal site's energy grew steadily until he saw the split boulder off the trail to left. He steered Patch toward it. Some immense power had sliced the granite behemoth, as big as a two-story house, cleanly down the middle. Fatigue washed over him, the aftereffects of sustained high magic. He closed his eyes for a moment and breathed steadily in and out.

He dismounted and led Patch under a tree. "You're not a unicorn, or any kind of mage, but I wish you could understand me." He gave the horse a rub between the ears and a tug on the forelock. The animal still resonated with Gryph's faint energy. "I don't know when I'll be back, or if I'll be back through this portal. If you don't wait for me, I'll understand." Patch snorted. He and Gryph hadn't talked about what to do with his horse. Maybe he'd find the way back to Moonstone.

Ash walked to the boulder's split center where the energy signal throbbed strongest. He fished another soggy paper from a pocket. Myst's scrawled words of the chant were barely readable, and then the note ripped along a fold.

"Didn't we just talk, One Mother? Can I get a break? Please."

He put the two pieces of the tissue-thin note together, then squinted at the words, reciting them while gathering strength. Sputtering power bubbled through him like the start of an old, rusty Chevy. *Come on. Come on.* The vortex materialized from the split, spinning, and growing one arc at a time. There was no rushing it with his low energy.

Myst better be on the Haven side of this thing. She might need to catch him.

Chapter Twenty

Strong hands tugged on an arm and a voice spoke in his ear. "Ash. You okay?"

Myst.

"Where's Parker?"

The portal had spit him out with a nasty thud on the floor. "She's with Gryph at Flip House." He squinted in the bright light of a nondescript space, empty except for the two of them. This would be the isolated back room deep in the Keeper wing. He breathed hard, trying to get oxygen flowing through his system to re-energize muscles.

"What happened?" She let go. "You're like a soggy noodle."

"Tired, but I'll live." He stood on unsteady legs, shook off the tingles. "Had to use some high magic back there."

"Can't wait to hear that tale, girlfriend." She spoke the ritual words to close the vortex. The spinning colors grew smaller and then winked out. "But first, lots happening here. I'm a rock star. Caught Thomas Blakely with lame help from the Council cops. You, on the other hand, are Haven's most wanted."

"I've got to question Blakely without anyone knowing I'm here."

"You doubt he's the one?"

"I have to be sure before I bring Skye back."

"So, it's Skye now." She raised both brows.

"Long story. Where's Mort?"

"He was still analyzing footage of Blakely at or near the crime scenes but had to leave for his clinic. He's conducting counseling sessions all afternoon."

"Hopefully I won't need him. What's the deal with Elizabeth? On our side or not?"

"Our side. She's sincere, Ash. She said she tried to stop Gray and Jada from issuing orders to have Parker grabbed up after you stormed out. *They* want Parker's memory erased. *E.T.* wants to help us."

"I thought so. Bring her here. I can use her as an energy shield. She can get access to the cell where Blakely's being held. And bring your laptop with all the incriminating footage."

Ash spent the next twenty minutes pacing the windowless room, looking at four blank walls, and re-energizing. The door opened, and Elizabeth and Myst entered. Myst carried a laptop case.

E.T. rushed to Ash and gave him a hug. "Glad you're back safe. Myst told me you left Skye in Moonstone until you see if we have the right man."

He nodded. "Can you get me to his cell, like, now. We'll go through the back door from the Keeper wing."

"It will be risky, but it's Sunday, so things are quiet in the halls."

"Surveillance cameras?"

"I insisted they be turned off before I left the Council room, and that they be taken down by the end of the weekend. I told them they'd have a real crisis on their hands should the general Haven population find out about them. I'd make sure they did."

"Good. I need to switch out my clothes."

E.T. waved a hand in his direction before he could summon a wardrobe. Beige hoodie jacket and jeans appeared on his body. He pulled the hood on and lowered his power level. No one else in the Haven could identify energy signatures. Alongside the powerful E.T., he'd be practically invisible. She opened the door.

Ash snagged her sleeve. "Listen, Elizabeth. Skye and I had to detour into Lumeria and the city." He took a breath. "I'm sorry, but I woke the dragonites by accident."

"No. How? They were in the long sleep in the sacred garden."

Ash looked at Myst, who had pursed her lips in a can't-help-you-dude expression. "I needed to speak with the One Mother."

"The tree." E.T.'s shoulders sagged but her eyes went kindly. "It's okay. I hope she guided you. If Tarig still leads the swarm, they'll be fine."

Ash nodded. "He took the rest to greener lands."

"Then I won't worry about them. There are serious matters right here."

They headed along the deserted Keeper hallway, passing one empty meeting room but hearing voices from another. The door was closed as they hurried past. A tall man entered the hall in front of them, closing a door behind him. Ash hunched his shoulders and kept his face hidden.

"Gavon," said Myst. "How the hell are you? You never called me for that drink." She stopped in front of the man.

Ash and E.T. kept walking.

"Is that Elizabeth—" Gavon asked.

Myst touched his cheek. "Yes. So, hey, call me. I'm available whenever."

Ash and E.T. turned the corner to another hall when Myst caught up to them. "I'm praying to the Mother he never calls."

Ash shook his head. Myst went through boyfriends like kids went through Halloween candy. She loved every one of them. Until she didn't and broke it off.

The Keeper entrance to the holding cells was up ahead, secured with a coded entry that only authorized security and certain Council members could open. Luckily, E.T. was one of them. She entered the code, used a push of her unique magic, and opened the door. "Wait. I'll check who's manning the block." She went through.

Ash hung back while Myst held the door ajar.

"How are you feeling now?" she whispered.

"I could run a marathon. What's taking her so long?"

"Give her five seconds. Stop worrying. You have an angry unibrow. This will be easy peasy."

He grunted. E.T. stuck her head around the door and waved them in. "Dickson's at the desk. But there are people."

Dickson was a distant cousin of hers and Ash's. Ash followed closely behind Myst to the large foyer, turning away from a group of suits deep in discussion at a round table to one side. They didn't even look up.

Dickson ushered Ash and Myst through the locked door to the cells. "He's in hold number seven." He pointed down the row of cells.

Ash followed Myst and E.T. as they walked past the cells, separated by solid walls. The fronts were clear, secured by an energy field only certain magic could open. The occupants looked as dejected as any prisoners in a Reg jail. In number seven, Blakely lay on the bunk with his back to them.

"Blakely, wake up," said Ash.

The man turned his head, then sat bolt upright. "What? What's happening?"

Ash recognized him from the Haven surveillance footage. Brown hair with a streak of white. His right shoulder slumped lower than the left.

Ash turned to Elizabeth. "I want us in there to talk to him without the whole block hearing."

She waved a hand. "We can pass through. I'll silence the space."

They walked into the cell, lit by recessed lights in the ceiling and a small window that let in weak, fake sunlight. Blakely, still clad in street clothes, stood. A wave of body odor wafted through the small space along with a strong hit of Elite energy. Blakely had no registered unique Elite powers, according to Mort. Mort suspected the guy had considerably more talent than he'd revealed.

Blakely's face, with its sharp angles and cleft chin, glistened with the sheen of sweat. His eyes were wide with fear. He rubbed both hands down his jeans and looked beyond Ash to E.T. "That's Immortal Elizabeth Trowbridge," he said, reverence in his tone.

"I'm Ash Hunter. Keeper and a Shadow Force leader. Sit down."

Blakely sat on the bunk, knees shaking.

Ash stood over him. "You know why you're here?"

"I—I'm accused of killing people." He shook his head. "*Me*. I've never hurt anyone in my life. Bless the

One Mother." He shot a glance at Elizabeth, who had stepped closer to Ash.

"Myst, sit beside him and bring up a couple of the videos."

She sat, took the laptop out of its case, and opened it on her knees. Her fingers tapped on the keys.

Ash crouched directly in front of Blakely. "Look at me." Blakely dragged his eyes from E.T. "You're an active member of that group that seeks greater restrictions on the use of magic and greater penalties for Public Displays of Magic. You want to insure the secrecy of our society. Maybe you decided to eliminate any threats to secrecy."

Blakely shook his head, flopping his white streak. "No. No. We protest peacefully. Take our concerns to the Council."

"What were you doing in the Haven?"

"I was—I was trying to find my girlfriend."

Myst brought up the shot of Blakely getting off the elevator and seeming to hide himself. "Why were you sneaking around?" she asked.

"I knew I wouldn't be welcomed into the Haven because of my views. I didn't want to be hustled out before I found her."

"Why were you looking for her?" asked Ash.

"To recruit her for our group. She's reluctant to join."

"Where were you on Wednesday, May twenty-fifth?" Ash figured the more recent date of Hetty's murder might stick in the guy's memory.

"I went over all this with security, man. All the dates they threw at me. I had alibis for a couple of them. They took my phone, so I can't check now."

"Who asked the questions?"

"A couple of goons, and some tall, thin guy. Mort, I think. He had a laptop, too. Kept showing me photos and videos."

"Do you have the ability to mask your energy signature? Make it so obscure you couldn't be identified by it?"

"What? I've never heard of that ability. That's crazy."

Myst brought up one of Mort's videos and turned the laptop toward Blakely. "Isn't this you?"

Blakely squinted at the screen. The image was just clear enough to make out a man with a slant to one shoulder walking briskly along a street and stopping at an intersection. You could make out the streak in his hair. "Mort showed me this one. Queens just over a year ago. Never been to that part of town. Not a year ago. Never." He looked straight at Ash. "I'm telling you, man. All the stuff he showed me? Looked like me, but I was not at any of those locations at that time, if ever." The knee shakes worsened. "There's someone out there that looks like me or is pretending to be me. Or those images have been altered."

Ash stood. He believed the guy for some reason. Maybe it was written in his eyes. The third option, messing with the images, niggled at him. Voices carried from the cell block door.

"I believe you," said Elizabeth. "We'll look at each possibility." She touched Ash on the arm. "We'd better go. They're serving lunch."

Blakely's eyes welled with tears. "Thank you."

"Don't thank us yet. You might be in here for a while." *Might be a long while*. Ash placed a hand on the man's shoulder, directing a mesmer to calm his hyper nerves.

E.T. restored the security on the cell and led the way. The novelty of having Elizabeth Trowbridge in the block allowed Ash and Myst to slip out without drawing the attention of the busy servers. Once in the Keeper hallway, they made their way to the Sanctuary and slipped into one of the pods. It was identical to the one Ash had used with Mort and Myst. Three of the walls undulated with calming images curated to each of them. He sat at the table across from E.T. and waved a hand to clear the walls.

Myst sat and opened the laptop on the table. "Which option do we tackle first? Doppelgänger? Impersonator? Video doctor?"

A hard ball of dread lodged in his gut like a bad case of indigestion. The burner phone chimed. "It's Jo." He clicked on speaker and answered. "Hi, Jo. How are you?"

"Fine. Got run out of Springfield by a two-year-old, so I'm in town. I can't reach Skye. She asked me to look into something."

In town. Not good. "Don't worry, she's safe. Where are you?"

"In the bitch bunker with my trusty Sig in my lap."

"Okay. Stay put. I need you to do some digging for us, too. You at the same e-mail address?"

"Yep, and I got a big shovel. Shoot."

"Myst, send Jo the whole Blakely file along with the videos and photos. All of them. Jo, we just interviewed the suspect, and he swears he didn't kill anyone."

Jo's laugh ended in a cough. "Yeah, they always

swear."

"We believe him. Do you have a quick way to tell if a video or image has been altered?"

"There are tells. Send them to me."

"Get it done fast and call me back." He clicked off the call.

Myst's fingers flew over the keys. "Sent. I can start checking the images, too. I'm not an expert, though. Mort's the guy."

Indigestion turned to flaming heartburn. He looked at E.T. She raised a brow.

"What?" Myst paused in mid-stroke. "I don't like that look."

Ash stood and paced. "We don't have anything yet, but I don't believe there's a Blakely lookalike out there."

E.T. stood. "I don't, either. While you're waiting to hear, I'll go back to my place and stand by in case any alarms are sounded. Call me when you're ready to leave the Sanctuary."

For the next hour, Ash sat beside Myst as she pored over the images, explaining date stamps, photo manipulation, and video metadata.

"This one," she said, pointing to a grainy photo taken near one of the so-called car accidents. "Looks like Blakely, but the—"

His phone chimed. He answered and put it on speaker. "Jo, what you got."

"Calling bingo. Everything's been altered. Every photo and vid. The techie is a wizard."

Ash shut his eyes. Common sense screamed, but the heart was deaf.

"Whaddya want me to do with all this?" She

coughed. "Ash?"

He opened his eyes. Myst sat rigid in the chair, nostrils flaring, cheeks reddening. She thought the same as he did but would fight to be wrong.

"Nothing. Just needed confirmation. Thanks, Jo."

"Yeah. No problem."

"Sit tight there, okay?" The last thing he wanted to do was grab Jo up and bring her into the Haven. Change her life forever. "Call me if you need anything."

"I've got a shitload of stuff to put together for Skye. There's a bunk here. Hey, I want to hear from her, and soon."

"You will." He clicked off the call. *A shitload of what stuff?*

"We can't be thinking who we're thinking." Myst sat back in the chair. "It's someone else. Gotta be. Definitely not…"

"Mort. You're right. It doesn't make sense. He's an empath."

"It would twist him up real bad if he hurt anyone. He counsels people in crisis, Reg and witch. It's who he is."

Ash nodded. "But he gathered all the evidence on Blakely. Took hours poring over surveillance pics and videos. With his talent, he could have altered everything. It's what he does every day when someone posts a PDM."

"Jo called the guy a wizard."

"That's Mort. Remember I asked him to hack into the Bureau's database listing witches in the area and their talents, look for someone who could mask their energy signal? He said none listed."

"Maybe he didn't even look because he's the

killer." Myst placed a hand over her heart. "I can't wrap my head around this. Mort brought me to one of these pods last year. Held my hand while I bawled like a baby wearing a week-old diaper over losing an asshole boyfriend. Checked in with me for days afterward."

"Sorry, I didn't…"

She waved a hand. "That's okay. You were kind of busy with the Witch Whisperer if you'll recall."

He tried not to. "We've got to find Mort. Get him here." *Mort.* How had he not seen this? Suspected even.

"He's supposed to be at his clinic. Sundays he schedules private consultations. I'll call him." She tried Mort's number on her cell and waited, mouthed the words *he's not picking up*. "Mort, need you to come to the Keeper offices stat. Call me back." She clicked off the call. "I can't wait. I'll go check on him in person and bring him in."

"No. We both go. Elizabeth will get me out of here."

Ash toyed with the idea of updating Gray but decided to wait till they talked to Mort. Found out the truth. He rang E.T. and let her know their suspicions. Her silence for several beats spoke of her shock.

He wanted the truth to be anything other than his trusted friend and coworker and empath being a killer. He sent up a prayer to the One Mother that his dad was not complicit as well.

Chapter Twenty-One

Skye let Freya lead her back into Flip House when all she wanted to do was watch Ash ride away up the road until he was out of sight. Or grab a horse and follow him. When had she become so lame? No man had ever had a hold on her like this one, this witch. And there it was.

Witch. She was in love with a witch.

"Perhaps I can show you how I braid my hair while Alain sleeps?" Freya entered the great hall, Gryph on their heels. "Of course, you do a lovely braid yourself, Skye."

Skye smoothed some frizz framing her face. "Thanks, but I'm all thumbs and everything is backward when I look in the mirror." She followed Freya into their quarters.

"May I come as well?" Gryph asked. "There be little can improve this"—he circled his face with a hand—"but we could try." He pulled the thin leather strip from his hair and let the partial tail join the rest, shaggy to his shoulders and shot through with polished silver streaks. Some women paid big bucks for that look.

Skye smiled. He was taking his job as protector of the Reg very seriously.

"I am up for such a challenge." Freya sat them at a round table near a large window. "Tiny braids might tame the fierce in you."

He grinned. "Nothing will blunt this warrior."

Outside, the wind had picked up, banging tree branches against the building, followed by the patter of rain. Ash was out in this. Well, he'd been through worse than getting soaked.

Freya disappeared into another room, returning with wide-toothed combs. Gryph took one and drew it through his tangles. Skye removed the ribbon from her ponytail, shaking out the mop. How she would twist her hair into artwork like Freya's she had no idea.

"By the Gods, you have a glorious head of hair."

"I have never seen the color," said Gryph.

"Don't any of the people of Tae-wen have red hair?"

Freya sectioned off a few strands of her pale hair, showing them how to set them in fingers. Skye followed suit. "'Tis rare. I have seen one or two. Folks from seaside Brimdom, far beyond the old Majiste lands of Lumeria."

"Tae-wen has an ocean?" She hadn't thought how vast this world might be. Her mind swirled with the possibilities, or impossibilities.

"'Tis where we get most of our fish." Gryph fought with the comb caught on a tangle.

Freya continued her instruction. Tiny braids to frame the face, thicker for the back. Gryph soon gave up, saying his fingers were too big. He'd managed a thin, scraggly braid that hung to one side.

"Gryph, tell me about yourself." Skye wove two braids together at the back of her head. "What adventures have you had?" She knew enough not to talk of his mage blood.

He frowned. "Adventures? 'Tis an adventure every day when you are Malgren and acquainted with witches and Faen."

"How did that happen?" She pointed a pinky, draped in strands of hair, toward his forehead.

"You are bold. Ash told me as much."

Freya huffed. "How would we know a thing in this world if we were not?"

"You and Skye are too much alike." He sat back in the chair, the comb still stuck in his hair. "The Malgren fight with other races and amongst themselves. In the last few years, the more warring among the Malgren, the ones still harboring a hatred of anything mage, have broken off from the more peaceful."

"Dark Raiders?"

"Yes. We battle each other. This bump on my forehead was sliced off many years ago in a fight with my best friend."

"How do you know when you encounter a Malgren you've never met whether they're on your side or not?"

"How do you know in Otherworld who is friend or foe? You trust your gut. If they didn't brandish a weapon upon meeting, be vigilant, anyway. I'm always hunted."

She nodded. "Basically, trust no one but yourself."

"A good rule."

Freya deftly wove tiny braids together in her hair. "Gryph, this is why you are alone at age, what? Thirty-five? You shall never find another heart mate if you don't trust. I shall be blunt."

"As you always are." He shook his head. His fingers strayed to a chain around his neck that held a gold ring. A wedding ring?

"You tragically lost a family a short time ago. Trust in the Gods and your heart that you will find another someone to love. We have all lost dear ones." Her eyes grew moist.

He touched Freya's arm. Skye's heart bumped. She thought of her mother, of Hetty. She didn't want to lose anyone else. *Ash better keep himself safe.*

Gryph took Freya's thin hand in his huge mitt. "I know, my friend. The scar, however old, is fresh pain every day. I'll try that trust thing out sometime."

"I'm sorry. I didn't mean to upset you both," said Skye, the word trust bouncing around in her mind like a loaded grenade. She held one, finger poised on the pin.

Freya smiled. She squeezed Gryph's hand, and he let go. "Words needed saying."

"Where's your home, Gryph?" Skye ran the comb through the loose hair covering her ears.

"Lyall Hill for now, at the edge of the Malgren land called Drekurk. It used to be the stronghold of a militant group, but we took it back last year. It's not far from here, where four lands come together, Drekurk, the Majiste's dead land of Lumeria, Faenstar, where we are now, and the Sandies' Wittensand over the Beset Mountains."

"Plenty of lovely ladies in Lyall, I hear," said Freya.

Gryph leaned toward Skye. "She never gives up. Now, if you were free…"

"She's not. Make no mistake." Freya stood and wagged a finger at him. "Ash the Keeper would turn you into a horse's arse, and well you know it."

Skye laughed. "I'm *free* to make up my own mind whether *I* want someone or not. I haven't decided on

Ash yet." Didn't she admit to herself she was in love? Maybe it was that witch thing. The novelty.

"And why is that?" asked Gryph.

"Because he—I don't…"

"You don't trust him, you told me." Freya yanked the comb from Gryph's hair and gathered the others from the table. "He has held things from you. But for good reasons. His kind must be kept secret."

"I don't know the rules of the mage in Otherworld," said Gryph. "Is it because he is mage and you are Reg? Are you forbidden?"

"Forbidden?" The question hit Skye like a lightning strike. Were there restrictions or consequences to a mage for loving a Reg? "Ash and I only just met recently. We aren't even thinking about being together." *Physically attracted, sure. Yeah, most definitely.* "I don't see a permanent future with him regardless of any restriction." Or my feelings for him. That thought brought an ache to her chest. No future, especially if she wrote the "magic is real" story.

Alain's mewling cry filtered through to the sitting area.

"My boss summons," Freya said. "You both did wonders with your hair. Gryph, you look an angel. Go get some refreshment. I will join anon."

Skye made sure her rounded ears were covered before leaving the Flip's quarters. For the rest of the day, Gryph shadowed her every move. Her heart tripped when Patch appeared before dinner, riderless, ambling down the cobbled street. Had Ash made it to the portal site? Gryph paid a young Faen to take Patch to the stable where Bings' big chestnut was housed.

She contemplated what to do about her story, about

Ash's role in her life, and life in Tae-wen. If she released her story, she'd need expert testimony that her video of Ash and Elizabeth hadn't been altered. The effects to both worlds would result in chaos. What would become of the Flips and the people she was beginning to care for? Maybe she could leave out any mention of portals and Tae-wen. Leave out the Haven. Did the Regs of her world really have a right to know? By dinnertime, her head ached and that lump in her stomach had solidified.

****

Thanks to Elizabeth's distracting presence, Ash was able to make it from the Sanctuary to the elevator and up without anyone recognizing him. Sam was waiting at the curb outside Ash's building when he came through the door with Myst. Sam turned to them after they settled in the back seat. "To the Brooklyn clinic, eh?"

"And hurry. But with your usual care." He wanted to get there alive, at least. "Then stay and wait for us."

"Still not answering." Myst put away her phone as the car sped away from the curb.

"I sure hope we're wrong." Ash's stomach churned like he'd eaten bad meat. Mort was someone he'd have bet his life on you could trust. Maybe Skye's philosophy of trust no one was valid.

"Me, too. How should we handle this when we meet up with him?"

"I'll tell him a bullshit story that the Council is having an emergency meeting about Thomas Blakely, and he's needed to demonstrate the video evidence. Something like that."

"And I hope he's genuinely glad you're back from

286

Tae-wen. He'll ask about Skye."

"I'll say she came back with me and is at E.T.'s because she's no longer in danger thanks to his documented proof of Blakely."

"Might work."

Myst kept busy on her phone for most of the drive, leaving Ash with his chaotic thoughts. What was Skye doing right now? Gryph would keep her safe. Eldrin and Freya were both fierce fighters, too. She'd be fine. He would feel a lot better when he could bring her back home.

With green lights magically with them, they arrived outside the clinic in a half hour. The rambling, beige brick house had seen many additions, renos, and added stories. He'd been to Mort's little apartment on the third floor only once about a year ago. Myst had been many times to look after Mort's familiar, Mercy.

"We'll go in by a side door. I want to avoid the front desk. Too many questions."

Myst nodded. They made their way through a gate to a locked door. A push of magic and they were through. They walked along a hall and peeked into the consultation and meeting rooms, all with open doors, all with not a soul inside. Being Sunday, the place was quiet, but if anyone needed counsel, a sympathetic ear would be found. Often it was Mort.

They went up the back stairs to the second floor and checked all the rooms, including Mort's office. Empty. They didn't meet anyone in the third-floor residence hall, either. Ash knocked on Mort's apartment door. No answer. He tried the knob. Locked. Another push of magic, and they both stepped into the living room.

A hint of stale garlic lingered on the air. His small apartment consisted of a living room stuffed with comfy furniture, a large TV on one wall. A bistro set sat in front of the tiny kitchen counter. Mort's cell phone sat on the round table. The bedroom door was closed, the door to the bathroom stood open. He detected tendrils of Mort's energy. He wasn't here.

Just in case he'd reduced his aura, Ash called out, "Mort, it's Ash and Myst."

Myst plopped into a red bean bag chair that almost swallowed her whole. "I've always said I gotta get one of these."

"Hello out there."

Myst struggled out of the folds. "Not Mort. That's Mercy."

Ash opened the bedroom door. A large white bird fluttered awkwardly out, landing on the back of the couch. Mort's white cockatoo sounded just like him.

"Mercy, where's Mort?" asked Ash.

Mercy ruffled his feathers. "Gone. Flew the coop. I didn't want him to go."

A knot of unease settled in Ash's gut. "Go where?"

"He was sad. So sad. Nothing I said helped."

"He's an empath, just like Mort." The bird stepped onto Myst's outstretched arm. "Why was Mort sad?"

"He said something had to be done. Bless the One Mother." Mercy flexed one wing, then the other. "I'll have a rough time with him when he returns from the Haven. Always do after his fatal interventions."

Ash stiffened. "Shit. He's in the Haven."

"He could go through a portal." Skye jiggled her arm. Mercy walked off onto the back of the sofa. "What are fatal interventions, Mercy?

"Keeping the secret at all costs, of course. Bless the One Mother."

Myst groaned. "We've gotta hurry."

Ash followed Myst out the door. As he closed it behind him, Mercy called out, "Don't hurt him. Don't hurt him."

They sped through the streets back to the office as the sun began to disappear behind the skyscrapers.

Myst looked up from her phone. "You don't suppose Mort has been counseling his victims' grieving relatives, do you?"

"Wouldn't surprise me." Nothing would surprise Ash anymore about his coworker.

Myst tapped out a text. "I asked Elizabeth to meet us at the bottom of the elevator."

"No time to finesse a sneak-in. I'll risk it and go right to Gray's office. He needs to hear me about Mort. If Mort goes to Tae-wen, we'll need help. Gray will have to release some men from Shadow Force."

E.T. hadn't answered Myst's text and was not there to meet them at the Haven elevator. "I'll go look for Elizabeth. We're going to need her, too. Meet you at Gray's." Myst took off along the hall that offered lapping waves on a sandy shoreline.

Mort must have used another elevator to access the Haven. Ash hadn't detected the empath's energy signature so far, but he kept his senses open. He walked quickly through the main hall past the cafeteria. The over-spiced aroma of vegan pot roast lingered on the air. He'd avoided the Sunday special as vigorously as Fast K's impossible burger.

He kept his head down as he passed through the busy central dining hall and the Magic Arts. A couple of acquaintances called out to him. He raised a hand in greeting but kept walking. He was a wanted man, so someone could raise the alarm at any time. He made it through the Bureau's doors, letting himself into Gray's office, where Mort's energy signature mixed with the Councilman's slammed his receptors. Mort had been in here recently. Why?

Gray stepped in from another room. His nostrils flared. "You have a lot of nerve."

"We've got to stop Mort. He's the killer, not Blakely."

Gray barked out a harsh laugh. "Mort was just here. He told me you've fallen in love with that journalist. You're obsessed. You took her to Tae-wen, and not because I talked about sending her there for good, but thanks. Saves me the trouble."

Had Mort been reporting to Gray all along? "What I feel for Skye is irrelevant. Mort's videos of Blakely are deep fakes. Blakely isn't the killer. Mort is, and he's after Skye."

The door behind Ash opened and two burly security goons entered.

Gray pointed to Ash. "Take him."

A force pitched Ash forward to his knees and brought both arms behind his back. He struggled against the power bindings that wrapped around his wrists like steel bands. Few witches had the magic to break these shackles. "What are you doing? Gray, listen to me. We've got to stop Mort before he goes through a portal." He lurched to his feet.

"Don't be ridiculous. Mort is an empath. He hasn't the will to be anything but. He expressed his sorrow at having to tell me, your father, what you've done. His loyalty to the Bureau won out."

"Elizabeth—"

"Has no say in this!" Gray pounded a fist on the desk. "Her time has long passed. Take him to the cells."

The irony was not lost on Ash when he found himself two cells down from Thomas Blakely just a short while after he'd questioned the man. They'd removed the bindings before shoving him inside. Ash sat on the cot and contemplated the four walls. One wasn't a wall as such, but the clear energy shield.

He lay down on the thin mattress, placing both hands behind his head. Magic would not work inside the cells. He couldn't conjure a better bed or fluffy pillow or cup of coffee. It was probably after eight. Dinner would be over at Flip House. What was Skye doing? Asking questions, dreaming about that publishing prize. Tilting the world on its axis. Both worlds. She'd promised E.T. she wouldn't write about their society. He wanted to believe her. Did believe her. He was letting his feelings cloud better judgement. Trust and love needed to go hand in hand. But he had to get her home first.

Mort hadn't gone through a portal yet. Ash's only hope was that Myst found E.T., and they'd come get him out. He closed his eyes. Gray don't-call-me-dad hadn't hesitated to lock up his only son. Did Gray really condone killing off those who would reveal their secret?

Red snowsuit.

The grim images and the burning pain skewered his heart. He forced his thoughts back to Skye, their night of lovemaking, her wild red hair spread across his chest. Tension eased, muscles relaxed. He'd bring her home.

He awoke to someone shaking his shoulder. *Myst.* "How did you—"

"Shh. Elizabeth put the guards to sleep and opened the wall. Come on. Mort went through a Keeper portal."

His worst fear. He jumped up and rushed out of the cell. At the end of the aisle, E.T. waved for them to hurry. Once through the doors and past the sleeping guards, Ash touched Myst on the sleeve. "What time is it?" They were headed down the deserted Keeper hallways.

"Close to four a.m. We figure Mort went through around two."

"Shit. Mort has a two-hour head start. No time for Shadow Force even if I could convince a couple of them. I go alone."

Myst stopped outside darkened offices, wearing a don't-fight-me-or-I'll-deck-you expression. "I'm going with."

He nodded. There would be no use arguing with her.

"I'll keep Gray in the dark about your disappearance from the cell block, Ash. Go," said E.T. She turned and hurried away.

Ash led Myst deeper into the Keeper wing toward the portal site.

"You sure, Myst? No familiars allowed. It'll be rough. Dangerous. Mort was more your friend than mine."

"I've been to Tae-wen more times than you. So has Mort." Myst closed her eyes for a moment. Her shoulders sagged. A range of emotions flickered across her face. When she opened her eyes, they glistened.

"When we catch up to him, promise you'll let me talk to him. Don't go slicing up his memories. Or worse."

He couldn't make such a promise because he had no idea what he planned to do to stop Mort. Mort wasn't the great empath they knew. He was a killer and would kill again.

Mort's strong, sharp-edged energy overlay the vibes from the portal site as they neared the room. He'd been here and never bothered to fuzz out his signature. Ash prayed. *Let Skye be safe. Bless the One Mother. Keep her safe.*

Chapter Twenty-Two

Skye shifted the porch chair into the light, careful not to spill liquid from the steaming mug. The morning sun tinged the sky above the treetops at the rear of Flip House. She breathed in the air, fresh and still moist from yesterday's rain, bringing with it memories of her and Mom every morning in every campground. They'd stretch out the sleeping bag kinks, inhale the scent of pine so pungent, it tweaked your nose, then hug each other in silent blessings. *Oh Mom, look where I am now.*

Her sigh turned into a deep yawn. She'd slept like shit, alone, wanting Ash's warm body to curl into throughout the night, his lips kissing the purple bruises, making them all better.

Jeez, what a wuss. She counted on this herbed brew to perk her up, bring her back to reality. She sniffed and sipped. Intense flavors of hickory, charred bark, and maybe a few grains of gunpowder. *No one light a match.* It was enough to curl your short ones, as Jo would say. God, she missed old White Fox, and it had only been like three days since she'd texted her with that exploding head emoji.

The back door opened. Gryph came through with a steaming mug and a broad smile. He wore a fresh shirt under a metal-studded leather vest. "May I join you?"

"Sure. Pull up a chair."

He dragged one of the rough-hewn wooden chairs to her side and sat. "I slept as in a rock pile, even though the bed be clouds. What about you?"

"My mind thought I was back in debate class."

"I don't know what that be, but it sounds full of dread. You have many worries."

She sighed and sipped. The liquid main-lined straight to the brain. "I do. Aside from some deranged killer out to murder me, there's another man killing me softly every day."

He chuckled. "You said you hadn't decided on Ash. To be with him. To love him."

"Yeah. I talk a good game, but I can't get him out of mind."

"You mean out of your heart." He fingered the chain at his neck, the ring she'd noticed earlier now hidden beneath his shirt. She was sure he had no idea how many times a day he touched it.

"You're right. But since you mentioned it yesterday, I need to know what the restrictions are, if any, for Reg and mage to be together."

Someone, a man, broke through the nearby brush with a rustle of branches about twenty feet away. Gryph jumped up and moved in front of her. "Who goes there?"

Mort. Skye set her drink down and stood, her heart hammering an oh-God-what-happened-to-Ash tattoo. "What are you doing here? Where's Ash?"

The tall, skinny Keeper staggered toward them. His dark hair hung in damp strings to his shoulders. The home-spun tunic and wrinkled pants were spotted with some kind of gunk.

Gryph rushed down the porch steps and took his

arm. "What happened to you?"

When they reached the porch, Skye pushed a chair under Mort's legs, and he plopped into it. A familiar stench rose up. *Hell creeper.*

"It took me hours to walk from the portal. Didn't come by way of Twilda. Eluded some Malgren Dark Raiders, but I just ran into a creeper. Stupid." Mort took a deep breath, closing his eyes. The fabric of his clothing rippled and changed from neck to ankle. Gone were the wrinkles, the creeper crud, the smell.

"Magic. The miracle of it never fails to astound me," said Gryph.

Amaze and terrify. Skye's nerves twitched. "What's happened to Ash? Why isn't he with you?"

Mort opened his eyes, a tentative smile tilting his mouth. "Don't worry. He's fine. Councilman Gray is holding him, though. He sent me to bring you back to the Haven."

Somehow his words didn't make her feel any better. "What'll happen to him? Is he in big trouble?"

"He's always in trouble. But Thomas Blakely has been charged with murder after a full confession. The danger is over for you, but we should leave now."

Skye wouldn't feel relief until she was in Ash's arms again. "Let's hurry, then. I'll say goodbye to the Flips."

"I go with you to the portal," said Gryph. "I'll get Mort a horse. They'll take us much quicker."

"No." Mort stiffened. Irritation flickered across his face. "I mean, you don't need to come, Gryph. I have magic. I can take care of her."

Gryph's mouth set in a firm line. "Ash entrusted me with her safety. I will see her to the portal."

Mort nodded. "Of course, but horses? I don't ride."

"You'll be fine," said Skye. "With those long legs, you can't fall off."

Skye found Freya in the kitchen seeing to breakfast. A dozen eggs spluttered in a skillet alongside strips of bacon. The familiar aroma was comforting. She gave the Faen a big hug that dislodged her glasses.

"What's this, eh?" Freya held her close.

Skye pulled back. "I came to say goodbye. Mort is here to take me to the portal with Gryph. Ash's dad, the head of Security, is keeping him, but I'm out of danger."

"A relief. You can stay for breakfast, surely."

"No. We're leaving now."

"I shall miss you. You must return to us."

Guilt jabbed at her soul. "I'd like that." She drew in a shaky breath. "Thank you for helping us, for your hospitality."

Eldrin strode into the kitchen. "I need food, my lovely." He stopped. "Oh, I am interrupting."

Skye pulled free from Freya's arms and wiped an eye. "I was just saying goodbye. Mort is here to take me home."

"He is? Ash is—"

"In trouble again," said Freya. She wrapped some pastries, setting them in a small sack that she handed to Skye.

Eldrin nodded. "I hope to see you again, Miss Skye."

She hugged the burly Faen, who smelled like vanilla-flavored pipe tobacco. "I hope under different circumstances." She let go. "Gryph is getting the horses."

"I'll come to see you off. I haven't seen Mort in a while," Eldrin said. "You go and I'll bring some water flasks out."

Freya turned a few eggs over with an expert flip of a spatula. "I must stay. Min won't be here for a bit. Safe travels, and, Skye, may you find trust and love."

Skye's eyes teared as she went through the great room to the back door. A grim-faced Mort stood when she stepped onto the porch. He must have worked more cleanup magic on himself. "Damn. You look a lot better than you did a few minutes ago."

"I confess that I took a sip from your mug. That stuff would revive a zombie."

Eldrin came through the door carrying three flasks with looped leather handles. "Mort, 'tis great to see you, my man. You do a good thing here today." He set the flasks on the small table. He grabbed Mort's arm and moved in for a half hug. "You and Gryph take the best care of Miss Skye."

Mort nodded. "We don't need Gryph. He should stay."

Why doesn't Mort want Gryph with them? Pride?

"He will not be staying behind. Might fix your mind to it." Eldrin clapped him on the shoulder. "You know how he is."

Hmm. Friction between Gryph and Mort. The man in question came around the corner of the building leading Bings' chestnut and a buckskin with a flowing black mane and tail that touched the ground. Patch followed behind like an obedient puppy. Skye stepped off the porch.

"Found a pretty one for you, Skye. Her name's Fallon." Gryph held the buckskin's reins out to her.

"Thanks, but I like Bings' horse. Me and chonky boy built a rapport." She handed Gryph the sack of pastries and hugged the big animal around the neck. "I'll call him Chunk."

"Suits 'im," said Eldrin. "Tie a flask to each saddle." He gave one to each of them.

Mort's face squeezed out another smile, but his shoulders remained rigid. He wasn't happy he was left with the "pretty" horse, or a horse at all. Something else was going on besides this ride and Gryph. Skye couldn't put a finger on it.

"Thank you, Eldrin," Mort said. "How's the baby? Last time I saw the precious little he was newborn."

Right. Mort's an empath. Skye shook off her unease. Ash trusted the guy. She needed to start following Freya's last words of advice. She tucked loose strands of hair back into the low ponytail that hid her ears.

"Alain is full of piss and farts and is the light of my life."

Everyone laughed. Skye accepted a leg up from Gryph, and the three said their final goodbyes before turning to Twilda Road. She settled into the rhythm of the horse's easy walk as she followed Gryph past Eldrin's field. Mort trailed behind, shifting in the saddle, and fussing with the stirrups. He tugged the broad-brimmed hat Eldrin had given him down over his ears. She couldn't make out his muttered words. Likely cursing Gryph and the horse he rode in on.

Gryph touched heels to Patch. They were off at a lope. She turned her head to watch Mort bounce like a paddle ball toy while holding tight to the saddle horn. Fallon refused to canter until finally she was too far behind and broke into a dead run to catch up. The horse swept by Chunk and Patch. Mort's hat flew off into a field while Fallon's long mane whipped in Mort's face. The only thing holding him to the saddle was his long legs.

Gryph caught up to him, grabbing a rein. They slowed to a walk. She couldn't hear their exchange, but she guessed it was spirited by Mort's mottled face and Gryph's huge grin.

Things settled down, and they lined up again as before. Matching grays pulled a wagon past them, the Faen driver tipping his hat. A lone rider cantered by. The heat rose with the sun, chasing the goosebumps. If only Ash had come to get her. Why was his dad holding him? They had to let her see him when she returned. What would they do with *her*? Most importantly, what were the consequences of a witch marrying a Reg? Just wondering.

Her life had become a series of questions. It had always been her job to find the answers, good or bad.

Gryph pulled up his horse. "We turn onto this trail. Still looks muddy from the rain, so be careful. 'Tis not called Dead Man's for no reason."

He led the way, keeping to the right of middle, where a thin stream of water trickled. The trail, hemmed in by thick trees and brush, ascended gradually. Skye turned in the saddle. "Mort, how did Ash look when you saw him last?"

"Mad as hell at Gray. Anxious to get you back home. It killed him that he couldn't come himself."

"I bet. Was he in his office or Gray's?"

"Uh, Gray's. We were telling the Councilman that it was safe to bring you home. But Gray wouldn't let

Ash go. He'll probably get off lightly, anyway, for all the infractions, especially with Elizabeth Trowbridge vouching for him."

"What will they do with me when I get back?" Visions of some dark dungeon where she couldn't even remember her name sent a shiver up her spine. Banishment to Tae-wen? Well, the place didn't hold the horror it once did now that she'd been here, had fallen in love with the people and the creatures. Hell creeper aside.

"I don't honestly know unless Elizabeth can work her persuasive magic on the whole Council. They will be involved, not just Gray."

She'd better convince *herself* she'd never reveal the witches to the world nor write the Big Story if she had any hope of convincing the Council of her sincerity. If keeping her own life as she knew it came to pleading her case, could she lie as smoothly and convincingly as Ash seemed to do? Maybe it wouldn't be a lie.

The trees had thinned, the ascent steeper. The trail, curving left, came perilously close to the edge of a sheer precipice. A sea of trees and rocks undulated in the gorge hundreds of feet below. The horses plodded on, heads low and bobbing, unconcerned with sheer death a misstep away.

"Hold up," said Mort. "I need to go. Forgot before we left."

Gryph drew up Patch. "Here? Wait till we get back into the thick trees."

But Mort had already clumsily dismounted. Gryph shot him an annoyed glance as he turned Patch, so his back was to the Keeper. She did the same.

Sizzle—bang! A flash of light blasted by her, knocking Gryph from his horse. Chunk snorted and reared, but she hung on. Rocks slipped out from under his hooves.

The edge—where's the edge?

"Mort!" Skye hung on as Chunk pranced. "What the hell?"

Gryph got to his knees, shaking his head. Mort stood with hands outstretched. His face contorted. He mouthed some words she couldn't hear. Another flash slammed into Gryph's back. He disappeared over the edge.

My god. "Gryph!" *What's happening?* "Mort— why?" Her voice croaked as her throat seized.

Mort turned those lethal hands her way. She dug both heels into Chunk's flank. She kept kicking as Chunk surged up the trail.

Sizzle. A blast blew by her into the trees. She rode low over his neck with a loose rein. Thank God the well-muscled horse had sure-footedness to spare. She turned him into the woods off the main trail onto a narrow, rock-strewn path. Where were Patch and Fallon? Hopefully both horses had taken off, leaving Mort on foot.

Her heart hammered, matching Chunk's gallop as she charged through the woods. She gulped air. *Get control.*

Mort killed Gryph.

She squeezed her eyes shut. Gryph, full of honor and bravery and pain. Not trusting the world. Now he was gone. Tears streamed down her face.

Mort was the killer after all. Ash hadn't sent him, or at least, didn't know his friend, a fellow Keeper, was the one behind the murders.

A crack sounded behind her. She turned to look. *Wham*. A sharp pain slammed her head. The world went dark.

Chapter Twenty-Three

Ash hurried along the kuda trail with only the moon as a guide, dawn a mere suggestion. Myst followed, a knitted cap tugged over her ears, water flask tied to the belt of the Faen clothing.

"This is where I caused an earthquake and scared a couple of Malgren shitless. We shouldn't see any here, at least."

"Do you still detect Mort's energy?"

"Faint. He might have taken a nearby trail." He balled his hands into fists.

"We'll get him. Don't worry."

His opti-Myst on the job. If only they had horses. It was too much to hope that they'd come across Patch. Gryph's horse had probably trotted back to Moonstone as soon as he'd released the animal.

The woods smelled ripe and rich after the rain, but still heavy with humidity. Soon he was drenched in sweat. He avoided the puddles when he could see them. Myst splashed close behind while keeping up a steady stream of positive self-talk for the next hour. The sky lightened, making the going easier.

Crashing sounds back in the trees had them moving into the brush and crouching. Ash held a finger to his lips. He mouthed the word *Malgren.* Myst nodded. A riderless white horse thundered past them trailing vaporous energy, then more swept by single file on the narrow trail, eyes wide, nostrils flared, snorting and grunting. Ash held an arm up to deflect the wet clods of dirt that their hooves kicked up.

Myst's breath caught on a whispered "Unicorns."

The wild beauty of the beasts dazzled him. He'd never seen them on any of his trips to Tae-wen. He nodded. "Malgren are hunting them. Listen."

Distant shouting—*this way. Catch the stallion.*

Ash counted ten mares. A trumpeting call reverberated through the trees from another direction. "Sigil. He's leading the Malgren away from his mares."

"We'd make a better catch." Before he could stop her, she stood and shouted. "Over here."

"Get down. Are you crazy?" Her damn love of animals would get them killed, or worse, nulled. He stood.

She tossed her ear-hiding cap, waving her arms as she moved along the trail toward the Malgren, who had gone quiet.

"Myst. Stop."

But she continued, collecting flowers that held butterflies, then directing them to float in front of her. She sent a shaft of light zinging along the trail. "Goddess where are you?" she called in a loud, sing-song voice.

"Gah." Ash strode after her and grabbed her arm. "You *are* crazy."

"Halt," a piercing, high-pitched voice commanded.

He turned, keeping Myst from the guy's sight. He held his hands out palms up. And groaned. This was one of the Malgren from the Dark Raiders he'd encountered before when he'd made the earth move. Dilly, wasn't it? The Malgren was on foot, unafraid now that he had the gang with him, but were some on horseback? He bristled with sharp metal points on leather straps crisscrossing a narrow chest, knife in hand, quiver of arrows slung over a shoulder.

"We are Faen. Lost in this forest." Ash amped his power.

"Eh, I knows you," Dilly said. "Where's yer pretty horse?"

Myst stepped out. Her short hair fully exposing rounded ears. "*I* am not." She directed the stream of light full of flowers and butterflies to swirl in the air between them, then waved them away.

Dilly gasped. "Witch."

Ash removed his cap. "We both are. We come in peace. If you don't turn around, leave us, we can—"

"Turn you into a pig," said Myst. She wiggled her fingers at Dilly.

The bushes erupted in movement as many men, bristling with weapons, stepped onto the trail in front and behind them. There had to be over thirty of them. Myst wheeled, pressing her back to Ash's. *Protect the neck from Malgrens' nulling hands.* The men left a ten-foot circle of space around them. Some nocked arrows in bows.

Shit. There would be no way out of this without some destructive magic. The potential to harm a Malgren became almost a certainty, killing not an option. *Bless the One Mother.*

"Plan?" said Myst through her teeth.

"The usual."

"Right. No plan."

"Shut up." One of the men bulldozed his way past the others, pushing Dilly out of way. He was big as an earth mover. "We are too many for you and your stupid magic."

"I seen 'er magic. A streak of light shot from 'er hands. Butterflies—"

"Sunbeams? Butterflies? Oh, I'm trembling, Dil." The big guy threw his head back and laughed. The rest glanced at each other, snickering nervously.

Some might have been with Blaise in the past, a rogue witch banished to Tae-wen. They might have seen some powerful magic and know their leader should be afraid. Very afraid.

"Because of you, we lost the unicorns." He waved a beefy arm to his troops. Take them."

"Low blasts, low energy," said Ash as Myst pulled away from his back.

He crouched, throwing his hands forward. An arc of brilliant light shot toward the advancing men. The ground exploded at their feet. They jumped back, bumping into each other. Myst had done the same in her direction. They turned in a circle. The steady spray of explosive energy blasted low to the ground, hitting trees, bushes, men's legs. They howled in pain. Some let arrows fly. Ash dodged and deflected. Didn't have time to check on Myst.

A loud buzzing filling the air soon became deafening. "What the hell are those?" Myst pointed to a spot between the trees.

"Dragonites. Elizabeth's pets I accidentally awakened."

The creatures swarmed the men, fingers of fire singeing heads, shoulders, and arms. The Malgren ran howling from the horde of tiny flame throwers.

One buzzed in front of Ash's face. *"To thank you*

for awakening us."

"Tarig."

The creature flew off to join the rest of his kind harassing the fleeing horde. The trail cleared ahead of him. He glanced behind. No one. "Come on."

He tugged on Myst's sleeve and took off running along the trail. She followed, turning often to shoot a burst of energy into the ground behind them.

The trail had been churned up by the unicorns' hooves, making tough slogging. After fifteen minutes at a stumbling jog, he stopped to listen.

"I don't hear them." Sweat beaded Myst's forehead and upper lip. She smiled. "You're lucky E.T. didn't kill you. Dragonites. Awesome." She groaned, winced, pressed a hand to her side.

"What's wrong?"

She removed the hand. Blood. "What the hell?"

"Lift your shirt."

She tugged on the fabric. A shallow red line slashed across her skin.

"I hope that's from a thorn, not an arrow." He bent to examine the wound. Inflammation crept outwards from the slash, sending lethal tendrils of fire along capillaries. He sucked in a breath.

"What?"

"Poison."

"No. No-no-no." She clenched her fists.

"We'll go back. Through the portal—"

"No, we keep moving. We've got to catch up to Mort. Get Skye." She took a drink from the flask.

"The poison will spread, Myst. It's usually fatal." The choices were agonizing—get Myst help through the portal or press on to Skye. He even thought of the

Witch Whisperer's portal, take her to Willow the healer, but it was even farther away. Besides, he'd sealed that portal last year.

Myst made the decision for him. She pushed past and marched along the path toward the main trail that led to Twilda Road.

He followed as the morning sun crept higher, steam rising from wet leaves. The trees, the underbrush thinned out. They were getting close to the main trail. Myst's steps slowed, her breathing labored. He should have insisted they turn back.

He heard what sounded like a horse's snort. Malgren? He touched Myst's shoulder. They crouched behind a straggly, thorn infested bush. Hardly good cover. Sweat beaded on her flushed face. The poison was taking its toll. He prayed to the One Mother to save her. She took a drink from the flask.

Maybe that wasn't a Malgren on a horse. Maybe it was a unicorn. The stallion could heal. He stayed her with a hand and snuck out from the brush. Crouching low, he crept along the trail. In a small clearing to his left, a brown horse cropped the tough grass. Not Sigil or one of his mares.

Wait. Bings' horse. The big chestnut. What was it doing here alone, all saddled and…

"Myst, come here."

The horse raised its head, looked at him while chewing a tuft of grass.

Myst came beside him. "Cool. Equine Uber is here."

Her shoulders slumped, she looked like shit, yet she could make funny.

"This is the horse Skye and I rode." Ash

approached the animal with a hand outstretched. "Good boy." He patted the soft nose with the wiry hairs. "Where's your rider, eh?" No hint of Mort's energy. He picked up a trailing rein while Myst stumbled over to pat its neck.

It flicked an ear. A torn ear. "Look, the ear has been seared." He gently pulled down the horse's head.

"From a dragonite maybe?"

"The damage is too large. More like an energy blast. The rider had been under attack." The possibilities, each more frightening than the last, tore through his mind, twisting his gut.

"There's nothing in this clearing. Let's go. We'll be faster on horseback." Myst held her side. "Don't give me that look. I'm doing—lousy, but I'm still breathing."

Ash mounted, then helped her struggle up behind him. She groaned. He remembered the last time on this horse, with Skye snuggled close. Was that only two days ago? Heat from Myst's hands scorched his sides. If she hugged, he'd go up in flames. He turned the chestnut onto the trail, every sense attuned to the surroundings, listening with ears, nerves and magic antennae.

He wanted to dig in his heels, tear along the trail shouting Skye's name, but he needed to focus. No more Malgren surprise attacks on his watch. Or Mort's sudden malevolent magic. No one was nearby judging by the high whistling call of a bird and chatter of squirrel-like creatures in a nearby tree. He remained vigilant.

Myst's groan was long, low, and filled with suppressed pain.

"You need to drink," he said.

Her body sagged against his. Despite the fever heat, he drew her arms tighter so she wouldn't fall off. "Myst, stay awake."

"I'm okay." Her voice shook.

Shit. She needed help. He couldn't lose her. He urged the big horse into a faster pace on the uneven path, ducking under low-hanging branches. The noise of the outsized hooves sucking through mud twitched his nerves. Maybe Skye had been hit by a blast while riding Bings' horse.

No. Focus.

The horse snorted, tossing its head. Ash brought the animal to a stop and listened, amping his senses. Something rustled in the brush ahead. An animal? *There, by the tree. Something big. No tingle of energy. Not mage.*

"Come out. Keep your hands high," he called.

A figure stumbled out from behind the tree. The horse startled. It was all he could do to keep Myst from slipping off.

"Ash. Omigod. Ash."

Skye. Relief was a shot of Xanax. Mud-soaked clothes. Hair caked with blood. The twisted, wire-rimmed glasses barely hung onto her ears.

"You okay?" He needed to touch her. Crush her to him. Never let her go. He couldn't dismount with Myst clinging like a desperate nettle.

She nodded. "I escaped Mort, but a branch knocked me off Chunk. Don't know where Mort is now." With a shaking hand, she swiped at blood trickling down a cheek. "He told me you were being held by Gray."

"I was, but E.T. and Myst broke me out."

"Mort said you'd asked him to come to Tae-wen to bring me back." She worked at twisting the glasses into shape.

"A lie. The bastard." Anger surged through him, settling a toxic mix of chemicals in his gut.

Tears tinged with blood dripped watery red from Skye's chin. "And, Ash, Mort killed Gryph. Blasted him over the edge at the gorge."

"No." He set aside the wave of black rage that swept through him, setting fire to his blood. He would grieve for his friend later. Right now, his focus was on Myst and Skye. Then he would go after Mort and kill him.

Chapter Twenty-Four

"Help me with Myst. Poison from an arrow." He loosened a fist that clutched his shirt. At least she had some strength left. Skye reached both hands up to Myst while he threw a leg over the pommel and slid down. They both eased Myst off the horse onto a soft bed of weeds to one side of the path. A creek burbled through the trees somewhere nearby. Good. They'd need lots of water.

Ash crouched beside Myst. He lifted her shirt. Fingers of red infection had spread outward from the wound.

Skye touched the flushed forehead. "She's burning up." She pulled the flask from Myst's belt and held it to her lips.

Myst took a few sips and coughed. "Yeah. Not feeling so good now," she said. "Good to see you, Skye." Her smile was weak, red-rimmed eyes glazing over.

"I wish I had healing powers." Ash had never felt more helpless.

"Healing powers. Didn't you say unicorns could heal?" asked Skye.

"The stallion can. He's the one with the horn. Did you see him?"

"A herd of white horses galloped by here earlier. I don't know if one of them had a horn or not. I jumped out of the way."

"They could be miles away by now." Had Sigil caught up to his mares?

As if desperation could summon, a horse walked out from the trees. A spiraled horn protruded through the long forelock. *Sigil*. The animal approached them, an invisible aura of energy shimmering around him as he tossed his head. The big chestnut neighed and pawed the ground nearby.

"Magnificent. The horn." Skye plopped onto the grass, mouth open. "That mane and tail."

Both trailed the ground, having never seen clippers. Ash rubbed the soft muzzle and wiry hairs, the skin phosphorescing under his fingers. He couldn't interpret any message from the mage creature like he could from some others, but when he patted the neck, sizzling energy fired his senses.

The chestnut whinnied. Two horses took tentative steps out of the trees, following Sigil. A *buckskin and Patch. Oh, Gryph.* A fresh grief swamped him.

Myst moaned.

"Does it know what to do? Have you…" Skye cradled Myst's head. She tried to get her to drink.

Ash's focus returned to the living, and Sigil. "Can you, big guy?"

Sigil walked to Skye. He lowered his head, the spiral horn coming within inches of Myst's wound. A low, rumbly nicker issued from his throat.

"Maybe Myst should touch the horn." Skye lifted Myst's limp hand, wrapping it around the horn.

Sigil went still. The animal's energy spiked, buffeting Ash's senses in waves. Myst moaned. Within moments, her face lost its scarlet flush. The fingers of infection began disappearing, the wound closing.

Ash crouched and felt her forehead. "Cooling down."

Skye still held Myst's hand on the horn. "I have no words."

Ash wanted to crush Skye to him. Skye, face bloodied, dirt-streaked, glasses crooked. He'd put her through all this chaos.

Sigil pulled away slowly from Myst's hand. She opened red-rimmed eyes, the glaze of fever gone. "Unicorn," she said, smiling. "Now that's cool."

"Yes, a unicorn." Relief nearly knocked Ash on his ass.

"It's so good to have you back, Myst. I'll get more water. I hear a stream." Skye grabbed the flask and headed into the trees.

Sigil walked back through the brush. The forest swallowed him up.

Ash scooted closer, tipping his flask so Myst could drink the final dribbles. "We can thank the One Mother for summoning Sigil."

"Already did." Myst rose on one elbow. "I hate that I'm so weak."

"Give it time. We have Skye now. We'll leave Mort to his fate."

"Won't work. Let's find him, then deal with him."

Another energy signal tickled his senses. "Wait. Stay put."

He jumped to his feet. The signal was muted like it came from a distance, or deliberately suppressed. A witch, not some other mage creature, moved in the woods. He sorted through the vibrations.

Mort.

A muffled shout came from the same direction.

"Skye!" He took off at a run toward the creek, scattering the horses. He should have noticed she'd been gone too long. *Stupid.* Mort would kill her.

The flask lay on the ground by the creek where a rush of water tumbled over rocks.

"Don't come any closer." About twenty feet away, Mort held Skye in front of him, face gone feral. He'd tied her hands with power bindings. She tried to speak but nothing came out.

Searing rage boiled up Ash's chest. "Let her go."

"I'll stop her heart. You know I can."

Ash detected Mort's energy powering up. He did the same.

"Don't try to wipe my memories. It'll take you too long. I'll sense your attempt."

Mort was right. "Then what? You'll kill me like you did Gryph and all the others? Why? Reverence for life, Mort. The One Mother oath."

Every emotion flashed across Mort's face before it crumpled. His thin shoulders slumped. "What good will that oath be when we're found out? At best we'll be lab rats. At worst"—his voice cracked—"exterminated."

"Not going to happen. We're Keepers. We keep the secret as we have been, without violence."

Mort's eyes welled with tears. "But it's getting so hard. This one"—he stabbed a finger at her—"she'll write her damn story."

Skye shook her head and tried to speak again.

"She won't. Let her talk."

"I saw on her computer what she's written. Read her mother's files."

"You were born an empath, Mort." Ash focused a

low hit of magic on Skye's bindings. "Let her talk. Please."

Tears trickled down Mort's sallow cheeks. "You love her, don't you?"

"Yes. She's everything to me."

She stood bravely, chin up, then she smiled at him. His heart did a flip.

Skye cleared her throat and half turned to look at Mort. "Thanks, Mort. In spite of all the damn secrecy, in spite of all the lies he's told me, I've fallen in love with Ash. I would never do anything to harm him or your society."

Was she telling the truth? She loved him? *Focus.* Another hit on the bindings. Skye should realize they'd become loose.

Mort swiped at his wet cheeks.

"When did you know you were an empath?" asked Skye, her voice still rough.

"I—what? When I got my powers."

"How did it make you feel?"

Ash took a few steps closer.

"Terrible. So much suffering."

"How did you possibly cope with those feelings?" Her face softened.

"I had to help the anguished. Mage or Reg, it didn't matter."

"But something changed. You've killed people."

Ash moved closer. *Why doesn't she step away?*

"I had to. How could I keep helping the ones who needed me most if we were found out? I agonize over my actions. I try to counsel the families of the fallen."

Ash shook his head. Mort would give comfort to his victim's families. *Twisted.*

"You were the one who broke into Ash's place, right?" Skye's voice remained gentle.

Mort nodded.

"My friend Hetty, and my mother, Diana Parker. Did you kill them?" Those words were said with deadly calm.

Mort touched her arm. "I'm sorry. So sorry. She—both of you—"

Skye smashed her body into Mort's, grabbed his arm and flipped him face-first onto the ground. She was on him, pinning Mort, twisting an arm behind his back before Ash could react.

She could have warned him somehow. Ash lunged forward. "Get out of the way!"

Mort surged upward, then twisted. Skye tumbled off with a shout. Mort stood and directed a power arc that sent her flying backwards.

Ash glanced at Skye slumped on the ground. She groaned, holding her shoulder. She was alive. He grabbed Mort by the shirt front and shook him like a mad dog shakes a rat. "I should have killed you while you blubbered like a baby."

"I wish you could," Mort rasped. "But you can't."

"Can't I?" Ash shoved him away and stood in front of Skye.

Ash raised an arm. He called on the magic. A searing white blast of energy rocketed from his palm. Slam. Mort staggered backward. A roar blasted through Ash's body and rushed his ears, flashing random images on the brain. Bodies of the dead. Myst. Skye, bloodied, lying in agony. He threw out another hit. A return volley punched Ash's chest like a sledgehammer. Breath left him in a whoosh. He gulped in air. Someone shouting his name through the ringing in his head. *Skye. This—ends—now.*

A powerful energy crackled through his body, sizzling along nerves, sparking through his fingertips. He blinked trying to clear his vision as he summoned the darkest of his magic.

A body slammed into Mort. They both went down as Ash's deadly bolt went wide. The two wrestled.

Ash took several running steps forward. "Gryph! Stop!"

Gryph held Mort in a choke hold. The Keeper gasped for air, his arms pinned by the hefty Malgren. Mort went limp.

Ash left them and rushed to Skye. He crouched, helping her sit back against a tree. "How bad is it?" Lines of pain creased her face. He was afraid to touch her when all he wanted to do was hold her, feel her warm body, feel her heartbeats close to his.

"Like I got hit in a Kevlar vest by a shotgun blast." She sucked in a shallow breath through her teeth.

"I'm not even going to ask how you would know that." He brushed the hair back from her face.

"I'll be—ugh—fine."

"Hey, mage. Over here." Gryph released Mort, who lay prone, gasping while tears streamed down his face.

Ash approached them. "What the hell were you thinking, Gryph? I had him."

"I needed to pummel the bugger a bit. He sent me over the gorge. Luckily, I landed on a ledge." He rubbed his chest. Deep scratches crisscrossed his cheeks. "And, my mage friend, I could not let you kill."

Ash went still. Yes, that last amped volley would

have killed Mort. He was no better than Mort, worse than Mort—willing to kill in fevered anger and a lust for revenge.

Forgive me, One Mother. He'd been willing to betray Her. The pain of this weakness lodged a sharp thorn deep in his soul to lay alongside another.

A low keening sound came from Mort. He sat up with both arms wrapped around his middle.

Ash grimaced. "How badly did I hurt him?"

"*You* didn't. *I* took away his magic."

"You what? No. Magic is who we are."

"Before you incinerate me, it might be temporary. I don't know."

"Shit."

"He's alive, is he not? He can no longer hurt Skye, or any of us. At least till my nulling wears off. If it ever does," he added under his breath.

"I may thank you someday." Ash clamped a hand on Gryph's shoulder.

Mort's low moans morphed into wails. Gryph put both hands over his ears. "You can thank me by making him stop. Use your magic."

Ash ignored the request, binding Mort's hands behind his back with power bindings, just glad he'd been stopped from…

He turned to Skye, who rose unsteadily to her feet. "Are you okay? I need to check on Myst."

She nodded. "Go."

"Myst? She's here?" Gryph rushed to his side. "Where?"

"Back through these trees. She got hit with a poisoned arrow—"

He took off calling Myst's name before Ash could

finish.

Skye smiled. "Gryph has a thing for Myst."

"He would never admit it to himself or her. I'll let him see to her." He pulled Skye close in a gentle hug. "*I* need to see to *you*," he whispered into her hair, taking from her a comfort he so badly needed.

"Are *you* okay?" She wrapped her arms around him. "You're looking like we lost the battle."

He pulled back and whispered, "I would have killed him."

Her face went soft. "You were saving our lives."

He nodded but knew there was more to it than kill or be killed. There was no fear, just that mind-blasting roar of anger fueling the uncontrollable urge to end Mort.

She brushed a hand across his forehead, trailing light fingers down his cheek. "You were trying to save *me*, but no worries now. Smile. I'm good."

Her gentle touch eased his mind. Maybe she could mesmer. "You're more than good. You're impressive. And crazy."

"I know." She kissed him, a lingering touch of lips that sent a jolt of heat straight through him. "I love you."

"I heard. I love you, too."

"But?"

"Let's talk later. When we're back home."

Home. Where reality would sink in damn quick. Where she'd hear his "but" and probably add her own. He was mage. She was Reg. Maybe she wouldn't want him after she learned about the rules. He'd face the consequences of his actions deep within himself and with the Council, where the bigger question would be

Skye. Did she have her irrefutable proof? Would she write her story that would reveal their existence? The Council would never give her that chance.

And he had to find a way to accept the fact he was capable of killing. Accept the fact that he was closer to being his father's son than he ever thought possible.

Chapter Twenty-Five

Ash landed on his side on the floor along with Mort, whose hands were still bound behind his back. Skye and Myst tumbled through the vortex after them. The Keeper portal room was empty. He stood, grabbing Mort by the arm, lifting him to his feet where he balanced on two wobbly legs. The empath's eyes were glazed over, his head downcast. He would be in shock over the loss of his powers. He gave off no energy signature. Ash was glad he felt some sympathy for the man he'd wanted to kill a few short hours ago. He hoped Gryph hadn't permanently erased Mort's powers.

Ash focused on the women. "Are you two all right?" They'd had a rough time in Tae-wen as well.

Myst staggered to stand. "Nothing a twelve-hour nap won't cure."

"I'm good. I'll inventory my bruises later." Skye shot him a saucy glance while holding onto Myst's arm.

Yeah. He'd be glad to do that for her, then kiss every one of them better. He closed the portal churning away on the back wall.

Elizabeth strode through the door, shutting behind her, filling the space with her powerful vibe. "By the One Mother, you all look like you've been through the tortures. You have Mort."

Ash gave her the short version of the happenings in Tae-wen, the capture of Mort, Gryph's near death, and the nulling of Mort's magic. His chest tightened. He left out the part where he would have killed the man in a blind rage if it weren't for Gryph.

Skye got up in Mort's face. "He deserves to lose his magic. He killed my mother and my friend Hetty." Rising color blotched her face. Fists clenched, she let out a breath before turning away.

"Mort." E.T. lifted his chin with a finger. He raised bleak eyes a moment before lowering them again. He'd shrunk in height, jaw and shoulders slack. "I'm sorry your magic was taken away. Perhaps that would have been your fate in any case." She turned to the women. "Myst, take him to a cell. My cousin, Dickson, is manning the desk. Ash, Skye, come with me. The halls are busy, so stick close."

"Will do," Myst said. "Afterward, I'll go to Mort's place. His familiar, Mercy, will need a lot of comforting."

Ash would have liked to throw Mort into a cell and see to the release of Blakely himself. Myst hauled Mort by the arm out of the room.

Ash waved a hand over Skye. Jeans and a long-sleeved blue t-shirt appeared on her body, a pair of black sneakers on her feet.

"Thank God. I couldn't wait to get out of those funky Faen clothes." Skye pulled her hair back, twisting the whole mess into a braid. She tried to straighten the wavy wire frame of the glasses, but only made them wonkier. She managed to fit them over her ears. "These glasses have been through a lot."

"They have, right along with you." Ash fought the pull of her. The overwhelming desire to hot kiss her until the glasses fogged over. Instead, he concentrated on changing his clothing into jeans and a t-shirt.

"Take Skye to your place, Elizabeth. We'll talk later about our misadventures in Tae-wen, including Tarig and the dragonites saving our asses. I'm going directly to Gray's office."

E.T. shook her head. "Wait, look what happened to you just yesterday when you went to talk to your father. I should—"

"No. He has to listen to me this time."

"Elizabeth's right. He threw you in a cell." Skye touched his arm. "And, every time you leave me, shit happens. I don't want to lose you."

She didn't want to lose him. Her words hugged his heart. He set control aside, pulled her close, wrapped his arms around her. The warmth of her body seeped through to the frazzled nerves. "You won't lose me. We won't lose each other," he whispered.

He looked at E.T. over Skye's head. She raised both eyebrows and pursed her lips. He got the message. The rules. The damn rules for Reg and mage. Rules he'd kept from Skye. Maybe he was making promises he couldn't keep.

"We'd better go." He released Skye, avoiding her eyes.

E.T. took Skye one way while he headed along the Keeper wing hallway in the opposite direction. He got lucky in the halls, only passing a couple of people, but the common areas bustled with traffic. He kept his head down, making it to Gray's office without anyone shouting for security.

His dad's energy signature spilled through the closed door, and then his voice in a shout. "Get the hell in here!"

This should be good. Ash strode through the door. Gray sat behind the ornate desk wearing a scowl and the damn ritual vest. He didn't have the courtesy to lower his powerful vibe. Ash didn't, either.

"Just got off the phone with Elizabeth. She said you caught Mortimer Payne in Tae-wen after he got ahold of Skye Parker. He's heading for a cell."

Ash sat in one of the plush chairs in front of the desk. "It was a group effort. Gryph Kazlo, our Malgren informant, nulled Mort's powers while we fought." He leaned forward. "Mort confessed. He's our killer, not Blakely."

Gray steepled his fingers. "I'll convene the Council. There isn't precedence for dealing with a mass murderer."

"Why didn't you believe me before when I told you he was the one?"

"How could I? I couldn't reconcile the fact that murders had even been committed, never mind by one mage, an empath. Add to that, you didn't keep me informed as I demanded."

"I didn't trust you. I thought you condoned the murders to keep our secrecy."

Gray rose from the chair. "I would *never* sanction murder." He straightened, shaking his head. "You can't let go of that child twenty years ago, can you? I—could—not—save—that—kid!"

Red snowsuit. He shut his eyes against the heavy pain that sat on his chest, one he'd carried forever. The child in the air. The thud as the small, limp body hit the pavement. The screech of tires. Crash of metal. The scream. His.

Dad, once his hero, turning away.

A hand touched Ash's shoulder. He opened his eyes. Gray stood next to him, suddenly looking ancient and haggard as if the weight and the fate of the world hung on his shoulders.

"I need to tell you something, Son, something I haven't told a living soul. Not even your mother."

Ash stood, a confused jumble of questions rolling around in his mind.

"My powers are—unreliable."

"Unreliable? What are you talking about?"

His dad paced. "My powers came in strongly Elite as expected in my teens. But then, in later years, I couldn't summon magic every time I called for it. Maybe I'm one of those mages whose magic spoiled, broke, like many others we're hearing about." He stopped and ran a hand down his face as if he could erase the years, the memories that had etched themselves in every worry line. "That day on the street, I couldn't summon a spark of magic."

"No. You're lying."

"If you think that, then I've hidden my inadequacies successfully."

Ash couldn't make his limbs work while he thought back to years of living with this man, with his magic, with his—excuses. Yes, there were times when his dad refused to use magic in one instance or another. Inconsequential commands, like putting out a fire in the barbecue, summoning lost keys, hanging up a jacket that had fallen off a hook. Soul-shattering things, like letting a child die.

Because he didn't have the magic.

"You let me believe all this time that you were—"

"A monster? Better than the alternative—a fraud, a

failure. No familiar would bond with me. Half the mage I let on to be. Not fit to be a leader."

Ash forced his legs to move. He stepped back, away from the man he thought he knew. That child's death had informed Ash's life. Made him passionate to help mage and Reg alike regardless of the consequences. Led him to accepting the role of Keeper so he could fix his own PDMs while he tried to save people. He'd need time, a long time, to process what his dad had confessed. To forgive.

Then the thought slammed him like a line drive— he, Ash, had tried to kill someone, end a life. He doubted he could ever forgive *himself*.

But right now, he needed to focus on Skye. "When will the Council convene? I want to know that when I take Skye out of here, she won't be hunted down by your goons."

Gray let out a breath. "You love her, don't you?"

"Whether I love her or not is irrelevant to the question of her freedom."

"I can't say what the Council majority will decide, but probably they'll want her memories erased before release over sending her permanently to Tae-wen. Elizabeth and I are only two votes out of eleven."

"Neither alternative is acceptable. Make sure the option of release with promise not to reveal us is on the table. With that, I agree to have my powers nulled. Add these stipulations or I'll tell the Council you're a fraud."

"I can't—"

Ash rounded on him, balling his hands into fists. "You will!"

"How can you know she won't reveal us to the world?"

"I trust her."

Ash *did* trust her, but how to convince a skeptical Council would take some work.

****

Elizabeth sent Skye right to her room to freshen up as soon as she opened the door to her place, saying Blunt would make them a soothing tea. The aroma of baking bread followed Skye along the hall. Her stomach rumbled. She'd missed Freya's sizzling breakfast this morning.

She picked up the folded denim shirt that someone had placed on the bed. Maybe Blunt put her clothes there. No one could have seen the button camera, or the reception she'd gotten would have been very different.

On the ride to the portal, hugging tight to Ash's warm body, listening to Myst and Gryph hide their attraction to each other, she'd decided she was done. Done waffling like an IHOP between writing the story and keeping silent. She would *not* write the story. Wouldn't reveal to the world that a society of witches lived among them. She'd hold this secret in a corner of her heart. Ash took up the rest of the space. Hopefully, Gray hadn't thrown his son into a cell. She wanted a chance to show Ash her love and support. He would have killed for her and the other victims of Mort's twisted logic. Ash would be hurting to the depths of his soul.

She yanked the camera out of the buttonhole, then stuffed it in the tote. It had stopped recording at some point. She'd erase everything as soon as she could. She needed to call Jo sometime today. Ash said she was in the bitch bunker. But first, a quick shower, then food.

Not long after, Skye winced as she sat down in a

bistro chair on Elizabeth's patio with Trinket on her lap. The dog had kept his enthusiasm at seeing her to a minimum, as if sensing her pain. She still couldn't take deep breaths. The wallop to her chest maybe four hours ago had left it tenderly bruised.

Elizabeth came through the slider. "I see Trinket found you. I had him in my room, so you'd have a chance to shower in peace. Blunt is making us tea. He baked a nice loaf of crusty bread and a quiche Lorraine. You must be hungry."

"Quiche sounds great. I've only just thought about food when my stomach reminded me. I was too busy running for my life." Skye pulled at Trinket's topknot.

Squawk. Strike flew past Skye's ear, ruffling her hair. "You're alive." He landed on the back of the empty chair, regarding her with his one good eye.

"I am very much alive, and thankful."

"You look like hell, though."

"Strike, don't be rude." Elizabeth wagged a finger at him. "She'll tell us her tale."

"Strike speaks the truth," said Skye. Her damp hair cork screwed like she'd used a mad curling iron. Blotchy face and blood-shot eyes. *Nice.* She tucked a strand behind an ear. "So much happened in such a short time. Tae-wen is amazing, death defiance aside. I don't think we were there three hours before a hell creeper almost ate me."

She continued with the tale of Malgren encounters, the fight in the city of Elysium with Bings, Gryph the hero's supposed death, her flight from Mort, Myst's injury. "I'm still dazzled by the miracle of a unicorn's healing. After Mort hit me with an energy blast, Ash weakened him with crazy arcs of energy."

Elizabeth and Strike punctuated with oohs and aahs.

"Then Gryph jumped into the fight out of nowhere. He grabbed Mort's neck." She'd let Ash tell Elizabeth his side of things if he chose.

"Nulling his magic," Elizabeth said.

"What's going to happen to Ash? Tell me your honest opinion."

"Ash will be fine. The killer has been found. You—"

Blunt came through the door carrying the tray of refreshments and set it on the table.

"Thanks, Blunt," said Skye. The fluffy quiche sent up a delicious aroma. "Smells wonderful."

Strike hopped along the edge of the chair back. "I'm sensing a lot of tension. We all need some lovely bread to calm down."

Elizabeth poured iced tea. After giving the raven a bit of her bread, placed a plate of quiche in front of Skye. "To continue, I'm *one* vote in a Council of eleven. Gray makes two on your side if Ash convinces him that you can be trusted to keep our secret. It's a majority vote that decides the outcome. The Council has two options on the table—banishment to Tae-wen or erasing of your memories." She spread her hands. "I know, both are unacceptable."

The forkful of quiche she'd just swallowed soured in Skye's stomach. She set Trinket on the ground after giving him a morsel. "Ash told me the options, but which is most likely? All this is just so crazy! I can't…" Every beat of her heart pulsed in her temple. "But *you* trust me, don't you?"

Elizabeth tilted her head, pursing her lips. "When

we first met just three days ago, you promised me and Ash that you'd tell no one about us. I trust you'll keep your promise."

"Hmm, I don't know," said Strike. "She is conflicted, like Walter White."

"Pfft. I'm cutting you off the *Breaking Bad* binge watch."

Skye shifted in the chair, trying to find a comfortable spot among the butt bruises. "I'm no longer conflicted, Elizabeth. I'll keep my promise. But will I get a chance to speak at this Council meeting to convince them, too?"

"I'll make sure you do."

"One more thing. Ash and I—we love each other."

"Told you," said Strike. He fluttered up a foot in the air before settling back down.

"I know." Elizabeth sighed.

"I don't want to get ahead of myself, but is there some kind of rule against your society's witches being with or marrying a Reg?"

Elizabeth set her glass down with a bang. "I thought he'd have told you by now."

"Told me what?"

"Reg and witch can marry, but it's highly discouraged. There are consequences to consider. They're similar to what you'll face with the Council over keeping your silence." Elizabeth covered a hand with hers. "The witch's magic must be nulled. Offspring never develop powers in any case. The couple could be sent to Tae-wen, but if they remain in this world, the Reg's memories of magic would be erased."

Skye pulled her hand away. "No. I can't—won't—

accept any of these so-called consequences." Lose her memories? Ash lose his magic? No way she'd let that happen. "No wonder he didn't tell me. Damn him."

"Well, you can tell him to his face how you feel. He's here."

Ash strode through the patio door accompanied by Blunt and a prancing Soot. Strike screeched a greeting or a warning to the cat, who made a beeline for the garden. Trinket charged after Soot.

"Nice. A tea party," he said, sitting in the chair next to Skye. He hadn't taken his eyes off her. "How are you feeling?"

"Like I want to slug you. Or worse."

"What did I do this time?"

"Goddammit, Ash. You didn't tell me the rules."

"The rules?" He glanced at Elizabeth who raised her brows. "Oh, *those* rules."

Strike fluttered his wings and squawked. "You are in deep shit." A tattered, black feather drifted down onto the loaf of bread.

"Strike, you and I will leave these two to their discussion." Elizabeth stood. Strike hopped onto her outstretched arm and complained all the way through the patio door.

Ash took Skye's hand. "I had a long talk with Gray. He's thankful that the real killer has been caught. I was allowed to go. One thing I want you never to forget. I love you with all my heart and soul."

"Never forget? What? Is this, like, goodbye or something?"

"I don't know."

She jerked her hand from his as tears formed. *I'm not going to goddamn cry.* "Why didn't you tell me about the rules? You had a ton of opportunities."

"I'm sorry. I was going to so many times. None seemed right."

"None seemed right? How about when we were in Elysium. Or at Flip House, before or after we made love. Or when you told me the Council rules for a Reg knowing about your magic. You had dozens of chances." She stood, sending the metal chair screeching along the patio stones. "Finally, I trusted you. Trusted that there were no more secrets."

She strode to the edge of the garden where a small, three-tiered fountain trickled water into ceramic bowls. The musical sound should have been soothing. Her rigid body was as tightly wound as her hair and mind that charged along impossible paths.

Ash came behind her. He touched an arm. "You *can* trust me. Trust that I love you. Do you love me?"

She turned. Dark eyes searched hers. "Shit, yes. Can't believe it, but I do. What a sucker." She wound her arms around his neck and winced. "Be gentle, magic man."

He gently wrapped his arms around her, their bodies lightly touching. "Is this okay?"

Soot bumped against her leg. Trinket nudged the cat with a nose. "It'll do until later."

"There will be a later for us. We'll fight this." Ash pushed strands of hair from her cheek.

He pressed his lips to hers in a gentle kiss, as if she were made of crystal. Was she melting? Did someone in love actually melt? Before she became a gooey puddle, she pulled back.

"Fight? Bloody right, we'll fight. Elizabeth says she'll make sure I get a chance to plead my case.

Anyway, what are they going to do, lock us up?"

"Yes. Then they'll null my powers and wipe your memories."

"That's cruel. Even criminal. I thought you people were pacifists. Reverence for life and all that."

Ash winced. She was sorry as soon as the words left her mouth.

"We're becoming more like Regs every day," he whispered.

She blew out a breath. "Sorry, Ash. I need time to think. Alone." She pulled from his arms. She desperately needed to talk to Jo.

"Wait. There's a chance Gray will put a third option on the table—your complete freedom, memories intact, for your *promise* not to write about us or reveal our society."

"What? You could have led with that. But why should they take my word?"

Elizabeth stuck her head out the door. "Security is here to escort you two to the Council."

"Already?" Skye had no time to think. No time to call Jo. What should she do? What could she do? She wanted to be with Ash. Wanted a life with him. But how? He didn't say he'd have his magic nulled to be with her. She didn't say she'd be willing to have her memory wiped, either, or go to Tae-wen.

"If I convince the Council to trust that I'll never reveal the society's existence, then they should let us, uh, be together with no consequences. They wouldn't need to take away your powers, right?"

Ash gave her that side-tilted smile that always charmed her heart. "Don't see why they would."

She grabbed his hand. "Listen, I'm pretty good

with words. I can do this. Get us out of this mess."

"I trust you." He tangled his hand in her hair, pulling her in for a brief, deep kiss that rocked her world.

Trust—the minute she let down her guard, bam. All she knew was, she had to be with Ash.

A fight was coming. If not for her life, for her freedom, for her memories, and for the love of this magic man.

Chapter Twenty-Six

Skye walked beside Ash in front of the guards along the wide corridor. They followed Elizabeth's straight back. The immortal had quickly changed into a long ceremonial robe of ice blue silk that shimmered with each confident step. Something right out of Middle Earth, which was where Skye thought she might as well be. She was underdressed for sure.

Ash took her hand, giving it a squeeze, throwing her a cautious smile. "It'll be okay. I've been here before."

"And lived to talk about it." She tried to sound bright and nonchalant at the same time. If she lost focus, she'd have a full body spasm.

He held her hand all the way, through one door then another, until they reached a set of closed, heavily carved double doors. The two guards went around them to open the doors wide, revealing a high-ceilinged, courtroom-like space. Lots of polished wood in the rows of empty spectator seating. Ten Council members were seated behind a long table on a raised dais across the room. It could be a Reg courtroom except for statues of the One Mother deity sitting in niches in the wall behind them instead of a display of noble American and State flags. A black cat peeked out from around a bench. Soot?

Elizabeth turned to Skye and Ash. "Trust in the

process," she whispered.

She strode through first across the white marble floor to take the prominent middle spot among the other ten. Six women, five men, all grim-faced. Surely the immortal held more sway than the others, right? The guy to Elizabeth's left—yes, that was Ash's dad. She recognized him from Jo's research. Skye's heart drummed a death march. She knew Ash was nervous, too, by the frequency of the hand squeezes, even though his posture was relaxed. His gift.

A courtroom attendant came down the aisle between the benches, motioning them to enter. Ash's lips were set in a firm give-them-hell line. She walked by his side until she was directed to stand behind one podium and he behind another a few feet away. The loss of contact was like losing the main chute. She faced the inquisitors, all stern except for Elizabeth, who smiled gently, her countenance softly welcoming.

Skye forced breaths through a tight chest. She'd spoken in front of many audiences, but this time was different. This time she'd be begging for her life, not physical life, but an unrestricted life. One with Ash in it. She'd be asking these strangers, these magical people, to trust her with a secret that would turn the world upside down should they be revealed. She, who trusted no one, had to convince, maybe beg, to *be* trusted. The irony wasn't lost on her.

Elizabeth banged a dragon-headed gavel to stop the murmuring voices on either side. "Let's begin." She stood. "Bless the One Mother. Ash Hunter, the Council recognizes that desperate measures were needed to protect this Reg, Skye Parker, from one of your own once-trusted Keepers, a serial killer intent on murdering her and any others that stood in his way. Those measures included revealing our society to her, bringing her to the Haven on my request, then ultimately to Tae-wen. Unfortunately, the killer entered Tae-wen to pursue her. He was apprehended and brought back to be prosecuted for his crimes. The Council thanks you and those who helped in his capture."

Ash knocked his knuckles on the podium. "Including Skye. She—"

"Yes. But let me continue. The Council has read about Skye's brush with a member of our society when she was a child, how that event helped guide the trajectory of her life, leading her to be here today. I have the same question for both of you." She turned to Skye. "I only need a one-word answer. Skye Parker, do you intend to continue an intimate relationship with Ash?"

Skye looked at Ash and her heart squeezed. "Yes." She wanted to say so much more.

Elizabeth turned to Ash. "Ash Hunter, do you—"

"Definitely."

A tingling warmth spread through Skye's body. This sounded like a marriage ceremony, until it didn't.

"Then I'll place the rules for such unions as set forth in our tenets on the record, as we will be only addressing this issue. Bless the One Mother." Elizabeth cleared her throat. "The mage will have his or her powers permanently nulled. The couple could be sent to Tae-wen, but if they remain in this world, the Reg's memories of our society and magic will be erased."

"Wait." Ash raised his voice. "There's another option. Councilman Hunter?"

Gray shrugged and glanced at Elizabeth.

Ash's face reddened. Both hands clutched the podium. "You said you'd add the option of letting Skye keep her memories and stay in this world on her *promise* not to reveal us. I agreed to have my powers nulled as part of that agreement."

What? She would not be part of any agreement that would take away Ash's magic. No way in hell.

Gray half rose from his chair. "I want to amend that option."

The Council members erupted in conversation. Elizabeth banged the gavel. "Let us have order." The room quieted.

Gray cleared his throat. "Remove the stipulation that my son's powers be nulled."

Ash relaxed his killer grip on the podium, his face registering surprise and relief.

The uproar resumed. It took Elizabeth several seconds to regain order. "We'll take these amendments into consideration."

Skye held up a hand and raised her voice. "May I speak now?" She'd have to be brilliant to sway most of this rowdy Council to her side.

Elizabeth nodded.

All eyes focused on Skye. Her knees went weak. "Thank you. So, you all know *part* of my story. Facts. What you don't know is what's in my heart." *Eye contact. Breathe.* "I've spent all my adult life searching out truth. Reporting my findings. Why? Because I felt the public should know the truth. I needed people to read my stories and *believe* them." She took a breath. "Because no one believed a little girl who said a man had saved her from drowning with magic. No one believed the teenager or the adult. Instead, I suffered

340

ridicule, bullying. No one believed me except my mother. She desperately wanted validation for me. Together we searched for that validation. As I look back now on all our investigations of the paranormal, I'm struck with how effective your Keeper network must be. How easily most people, Regs, discount anything out of the ordinary, even when the evidence is right before their eyes. I intended on writing a story about magic in the world until quite recently."

One of the Council members, a sharp-featured woman in dark burgundy robes, rose. "Council Jada Gladstone. None of what you're saying is helping your cause. We shouldn't have to work so hard to keep our society a secret. We don't have enough Keepers."

The members murmured among themselves until Elizabeth brought order once again. "Continue, Skye."

"My mother, my—dear mother, was murdered. My world was turned upside down. Then I met an incredible man, Ash Hunter." She glanced at his face that still wore a look of wide-eyed bewilderment. She smiled and his face softened. He nodded. "I believe I fell in love with him the day I met him. He stalked me, infuriated me, kept secrets from me. In the end, he loved me. Trusted me. He took me to an extraordinary place, Tae-wen. Who here has been to the land of your origins?"

The only member of the Council to raise a hand was Elizabeth.

"It's both strange and familiar, terrifying, and welcoming. From Malgren marauders to man-eating cabbages, the place keeps you on your toes. Believe me when I say you do not want to be anywhere near the foul mouth of the hell creeper." She waved a hand in front of her nose.

That drew chuckles from the Council.

"In Tae-wen I met some amazing people. People from different lands, cultures, and faiths. What did they all have in common? They were human. They were passionate. They were proud. They were brave, loving. Generous to a fault. Hear me." She let her gaze rest a moment on each set of eyes. "I could never write my story now. I would *never* jeopardize their safety any sooner than I would jeopardize Ash's, or any of you. I have my validation right here." She placed a hand on her heart. "And my mother's killer has been caught. I trust *you* with his punishment as I'm asking you to trust *me* to keep your secret, and to let Ash keep his magic. It's who he is. It's as part of him as your faith in the One Mother. He's my magic man. I can't imagine living without him."

Skye's gaze swept across the Council. Some were still grim-faced like the Gladstone member. They began talking among themselves. Ash's dad was in quiet conversation with Elizabeth. Had Skye convinced the majority? Ash looked over at her, a smile on his lips. Her heart tripped double time in her chest. She understood that part of his sudden lightness of being involved don't-call-me-dad Gray referring to him as son.

The burner phone vibrated a call in her pocket. It would be Jo. She still didn't know what to tell her. Jo would call BS on any concocted story of where she'd been that she couldn't have contacted her at some point.

"Attention," called Elizabeth. "We shall include Council Hunter's suggested option into our deliberations. We're ready. Attendant, please take Skye and Ash to the side room. We'll get word to you if deliberations will be protracted." She gave Skye a slight smile.

Ash grabbed her hand as soon as she came beside him. The attendant led them out another door into a lounge-type room with comfy, overstuffed chairs. He left them alone. Ash pulled her into his arms. The warmth and solidness of his body reassured her.

"You were amazing," he whispered in her ear.

"I spoke from the heart. I hope they heard me."

He gave her a gentle hug. The tummy quivers resumed along with the vibrating phone.

"Jo's calling me. Let me answer. I need to let her know I'm ok."

Ash gave her just enough space to grab the phone from a pocket. "Jo, sorry I haven't checked in."

"Friggin' hell. You're alive." Her voice came through loud and clear. Too loud.

"Very much so. But I'm in a sitch. I need to call you back."

"Wait—imminent danger sitch? 'Cause I know, Skye. I saw your videos. Ash is a witch, that woman Elizabeth is too. Are you in the Haven?"

Skye's blood ran cold. Ash had heard. He dropped his arms and narrowed his eyes. *Shit.* "Listen, Jo, erase all the videos. I have no intention of using them."

"You've got to be kidding, right? Erase them? You're in danger. I can smell it."

Ash's face went hard, his body rigid.

Skye's heart beats pounded in her ears. "I'm fine, Jo. Tell no one about this. Erase all the videos. I'll call you back." She clicked off the call, then pocketed the phone. It began vibrating almost immediately.

Ash flinched away from her outstretched hand.

"What was that all about? A video?"

"She was never supposed to see it. I was going to erase it as soon as I could. I didn't even know *if* the cam was recording."

"What did you tape?"

"It doesn't matter. It'll be gone."

"What-did-you-tape?"

Her throat constricted. "I had the hidden camera in my shirt at the hotel. It was recording when you revealed what—who—you are."

"How did she know about Elizabeth?"

"It was still recording when you took me to the Haven to meet her."

His breathing was rough, like something pressed on his chest. She touched his arm, but he pulled it away again. "You've put us all in jeopardy. Everything you said in there—"

"—was the truth. I love you. I would never endanger you and your world. Jo will do what I tell her."

"That was going to be your irrefutable proof, wasn't it? You'd have the video authenticated, deemed unfalsifiable by the authorities, the government."

"My intention at first. Not now. I said as much in the courtroom. I regret ever clipping on that damn camera." She grabbed both his arms. "Believe me. I love you. I will *not* reveal your society."

His eyes searched hers.

The door opened. "They have come to a decision," said the attendant. "Follow me."

Too quick. Did this mean the verdict wouldn't be in her favor like regular trials? Ash didn't take her hand this time. He marched on ahead. She entered the courtroom, mind detached from body. She stood behind the podium while he went to his. He stared straight ahead. *Look at me*. She held back tears, the effort bringing the blood back to her face, and the heat.

Elizabeth was speaking. Skye tore her eyes away from Ash's harsh profile.

"I will pass the proceedings on to our Head of Security, Council Gray Hunter."

Gray stood, his expression blank. He looked from Skye to Ash and cleared his throat. "The existence of our modern society, based on the ancient Majiste customs, our faith in the One Mother, is reliant upon secrecy in this world. Technological and electronic advances have made maintaining this secrecy both easier and infinitely harder."

Skye swallowed, every muscle quivering, but she managed to straighten her shoulders and lift her chin.

"Should we be revealed, not only our society, but the world would be thrown into chaos. Perhaps even our ancient homeland, Tae-wen, would be devastated." He looked directly at Skye. "Skye Parker, you came to our attention months ago due to your social media postings, and the fact you're an investigative reporter. Keeper Ash Hunter was assigned to watch over your activities. All of this has resulted in you coming before us today."

Skye glanced at Ash. *Look at me, dammit*. He didn't, splintering her soul. Elizabeth poked Gray on the arm and mouthed something she couldn't decipher.

"All right," Gray said. "Skye Parker, the option under vote was to allow you to keep your memories on your stated promise while Ash Hunter would keep his magic because you intend to make a life together. The Council vote was split five for, five against. As head of security, I was the tie breaker." He paused, looking from her to Ash, then back to her. Elizabeth poked him again. "I listened carefully to your words, what was in your heart. I voted—for." His face split into a wide grin.

Skye gasped. Had she heard right? She would keep her memories, Ash his magic, even if they stayed a couple. Ash nodded in her direction but didn't make eye contact.

"Thank you, Council Hunter," Elizabeth said. "Skye Parker, the decision in your favor came about because, in the end, we trust your words. We trust they come from your heart and soul. You are free to go."

Relief was like cool water dousing scald-blistered skin. "Thank you, Council." She couldn't think of anything more to say. Words, her specialty, eluded her. She'd need to come up with some good ones for Ash. Now.

She hurried to catch up as he walked through the open doors. She took his hand. "We need to talk. Your office?"

He wore his scowly face. "Okay. This way." He still hadn't made eye contact. He dropped her hand when they came to the hall of the Keeper wing.

Trust. She never would have believed that her fate would rest on her own trustworthiness. *But here we are.* She'd deeply hurt Ash. She needed him in her life, heart, and soul.

Chapter Twenty-Seven

Ash amped up his aura to make up for Skye's lack as they walked to his Keeper office. It was still not widely known that a Reg had infringed on the sanctity of the Haven. Every emotion roiled through him—knee-weakening relief, hot anger, crushing hurt. Nothing she could tell him would ease any of them. Nothing she could do would heal the Grand Canyon opening in his heart.

He ushered her through the office door, turning the windows opaque with a thought. Soot sat on the desk, tail thrashing, and pushing thoughts Ash didn't want to receive. They found a way in, anyway.

"You look crazy. Why aren't you happy?"

Ash shook his head. *Later, Soot.*

Skye's eyes filled with tears. "I am *so* sorry. I wore the camera when I was still uncertain what to do. I was doubtful it was even recording."

"That was what, all of three days ago? Why should I believe a thing you say now?"

"Because I love you. Because everything I said in court is the truth."

"Now Jo knows. Maybe she told others, shared the video."

"She wouldn't. You heard me. I told her to erase the videos."

Ash groaned. "You realize if the Council had

known you videotaped *anything*, they'd have come to a much different verdict." He ignored Soot's pithy comments.

"Thank you for not telling them."

He searched her eyes, still glistening, full of hope. "No, I won't. But they'll be watching your every move when you leave here."

Her shoulders sagged. "Probably forever."

She took a step closer. His fingers wanted to brush back some of that wild, flaming hair. Remove the glasses, hold her close, bruise her lips in a fierce kiss. He did none of that. His seething emotions had flatlined.

"You should go. Jo won't stop calling until she sees you." Ash detected Elizabeth's energy beyond the door.

Skye placed a kiss on his lips. He crushed the sudden longing beneath a veneer of indifference.

"Will I see you later?"

He hesitated. "I need some time."

She nodded. "I'll get my things from Elizabeth's. Will you take me there?"

"Elizabeth's here. She'll take you." He willed the glass to clear and the door to open.

Elizabeth strode through, smile fading. "This is not the happy scene I anticipated."

"We're working out a couple of things," Ash said. "Thanks for your support. I'm sure your influence swayed more to our side."

"A couple of the Council members are stubborn, hardline asses. Nothing I said made any difference, not your love for one another or your trust in one another. I spoke of your unique talents, Ash, how our people need them now more than ever. Council Gray agreed with me."

Ash wanted to quit the Keeper job. Could he now? Should he?

She'd videotaped him. Secretly. He'd be a long time getting over that punch to the gut.

Skye hugged Elizabeth. "Thank you for championing us. I'd hate to think what would be happening right now if you hadn't."

"Would you mind taking Skye to your place to collect her stuff and the dog, then to the elevator? I need to clear off a few things here. Reports need to be filed." No Mort to help him. A roil of emotions left him uncertain what to feel.

"Of course."

Ash sank into a chair as soon as Elizabeth closed the door. Soot jumped into his lap.

"You're an asshole, you know that?"

"Probably." He stroked Soot's smooth back. The cat arched up to meet his hand.

"How long are you going to torture her?"

"I'm the one being tortured."

The door opened. Myst strode through with a raggedy white cockatoo clinging to one shoulder, Lucien at her heels, her big bright smile fading. "I'd say congrats, but I don't feel the party."

"We're saving the party till later." *Maybe much later to never.*

She dragged a chair closer and sat. Lucien jumped onto her lap, his smoky, dense fur like a storm cloud, glittering don't-mess-with-my-witch yellow eyes fixed on Ash. It took him a moment to recognize Mercy, Mort's cockatoo. His head hung low, eyes closed. The faithful familiar was in mourning.

So was he. An ache spread from the hollowed-out space in his heart. Soot bumped his head against Ash's chest, then curled in a rumbly purr ball on his lap.

"I snuck into chambers. Heard Skye, and later, the obvious verdict. So, what happened since?"

Ash cleared the lump from his throat. "She videotaped me before I took her to Tae-wen. And Elizabeth. The Haven. You."

Myst's eyes widened, then narrowed. "O-kay. She's a reporter. I get that. But, Ash, she loves you. You heard what she said. Tae-wen, and you, changed her. I believe her."

"You would. You're little Miss Sunshine."

"Do you really think she was lying in there? She said she'd never do anything to put any of us at risk." She took his hand. "She can't live without you. You're her magic man."

"I am, aren't I." He felt himself thawing, muscles relaxing, as if he'd stepped inside a warm room after hours in frigid weather. Myst didn't have the mesmer, so the defrost was all his own.

She squeezed his hand and let go. "There you are. Your face just lost that frowny scowl. You can't live without Skye. Go to her. Let her prove she's telling the truth." Myst stood, dumping Lucien to the floor. She stroked Mercy's bowed head with two fingers. He could relate to that poor bird.

He held up a hand. "Okay. Get out of here. Let me think for five minutes."

Her grin was ear to ear as she ushered the fluff ball out the door, closing it softly behind her.

It seemed he'd known Skye for years instead of a

few weeks. Good weeks. Crazy weeks. They'd made love. The memory of her warm, naked body wrapped around his, her willingness to share every bit of herself, the willingness to pleasure him, stirred his blood. But what he felt, had felt, for her was more than physical. Skye was courageous, fierce, formidable. More than that, she was tender, loving, and kind. She experienced the world with all her senses, all her emotions.

Ash leaned back in the chair, closing his eyes. The quiet enveloped him in a cocoon of solitude for long minutes while he thought about Skye, leaving her be, loving her. Soot stirred, the rumbly purr stuttering.

"You hardly ever purr."

"You needed it. Too bad humans can't purr."

He gathered Soot in his arms, cradled the cat like a baby and scratched under his chin.

"You love her. Go to her. I won't be able to live with you if you're miserable."

"Thinking about it. I guess I should make sure she's okay."

"Anything could have happened to her. Better hurry."

Poof. Soot winked out, leaving him with empty arms. He grabbed the burner and called Elizabeth. Skye had driven away with Sam fifteen minutes ago. She'd head for the bunker.

He rushed out of the Keeper wing to the elevator. He had one thing to do before leaving.

****

Skye sat at the desk in the bunker, swiveling the old chair that squealed in protest. The reunion with Jo had involved more than a few tears. After telling her about Tae-wen, her love for Ash, and the Council

351

verdict, shock and awe had set in. But Jo, who'd seen a lot of extraordinary things in her life, quickly regained composure. She was a tough old bird. In the car on the way to Springfield, she'd realized that Hetty had probably been murdered.

Skye checked her phone again, stomach knotting up like Mom's Christmas lights. It had been almost an hour since Sam had dropped her off.

"Give him a minute." Jo sat at her own desk with Trinket in her lap. A shot of hot pink streaked through the white hair. "Again, sorry for putting my size nines directly in my big mouth."

"Don't worry about it. I would have told him anyway. The outcome might have been the same." Yeah, she would have come clean. She wanted to prove he could trust her.

"Holy shit. Magic is real," Jo muttered, turning back to the computer.

A banging on the metal door made them both jump. Skye's hand went to her chest, heart thumping against still tender ribs.

Jo harrumphed. "Answer it before I have to haul my ass out of this chair and hobble."

Swallowing hard, Skye smoothed shaky hands down her jeans and went to the door. After settling her breathing, she pulled it open. Ash stood with hand raised, about to knock again. The stern face set in harsh lines, the fathomless eyes unreadable, the stiff posture—the knots in her stomach twisted and tightened.

"Can I come in?" He had her rolling bag gripped in one hand, the one she'd left in his apartment all those days ago when she'd escaped the killer. Mort.

She held the door open wide. "We've been waiting for you."

He swept by her, the wheels echoing loudly on the cement floor. She followed his lengthy strides along the aisle of metal shelves to Jo's desk.

"It's great to see you, Jo," he said, sharing a fist bump, then setting the bag upright.

"Likewise. Uh, do you two want me to get lost, or…"

Skye came beside Ash. "No. Now that he's here, you can begin erasing all the videos, all my files on the paranormal, everything, even my mom's files, while he watches. I'll shred my hard copy notes."

"That's not what I came here for."

"What did you come here for?" *Me. Say me.*

His erect posture loosened. Face softened. His eyes went to her mouth. He wet his lips with a tongue, igniting a pilot light in the girly parts while her heart bumped along on rickety rails.

"I don't know."

She nodded. "Somehow, I understand." She touched his arm. "I hurt you. I'm sorry."

"How sorry are you?" A lip twitched.

"Really sorry. Never been sorrier in my life."

He nodded. "I accept your apology."

"And I accept yours."

"For what?"

"Lying to me. Wasting my time and Jo's on endless rabbit holes. Then not believing me today at Council."

"Wow. We are a sorry pair." He took her hand. "Maybe we're even."

"Hmm. Maybe. So, what now?" The thumb rub

across her knuckles sent lovely tingles to every part of her body.

"We have some stuff to work on, you and I."

Yeah. Trust issues. Soul-shifting revelations. Ash would need time to process the whole Mort implosion. "How about we work on them together?"

His mouth tilted in that sexy, innocent, irresistible smile she loved. "Perfect. I love you, Skye. I want us to—"

"Yes!" The next instant, she was in his arms, lifted off her feet, or maybe pure joy sent her flying. Jo was clapping. Tinker barking. Her heart soared. She had no idea what life would be like from now on. She only knew that she'd be living it with Ash. Her magic man.

Epilogue

Six Months Later

Skye said goodbye to Jo and slipped the cell phone into a back pocket. Jo had finally found the courage to endure the last of the needed shots for the trip. She would meet them at the airport. She closed the lid on the bulging suitcase that sat at the edge of the bed.

"Ash, I need you in here to zip up this beast." She scanned the bedroom for any missed items. The old room, filled with memories of nightly tuck-ins from Mom, of teenage tears over lost loves, of pillow dreams never realized, looked like a hotel room now, professionally staged for the house sale. The lump in her throat felt like a giant warty toad.

Ash walked through the door. "Myst picked up Soot and Trinket." He stopped, eyebrows raised. "You know, we could take two suitcases."

She swallowed hard, lifting her chin. "We want to travel light."

He laughed. "Too late for that." He tugged on the zipper, pressed, and tugged. "I'm gonna need a bit of help." Fingers circled the air over the bag. Z-i-p.

She pulled him close, as close as the mini baby bump allowed, and wrapped her arms around his neck. "I love your magic fingers."

"You do?" He kissed her nose, fogging the new glasses. "We have fifteen minutes before Sam takes us to the airport."

"Sorry. I have a few things to do in those minutes."

"And I'm not one of them." He faked a tragic face.

She unwound her arms, setting him back. "You're busy, too. You need to call your dad. It's his birthday. Don't forget." She headed for the bedroom door. "Grab the suitcase."

"I'll call him on the way. I still can't believe he quit Security." He waved a hand. The bag disappeared.

"*You* quit. *He* retired. If you want to call returning to a sixty-hour week at a madhouse brokerage firm retirement."

She led the way down the old wooden stairs. The empty wall where the photos of her youth had hung held only the outline of ghostly frames.

"Did you call your clients, Ash Hunter, P.I.?" She passed through the staged living room and into the kitchen on a final search for anything trip worthy. The white appliances gleamed, and the Formica countertop—would need to be replaced by whoever had bought the place. Their new, modern condo just off Central Park South awaited their return. She'd loved the place the moment she'd stepped off the private elevator into thirtieth floor views of the city and park.

"Every one of them. None of my cases are urgent. We'll only be gone two weeks."

"My assignments never last just two weeks, but we'll go with that for now." She checked the fridge for the tenth time. Still empty. Her throat clogged again. "We'd better go before I start blubbering like a baby."

He reached for her, but she dodged his arms. "Jeez. If you hold me, I'll lose it for sure." *Damn hysterical hormones*.

"Okay. Follow me. Stare at my back. Do not look right or left."

She did as ordered, making it out past the "In Escrow" sign on the postcard-sized lawn and into the back seat of Sam's car without making a fool of herself. Apparently, the bulging bag and all their gear had magically fit into the trunk. Ash slid in beside her.

Sam turned, an elfish grin appearing between bushy mustache and beard. "Next stop JFK, eh?"

"Yep. We're not in a big hurry. We need to get there alive," Ash said.

The force of rapid acceleration pressed her into the seat. Ash brought her hand to his lips, dark eyes lit with excitement. "Africa. You don't mind mixing our honeymoon in with business, Mrs. Hunter?"

"Not at all, magic man. This will be just the first of many adventures." She squeezed his hand. "Trust me."

www.ingramcontent.com/pod-product-compliance
Lightning Source LLC
Chambersburg PA
CBHW072309020726
47501CB00002B/451